Art for Travellers
ITALY

**The Essential Guide to Viewing
Italian Renaissance Art**

Verrocchio's Statue of Colleoni, Venice

Art for Travellers

ITALY

The Essential Guide to Viewing Italian Renaissance Art

ANN MORROW AND JOHN POWER

ILLUSTRATIONS BY

MATT MORROW AND ERIN ROUND

Interlink Books
An imprint of Interlink Publishing Group, Inc.
New York • Northampton

709.45
MOR

First published in 2004 by

INTERLINK BOOKS
An imprint of Interlink Publishing Group, Inc.
46 Crosby Street, Northampton, Massachusetts 01060
www.interlinkbooks.com

Text copyright © by Ann Morrow and John Power 2004
Photography copyright © by Felix Oppenheim 2004
Edited and designed by Ed 'n' Art, Newport, Sydney

Cover painting: A detail from Sandro Botticelli's *Primavera*.

Library of Congress Cataloging-in-Publication Data
Morrow, Ann 1940– .
   Italy : the essential guide to viewing Italian Renaissance
   Art / by Ann Morrow and John Power
   p. cm. – (Art for travellers)
   ISBN 1-56656-510-3 (pbk.)
   1. Art, Italian–Guidebooks. 2. Art, Renaissance–Italy–Guidebooks.
   I. Power, John M. 1933– . II. Title.
   III. Series.
N6914.P68 2003
709'.45'09024–dc21

                2003000440

All paintings are used in this books with the kind permission of:
The Bridgeman Art Library, Branacacci Chapel, Florence; Ca d'Oro, Venice;
Galleria Borghese, Rome; Galleria dell' Accademia, Venice; Galleria dell'
Accademia Carrara, Bergamo; Galleria degli Uffizi, Florence; Museo Civico, Pesaro;
Museo Correr, Venice; Museo dell' Opera del Duomo, Florence; Ognissanti,
Florence; Palazzo Barberini, Rome; Palazzo Ducale, Mantua; Piazza del Santo, Padua;
San Francesco, Arezzo; Scrovegni (Arena) Chapel, Padua; Santa Maria della Grazie,
Milan; Vatican Museums and Galleries, Vatican City.

Printed and bound in Korea

To request our complete 40-page full-color catalog, please call us toll
free at **1-800-238-LINK**, visit our website at **www.interlinkbooks.com**,
or send us an e-mail: **info@interlinkbooks.com**

Acknowledgements

We would like to thank the colleagues, friends and family members who road-tested sections of the text, especially Bryon and Winifred Cunningham, Di Sisely and Philip Craig, but also the Travellers we met en route in Italy who were happy to give us on-the-spot feedback! Thanks, too, to Bill Hannan, Ian Guthridge, Warwick Forge, Max Dumais, Geoff Holden, Faith Fitzgerald, the Cavalier family and Carol Floyd for their advice and support.

Detail of Brunelleschi's Cupola of the Duomo *in Florence*

Self portrait incorporated into the decorative frieze of the Camera degli Sposi or Camera Picta, by Andrea Mantegna, Palazzo Ducale, Mantua, Italy

Table of Contents

Introduction

About the Trails

When visiting a gallery like the Uffizi in Florence, most of us are completely overwhelmed. Of course we appreciate that we are surrounded by some of the world's greatest art treasures. But, because we may not ever pass this way again, and perhaps do not have the background to make a confident selection, we try to squeeze in as much as possible. The result is that we soon lose our powers of discrimination, fatigue sets in, and eventually we stagger out of the gallery with glazed eyes and weary body and mind. And this was supposed to be a highlight of our trip!

That is why we have designed a series of Trails – to help you plan the art-focused part of your trip and to make it more manageable and enjoyable. Each chapter will take you on a different Trail, with suggested itineraries, and each concentrates on the most significant art you will see. From Giotto to Caravaggio, the Trails take you from the precursors of the Renaissance to the beginnings of the Baroque period. This book is not intended to replace a more conventional guidebook, as we do not provide information about eating or accommodation, and our maps are simply guides as to the order in which to visit sites or towns.

Art historians commonly list more than 200 Italian Renaissance artists, so we have had to be selective. We focus on 17 artists, but with brief reference to quite a few others. You'll find profiles of each of them in this chapter. Brief biographies of other artists, writers, and characters of note are in an appendix at the back of the book.

When 2000 Italian Renaissance paintings executed between 1420 and 1539 were catalogued, it was discovered that nearly 90 percent had a religious subject, and nearly half of these were devoted to the Virgin Mary. You will find that most of the works you see focus on New Testament themes – the main source of inspiration for most of the Renaissance masters. (There are references to Biblical stories, characters, terms, and saints at the back of the book to help you interpret and

INTRODUCTION

understand these works). However, there is some relief in the paintings of Botticelli and others.

If you are primarily interested in the painters of the Early Renaissance, you can satisfy your interests without leaving Florence and its surrounds. However, if you are also attracted to the later artists, you will have to travel. Michelangelo and Raphael were the stars of the High Renaissance, which peaked in Rome in the early years of the 16th century. Later on in that century, during the Late Renaissance, the focus shifted to Venice, with Titian and Tintoretto.

The Trails highlight the six major concentrations of Italian painting – Florence (Firenze), Rome (Roma), Venice (Venezia), Assisi, Padua, and Milan (Milano). We also visit other towns along the way in the three intercity Trails. If you can manage to get to some of these out-of-the-way towns – even if they contain only one or two Renaissance paintings of note – you will enjoy interpreting those works on the basis of what you have learned on your visits to the major centers. And along the way, you'll see a lot more of Italy.

Tips for the Traveller

- When planning your itinerary, check opening days first. Many Italian galleries are closed on Mondays. You'll find opening times and charges listed for the major museums as they were in mid-2002, but these change frequently. For brevity's sake, we have listed only the summer hours of opening, have not listed holiday closures, and have not gone into the details of discount entrance charges. We don't always provide opening hours for the briefer, small-town visits or for every church.

- Whenever you arrive in a new town, head first for a tourist information center (often attached to the railway station). They will usually be able to supply you with a free town map. We have written our directions on the assumption you will always have such a map.

- Prices are subject to change – mostly upwards! An increasing number of churches charge strangers who are visiting for tourist, rather than liturgical, reasons. Others manage to raise a bit of revenue by forcing you to feed coins into machines that illuminate the paintings. If you are over 65, ask the *museo* (especially if it is state-owned) whether there is a discount. Some offer student discounts – though mainly for residents of the European Union. For churches and minor museums whose charges we do not specify, allow a maximum of around 4 Euro per person.

- Make a realistic assessment of your stamina. Art touring shouldn't be treated as a test of endurance or self-denial. Most museum tickets are valid for the whole day so you can go out for a meal if you want, then come back – that's if the *museo* or *chiesa* doesn't close for the siesta. (Best to check that you will be allowed back in – without lining up again.) A few museums have their own cafeterias (though you may have to mortgage your house to eat in the Uffizi!) Carry some water if you can.

- Of course, the big museums don't have to be done in one single visit, though the entrance fees since the introduction of the Euro may deter you from spreading your visit over two days. But be warned: big collections can be exhausting. (Ever since Stendahl claimed he got physically ill in Italy from too much cultural stimulation, museum fatigue has been called "Stendahl's disease"). This book has been designed to combat Stendahl's disease: basically, to help you decide beforehand what you're going to concentrate on and more or less to stick to it.

- Decide whether and how you want to make a record of the Trail. Notes? Sketchbook? Photos? Flashes are forbidden – you will be reminded of this by an attendant just about every time you take out the camera. Many places forbid all photography – flash or no flash. To get a good view of sculpture, and high-up frescoes, low power binoculars are a great help.

- To avoid museum fatigue, focus on a manageable section, take your time, and plan some rest periods. Stretching exercises performed periodically can really help that low back pain that some people get after long periods inching their way along walls of paintings.

- A note about translating from the Italian: in most cases, we offer the names of the paintings in English only. Many of the words are easily translatable, even by someone who speaks not a word of Italian.

- The word *chiesa* means church. These Trails refer to dozens, each of which contains at least one major work of art. Where we have not translated the names of these churches into English, it is because you will never hear (or see) them referred to in this way. We have often provided details of their location, (churches are usually located in a *piazza* or *campo* of the same name as the church) but, with few exceptions, 'opening times' are variable, usually meaning between religious services. (In the smaller towns and in the southern regions of Italy, churches may be closed during the siesta.)

The Italian Renaissance and its Painters

The Renaissance – meaning "rebirth" – is a label devised in the 19th century to describe what happened during a spectacular period of cultural creativity, namely, the 14th, 15th and 16th centuries in Europe. The idea of rebirth refers to a renewal of enthusiasm for the arts and philosophy of ancient Rome. Classical culture had been conserved and adapted throughout the Middle Ages, in Byzantium and Western Europe, but many artists and thinkers of the Renaissance began to see ancient Rome as an ideal model for building and sculpture, and classical philosophy as a source for humanist thinking.

Several painters began the transition from the Middle Ages to the Renaissance; among them were the Florentine, Cimabue, and the Roman, Cavallini. It was the next generation, however, which is usually recognized as having provided the bridge into the Renaissance – especially Giotto, who was reputed to have been a pupil of Cimabue, and the Sienese painter, Duccio.

Throughout much of the 15th century, a progression of great artists – from Fra Angelico to Michelangelo – ensured that the center of the Renaissance remained in Florence. In that city, there was no shortage of patrons. The ruling families, such as the Medici and the Pazzi, and the increasingly influential mendicant orders of the Dominicans and the Franciscans were sympathetic to the new forms of realistic representation in art. These new forms long remained largely in the service of religion: even secular patrons typically gained the greatest prestige by commissioning works of art in the principal places of worship.

A generation or so after Florence, Venice began to develop its own system of cultural production, in which the Bellini family was the early leader. But the biggest challenge to the cultural dominance of Florence was to come from its south. The greatest potential patron of the arts in Italy was the papacy, and under the leadership of Pope Sixtus IV (after whom the Sistine Chapel was named) this potentiality began to be realized. For half a century – until the sack of Rome by French troops in 1527 – the greatest Italian artists of the day, among them Botticelli, Michelangelo and Raphael, were lured to Rome to work for the papacy.

Then the leadership passed to the wealthy city-state of Venice, whose greatest painters were Titian and Tintoretto. By the time they died at the end of the 16th century, the Renaissance was being displaced – in the somewhat arbitrary labeling of later generations – by the Age of the Baroque. So long as their limitations are recognized, these labels have their uses, but we must always realize that a late Renaissance painter like Tintoretto had much more in common with the Baroque Caravaggio than he had with the pre-Renaissance Giotto.

The Renaissance was by no means confined to Italy. At about the same time as the Early Renaissance was getting underway in Tuscany, the countries of northern Europe were similarly experimenting with new techniques and the new naturalism. Artists such as Albrecht Dürer from Nuremberg and Van Eyck from Bruges were making their mark. Painters, sculptors, and architects from either side of the Alps gained from a vigorous interchange of ideas.

About Painting in Italy at the Time of the Renaissance

Why did Italy play such a pivotal role in the development of the Renaissance? From a bewildering complex of possible reasons, we single out three:

Classical identification

Rome had of course been one of the great centers of classical civilization. In the 14th century, Italy differed from such other classical centers as Egypt, Persia, and Greece in a number of important respects, especially in:

Levels of prosperity

Both Florence and Venice were thriving centers of trade and commerce, which produced many entrepreneurs of great wealth. Rome was the center of the great wealth of the papacy. The prosperity of these cities was in turn linked to:

Political autonomy

Although Renaissance patriots such as Machiavelli understandably longed for the unification of the network of small states and principalities that then occupied the Italian peninsula, the very fragmentation of governance may have stimulated the emergence of new forms of cultural experimentation.

INTRODUCTION

Why was painting so prominent among the accomplishments of the Italian Renaissance? That there were many more great paintings than there were great sculptures or great buildings may be attributed to the simple fact that they were much cheaper to commission. Even this, however, began to change as the status of painters continually rose throughout the period. By the time of Titian, painters were commanding very considerable remuneration – which international patrons were all too prepared to provide.

Another interesting development in Renaissance painting came with the shift of interest from frescoes to discrete, portable paintings. Traditionally, discrete paintings had been favored for more devotional themes, as in Byzantine art, with its more stylized figures and gilt backgrounds. Frescoes were favored for narrative purposes; but they required well-heeled sponsors, who usually owned the houses and palaces whose walls were being adorned. The decisive shift away from the narrative fresco tradition came with Piero della Francesca in the 15th century. While he continued to produce frescoes, his discrete paintings lost their traditional stylized character, even when they focused on devotional themes. The distinction between the subjects proper to frescoes and those appropriate for discrete paintings meant little to Venetians such as the Bellinis, who were coming into national prominence at this time: the Venetian climate had never favored the fresco form of painting. By the beginning of the 16th century, when the papacy became the major patron of the arts, the traditional distinctions between discrete devotional paintings and narrative frescoes had all but disappeared.

Profiles of the Artists

GIOTTO (c.1266/7–1337)

Giotto di Bondone is commonly described as the "first" painter of the Italian Renaissance, and sometimes as the father of modern painting. His importance lies in his revolutionary departure from the comparatively stylized representation of the earlier Christian art of Western Europe and the iconic tradition of the Byzantine art of the east. While early Christian art is by no means devoid of emotion, it is easy to understand why Giotto's paintings caused a sensation among his contemporaries. Never before had art imitated nature in just this way. Never had the events of sacred history been placed in such spacious settings. Never had God been made so accessible – and ordinary people encouraged to view sacred figures as capable of the same feelings as they themselves.

The earliest intensive work by Giotto is at the great Basilica of St Francis at Assisi. Between 1296 and 1300, he and the members of his workshop painted, on the walls of the Upper Church, 28 frescoes depicting events from the life of St Francis. From 1302 until around 1305, he painted the walls of the Scrovegni (Arena) Chapel in Padua. This remains the most monumental (and best-preserved) concentration of his work. Around 1314, he began work on the Peruzzi Chapel in the Church of Santa Croce in Florence. Between 1319 and 1328, he returned – at intervals – to Santa Croce to paint the adjacent Bardi Chapel. In 1316, he went back to the Basilica at Assisi to work in the Lower Church for the next four years. After a prolific career, he died in 1337 in his early 70s, leaving a brilliant design for Florence's famous Campanile of the Duomo.

Comparing Giotto's three major cycles – in Assisi, Padua, and Florence – provides fascinating insights into the ways in which his art developed during his long career. His growing interest in architecture and with it, ever more detailed contexts for his figures, is just one of the features of his developing style. The Bardi and Peruzzi frescoes, for example, are full of very elaborate architectural treatments, with urban buildings, fortresses and decorative loggie framing the three-dimensional spaces in which simple and dignified characters pursue the drama of their lives.

DONATELLO (DONATO DI NICCOLO' DI BETTO BARDI) (1377–1446)

Throughout Donatello's long life, Florence remained his center. Although he travelled widely, he always returned to his home town and is buried in the crypt of the Chiesa di San Lorenzo. From an early age, Donatello acquired a mastery of the various sculptural media, being equally at home with stone, wood, and metal. He is today recognized as the leading sculptor of the early Italian Renaissance. Because sculpture was at the cutting edge of that movement, his influence extended well beyond his chosen field. Several of the leading painters of the Quattrocento, such as Masaccio and Mantegna, were deeply indebted to him, especially for his use of perspective, as were the sculptors who were to follow him. Vasari captured nicely the relationship between Donatello and Vasari's own hero, Michelangelo, when he observed that: "Either Donatello's spirit inspired Michelangelo, or the spirit later manifest in Michelangelo's work was anticipated in Donatello."

FRA ANGELICO (1395-1455)

Guido di Piero, later to become Fra Giovanni da Fiesole, then Fra Giovanni Angelico, and finally, simply: Fra Angelico (Angelic Brother) or Beato Angelico, was born just outside of Florence. He became a painter while still a child, and continued to paint after joining the Dominicans at the age of 20. How delighted he must have been to receive the commission to decorate the walls of his own monastery! The Dominicans lived according to a strict rule that emphasized charity, humility and voluntary poverty. Fra Angelico's genius was to produce great paintings that were full of piety and moral virtue, and theologically correct in every respect, but which radiated human sentiment.

Vasari, the painter, architect, and biographer of the Italian Renaissance artists, said of Fra Angelico:

> It was his custom never to retouch or repaint any of his works, but to leave them just as they were when finished the first time; for he believed that such was the will of God. It is said, indeed, that Fra Giovanni never took a brush in his hand until he had first offered a prayer; nor did he ever paint a Crucifixion without tears streaming down his cheeks.

Fra Angelico died in Rome. He is buried in the Church of S Maria Sopra Minerva – a couple of hundred yards from the more prominent tomb in the Pantheon of the High Renaissance painter Raphael – who was in many ways his successor in the limpidity of his work.

MASACCIO (CASO DI SER GIOVANNI) (c.1401-1428)

Masaccio was born in San Giovanni Valdarno, a village to the south of Florence. There is no evidence that he underwent the traditional apprenticeship for his craft. By 1422, however, he had registered with the Florentine guild of painters. Initially, he seemed a conservative artist, for he rejected the popular ornate International

Gothic style, instead trying to revive the long dormant Florentine tradition of Giottoesque realism. But at this very time, the Florentine tradition was itself being renewed, initially not by painters but by sculptors – such as Ghiberti, Brunelleschi and Donatello. It was Masaccio's role to translate into painting much of the innovatory progress that had been made by sculptors such as these.

Virtually nothing is known about his tragically early death in Rome. Masaccio left only a small body of work, and this is dominated by one set of frescoes –in the Brancacci Chapel in the Florence's Church of Santa Maria del Carmine. Here Masaccio was to have two great collaborators: Masolino, an older man who was however never his master, and, posthumously, Filippino Lippi, who completed the frescoes in the latter part of the 15th century. One of the most memorable of all the images in Italian Renaissance painting is there: Masaccio's: *The Expulsion of Adam and Eve*. Less than 20 years before Botticelli was born, the great Masaccio had painted his groundbreaking fresco of the *Trinity* in the church of Santa Maria Novella. Following the radical path laid down by Giotto, Masaccio took realism to new heights: he was the first Renaissance painter to study seriously the sculptures of antiquity, and he was the first to apply the laws of perspective to the art of painting. He was one of the great innovators of the early Renaissance, whose tragically short life was to prefigure that of his equally talented successor of the early Baroque period, Caravaggio.

FILIPPO LIPPI (1406–1469)

Fra Filippo Lippi was one of the artists who thrived under the patronage of the Florentine Medici family, but he quickly established a reputation that extended well beyond Florence. Vasari informs us that Michelangelo admired Fra Filippo. The father of Sandro Botticelli placed his son as a garzone (assistant) with Lippi. Botticelli in turn became the master of Filippo's son, Filippino.

Fra Filippo created a huge scandal when he fathered Filippino to an Augustinian nun, Lucrezia Buti, in Prato. Vasari reports that the pope offered to release Fra Filippo from his religious vows on condition that he marry his lover, but that the friar politely declined, preferring his freedom. Subsequent historians, however, state that Cosimo de' Medici did, in fact, negotiate the release of Filippo and Lucrezia from their vows and that, following the birth of Filippino, the couple married. The citizens of Spoleto were apparently less scandalized. When Filippo Lippi died in their city, they refused to return his body to his native Florence.

Fra Filippo's contemporaries admired his paintings for their delicate color and decorative detail, for the splendor of the architecture they often contained, for the great dignity with which he imbued their sacred figures, and for the sensual grace of his women. Like his contemporaries, Filippo experimented (usually successfully) with perspective and foreshortening, especially in his architectural settings and grouping of figures. Although his people are physical expressions of an idealized spiritual world, he manages to give variety to their facial expressions. Poses are often reminiscent of Roman statuary adorned, however, with rather medieval drapery. His favorite theme is the Madonna – an excellent excuse for painting beautiful women! Lippi's paintings of St Jerome occupy a special place in his *oeuvre*. St Jerome was one of the most popular saints of 15th century Florence, in part because of the many roles he played – scholar, translator of the Bible, bishop, and hermit. Some have suggested that St Jerome was of special significance for Lippi because of the painter's own contrition about his sins of the flesh. (Jerome is seen by some religious historians to have been something of a misogynist.)

PIERO DELLA FRANCESCA (c.1416–1492)

Piero's painting almost single-handedly represents all those qualities which epitomize the Renaissance for us: use of linear perspective, visual references to Graeco-Roman architecture and sculpture and the humanistic concentration on individual identity and achievement.
— M.A. Michael, Piero della Francesco: The Arezzo Frescoes

Piero is unusual in that he is most heavily represented by paintings located outside the major cities. He was born, raised and lived most of his life in the small town of Sansepolcro, in southeastern Tuscany. Unlike Raphael, who was born two generations later across the Mountains of the Moon in the nearby city of Urbino, Piero was never a participant in the patronage mainstream. Like Raphael, he spent time in Rome, but papal patronage in the middle of the 15th century was not what it was to become in Raphael's day, and no trace of Piero's work in Rome survives. Viewing his work takes us on a gentle course from one hilltop town to another. Piero did undertake work for such noted (some might say, infamous) soldier statesmen as Sigismondo Malatesta in Rimini and Federico da Montefeltro in Urbino, but the major commission of his career came from the Franciscans and resulted in *The Legend of the True Cross* in the humanist center of Arezzo. Piero's work is primarily seen in two of the Trails: the major works are in Arezzo, Monterchi and Sansepolcro at the start of the Florence-Rome Trail, and the remainder – the other side of the mountains to the east – on the Rome-Venice Trail.

Piero was an intellectual of some note, and sought in all his work to place mathematics at the service of art – most notably through the development of new techniques of perspective. Some of his townscapes seem clearly to anticipate modern ventures in cubism.

GIOVANNI BELLINI (c.1435–1516)

As the Renaissance arrived late in Venice, that city's first great painter, Giovanni Bellini, was a generation younger than the Florentine masters, Fra Angelico and Fra Filippo Lippi. Indeed, it was his artist father, Jacopo, who was one of the most important early disseminators in Venice of the new Florentine style of painting. Giovanni was therefore extremely well placed to make his mark early, although in time he came to be seen by many as somewhat old-fashioned when compared with his star pupil, Titian. But Bellini retained the respect of many talented painters and critics right up to the end of his long life – and beyond. Just ten years before Bellini died, Albrecht Dürer, the German engraver, said of him: "Giambellino is very old and still the best in painting." And nearly four centuries later, the Victorian critic John Ruskin expressed the view that two of Bellini's paintings (which are included in the Trails) were the best in the world.

Giovanni was very close to his father, and also to his brother, Gentile, who was the third great painter in the family. And that extraordinarily innovative painter, Andrea Mantegna, was his brother-in-law. In the early part of the decade of the 1460s, Bellini painted dozens of versions of the theme of the Madonna and Child. Of these, more than half are now outside Italy. But from those that remain in his country, the Accademia in Venice has assembled an unmatched collection of the Madonnas from the differing periods of his life.

MANTEGNA, ANDREA (c.1430–1506)

Mantegna was born in the Veneto – in the village of Isola di Carturo, between Vicenza and Padua. Inevitably for a boy with strong artistic interests, at an early age he became an apprentice in the great cultural center of Padua. His earliest known work was devoted to the frescoes in the Ovetari Chapel in the Chiesa degli Eremitani in that city – work that, tragically was all but destroyed in World War II. Working at that site must have been a great educational experience for the young painter, for the Ovetari Chapel is next door to the Scrovegni Chapel, whose frescoes were one of Giotto's greatest feats. At this time, Mantegna was also made aware of the work of Donatello, for one of his collaborators in Padua had been a student of the great sculptor. Many critics attribute the strong three-dimensionality of Mantegna's paintings to this early influence. Most of Mantegna's working life was spent in northern Italy, as he moved between major commissions in Verona and Mantua, although he did spend some time in Rome.

Mantegna was also an important exponent of the art of copperplate engraving, and exercised a strong influence on Albrecht Dürer, who was a generation behind him. Though a painter of genius, Mantegna was never to attain the recognition of his brother-in-law, Giovanni Bellini. In part, this was because he worked for most of his life in smaller cities, such as Mantua and Padua.

GHIRLANDAIO, DOMENICO
(c.1449–1494)

For the entire 20th century, Ghirlandaio was the least fashionable of the major Renaissance painters. Throughout that century, the term that was most frequently used to describe his massive *oeuvre* was 'mediocre.' Admittedly, Ghirlandaio lacked the genius of contemporaries such as Botticelli, Leonardo or his student Michelangelo, who were able to fashion images that resonate with the collective unconscious of all humanity. But Ghirlandaio was a popular painter of his day, and is now acknowledged as one of the earliest Renaissance painters to experiment with perspective and foreshortening. Among his most noted works are his frescoes in the Sistine Chapel: these demonstrate clearly his great design skills and his ability to execute exquisitely detailed *tableaux* – an influence from northern Europe. He might very well receive a more sympathetic response in the new millennium, as art historians become increasingly critical about the last century's obsession with genius.

INTRODUCTION

SANDRO BOTTICELLI (1445–1510)

Alessandro Botticelli's surname, meaning "little bottle," was originally the nickname of his apparently well-padded brother but eventually it was adopted by his entire family. The son of a tanner, Alessandro was born in Florence near the Church of the Ognissanti. He enjoyed distinguished contemporary neighbors – people like the great explorer, Amerigo Vespucci, whose name was to grace the American continent. Vespucci, in turn, was very close to the Medici: both families were to become Botticelli's most important patrons. Others who were to prove very influential included Piero and Antonio Pollaiuolo (Botticelli spent some time in their workshop), and Andrea del Verocchio, who was also Leonardo's teacher.

Botticelli's own career began in the goldsmith's workshop – an experience that he was later able to draw upon in his painting (in the jewelry worn by Venus and the three Graces in *La Primavera*, for example). He was not apprenticed as a painter until the age of 18 – late by Renaissance standards. His master was the Carmelite monk, Fra Filippo Lippi, who showed him how to capitalize on the main achievements of the Renaissance: the use of perspective to create the illusion of depth and spaciousness, new ideas about composition, the depiction of "corporeality" – giving seemingly tangible human substance to painted figures. In his turn, Botticelli was to become the master of Filippino Lippi – Fra Filippo's son.

It seems that, late in his career, Botticelli may have become a devotee of Savonarola, the firebrand Dominican monk who organized a "bonfire of the vanities" on which books, works of art, extravagant clothing, opulent jewelry, and furniture were burned. Perhaps because of this, Botticelli's later paintings are less sumptuous than the earlier ones, and they deal with more sober themes. In the 16th century, Botticelli's popularity declined and he had to wait until the 19th century to be rediscovered. In part, his falling popularity was the product of misunderstanding: his early paintings were sometimes dismissed as being merely decorative and devoid of significant philosophical, political and religious content. As we shall see, nothing could be further from the truth.

LEONARDO DA VINCI (1452–1519)

Leonardo was born in the small Tuscan town of Vinci, the illegitimate son of a notary. By his middle teens, he had moved to

Florence and entered into an apprenticeship with the sculptor and goldsmith, Andrea del Verrocchio, with whom he developed a close collaborative relationship. As one of the supreme figures of the Renaissance, Leonardo da Vinci was jack of all trades and master of the lot – painter, anatomist, botanist, engineer, and artificer. Despite (or perhaps, because of) his mastery of so many disciplines, Leonardo left many of his works unfinished.

At a time of a huge expansion of human knowledge, Leonardo sought to embody the Renaissance ideal of the Universal Man. Indeed, he may be the last such Universal Man, for after him, the continuing expansion of knowledge put the ideal out of reach. Even at the end of the 15th century, it was a formidable aspiration, especially for one such as Leonardo who had not had the privilege of a formal education. He was thus the epitome of the self-made man, but one who always considered painting to be the highest of the sciences. Because of this, he was critical of those painters who sought only to produce beautiful works of art, for such a path led ultimately to superficiality. This was a lesson not lost on the painters of the 16th century.

As a painter, however, Leonardo's productivity lagged far behind his influence. While Vasari claimed that no one had ever shed such luster on the art of painting as Leonardo, Italy contains only six of his works, about one third of the total known to exist around the world. For this reason, we suggest that any serious follower of Leonardo should be prepared to travel (at least!) to the Louvre in Paris. Even so, those wishing to restrict their travels to Italy – or, indeed, only to Florence – will still be able to gain an appreciation of the universe of Leonardo the painter: lit by twilight, mysterious, and peopled with enigmatic characters.

In this respect, Leonardo resembled his great predecessor Piero della Francesca. Above all the other painters in the Trails, these two sought to integrate the arts and the sciences, and yet, strangely, to modern eyes, both painted the most mystifying figures. Such conjunctions are strange to modern people, because we tend to associate the natural sciences with technological certitude. Five centuries ago, however, the natural sciences and the art of painting may equally have been concerned with penetrating the realms of the mysterious.

MICHELANGELO BUONARROTI (1475–1564)

The most benignant rector of Heaven cast his merciful eyes
towards the earth and … decided to send into the world an artist

who would be skilled in every art and craft, whose work would
serve to show us how to achieve perfection in art ... to use
judgment in sculpture, and in architecture, make dwellings safe,
comfortable, healthy, pleasant, well-proportioned and rich in
ornament. He determined, moreover, to give this artist a
knowledge of true moral philosophy ... so that he may be
called divine rather than earthly.
— Giorgio Vasari, Lives of the Artists.

Although Michelangelo was born in Caprese – a village not far from Sansepolcro – he was in no way a "provincial" like Piero della Francesca. He came from an old Florentine family, which had temporarily fallen on hard times – hence his rural birthplace, for his father had been forced to take a position as a minor official of the city. Michelangelo's family was soon to return to Florence, and indeed, he was later able to restore the family fortunes. Although his father had wished him to take up a career in public service, Michelangelo asserted his intention of becoming an artist early. At the age of 13, he was apprenticed to the leading Florentine fresco painter – Domenico Ghirlandaio. Within two years, he had been taken into the service of Florence's ruler, Lorenzo de Medici, even being invited to reside in the Medici Palace. In 1494 he left Florence, and lived in Bologna for a year, after which he lived in Rome from 1496 to 1501. Returning to Florence in 1501, he was given many commissions for sculptures, among them the magnificent David. Michelangelo began work on the Sistine Chapel in 1508; and finished it four years later – except for the Last Judgment, which he painted between 1535 and 1541. In the intervening years he lived mostly in Florence.

Ever since his contemporary and friend, Giorgio Vasari, published his enormously influential *Lives of the Artists* in the middle of the 16th century, Michelangelo has been recognized as one of the great artists who most fully represented the ideals of the Renaissance. Greatly influenced by classical antiquity, he sought to realize himself through a wide range of creative activity – as sculptor, architect, painter and poet. He died at the ripe old age of 89, and is buried in Florence in the church of Santa Croce.

RAPHAEL (RAFFAELLO SANZIO) (1483–1520)

In the course of his tragically short life, Raphael came to occupy the pivotal position in the development of Renaissance painting. Born in Urbino, he derived from Piero della Francesca a profound concern for the placing of figures in meaningful spaces and for the mathematically rigorous definition of perspective to lend order to the treatment of these spaces. His youthful years in Florence gained him familiarity with the work of several Italian masters – Fra Angelico, Botticelli, Leonardo (whom he came to idolize) and Michelangelo (with whom he enjoyed a relationship of reasonably friendly rivalry).

In the 12 years in Rome – when he primarily worked on the Stanze, a series of rooms in the Vatican for which Pope Julius II had commissioned paintings, and on the Villa Farnesina, the house of his wealthy patron, Agostino Chigi – Raphael was able to reconcile the differing demands of classical humanism and the Church, of the sacred and the everyday, of *disegno* and *colorito*. In so doing he pointed the way forward for the Venetian masters of the late Renaissance, Titian and Tintoretto, and beyond them to the Baroque painters of the succeeding century.

TITIAN (TIZIANO VECELLIO) (1485–1576)

"Titian … is the only painter who expressed nearly all of the Renaissance that could find expression in painting," enthused the American art historian, Bernard Berenson. For a Venetian painter, Titian was extraordinarily successful on the international scene. Across Europe, the nobility vied with each other to retain his services. His favorite patron – Charles V of the Holy Roman Empire – ennobled him and appointed him court painter in 1532. Such spectacular successes meant that Titian, who after all was not a native Venetian, did not have to fit all that comfortably into the tight world of Venetian art, with its guilds and family dynasties. Some critics allege that his fierce ambition led to his falling out with the aged Giovanni Bellini, who had earlier been his master. The only master with whom Titian enjoyed a close collaborative association was his peer, Giorgione, also an outsider to Venice. When it came Titian's turn to be master, he mysteriously dismissed the young apprentice Tintoretto after only ten days. His most successful teacher-pupil relationship was with the even more alien El Greco (from the Venetian colony of Crete). Western art was to embark on a long journey from the dream-like mysteries of Giorgione to the surreal nightmares of El Greco, and Titian was its guide for that journey.

As the most successful Venetian painter, Titian had strained relations with some of his Florentine counterparts. Michelangelo, for one, was an admirer of Titian's style, but regretted that Venetian painters did not at the outset learn to draw well, and went on to characterize Venetian painting as rather effeminate when compared with the robust manliness of the Florentines. Certainly there were important differences in technique dividing the Venetians and the Florentines. While the latter typically prepared detailed sketch plans before starting out on the actual painting, the former were more inclined to begin with the placing of areas of color. In his early years, Titian took over from Giorgione the *alla prima* method of brushing paint directly on the canvas and building it up in layers. In this way he produced brilliantly and subtly colored works.

For the bulk of his immensely long career – his middle period may well be defined to cover the best part of the half century from 1518 – Titian's style in his religious paintings was monumental. The tone was set in 1518, with the appearance, in Venice, of his spectacularly successful *Frari Assumption of the Virgin*. In his early period he was heavily influenced by Giorgione. This Giorgionesque approach was informal, lyrical, and small-scale – at least insofar as the number of figures was concerned – and paid great attention to background landscapes. Unfortunately, the most outstanding examples of Titian's Giorgionesque work are now outside Italy, but two early paintings now in Rome can serve to represent this period. The first of these is his *Baptism of Christ*; the second *Salomé with the Head of John the Baptist*.

TINTORETTO (JACOBO ROBUSTI) (c.1519–1594)

Vasari described Tintoretto as "… extravagant, capricious, swift and determined, and the most awesome brain that painting ever had." Like Giotto two and a half centuries before him, Tintoretto stood at the end of a major phase of cultural history, and his work opened up possibilities for those who would be following on in the next stage. As the last great painter of the Italian Renaissance, Tintoretto is considered by some to be the major forerunner of the Baroque period. In some ways, he was the first painter whose career followed a modern trajectory. For reasons that are little understood, he was expelled from Titian's *bottega* after only ten days as a *garzone* (or apprentice). This experience did not blind him to the value of the work of his former master, for he adopted as his early motto: "The drawing of Michelangelo and the color of Titian." His *oeuvre* is innovative and energetic but uneven. Tintoretto was perhaps the only major Renaissance painter to portray honestly scenes of squalor and decay. Such scenes figure prominently in several of his paintings of St Rocco, the patron saint of the afflicted.

Tintoretto was also strongly attracted to themes concerned with the passion and death of Christ, and little interested in those concerned with the Madonna and Child. In his later years he was reported to have observed that the most important colors in the painter's palette were black and white. Here may be some of the origins of the tenebrist and chiaroscuro styles that were to attain such prominence in the work of painters such as Caravaggio in the following century. He also anticipated the Baroque in the vast scale and dynamic sweep of his paintings, and sought to obliterate much of the distinction between figure and background of earlier Renaissance paintings. Instead, he drew the eye of the viewer into the swirling totality of the actions he so powerfully portrayed.

CARAVAGGIO (MICHELANGELO MERISI OR AMERIGHI) (c.1570–1610)

There was art before him and art after him, and they were not the same.
— Robert Hughes

In a short, tumultuous life marked by fights, imprisonment, and quarrels as well as brief periods of dazzling success, Caravaggio effected a revolution in form and iconography. His exploration of chiaroscuro led to many followers, and he may be seen as a bridge between the classical academies of the Renaissance and the more illusionist and decorative character of Baroque painting. Strictly speaking, he is a Baroque rather than a Renaissance painter, but his importance within the art of Italy is undeniable.

He spent much of his life in Rome, although he was born in Lombardy and was an apprentice to Peterzano in Milan. By 1593, he was painting in Rome, where he quickly gained a series of commissions from prelates in high places, who apparently were unconcerned about the homoeroticism that was already apparent in his work. Caravaggio was a short-tempered man, prone to violence. Accused of murder in 1606, he fled to Naples, and later Malta and Sicily. In 1610 he disappeared forever. Whether he was murdered by one of his enemies, or died of a fever, as was rumored at the time, may never be known.

Just as Giotto is too early to be properly placed in this book, but too important to leave out, Caravaggio may also be considered out of place. He himself would not have cared where he was categorized, for he was the most unconventional of painters – themselves a fairly unconventional lot. And his art is too exciting to be left out simply because he was born a generation after Tintoretto.

BERNINI, GIAN LORENZO, (1598-1660)

No man has left so spectacular a mark on any city than Bernini on Rome. With the strong and continuing support of the Barberini family (especially when they occupied the papacy), Bernini transformed many parts of Rome. He was a prodigiously productive sculptor and architect, and one who worked well outside the years of the Renaissance. So we here offer a transparent compromise. We do not claim to have offered a comprehensive set of works by Bernini. Rather, we visit and briefly comment on four sites where he left his most prominent work: the Piazza San Pietro, the Museo Borghese, the Piazza Barberini, and the Piazza Navona.

SECTION 1

FLORENCE, ROME AND VENICE

Left: Brunelleschi's Duomo

View of Florence

TRAIL 1:
Florence and Surrounds

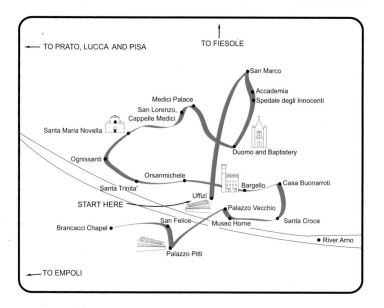

TO PRATO, LUCCA AND PISA

TO FIESOLE

San Marco

Accademia
Spedale degli Innocenti

Medici Palace

San Lorenzo,
Cappelle Medici

Santa Maria Novella

Ognissanti

Duomo and Baptistery

Orsanmichele

Santa Trinita'

Bargello · Casa Buonarroti

Uffizi

START HERE

Palazzo Vecchio

San Felice

Museo Horne

Santa Croce

Brancacci Chapel

River Arno

Palazzo Pitti

TO EMPOLI

Florence

Introduction to the Trail

For the cultural tourist, Florence is one of the few absolutely essential places to visit. It is the cradle of the Renaissance, home of two of the world's great art galleries, political and administrative center of the great region of Tuscany, and one-time capital of the Italian nation. It is an elegant, compact city bounded on the southern side by the River Arno and houses by far the greatest number of Renaissance art works of any Italian city. The Florence

Trail identifies the most critically acclaimed and · best-known paintings and sculptures. There is much more to see if you have time!

To do this Trail you will need at least two days. Spend one full day in the Uffizi: you will not be disappointed. The rest of the Trail can be covered in a day, but the art lover will be rewarded by a much longer stay in this, the greatest of all art cities, especially if you wish to sample the side trips we suggest.

Any first-time visitor to Florence should begin at its historic civic center – the Piazza della Signoria (just over half a mile to the southeast of the main railway station). Just off the Piazza is the first stop on this Trail: the great Uffizi Galleries, on the northern banks of the Arno river. After the Uffizi, we suggest you walk nearly a mile north, to the Museo San Marco, site of one of the world's greatest concentrations of the works of one genius – Fra Angelico, with some charming works also by Fra Bartolomeo. From there, you progress slowly and indirectly towards the south, taking in most notably a number of the works of Michelangelo, before crossing the Arno to visit the second great gallery in Florence, the Pitti, a must for any Raphael enthusiast. You are also invited to complete the Trail by making brief trips, northerly to Fiesole (for more Fra Angelico), and westerly to Prato and Empoli (for more Fra Filippo Lippi).

The Uffizi

Location: Piazzale degli Uffizi 6 – between the Piazza della Signoria and the Arno River – a little over half a mile southeast of the Stazione di Santa Maria Novella.

Contact details: Tel. 055 294 883

Opening hours: 8:30 am–9:00 pm Tues.–Fri., 8:30 am–midnight Sat., 8:30 am–8:00 pm Sun., closed Mon. For the most recent information, contact the Uffizio Informazione Turistiche, Via Cavour, 1 Rosso, 50129, Tel. 055 290832 or 055 2767383. For more information, you can also visit the website, which also features a few virtual tours: http://musa.uffizi.firenze.it)

Other information: Tickets can be purchased in advance, either by calling and paying by credit card; or in person, at either the Uffizi or Accademia Galleries, preferably two days before your intended visit. If you get your tickets on the day, be very early or be prepared to wait in long lines.

Admission: Euro 8.50 (+ Euro 1.55 for prior booking)

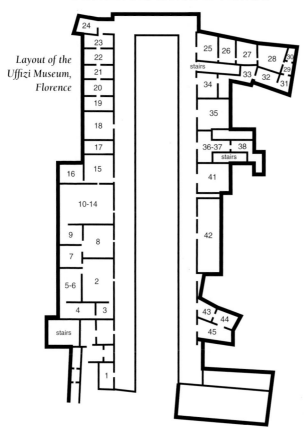

Layout of the Uffizi Museum, Florence

FLORENCE AND SURROUNDS

The pre-eminent status of the Uffizi (the "Offices") as a treasure-house of Renaissance painting is a result of the passion of those great patrons of the arts, the Medici family, who ruled for so long in Florence. The building was designed in the mid-16th century by Giorgio Vasari to house the administrative offices of the grand duchy – hence its name. Within 20 years, however, it had already begun to serve as the showplace of the greatest Medici works of art. To the present day it bears the stamp of its origins: it boasts the largest and most important collection of Renaissance art of any gallery in the world.

This Trail takes you through the most important rooms of the museum and concentrates on the most significant paintings. (There are 1,555 paintings in all, so we've had to be selective!) If you have time, return for a second day to view the rest of this remarkable collection, presented in over 45 rooms. *Sala* means "room" in Italian.

FLORENCE AND SURROUNDS

Sala 2

To enter Room 2 of the Uffizi is to be assured of a memorable experience, for there, displayed almost cheek by jowl, are arguably three of the most magnificent versions of the Madonna and Child enthroned, all painted at the dawn of the Italian Renaissance. This is a great opportunity to compare the three: Giotto's *Ognissanti Madonna*, the *Rucellai Madonna* of Duccio di Buoninsegna (1285) and Cimabue's *Madonna di Santa Trinitá* (c.1280–1285). Duccio was the greatest of the Sienese painters. Cimabue is commonly believed to have been Giotto's teacher, but, as Dante rather cruelly pointed out in his *Purgatorio*: "Cimabue was thought to have the mastery, but now the cry is for Giotto, so that the fame of the other is dimmed." As you enter Sala 2 from the corridor, facing you is Giotto's *Ognissanti Madonna*.

Giotto
Ognissanti Madonna (La Madonna col Bambino Gesu', Santi e Angeli), 1306–1310

The Madonnas of Cimabue and Duccio seem more closely tied to the stylized Byzantine tradition. However, some Byzantine features remain in Giotto's painting, too: the gold background and the serried rows of angels, for example. For all that, Giotto's Madonna sits more comfortably in her elegant Gothic throne, her head positioned at a more naturalistic angle. Giotto enthusiasts also like to point out

the "volumetric fullness" of his Madonna, which simply means that, in contrast to the other two, she really does appear to be taking up a dimensional space: look at the way the folds of her gown flatten over her knees and her breasts. The two angels at her feet offer her the Marian symbols of roses and lilies, while the two at her side hold out a crown and the eucharistic pyx, which represents the passion of Christ.

Giotto's **Ognissanti Madonna** *was one of the earliest three-dimensional Madonnas.*
Illustration Matt Morrow.

Turn and face the back wall of the room to view Giotto's famous polyptych.

Giotto
Badia Polyptych (Polittico di Badia), 1330

This polyptych, or multi-panelled altarpiece, originally sat on the main altar of the church of the Badia family in Florence. It is regarded as marking the end of Giotto's early phase. The Madonna and Child, in the central panel, are flanked on the (viewer's) left by St Nicholas and St John the Evangelist and on the right, by St Peter and St Benedict. The brilliant Byzantine gold backgrounds with their Kufic script and the Gothic architecture of the panels' frames nevertheless recede behind figures of great vitality. Giotto has used radical techniques of foreshortening to achieve this impression of sculptural relief.

After viewing the other Madonnas in this room, go straight to Sala 7 to view works by the "friar painter" Fra Angelico, Piero della Francesca, and Masaccio. However, if you intend later to visit Siena (Trail 4) you may want to spend some time in *Sala 3*, which contains works by the great Sienese painters, Simone Martini and the Lorenzetti brothers. Also go to:

Sala 5–6

Gentile da Fabriano
Adoration of the Magi, (1385?–1427)

This work, commissioned by the wealthy Strozzi family, is one of the most opulent of the Quattrocento. A fabulously accoutered procession, led by the Three Kings, winds its way down a mountain path to the manger. But there is more to admire in the painting than its lavish decoration: the exquisitely modelled figures, for example, and the gentle play of light on the scene.

Sala 7

Just inside this room, to your left, you will view two Fra Angelico paintings.

Fra Angelico
Coronation of the Virgin (Incoronazione della Vergine), c.1435

The gleaming setting for Angelico's Coronation is his version of paradise – a domed firmament which sends out heavenly rays that bathe all its occupants (and seemingly the viewer) in a golden light. The newly crowned Queen of Heaven and son are flanked by the faithful. Cordons of angel-musicians surround them: there appear to be great hosts of these, disappearing into the distance behind the elevated figures of Jesus and Mary. Two of the angels swing incense-burning censers, and a troupe of six angelic dancers sway gracefully around the divine couple. Fra Angelico, perhaps with his assistants, painted this radiant picture for the Church of Sant'Egidio during his middle years.

In this same room, there's another glimmering Fra Angelico:

Fra Angelico
Madonna and Child. After 1450

Mary sits on a red-brocaded throne, surrounded by a blaze of gold-on-gold light. Here is a further example of Fra Angelico's simultaneous acknowledgement of medieval tradition and contemporary innovation. The background is pure Byzantium, but the rest of the painting – the natural fall of the robes from the ample knees, and the life-like (if small-headed) infant – belong to the Renaissance.

Masaccio and Masolino
Madonna and Child with St Anne and Five Angels (Pala di Sant'Anna Metterza), 1424–25

Not many Renaissance paintings depicted the infant Jesus with his mother and grandmother, as Masaccio and Masolino have done here. Mary's mother, St Anne, a protective hand on her daughter's right shoulder, surrounds the Madonna and Child like a mother hen with her chicks. Most critics now accept that the Madonna, Child, and angel on the right were executed by Masaccio, and the rest by Masolino. St Anne was especially important to the Florentines because on her feast day in 1343, they had expelled a tyrant.

Masaccio
Casini Madonna, 1426–27

For reasons that are quite obvious, the alternative name for this charming picture is *The Madonna of the Tickle.* Much of what was original in Masaccio can be observed here: he was one of the first

Florentine painters to capture the playfulness that so often marks the interactions between mother and infant.

The panel has had a very adventurous career in the 20th century. Stolen by the Nazis during the World War II, it was not reclaimed until 1947, when at last it was authoritatively attributed to Masaccio. In 1971, it was stolen again, and was not recovered until 1974. Since 1988, it has been securely held in the Uffizi – although some of the museum's tourist catalogs haven't yet caught up with this development!

Among the many other treasures of the Uffizi's Room 7, you will find Piero's famous portraits of his patrons, the Duke and Duchess of Urbino, Federigo da Montefeltro and Battista Sforza.

Piero della Francesca
Diptych of the Duke and Duchess of Urbino (Dittico dei Duchi di Urbino), c.1465

Posed in solemn profile, like the heroes depicted on classical Roman medals and coins, they are painted on two double-sided panels that were originally hinged, like a book. The physical features of the two nobles are rendered with great precision: no attempt has been made to disguise the Duke's nose, which was hacked by an opponent's sword during a tournament. Behind them, unimpeded by window-frames or balustrades, stretches a magnificent vista that enables Piero to give full rein to his love of perspective: the hills and rivers of the countryside that comprised the Montefeltro estates. Don't miss the paintings on the reverse sides, which Piero executed after the death of the Duchess. Continuing the classical mood of the portraits, Piero has depicted the Duke and Duchess as allegorical figures, being conveyed in triumph like the ancient heroes of Petrarch's epic poems. They are each accompanied by four Virtues: Faith, Charity, Hope, and Modesty in the case of Battista Sforza, and Temperance, Fortitude, Justice and Prudence for Federigo. The unicorns pulling Battista's carriage symbolize purity and chastity, their reins held by a little angel. A grown-up angel seems to be crowning the Duke in transit.

You shouldn't leave Sala 7 without pausing before the famous *Battle of San Romano* by Paolo Uccello.

Sala 8

We now move into Sala 8, which contains paintings from the middle of the 15th century. In here, we can feast our eyes on the celebrated Madonnas of the friar painter Fra Filippo Lippi. Rather charmingly, the Uffizi has varied its normal practice of chronologically ordering its paintings in order to place Filippo's son, Filippino Lippi, in the same room as his father. This would once have been considered a scandalous co-location, because of the circumstances surrounding the conception of Filippino. His mother, Lucrezia Buti, was a nun who was Lippi's favorite Madonna model. Some scholars believe that the infant Filippino may well have been the model for several of Filippo's depictions of the Christ Child.

Filippo Lippi
Maringhi Coronation (Incoronazione della Vergine) begun in 1440, finished 1447

This opulent, gold-decorated work – a splendid example of Lippi's *ornazio* style – depicts the coronation of the Virgin Mary by God the Father. It was commissioned for the high altar of Sant'Ambrogio in Florence by Francesco Maringhi, the prior of the church. (Maringhi is pictured reverently kneeling in the lower right of the picture.) The overall symmetry of the ornate design reflects the love of pageantry in 15th century Florentine society. But note the naturalistic poses of the figures, despite their formal, gold-embroidered garments. The coronation is witnessed by serried rows of saints and angels, not unlike those depicted in celestial paintings of the previous century. St Ambrose, patron saint of the church, stands in rose-colored robe on the extreme left of the painting. The counter-balancing figure on the extreme right, in complementary rose-colored garb, is St John the Baptist, the patron saint of Florence. The monk kneeling in front of Ambrose and looking out at the viewer with his chin resting on his hand may be a self-portrait of Lippi. While the composition is somewhat traditional – especially in the use of the arches to separate the different groups of figures – the figures themselves are lively and their facial expressions animated and natural. The picture offers a feast of color – white lilies, sheer veils, gold embroidery and rosy, flesh tones against the intense blue-striped awning, lit from behind under the left-hand arch.

And now turn to the interesting little paintings in a predella from an altarpiece. It is situated underneath one of the Lippi Madonnas.

Filippo Lippi
Barbadori Altarpiece Predella, late 1430s

The theme of the three small paintings that comprise the Barbadori predella is the Christian triumph of life over death. The three panels depict St Frediano diverting the course of the River Serchio, the Annunciation of the Death of the Virgin, and St Augustine in his study. The three arrows piercing his heart are a reference to Augustine's life-long struggle to understand the Holy Trinity. In the painting of the Virgin, a dignified but saddened Mary receives the announcement of her death from the angel: a poignant reminder of the earlier visit to announce her divine pregnancy. As a prelude to her imminent assumption into heaven, angels have brought the apostles to bid her farewell. In other versions of this theme, the sign of Mary's impending death is a palm branch from the garden of paradise. Fra Filippo, however, pictures her receiving, from the hand of the angel, a glowing candle of the kind that was used in prayers for the dead and dying. The golden, metallic gleam of the taper immediately commands our attention in a scene otherwise suffused with natural light from the left of the pillars.

Above the predella are two panels.

Filippo Lippi
Virgin Annunciate (with St John the Baptist), early 1450s

The four figures are painted on two wooden panels that may have decorated a piece of furniture – possibly the doors of a cupboard. The Virgin is depicted in a moment of fluid movement: she has turned to receive the Archangel, her right hand raised in fright or protest. In the left-hand picture field, Gabriel has delivered his divine message, his deferentially lowered head completing the arc formed by the two figures. St John the Baptist, wearing animal skins and a troubled expression, stands, weight on his right foot and left leg forward, his right hand raised in the characteristic pose of the precursor of Christ.

The next picture is the one commonly regarded as the most significant of Fra Filippo's many Madonnas:

Filippo Lippi

Madonna and Child with Two Angels (Madonna col Bambino e due Angeli), mid to late 1460s

The theme for this very beautiful panel is the marriage of Christ as Bridegroom with Mary as the church. Mary is depicted, conventionally enough, as preoccupied by her sad, prophetic vision, and is believed to be modelled on Lucrezi Buti. As in many medieval paintings, the Holy Infant has the physical form of a baby, but the facial expression of an adult. His dignified gaze and mature gesture, far from being those of a doomed and helpless child, offer a dramatic contrast to the oblivious cheerfulness of the angel. The delicately subdued and harmonious coloring of the painting serves to unite its different planes: hazy azure background sky and water with the light fabric of the angel's chemise; light on rocky hills with flesh and hair and the carved arm of the Madonna's throne. The Madonna's beautifully rendered sheer veil is sometimes interpreted as a reference to the Child's swaddling cloth. The craggy landscape behind the figures may signify the harsh suffering that lay ahead, or the rock on which the church was to be established. Other symbols lurk in the mysterious background: the City of God, the sea of which Mary is the Stella Maris, the Tower of David, among others.

Lippi's Madonna wears Renaissance art's most intricate veil. Illustration Matt Morrow.

If you haven't yet tired of Lippi's favorite (or most frequently commissioned) subject for his paintings, there are three more Madonnas that deserve your attention before you leave Sala 8:

Filippo Lippi
Medici Novitiate Altarpiece, (Pala del Noviziato), mid to late 1440s

The serious expressions worn by the figures in this painting – especially that of the out-of-sorts Child, contrast with the rather more ethereal mood of his depiction of the Madonna and Child and two angels to the left of this work. But the picture is full of interest and innovation. For example, contemporary viewers would have considered it quite daring for Filippo Lippi to depict the saints as seated in the Virgin's presence, and of the same height as herself. In other ways, however – for example by elongating and idealizing all five adult figures – Lippi follows standard Renaissance practice. The chapel for which the panel was designed was dedicated to the physician-saints (and therefore patrons of the Medici) and early Christian martyrs, Cosmas and Damian, seated on either side of the Virgin. The Madonna is enthroned in an elaborate, vaulted aedicule, whose splendid architecture is reflected in the shell-shaped recesses on either side of her platformed throne. Scallop shells are sometimes interpreted as Marian emblems and also as pilgrim symbols, derived from the legend of the birth of Venus.

Filippo Lippi
Annalena Adoration (Adorazione del Bambino con SS. Ilarione, Girolamo, Angeli e La Maddalena), mid 1450s

In this picture of the Nativity and the Adoration of the Shepherds, the Holy Family is pictured, not in the manger, but in a flowery meadow in front of it. This is an example of a "Wilderness Adoration," whose special theme was that of penance – an act often associated with the deprivation voluntarily endured by holy men and women in desert and mountain wildernesses. Further clues as to the penitential purpose of the picture lie in the figures that surround the Holy Family. St Hilarion, an early Christian hermit is there. So is St Jerome, who was often depicted in Renaissance art as the penitent hermit. A bedraggled Mary Magdalene – an image from her time as a hermit in the Palestinian wilderness – kneels prayerfully against the ruin of the manger

Lippi's **Annalena Adoration**

wall. These figures and those of the approaching shepherds
provide the context for Mary and Joseph's grave contemplation of
the Incarnation. The Madonna has laid the Child on the folds of
her robe, freeing her hands for adoration, and perhaps presaging
the dead Christ on a winding sheet. A troubled St Joseph looks on.
A group of angels hovers overhead, holding a banderole inscribed
with the message *Gloria (in excelsis) Deo.* The warm vermilion of
the robes and the golden halos of the angels, saints and Holy
Family contrast with the darkly dramatic tones of Fra Filippo's
imagined wilderness. Broken tree-trunks, rocky crags and a forest
portend the hard journey that lies beyond the temporary comfort
of grass and flowers.

Filippo Lippi
*Camaldoli Adoration (Adorazione del Bambino con s. Giovannino e
San Romualdo),* mid 1460s

This painting, which derives its popular name from the cell that
once housed it in the hermitage of Camaldoli, is another example
of a Wilderness Adoration. As in Fra Filippo's *Annalena Adoration,*
(on the same wall in this room) the Christ Child lies in a flowery
field, resting on Mary's garments, while his mother worships. In

this case the penitential figures looking on are St John the Baptist, and, tucked into the bottom right-hand corner of the picture, St Romuald, the 11th century founder of the Camoldolensian monastic order. The beautifully drawn Camaldoli wilderness is a truly surreal backdrop to the pastel-toned figure of the Virgin. Behind John the Baptist lays a barren gorge with bare hillsides and dead trees. In contrast, behind the Virgin there flows a clear stream, separating her from more rocky crags, shadowy ledges and intermittent forest. From the skies appear the disembodied hands of God the Father and the Holy Spirit in the form of a dove at the apex of the triangle of figures. This is preparing the ground for the more fully psychedelic frescoes that were to crown Lippi's career in Spoleto.

The paintings of Filippino Lippi may also be viewed in this room, and there is one more in Sala 9. Also in Sala 9 are paintings of the Seven Virtues, of which the one on the far left – and the most vividly colored – is *Fortitude (La Fortezza)* by Botticelli. The bulk of Botticelli's magnificent canon can be seen in the following rooms.

Sala 10–14

Had the Uffizi stuck rigidly to the policy of ordering its painters chronologically, the artist who dominates the next rooms – Sandro Botticelli – would have split the Lippis, for Botticelli was in turn the

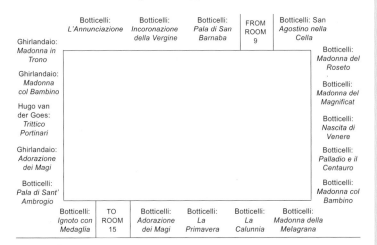

The Uffizi Rooms 10–14 (now one room).

student of Filippo and the master of Filippino. Rooms 10 to 14 in the Uffizi have been merged in order to accommodate the gallery's magnificent collection of Botticelli paintings (although other painters' works are housed there as well). Botticelli fans should also note that some of his works have been hung in Sala 8 (*Madonna del Rosario; Madonna della Loggia*) and in Sala 9 (the allegorical *Fortitude* and *The Discovery of the Body of Holophernes; The Return of Judith*). In any case, be prepared for the crush, for here are two of the most popular paintings in history – *Spring* (*La Primavera*) and *The Birth of Venus* (*La Nascita di Venere*). The map of the room will help you quickly identify the Botticelli paintings so you can decide how best to spend your time.

Botticelli
St Augustine Writing in his Cell (San Agostino nella Cella),
c.1490–94

This small painting is another of Botticelli's more austere works from his later period. No verdant Renaissance background landscape here, and no sumptuous interior. The painting is reduced almost to a two-tone treatment: the neutral, earthy, gray-browns of Augustine's cold, vaulted cell, and the contrasting red of the saint's robe which, heightened by the light, ensures our attention is drawn to the saint at his holy labor. You will find more of Botticelli's representations of St Augustine in the predella of the *Pala di San Barnaba* in the same room – in the *Virgin and Child Attended by Angels and Saints* and in *Coronation of the Virgin with Saints.*

Next is one of Botticelli's fine Madonnas:

Botticelli
Madonna del Roseto, c.1470

Under a vaulted arch, a beautiful, fair-haired Virgin sits with her chubby, but wise-faced Child. Contemplating her son's destiny, the Virgin's face is unutterably sad. The intricately arranged sheer veil of her headdress evokes Fra Filippo Lippi's treatment of the famous veil of the *Madonna and Child with Two Angels,* which you saw in Sala 8. Botticelli was Fra Filippo's apprentice and no doubt this was a technique that he learned to perfection from his master. The scene is suffused with the golden light of the Tuscan dying day: beyond the archway, the setting sun throws the foliage and the rose leaves into shadow.

And next is another of Botticelli's Madonnas – in fact, a magnificent Madonna!

Botticelli
Virgin and Child with Five Angels (Madonna del Magnificat), 1480–81

What is the Madonna writing? On the left-hand side of the book being held for her by two angels are the words of the hymn of St Zacharias on the birth of his son, John the Baptist (the patron saint of Florence). On the right-hand page are the first words of the Magnificat, Mary's own hymn of praise, from which the painting derives its name. This is possibly Botticelli's most famous Madonna and Child. And, if the amount of gold used to embellish the painting is any guide, it was also one of his most expensive. The artist has gilded the decoration on the Virgin's and the angels' robes; the divine light shines in rays of real gold; he has even given golden highlights to the hair of Mary and the angels! And, revealing his prior experience as a goldsmith, he has crafted the most exquisitely delicate crown of the Renaissance. It is a garland of tiny golden stars, loosely tied with gossamer-fine ribbons, themselves embroidered with the finest gold. With the possible exception of the angel on the extreme left, the composition is beautifully contained within the circle of the tondo: the Virgin and the angel embracing his two sitting brothers lean towards each other; and the arc they form is framed, first by the molding of the arched window frame, then by the hands holding the crown above Mary's head; the circle is then completed below by her left arm, the legs of the infant, and the arm of the angel holding the inkwell. This is a painting of great sensitivity and delicacy.

Now you come to one of the two most popular of Botticelli's pictures:

Botticelli
Birth of Venus (La Nascita di Venere), c.1486

It must have caused a sensation when the first large-scale Tuscan work to be painted on canvas had as its subject – for the first time in a thousand years – a life-sized naked woman! Botticelli painted the beautiful Greek Aphrodite, the Roman Venus, risen from the sea and, under a shower of roses, being blown to shore on a seashell. Despite the nudity, the picture is virtually devoid of eroticism. This is no real woman, but an inaccessible and statuesque goddess, her skin more alabaster than living flesh. Nor is she the promiscuous

FLORENCE AND SURROUNDS

In Botticelli's famous painting **The Birth of Venus,** *the goddess is gently blown to shore by Zephyrus, the god of winds.* Illustration Matt Morrow.

Venus of the Middle Ages. She is the Venus Pudica, the classical statue of the modest Venus. The picture is full of energy. Everything (with the exception of the marble-like body of Venus) is in motion. Zephyrus, God of Winds, carrying on his hip the breeze, Aura, flies through the sky, blowing the mythical craft to shore. The sea is choppy, roses drift down from the skies, the branches of the trees sway in the wind, the robes of the Goddess of Spring – and the cloak she is holding out for Venus – flutter behind her. The golden tresses of the two divinities fly in the air.

It is interesting to see how Christian iconography and classical symbolism overlap in the religious and allegorical paintings of the Renaissance. Roses were associated with both the Madonna and Venus. The seashell has a number of meanings in Renaissance paintings. Because of its shape – resembling that of the female genital organs – it can signify sensuality or fertility. But when inverted in the vault of an aedicule above the Virgin's head (as in Botticelli's *St Barnaba Altarpiece* found in this same room – look over your shoulder) the shell can symbolize virginity. It was thought that some molluscs were fertilized by dewdrops. Unfortunately, after Savonarola's period of theocratic power (1494 to 1498), Botticelli painted no more naked women and he ceased to depict pagan mythology. Botticelli may have been a member of Savonarola's sect – the *piagnoni* (the weepers). Certainly he believed that the public hanging and burning of Savonarola was unjust. He regarded the monk as a martyr and believed Florence would suffer for having executed him.

Adjacent is one of Botticelli's allegorical pictures: *Palladin and the Centaur (Palladio e il Centauro)*. And following that, another of Botticelli's numerous Madonnas:

Botticelli
The Virgin and Child in a Glory of Cherubim (Madonna col Bambino), c.1469

The Virgin, framed by an aureole of sublime angels, sits squarely facing the viewer, firmly holding her rather weighty infant. The Child's face is marvellously life-like: perhaps that is why he appears to have a bad case of the snuffles, rather than an intimation of his destiny. The Virgin, too, appears to be more intent on securing a restless baby than on contemplating their shared future. Again, the Madonna's head is covered with one of Botticelli's sheer, intricately folded, beautifully crafted veils.

The first painting on the left of the wall that contains the doorway to Room 15 is a Madonna that derives its name from the fruit that the Virgin is holding in her hand.

Botticelli
The Madonna of the Pomegranate (Madonna della Melagrana), c.1485

The pomegranate is a symbol of the Resurrection, especially when it is cut open to show the seeds inside. This sublime painting represents Botticelli's complete mastery of the tondo (round painting) form. The Virgin, in somewhat listless mood, sits facing the viewer, her sad-eyed infant in her arms. She is flanked by six beauteous young angels carrying floral symbols – the lilies of purity, the red roses of martyrdom – and books, possibly hymnals. Rays of divine light descend from a golden aureole above; the expressions on some of the angels' faces reflect the wistful mood of the Madonna. The painting again demonstrates Botticelli's genius as a colorist. The tones are those of the setting sun: a lavender background is picked up in the deeper shade of the Virgin's cloak against a palette graduating from whites and creams to flesh tones and yellows. Blonde and light brown hair colors and saffron clothing move thence to pinks and rose and through to the deeper red of Mary's dress.

On your way to study *La Primavera*, you pass a second allegorical painting by Botticelli *The Calumny (La Calunnia)*. After pausing there, move on to *La Primavera*. The second of Botticelli's two most popular pictures, it is popularly regarded as a 'pair' with the Venus and is regarded as one of the Renaissance's greatest paintings.

Botticelli
Spring (La Primavera), c.1482

Venus stands demurely at the center of the painting, framed, not by a golden halo like that of the Madonna, but by an aureole of trees. Above her head hovers not the winged Holy Spirit but her son Amor, blindly shooting his flaming love dart at the dancers below. On the right, the blue-skinned Zephyrus, blowing the breeze that heralds the coming of spring, is in pursuit of the nymph Chloris. Flowers issue forth from the mouth of the startled Chloris – a reference perhaps, to her final fate which was to be raped by Zephyrus, but then to be married to him, and finally, as a result of his guilt, to be transformed by him into the Goddess, Flora. Walking alongside Chloris is her final manifestation: Flora. Flora is wreathed in myrtle, her gown a riot of spring flowers as she smilingly scatters her blossoms over the earth. The flowers are wonderfully profuse. On the left, three diaphanously gowned women, perhaps the three Graces who often accompany Venus, are dancing. They are the embodiment of the Florentine ideal of feminine beauty – tall, alabaster-skinned, round-bellied, with elegant hand gestures, thin eyebrows and elaborately dressed blonde, bleached hair. Next to them, Mercury, the Messenger of the Gods, uses his wand to ward off the gathering clouds.

But the meaning of the picture runs deeper than a depiction of a mere spring frolic in a flowery grove. The dominant theme is love – but in particular, the victory of spiritual love over earthly passion. Perhaps that is why the dancing Graces are so solemn: the middle Grace actually turns her head away from Zephyrus' lustful chase, and away from her dance partners towards Mercury, whose own gaze has turned heavenwards. Venus, in the center, represents the balance between these two dimensions of love.

During the Middle Ages, the ancient gods of Greek and Roman mythology had been supplanted by the Christian God and by the Virgin Mary and the saints. However, by the time of the mid-Renaissance, the classics were enjoying a revival; sometimes the distinction between Venus and Mary was deliberately blurred. The Venus in *La Primavera*, for example, is not the amoral goddess of erotic connotation. On the contrary, her beautiful form is modestly

Botticelli's La Primavera

clothed, and even if her feet are bare, her head, at least, is covered in the manner of respectable Renaissance married women. She represents creativity, balance and harmony: she is the *Venus humanitas* described by Raphael's friend and author of *The Courtier*, Baldassare Castiglione (1478–1529).

Botticelli's *Primavera* was painted as a wedding present for Lorenzo di Pierfrancesco (The Magnificent's cousin) and his bride, Semiramide Appiani, a mining heiress. The 19-year-old bridegroom was well educated and would have delighted in interpreting the classical symbolism in the painting. He most surely would have discerned that the laurel trees were a reference to his own name. And it would not have escaped him that Venus's customary golden apples here are replaced by oranges – the *medica mara*, or health fruit – a reference to the Medici.

Whether or not Botticelli, the tanner's son, was *au fait* with the classics, we don't really know. But we do know that, in the year before *La Primavera* was painted, Poliziano gave a series of very popular public lectures on Ovid's festive calendar. Some of the themes of the calendar are to be found in the painting. Perhaps Botticelli drew his inspiration from the lectures.

Here, now, is one of Botticelli's commissions from the Medici (a fact that becomes fairly obvious when you count how many Medici portraits it contains):

Botticelli
Del Lama Adoration (Adorazione dei Magi), c.1475

This altarpiece, which Botticelli painted for the funerary chapel of Guasparre di Zenobio del Lama in the Church of Santa Maria Novella, won him instant fame and secured his reputation as a major Florentine painter. Del Lama was the official broker of the money-changers' corporation – a profession often equated with usury in the second half of the 15th century. He appears in a group on the right of the painting as a white-haired, elderly man looking out of the picture. The painting is a richly populated composition containing wonderful color and beautifully rendered detail. The three Magi are actually portraits of Cosimo de' Medici (who kneels at the Virgin's knee) and his two sons, Piero (whose back you can see in the brilliant red, ermine-lined cloak in the center of the picture below the Virgin) and Giovanni (in white gown with gold-embroidered sleeves). Two other members of the Medici family – Lorenzo (in the white, gold-embroidered cloak, glancing at Giovanni) and Giuliano (in dark tunic and red sleeves) – appear as the men of high rank standing in front of the courtiers on the left and right of the picture. The orange-cloaked figure on the extreme right of the painting, staring out of the picture, may be a self-portrait of Botticelli.

Golden light from the star shining through the roof of the manger falls on the very tiny babe, who, with the figure of Cosimo, unites the two sets of figures in the lower half of the painting with those of Joseph and Mary at its apex. The picture contains evidence of Botticelli's developing skills, especially in relation to composition: the figures are set on different planes so that almost every face can be seen distinctly. Perhaps responding to the requirements of his client, Botticelli seems more intent on achieving a picture of courtly grace than on emphasizing the Holy Family. But the formality of the scene is relaxed by more natural and subtle departures – like the young man in the left foreground leaning on his friend to gain a better view – as well as by a great variety of individual attitudes and responses.

Walk past the doorway to Sala 15 (for the moment), and you will come to Botticelli's Portrait of a Young Man with a Medallion (Ignoto con Medaglia di Cosimo Il Vecchio). On the right of the portrait is Botticelli's first altarpiece (or pala):

Botticelli
Virgin and Child with Six Saints (Pala di Sant'Ambrogio), 1470–80

Botticelli depicts an elegant and elaborately draped Virgin and lively Child engaged in *sacra conversazione*. Sts Cosmas and Damian, the patron saints of doctors, are kneeling in the foreground. St Mary Magdalene and St John the Baptist, patron saint of Florence, stand on the left of the painting; and on the right are St Francis of Assisi and St Catherine of Alexandria, the latter's hand resting on the spiked wheel that was intended as the instrument of her martyrdom. We can see that, by the age of about 25, Botticelli had learned how to compose a complex group of figures, place them in a pleasing and plausible relationship with each other, and vary their attitudes and poses to add interest to the picture.

Because they are in this same room, you have an opportunity to compare this pala with that of *San Barnaba*, painted some seven years or more after the completion of *Sant'Ambrogio*. The tones used by Botticelli in each case are similar – off-palette greens and browns, red robes offset by the rose-colored garments, the whole softened by the sheer veil of the Virgin's headdress and, in this picture, Mary Magdalene's shift.

The next picture on the same wall as Botticelli's *Pala* the *Adoration of the Magi (Adorazione dei Magi)* is by Domenico Ghirlandaio, teacher of Michelangelo. You will then see a painting by the Flemish painter, Hugo Van der Goes, followed by two further paintings by Ghirlandaio, both Madonnas. The Uffizi's placing of Van Der Goes' *Trittico Portinari* in The Botticelli room is quite deliberate. The purpose is to show two different streams of artistic influence coming together at the end of the Quattrocento (1400s).

Ghirlandaio
Adoration of the Magi (Adorazione dei Magi), 1487

This tondo is as good an introduction to the work of Ghirlandaio as you could get. The composition is skillful, the figures are in natural poses, the neutral tones of the architecture and the stony rise behind the Virgin are enlivened by a sea of red and orange garments. Even the livery of the white horse is red. The background, with its ornate broken archways before a finely executed portscape (some believe to have been Naples), frames a

very complex arrangement of figures while simultaneously emphasizing the centrality of the Virgin and Child.

Ghirlandaio
Madonna and Child with Angels and Saints (Madonna col Bambino, Angeli e Santi), c.1482

This conventionally symmetrical rendering of the theme of *sacra conversazione* honors four saints of special significance for the Dominican order (from the left of the viewer) Saints Dionysius, Dominic, Clement and a plump and bookish Thomas Aquinas. There is one unusual feature in this *sacra conversazione*, however, and that is that the Virgin and Child and their attendant angels (carrying the lilies of purity) are almost upstaged by the more volumetric figures of the saints.

Ghirlandaio
Enthroned Madonna and Child with Saints (San Giusto Altarpiece), (Madonna in Trono col Bambino e Santi), 1485

In this painting, Ghirlandaio provides a skillful summation of the productive Quattrocento which was coming to an end. The serene Virgin and Child and their angelic entourage are framed by Saints Michael (in his armor) and Saint Justus on the viewer's left, and Saint Zenobius and Raphael, the Archangel, on the right. Here's an opportunity to compare the work of Ghirlandaio with that of his contemporary, Leonardo – and indeed, with that of Leonardo's master, Verrocchio, who is also represented in the next room. In contrast to the meticulous conventionality of Ghirlandaio, the restless energies of Verrocchio and Leonardo were pointing the way forward to the next century.

The three remaining pictures in Sala 10–14 are all by Botticelli.

Botticelli
The Cestello Annunciation (L'Annunciazione), c.1489

What is particularly striking in this version of the Annunciation is the marvellous plasticity of the two figures. Not content with relying on mere facial expressions to convey the emotion of the scene, Botticelli uses the postures of the two figures to express profound feeling. Although Botticelli is widely regarded as the first of the Renaissance painters to depict mythological themes, he

was also greatly attracted to the Madonna as a subject. This painting suggests that these two themes were intimately connected. The Virgin here has some resemblance to some of his mythological figures: the same reticent grace and sublimated sensuousness.

A really interesting aspect of this painting – and, in a way, the central focus of it – is the relationship between the two outstretched hands. The Archangel has raised his hand to emphasize his announcement: the hand is vertical, reflecting Mary's standing posture. The Virgin's arm is outstretched, but her hand does not actually bridge the gap between herself and the angel. It inclines towards the lateral, following the horizontal line of the angel's head and wings; but is that a gesture of protest and resistance? Or is it a gesture of acceptance and resignation? You have to decide.

During the 1970s and '80s, the next painting was lovingly restored from a near ruinous state. It is now recognized as a very significant work from Botticelli's later life.

Botticelli
Coronation of the Virgin with Four Saints: St John the Evangelist, St Augustine, St Jerome, and St Elegius (Incoronazione della Vergine), c.1490

Against the gold background of a vividly colored celestial scene, God the Father, gesturing dramatically, places the crown on the Virgin's devoutly bowed head. Around these two figures, a circle of angels dance, their robes billowing as they whirl around. The circle is completed by the angel who, hovering between them, peers at the scene from behind a curtain of golden rays. Rows of navy blue and vermilion-winged cherubs form an arc over the heads of God the Father and the Virgin. Below, the earth-bound saints react to the Coronation in various ways: St John the Evangelist holds his Gospel and gestures heavenwards, drawing our attention to the truth of the written word. St Augustine appears to be oblivious, lost in his own meditations. St Jerome seems deeply emotionally affected by the scene, and St Eligius (who was the patron saint of the Goldsmiths' Guild that commissioned the work) stares out of the painting, making the link between the viewer and the events depicted. This large painting is from Botticelli's more ascetic period – after he had become influenced by the conservative teachings of

Savonarola – and it has a dramatic intensity that was not always present in the earlier paintings.

The final Botticelli work in Sala 10–14 is another altarpiece:

Botticelli
The San Barnaba Altarpiece (Pala di San Barnaba), 1487

The painting was originally executed for the main altar of a chapel in the Church of San Barnaba in Florence – a 14th-century church built to commemorate Florence's 1289 victory over Arezzo. The Florentines were able to boast that Dante had fought in the battle, and the quotation inscribed on the base of the Virgin's throne is from Dante's *Paradiso*: *Vergine madre, figlia del tuo figlio.* (Virgin mother, daughter of your son.) As the chapel was the responsibility of the Florentine Guild of Apothecaries and Doctors (which happened also to be the Guild for the painters), it is thought that the Guild probably commissioned the altarpiece.

This is another *sacra conversazione* Virgin and Child: very popular during the Quattrocento. The saints standing on the marble-tiled floor at the foot of the Virgin's throne are, from the left, St Catherine of Alexandria – the patron saint of philosophy and education; St Augustine, one of the Doctors of the Church, and St Barnabas, after whom the church was named. On the right are: the patron saint of Florence, a haggard St John the Baptist who obviously owes much to Donatello's sculpture of the saint; St Ignatius, one of the early

Leonardo's Virgin listens with great restraint to the Archangel's message that she is to become the Mother of God. Illustration Matt Morrow.

theological writers, and the Archangel Gabriel, in his suit of armor. Note the varied facial expressions of the saints.

The picture is a rich study in olive greens and dark, ruby reds, blending into rose tones, soft oranges and cream. The only blue to be seen is in the Virgin's cape. The Virgin sits in an elaborate green and gold marble throne under a vaulted ceiling shaped like an upturned shell – a symbol of her purity. Angels pin back the curtains and ominously display the instruments of Christ's passion. The wide-eyed Holy Child leans forward with his blessing. The predella contains a marvellous treatment of the eager Salome with the head of St John the Baptist.

Sala 15

We now come to the one Renaissance painter who can challenge Botticelli in the popularity stakes, although his two most famous paintings are elsewhere – *The Last Supper* is in Milan (see Trail 6) and the *Mona Lisa* in Paris. He is the universal genius of the Renaissance – Leonardo da Vinci.

Leonardo da Vinci
Annunciation (Annunciazione), (1475–1480)

Leonardo's treatment of the Annunciation – one of the grand themes of the Renaissance – is full of dignified restraint. This was intentional. He was very critical of the more dramatic versions of other Renaissance painters, and particularly of Botticelli's *Cestello Annunciation* (Room 10–14). When he saw this work, he said:

> … *some days ago I saw the picture of an angel who, in making the Annunciation, seemed to be trying to chase Mary out of her room, with movements showing the sort of attack one might make on some hated enemy; and Mary, as if desperate, seemed to be trying to throw herself out of the window. Do not fall into errors like these.*

Leonardo's own version of *The Annunciation* was therefore much tamer, with the Archangel proffering a respectful salutation, and a composed Virgin reflecting on his message. Despite continuing debate about the attribution of the painting (it was once thought – incorrectly – that Ghirlandaio painted it) it nevertheless contains many Leonardo trademarks. The dark Tuscan cypresses in the background draw the viewer's eye to a misty, but minutely detailed city on the shore of a lake framed by rocky outcrops. The Virgin's drapery has a sculptural feel, and the two figures are idealized: look at the length of the Virgin's arm which has been extended to rest on her *prie-dieu*; and at that of the shadow of the Angel, which seems a little excessive in the weak, early morning (or even late afternoon) light depicted in the painting. The beautifully ornate base of the *prie-dieu*, too, seems to have been painted by someone who has also sculpted marble: its shell motif refers to Mary's virginity.

Leonardo's next painting is an Adoration. It has been claimed that when Leonardo's master, Verrocchio, first saw this painting, he was so impressed by the talent of his star pupil that he resolved henceforth to stick to sculpture.

Leonardo da Vinci
The Adoration of the Magi, 1481–2

Originally commissioned by the Augustinian monks of San Donato a Scopeto in 1481, this large painting was left unfinished when Leonardo took off for Milan in the following year. (After 15 years, the long-suffering monks finally commissioned Filippino Lippi to paint an alternative Adoration: you can see the splendidly colorful

da Vinci's Adoration of the Magi

result in Room 8.) Notwithstanding, the unfinished work is generally regarded as Leonardo's first masterpiece. The composition is extremely complex: nearly 30 figures occupy the bottom half of the canvas. Elderly, bearded faces lean forward to gaze intently at the Child. Some simply worship; others interact, engaged in earnest discussion about the significance of the event. The flow of adoration from the Magi angled towards the Virgin is accentuated by the contrasting upright figures of the philosopher on the extreme left of the picture and the soldier (who may well have been Leonardo himself) on the extreme right. These figures have often been interpreted as the neo-Platonic opposites of contemplation and action. In the background, the architecture of a once-grand palace stands against dark cypresses. Under its broken arches, horses rear and jostle, conveying a turbulent mood.

We now come to a work in which Leonardo collaborated with Verrocchio:

Leonardo da Vinci and Andrea del Verrocchio
The Baptism of Christ 1475–8

Christ stands ankle-deep in the clear waters of the Jordan, while a gaunt John the Baptist reaches forward to pour water on his head. The hands of God the Father reach down from the celestial heights, apparently releasing the Dove of the Holy Spirit. Golden light radiates from the Dove, which hovers over the head of Christ. In a craggy wilderness setting, a lone palm tree balances a treed hill, towards which flies a solitary bird. In the distance, a mysterious fortification – Jerusalem? – begins to glow in the setting sun. While this painting is generally attributed to Leonardo's master, Verrocchio, there is wide agreement that at least one figure was executed by the apprentice. This is the angel on the left. When he is compared with his companion, the future of Italian painting can be seen to confront its past. Verrocchio's angel is conventionally pious, while Leonardo's is defined and molded in such a way as to convey the character of a boyish hero of classical times. Nevertheless, it would be going too far to say that Leonardo's angel is superior to the rest of the painting. The young apprentice (he would have been 20 or so) undoubtedly contributed to the design – if not the painting – of the background.

If you are game to brave the slow procession that inches around the red-walled Tribune Room, you will be rewarded with Giorgio Vasari's interesting portrait of *Lorenzo Il Magnifico*. Peer into its dark background to find three mysterious visages: on the left, the skull of mortality; at bottom right, vice and greed; and at top right, the face of goodness forms the profile for Lorenzo's own face.

The Trail next takes you to the room containing two of the great early Renaissance Venetian painters (somewhat out of chronological sequence) – Giovanni Bellini and Giorgione. Giorgione's work continued to influence Renaissance painting long after his premature death at the age of 30. On the way to Sala 21, you may well want to visit Sala 19 (containing works by the great painters of Umbria, Signorelli and Perugino) and Sala 20 (devoted to Dürer and the German School).

Sala 21

Giovanni Bellini
Sacred Allegory (Allegoria Sacra), 1490–1500

Although Bellini painted several classical allegorical pictures, this work, representing a Christian allegory, is unique in his *oeuvre*. You may consider that because of its scale and composition it lacks the immediate dramatic and emotional impact of his other paintings. But as a devotional vision it is deeply fascinating. Contemporary viewers, well-versed in the Christian iconography of Renaissance religious paintings, would have enjoyed it immensely, no doubt enjoying spotting the symbol. It is a work that looks more like a diorama than a painting. The background landscape looms large: it is an important part of the picture. The human figures, on the other hand, are small, and set back, like paper cut-outs of actors on a stage. In the left-hand corner of the terrace, the Virgin Mary sits enthroned under a surrealistic baldachin (which is a little hard to see in the poor light). Her praying hands are pointed towards the Christ Child, who sits playing at the foot of the throne, examining a golden apple, apparently oblivious of his surroundings. His companions are the Holy Innocents – Christianity's first martyrs. The apple, of course, is the symbol of original sin, especially when associated with Adam and Eve. But it can also signify redemption or charity. Notice that this golden, apple-bearing tree flourishes, while the trees beyond the balustrade are dead. St Peter leans his elbows on the balustrade and looks in towards the children, his hands joined in prayer. On his right, St Paul seems to be using his sword to menace a retreating, turbaned man. This may be a reference to the conflict between Christianity and Islam. The identity of the women has been much debated. The saint wearing the crown may be St Catherine of Alexandria or St Lucia. Could one of them be Mary Magdalene? Or are they martyrs? Turning our attention to the middle ground, we notice, on the right, a wooden cross – a reminder of the sacrifice that is to be made by the presently playing Christ Child. The man walking down the stairs on the right (also difficult to see) is probably the hermit, St Anthony Abbot. The clue here is the centaur waiting for him below the steps. (St Anthony's legend includes a story about a friendly centaur rendering him assistance when he was searching for Paul the hermit). The picture is lit from the left. This causes the Christ Child to throw a shadow – perhaps to remind us that his life on earth was always overshadowed by the inevitability of his human fate.

Sala 21 also contains a small Bellini portrait: *Ritratto do Gentiluomo* and two paintings from the workshop of Giorgione. Sala 22 contains works from the Flemish and German Renaissance, including those of Hans Holbein the Younger. In Sala 23, the last room on the first corridor, we see paintings by Mantegna as well as the Emilian painter Correggio. Walk into Sala 23 now to see pictures by Mantegna.

Sala 23

Mantegna
The Mantova Triptych (Adorazione dei Magi, Circumcisione, Ascensione), c.1489

Although this work is now described as a triptych, the three paintings were first assembled in this manner in the 19th century. The panel on the left is a rather stiff rendering of the Ascension, with little of the dynamic tension achieved in later treatments of this theme, like that of Raphael (in the Vatican). Christ ascends, surrounded by rose-colored *putti*, like the ones that his brother-in-law, Giovanni Bellini, liked to paint. In the concave center panel, an elaborately composed *Adoration of the Magi* unusually places the Magi, rather than the Virgin and Child, as the primary focus. On the right is an elaborately posed Circumcision, in which the actors are dwarfed by the massive architecture of the Temple.

Mantegna
Madonna of the Quarries (Madonna delle Cave), c.1489

Although the Virgin and Child are sensitively rendered in this small painting, the main interest lies in the unusual and mysterious background. They are removed from the busy activity of the distant quarryworkers, as they are in turn removed from the faraway hilltop township.

Once you make a U-turn at the river end of the galleries, you enter the world of the High Renaissance, where the Uffizi is much less strong. Nonetheless, there is enough here to help you to decide whether or not to explore the further works of Michelangelo and Raphael elsewhere in Florence and in Rome, and of Titian, first and foremost in Venice.

Sala 25

This is the first of 11 rooms devoted to 16th-century painting.

Michelangelo
Doni Tondo (Sacra Famiglia), 1504–06

This famous *tondo* is Michelangelo's only painting on wood. Above all, it is the painting of a sculptor: the figures are substantial and related in complex ways along all three dimensions. Mary, in particular, looks as though she has been carved from a block of marble. One interpretation is that the arrangement of the members of the Holy Family symbolizes its status as a bridge between the Old and the New Testaments: the infant Jesus is being hoisted onto the shoulders of the parents as a sign of an emerging ascendancy. (In medieval Europe, such ascendancy was typically represented in this way, as in the placing of apostles on the shoulders of prophets.) Another is that Michelangelo derived his inspiration for the intricate, intertwined arrangement of the three figures from classical Roman sculptures like the Laocoon – which may also have provided the model for the standing youth in the right background. And who are these five mysterious naked young men? Are they pagan fauns? Or prophets? Certainly, the classical allusions are very strong: the grave young mother is a forerunner of the sibyls that Michelangelo would later paint on the ceiling of the Sistine Chapel. The somewhat sullen expression on the face of the Christ Child contrasts with the wistful smile of Giovannino – the young John the

Baptist, crouching in the background. Christ's nakedness emphasizes his humanity – and evokes his future passion and death on the cross to redeem the sins of the world. It is this that accounts for the seriousness of his earthly parents, and their tenderness towards him. The tondo is also interesting because of the prominence given to Joseph – an innovation in 15th-century Florence. His orange cloak surrounds the family, its brilliant sheen contrasting with the green-lined, blue cloak that has slipped from Mary's shoulders. The tufts of grass and clover-like plants at their feet are drawn with Michelangelo's customary precision.

Before leaving the room, you may wish to look at the three Fra Bartolomeo paintings. Fra Bartolomeo was a Dominican monk, born soon after the death of Fra Angelico, whose continuation of the Fra Angelico tradition is very evident in Florence's San Marco.

Sala 26

So central to modern images of the High Renaissance has Raphael been, that 19th-century romantic painters yearning for the mannerist piety of earlier times defined themselves in opposition to him, calling themselves the pre-Raphaelites. Raphael is much more strongly represented elsewhere – in the Pitti in Florence and in the Vatican in Rome. There are several paintings here only attributed to Raphael, as well as several from the Florentine painter Andrea del Sarto. The most notable Sarto is *Madonna of the Harpies*, called this when Vasari mistook the creatures on the plinth as monsters. In fact they are meant to be the locusts described in the ninth chapter of St John's *Apocalypse*.

Raphael
The Madonna of the Goldfinch (Madonna del Cardellino), c.1506

One of Raphael's beautiful, golden-haired, oval-faced women, the Madonna – the universal mother – sits with children at her knee. John the Baptist offers the infant Jesus a goldfinch – a symbol of Christ's Passion to come. The child, with a look of sadness, nevertheless gently caresses the bird. The picture conveys profound tenderness, from the Madonna's loving arm encircling the shoulders of her nephew to her foot gently supporting that of her little child. Raphael's debt to Leonardo is obvious in the painting: particularly in its pyramidal composition, the color and shading of the

FLORENCE AND SURROUNDS

garments, and the smoky background landscape. The slender, linear trees are like those in his portrait of Maddalena Strozzi Doni (in the Pitti Gallery), which was painted about the same time. The clear Tuscan light that produces such warm flesh tones can be seen also in Raphael's *Granduca Madonna* (also in the Pitti).

Raphael was a fine portraitist and there are several examples of his work here, the most famous of which is probably his picture of Pope Leo X with Cardinals Giulio de' Medici and Luigi de' Rossi. There is a portrait of Pope Julius II (by him with assistance from his *bottega*) plus three other portraits attributed to him.

Sala 28

Sala 27 contains Bronzino, Rosso Fiorentino and Pontormo paintings, but we have proceeded past them to the next room, devoted to the great Venetian, Titian, and Sebastiano del Piombo. Although he was a contemporary of Raphael, Titian – at least in his early years – was in his shadow, and indeed, he shamelessly copied some of Raphael's work. However, Titian came into his own after the deaths a few years apart of his early master, Giovanni Bellini, and of Raphael (whose lifespan Titian more than doubled).

Titian
Venus of Urbino (Venere di Urbino), 1538

This has to be one of the most beautiful erotic pictures ever painted. One story has it that the Duke of Urbino commissioned the painting to motivate his young wife, Giulia Varana, to enhance the domestic bliss of their summer villa. Outside the window of Venus' bedchamber, the rays of the setting sun are turning the sky to violet and the clouds to pink. She reclines on a bed with decidedly rumpled sheets. Her long, golden tresses fall across her right shoulder. Otherwise, she is completely naked, except for an ebony bracelet and a single pearl droplet, which shines from her left earlobe. Her left hand, complete with wedding ring, hides her pubic area – or does it extend an invitation? Her head begins to rise from her pillow, as though we have just disturbed her, and her languorous eyes meet those of her observer with an intimately ambiguous gaze. Her right hand loosely holds a spent posy of roses – flowers that symbolize love. At her feet, her small dog sleeps peacefully – the symbol of fidelity. In the background, against

Titian's Venus of Urbino

sumptuous wall hangings, two servants extract luxurious clothing from a row of commodious trunks.

Sala 32

After an abortive early attempt to secure an apprenticeship with Titian, Tintoretto went on to develop his own unique style. With his massive and gloomy paintings of *The Last Judgment* and *The Crucifixion* (Trail 3), he foreshadowed much of what was to come in the Age of Baroque. Unlike Titian, Tintoretto had strong local roots, with the result that his finest work is without exception to be found in Venice. In this room, the Uffizi offers eight Tintorettos. Of these, five are portraits, and of these the most interesting is that of the Venetian sculptor, Sansovino. Hanging over the two doors of the room are renderings of Christ and the Samaritan woman at her well. The remaining painting provides the best introduction to the nature of Tintoretto's work.

Tintoretto
Leda and the Swan (Leda e il Cigno), 1550–1560

In a strange interior, Leda sprawls (none too comfortably) on the steps leading to her bed. She is surrounded by domestic animals: a parrot hangs in a cage; from a crate on the floor, a duck unwisely pokes its beak towards a black cat, and a small dog yaps at the swan. Despite this incongruous menagerie, Leda, adorned only with her jewels, manages to convey a certain sensuality. Her hand has reached out to caress the swan between neck and wing. Her servant turns her ringleted head towards her mistress. What can their conversation be about? The painting was produced in part by Tintoretto's workshop. Apparently, the Uffizi depository holds a second, superior version – painted as a prototype for this picture.

Sala 35–45

It's well worth pausing in Sala 43 to look at one of the very few pictures in the Uffizi painted by a woman. This is Artemisia Gentileschi's *Judith and Holofernes (Giuditta e Oloferne)* – perhaps the only Judith and Holofernes anywhere painted by a woman – and it rivals that of Caravaggio for sheer gore. Hers is easily the most determined Judith.

The last stop in your Uffizi tour is to view three Caravaggios.

Caravaggio
Bacchus (Bacco), c.1595

Caravaggio has dressed the hair of his lover, Mario Minetti, with over-ripe grapes and brown and wilting vine leaves. Reclining on a grimy mattress covered with a crumpled sheet, Mario wears a second sheet, toga-style, fingering its black sash – according to some – suggestively. On the table in front of the viewer is the famous basket of rotting fruit – a marvellous still life. The sleepy-eyed Bacchus extends his left, less-than-clean hand to offer the viewer a glass of dark wine. If the picture were better lit, you would be able to see a self-portrait of the artist in the carafe in the left foreground. What is it that is so compelling about this picture, despite its indisputable seediness? Is it the photo-real detail? (The different tones – pale and weathered – of Mario's flesh; the rotting pomegranate spilling its glassy seeds …) Is it Caravaggio's unequalled mastery of light? Is it the psychological complexity of his facial expression? Whatever it is, there is no doubting its power.

Caravaggio
The Sacrifice of Isaac (Sacrificio d'Isacco), c.1600

Abraham, commanded by God to sacrifice his own son, Isaac, is interrupted by the angel, who tells him that God, impressed by his obedience, has allowed him to substitute a ram. The viewer's eyes are drawn immediately to the trussed and terrified boy, screaming in fright and in real pain as his father violently presses his head down on the sacrificial altar. The model for the young Abraham was Cecco Boneri, another of Caravaggio's lovers.

Caravaggio
Medusa, 1595–1600

This is a very male image of the terrifying female Greek gorgon who turned people to stone with a single glance. Her expression is one of disbelieving horror at her decapitation by Perseus: her severed neck gushing blood, and her writhing snake-tresses in their final throes. Caravaggio has painted in oils over a leather-covered, poplar-wood shield.

Caravaggio's **Medusa**

This completes your Uffizi visit. You now deserve – though you may not be able to afford! – a cup of coffee in the café at the northern end of the gallery, from which you'll have a bird's eye view of the tower of the Palazzo Vecchio. If this hasn't taken up a full day, you can, now appropriately fortified, return to view any rooms you have missed, or leave the Uffizi. You can start afresh the next morning, visiting the Museo di San Marco.

The post-Uffizi Trail in Florence has the shape of an inverted "Z": it starts at the northeastern edge of the city center, progresses westerly across its top, then slices diagonally until it reaches the southeastern edge, and then proceeds a little south of west, crossing the Arno in the process. Start at the Piazza San Marco.

Museo di San Marco

Location: Piazza San Marco 1
Contact details: Tel. 055 2388608
Opening hours: 8:15 am–1:50 pm, Tues.–Fri., 8:15am–6:50 pm Sat.;
8:15 am–7:00 pm Sun., closed 2nd and 4th Mon. and 1st, 3rd and 5th Sun.
of the month.
Admission: Euro 4

In this museum you will encounter one of the world's greatest concentrations of the works of an artistic genius – Fra Angelico. For visitors to Florence, a leisurely walk through the monks' cells in this former Dominican monastery is an absolute must. Each cell has its very own fresco depicting a scene from the life of Christ, and many of these were painted by Fra Angelico. There is a grand collection of his work in the Sala del Capitolo (Chapter Hall) and in one of the cloisters, and he also painted the altarpiece for the high altar.

The Cloister of St Antoninus calls to mind a story about Fra Angelico that tells us much about the way the church distributes its honors. Late in his life when he was working in Rome Fra Angelico was asked by the pope if he would like to be the Archbishop of Florence. The monk modestly declined, suggesting instead that the office be offered to his fellow Dominican monk, Antoninus. Antoninus duly became Archbishop, and within a few decades of his death was canonised. Six hundred years later, Angelico is still waiting for this highest of honors.

Even if you are not a fan of Fra Angelico, you will enjoy the serenity of the building itself. Pope Eugenius IV took the San Marco Monastery

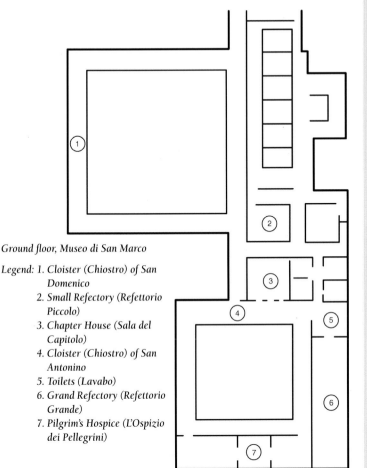

Ground floor, Museo di San Marco

Legend: 1. Cloister (Chiostro) of San
Domenico
2. Small Refectory (Refettorio
Piccolo)
3. Chapter House (Sala del
Capitolo)
4. Cloister (Chiostro) of San
Antonino
5. Toilets (Lavabo)
6. Grand Refectory (Refettorio
Grande)
7. Pilgrim's Hospice (L'Ospizio
dei Pellegrini)

from the Silvestrines, the Order that had founded it, and gave it to the
Dominicans of Fiesole. Cosimo de' Medici, the mercantile magnate and
political ruler of Florence, paid for its restoration. The architect for the
restoration works was Michelozzo di Bartolomeo (1396–1472) who had
worked with Lorenzo Ghiberti and Donatello on the Florence Baptistery
doors. Don't miss his beautiful library – the entrance is upstairs.

Other delights in San Marco include works by Fra Bartolomeo
(1472–1512) in the Fra Bartolomeo Room, Gozzoli and Baldovinetti in

FLORENCE AND SURROUNDS

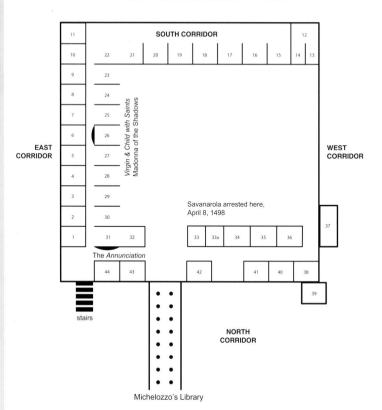

This diagram shows the cells of the Museo di San Marco, upstairs. The highlights are contained in the following cells: Cell 2: Lamentation Over the Dead Christ Cell 3: Annunciation Cell 4: Christ on the Cross with the Virgin and Saints Cell 7: The Mocking of Christ and Cell 9: Coronation of the Virgin. Cell 11 was once Savanarola's cell.

the Alesso Baldovinetti Room, Sogliani and Ghirlandaio in the big and small refectories. In the big refectory, too, there is a rare work – a painting by a Renaissance woman painter. *Lamenting the Dead Christ* is the work of Plautilla Nelli (1523–1588), who was a nun. The monastery is also steeped in the history of Savonarola, who lived there, at one time, as its prior.

The Cloister of Sant'Antoninus (Chiostro di Sant'Antonino)

You will enter the museum through a gateway in the south wall next to the Chiesa di San Marco into the cloister. When you walk from the street through the entrance to the monastery, you are facing the north wall. At the very end of the cloister is a dramatic sight:

Fra Angelico
St. Dominic at the Foot of the Cross, c.1442

This large fresco – at the far end of the St Antoninus Cloister – is the first painting by Fra Angelico that we see as we begin our visit to the monastery. It signals the central theme of the paintings on both the upper and lower floors: the mystical participation of the Dominicans (in this case, of St Dominic himself) in Christ's life and Passion. The naturalism of the figure of the suffering Christ is quite remarkable: the weight of the body stretches the muscles and sinews of the arms and the stomach relaxes in death. The impressive head leans to one side, the mouth still slightly open after the final breath, the facial muscles now at rest. Dominic's delicately veined hands encircle the crucifix, his anguished face a study of fervent love. Those who find this image interesting will have no shortage of opportunities in San Marco: you will find other versions of *Christ on the Cross Adored by St Dominic* in several of the first floor cells: 15, 16, 17,18, 19, and 21.

The south wall of the cloister is at your back, the east on your right and the west, on your left. There are lunettes dating from 1440 on the west (*St Peter Martyr Cautions for Silence*) and south (*Christ Clad as a Pilgrim Received by Dominican Monks*) walls.

Now enter the main part of the museum. The *Sala del Capitolo* (or Chapter Room) was the place where the monks, after confessing their sins, waited to hear what punishments they'd been given by their Superior. The painting in the lunette of *St Thomas Aquinas holding the Book of Discipline* sets the scene and Fra Angelico's *Crucifixion*, described below, is a suitably grave subject for the painting opposite the entrance.

The Sala del Capitolo (or Sala Capitolare)

Fra Angelico

Crucifixion with Attendant Saints, 1441–2

This composition has been described as one of the greatest in the history of Western fresco painting. On a barren Golgotha, a slender Christ hangs from the cross. He is flanked by the good thief, whose body seems to have lightened with his conversion – and the wild-eyed bad thief, who, hanging heavily and painfully, utters a final cry of damnation. The vivid red blood of Christ streams down the cross, over the skull of Adam, bringing spiritual sustenance to the dry earth and its future generations. At the foot of the cross are the Virgin and the patron saints of Florence and of the San Marco monastery, and the founders of various monastic orders. Mary is about to faint, her eyes tightly closed against her overpowering grief. She is supported by John, and by the wife of Cleophas, Mary, whose own tears of grief course down her face. Mary Magdalene, the fall of her golden hair like a shawl, has turned to support the Mother of Jesus. To the left of this group is seated a white-bearded St John the Evangelist, holding his Gospel, and standing to his left, a beautifully rendered John the Baptist, deep in thought. On the extreme left are the patron saints of the Medici, Sts Lawrence, Cosmas and Damian, the latter shielding his eyes. On the right of the picture are an anguished St Dominic, St Augustine, St Jerome (who has laid his red cardinal's hat on the ground in a gesture of humility), St Ambrose, and the philosopher, Marcus Aurelius. The humble St Francis kneels on the ground, hand raised to his thin, tragic face. The group on the extreme right includes St Peter Martyr with his constantly bleeding head, and the scholar, Thomas Aquinas. Over the apex of the crucifix is the pelican, the bird that symbolizes the Passion because it nourishes its young with its own blood. The carefully rendered figures in the hexagons are prophets and, in the predella, notable Dominicans.

The Pilgrims' Hospice (Ospizio Dei Pellegrini)

In addition to its many other treasures, the Pilgrims' Hospice houses the world's most significant concentration of panel paintings by Fra Angelico. Take time to enjoy at least some of the following:

Fra Angelico
Deposition, c.1443

Almost more than any other of his works, this altarpiece demonstrates Fra Angelico's capacity to live comfortably within the medieval tradition while embracing contemporary artistic values. Confined by a conventional Gothic triptych frame, Angelico refuses to allow it to dictate the composition of his painting. This *Deposition* is one of his best-known works.

Using the height of the central arch to house the crucifix and ladders, Angelico allows the scene to spread across the full width of the panel. As if to underline his intent, the wonderfully realistic body of Christ forms a diagonal with the figure of John, standing on the right-hand ladder and supporting the dead Christ at its head, and that of St Mary Magdalene, kneeling at his feet. A further diagonal line is formed by Nicodemus, gently lowering the body from the top of the ladder into the waiting arms of the blue-robed saint and the figure at right, whose kneeling form corresponds to that of Mary Magdalene, and, like hers, straddles what otherwise would have been two separate panels.

The three arched sections of the panel are further unified by a spreading Renaissance landscape intersected by vertical trees and towers that echo the pilasters' strongly lineal figures. A further interesting feature is the upwards and downwards perspective of the golden plinths on which the saints stand.

In the Pilgrims' Hospice, too, you will find this triptych: the earliest datable painting by Fra Angelico.

Fra Angelico
Virgin and Child Enthroned with Saint (Saint Peter Martyr Triptych),
1424–5

This work foreshadows what was to be the painter's continuing attempt to reconcile the medieval tradition of painting with Renaissance innovation. The naturally full figure of the Virgin sits, at a slightly oblique angle to the viewer, on a gold-brocade covered throne. Her Child stands in her lap, golden orb in his left hand, right hand raised in grave benediction. The saints, despite the arches above each of their heads, are actually arranged in *sacra conversazione* mode: their bodies, realistically voluminous and plastic, overlap and relate to each other, rather than being presented as independent panel paintings. Interestingly, the three finials are united by a curved line of trees and scenes from the life of St Peter Martyr. The green forest at the sides of the finials are an early intimation of Fra Angelico's love of nature.

A small panel from a predella repays closer examination:

Fra Angelico
Naming of Saint John the Baptist, before 1435

The story of the birth and naming of John the Baptist are popular themes in early Renaissance art. Zacharias and Elizabeth were old and childless when the Archangel Gabriel appeared to Zacharias in the temple to tell him that his wife would bear a son who would be called John. The angel then took away the old man's speech, hence the many pictures of Zacharias writing down his newborn son's name. In this beautifully composed version, Fra Angelico's mastery of perspective is very evident – particularly in the archway which draws our attention past the group of women, through a vaulted passageway to the trees beyond.

Turn now to Fra Angelico's brilliant *Last Judgment*:

Fra Angelico
Last Judgment, c.1431

Christ the Judge sits in celestial glory surrounded by the heavenly host of angels and tribunals of apostles and prophets. He raises his right hand to beckon the faithful to the gates of the heavenly Jerusalem. With his left hand, he consigns the damned to the orifice of hell. Close by, the Virgin Mary and St John intercede for the souls of the dead whose tombs have burst open at the sound of the heavenly trumpets. On the right of the painting, hideous monster-devils thrust the unfortunate sinners into hellish caverns of unspeakable tortures while the horned mega devil – Satan himself – devours them whole. What a contrast with the radiant souls on the left of the divide of tombs! They gaze enraptured towards the celestial scene above. Some are embraced by welcoming angels. Other are led in a courtly dance through fields of flowers to the heavenly city. The scene is ablaze with color – the brilliant reds of the garments of the participants are repeated in the hellfires on the right and reflected in the flowers and the pink gates of paradise. Golden rays shine forth from the aureole behind Christ, from the haloes of the saints and from the gates of paradise. Even the humble tonsured monks have sprouted golden tassels on their hitherto modest robes. There are references, in this monumental work, to Plato's myth of Er (which seems to be about the procession of souls to paradise), and to Pythagorean theories that the circular movement of spheres in the heavens generates musical harmony. Some think, too, that the strange path of death that separates the damned from the elite may contain mathematical or numerological symbols.

Look now, for the scenes from the doors that decorated the silver chest that once held offerings donated to the oratory of the Santissima Annunziata. Displayed in four sets, these jewel-like little pictures contain 35 scenes from the life of Christ. Fra Angelico is the author of at least nine of the panels, and probably had a hand in the production of several of the others. The set of just three pictures was executed by Alesso Baldovinetti.

Fra Angelico's narrative power is very striking when the series is read as a whole. The most unusual is the wheel within a wheel that depicts the vision of Ezekiel. But look particularly for an Annunciation (in which Gabriel has wings striped like a football sweater). There's a Nativity (with a Holy Infant who glows like a star), and a Circumcision of a seemingly protesting (and understandably rigid) Christ Child. There's a colorful Adoration of the Magi against a background of green, rolling hills. And look for the Presentation in the Temple (designed like a Gothic cathedral). The Flight into Egypt is there, with an orange-frocked, plodding Joseph. Note the horrific Slaughter of the Innocents in which one desperate mother has been able at least to draw blood on the face of the soldier who is decapitating her baby.

Fra Angelico
Last Supper (Door of Annunziata Silver Chest), 1452–53

The Last Supper, which is one of the panels that may not have been the sole work of the master himself, is our only example of Fra Angelico's treatment of this theme. Christ and the apostles sit at table. Behind them, hanging from a line of rings, is a most unusual curtain. Edged with a red embroidered vine, it carries an unusual eastern pattern of white, spiky-foliaged trees and blossoms, but its predominant color – black – throws Christ and his brightly robed apostles into high relief.

John has collapsed on the breast of the Savior on hearing that one of the apostles will betray their Lord. We know that the gray-cloaked figure with his back to us is Judas: he is the one receiving the payment of silver in a subsequent panel.

Look, also, for the three gold-encased reliquaries that contain Fra Angelico's depictions of the Coronation of the Virgin; the Annunciation and Adoration of the Magi and the Madonna della Stella, with its gorgeous diaphanous angels.

Fra Angelico
Coronation of the Virgin, c.1435

It seems that Fra Angelico drew the cartoons (preparatory drawings) for this beautiful picture – one of three reliquary panels in the Pilgrim's Hospice at San Marco – but that he received at least some studio assistance with the painting. Christ, sitting on a brocade-covered throne on the platform of brilliantly painted steps, places a supremely elegant crown on the head of his mother. Angels sound trumpets and wave censers, while below kneels a celestial audience of saints, the Dominicans' robes having been specially gilded for the auspicious occasion.

The Linaiuoli Tabernacle, produced for the flax-workers' guild, is a mini-gallery of Fra Angelico's work:

Fra Angelico
Linaiuoli Tabernacle, 1433–5

On the central panel is a dreamy Madonna, her icon-like infant standing formally in her lap. Yet the stiff-bodied Christ Child rests lightly on drapery that flows naturally over the Virgin's realistically turned knees. We can see that Angelico's intention was not entirely to abandon older artistic traditions, but to unite them with the new. On the inside of the wings are rather more interesting and realistic images of the two St Johns: the Baptist, and the Evangelist. On the outside of the wings are Sts Peter and Mark. Decorating the frame surrounding the central panel are 12 angel-musicians. On the predella beneath the tabernacle is a scene of St Peter dictating the Gospel to St Mark. In a detailed architectural setting, Peter preaches from a pulpit to an appreciative audience while Mark, assisted by a youth holding an ink-horn, sits with poised quill. In the right-hand panel, the martyrdom of St Mark is taking place under an intriguing hailstorm, which descends from a darkening sky. On the central panel of the predella is the Adoration of the Magi. In addition to its gay colors and courtly, almost festive, procession of worshippers, the Adoration is fascinating because of its unusual composition. The Madonna and Child sit on the extreme right, receiving a circle of prostrate, kneeling and standing worshippers. The circular arrangement of the figures is suggestive of a village dance – the flamboyant gestures and outstretched foot of the central figure in the rear inject the scene with an almost musical quality. One further point of interest: some art historians believe that the youth with the flaxen hair standing to the left in front of two horses may have been painted by the youthful Piero della Francesca, who, along with other young artists new to Florence, frequented Fra Angelico's studio.

Look, now, for two altarpieces. The first is very decorative. Fra Angelico painted it towards the end of his life for the monastery of St Bonaventura al Bosco ai Frati, a small village in Tuscany, hence its name.

Fra Angelico
Bosco ai Frati Altarpiece, c.1450

Angelico returned to Renaissance architecture to frame this *sacra conversazione*: the Virgin and Child and their guardian angels sit in a shell-vaulted aedicule against the backdrop of a golden brocade curtain, Corinthian pillars and arched recesses, the edges of which are all softened by a gentle light coming from the left. The focus of the picture is the Virgin, sitting square to the viewer: her brilliant blue robe, lined with green and edged with gold, forms a commanding triangle, modified only by the naked Christ Child on her knee. Against the brocade back-drop, the somber robes of the Franciscans (Sts Anthony and Francis) and the Dominican (St Peter Martyr) contrast with the angels' pinks and reds, the vibrant lavender and pink colors of the cloaks of Sts

Cosmas and Damian on the right, and the greens and reds worn by Bishop Louis of Toulouse on the left, between the two monks. The otherwise plain floor is decorated with five floral marble tiles. The heads of the mother and infant gently touch. His right hand holds the pomegranate – the symbol of his coming Passion – while his left tentatively caresses his mother's neck. However, their facial expressions are curiously bland in comparison to those of the emotional Cosmas and Damien. The predella contains a most moving representation of the dead Christ, and figures of six saints.

Go back into the St Antoninus Cloister and take the stairs diagonally across from the museum entrance. As you climb, prepare yourself for the magnificent experience that awaits as you reach the top.

Fra Angelico
The Annunciation, c.1450

Fra Angelico depicts the Virgin as a frail, young girl, piously inclining her head towards the Angel Gabriel, who now genuflects to her, his arms and hands mirroring her own prayerful gesture. The painter's love of proportion is expressed in the graceful symmetry of the composition, especially in the carefully rendered arches that frame the two figures. But the painting contains references to nature, too, in the flowery garden separated by a paling fence from a lush wood, and in the pheasant-colored feathers of the angel's wings.

You may wish to walk immediately to Cell 3, to compare a second version of *The Annunciation*. The cells all contain beautiful frescos. We have selected a sample of some of the best, all by Fra Angelico. Begin with the works in Cells 2, 3 and 4:

Fra Angelico
Lamentation over the Dead Christ, c.1440

The three Marys (the Mother of Christ at her son's head, the golden-haired Mary Magdalene, and Mary, the mother of James and John) are attending to the body of Jesus as described in St John's Gospel 19:41-42: "In the place where he was crucified there was a garden; and in the garden a new sepulcher ... There they laid Jesus." John is also present (with his back to the viewer), as is St Dominic, carrying a lily in his hand. The mood is disquieting: the body of Christ is already rigid; the women's faces mirror their great pain. Blood still streams from Jesus' wounds and this, and the women's brilliant red garments, are reminders of the violence of his Passion. The viewer's eye is drawn upwards to the strange, spiky foliage and the darkening sky, and inexorably, to the shadowy depths of the tomb.

Fra Angelico
Annunciation, c.1440

If anything, the Virgin Mary of this rendition of the Annunciation is more diaphanous, more luminous than the first. Again, the feathers of Gabriel's wings are painted in wonderful wild-bird colors but his expression, as he contemplates the young girl's humility, seems calmer, even more benevolent. The Virgin's loggia is filled with a pure, white light: only St Peter Martyr (the inquisitor) is in shadow. The room lacks the decorative capitals that graced the pillars of the version at the top of the stairs, its architectural design having been pared down to the minimalist vaults designed by Michelozzo for the priory itself.

Fra Angelico Workshop
Christ on the Cross with the Virgin and Saints, c.1440

This picture was painted not by Fra Angelico, but by one of his assistants. But it is certain that Angelico would have directed the work. The representation of Jesus on the Cross attended by the Virgin plus a group of saints expressing various reactions was inspired by St Thomas Aquinas, who wrote about Christ's simultaneous fear and longing for the Passion – as Man and as God.

In the east corridor, you'll find this treasure:

Fra Angelico
Virgin and Child with Saints (Madonna dell'Ombre), c.1440

The name of this exquisite picture derives from the delicate shadows cast on the white-washed walls by the finely molded pilasters. The Madonna and her mature-looking Child sit in an aedicule underneath a gleaming metallic vault. On the Virgin's left is St John the Evangelist, the patron saint of Giovanni de'Medici. The two red-clad figures on the Virgin's right (wearing their doctors' hats) are Sts Cosmas and Damian – patrons of Cosimo de'Medici, Giovanni's son. On the Virgin's extreme left is St Peter Martyr, patron of Cosimo's son, Piero. Next to him stands the patron of the

FLORENCE AND SURROUNDS

entire Medici family – St Lawrence – carrying the griddle of his martyrdom. Thus, every time the monks prayed before this painting, three generations of the Medici family stood to benefit.

Now proceed to Cell 7, and after that, to Cell 9:

Fra Angelico
The Mocking of Christ c.1440

This is an intriguing and intensely moving painting that demands your attention. A supremely dignified Christ, robed in the white of innocence and wearing the crown of thorns, sits on a mock throne. The disembodied hands of his torturers deliver blows to his blindfolded head; one brutish-faced assailant doffs his cap in a parody of respect while simultaneously spitting at him. What is intriguing is the way in which Fra Angelico has captured not just a single moment, but several. The mock staff in

Fra Angelico's intriguing, rather surreal depiction of The Mocking of Christ.
Illustration Matt Morrow.

Christ's right hand becomes another instrument of torture, just as reported in Matthew's Gospel (27:28-30): "And they spit upon him, and took the reed, and smote him on the head." It is also interesting to compare the two figures seated on the plinth. That of the Virgin – her sad face averted from her son's suffering – was painted by one of Fra Angelico's assistants. The youthful St Dominic, on the other hand, was painted by the master. You can see Fra Angelico's genius in the soft, natural fall of the saint's mantle; the light that falls on his tonsure; the gently bowed head and arched neck; the whisper of a light beard, the frowning concentration …

Fra Angelico
Coronation of the Virgin, c.1440

Framed by concentric circles of white, golden, green and ochre light, Christ lightly places a crown of gold and pearls on the humbly bowed head of his mother. In an arc of clouds below, six apostles and saints kneel in adoration, their faces infused with ecstasy. At the upper left is St Thomas Aquinas, the scholar, followed by St Benedict, who founded the first monastic order, and St Dominic, founder of the Dominicans. St Francis, first on the right, has, behind him St Peter Martyr, the patron saint of Inquisitors, (always shown with the axe wound in his head – and sometimes also the dagger wound in his back!) and St Mark.

This completes the tour of Museo di San Marco.

Fiesole: An optional extra for Fra Angelico admirers

For Angelico enthusiasts, an optional extra at this point is a short bus trip north (about 5 miles) to Fiesole, his home for most of his life. The most famous painting in Fiesole is Fra Angelico's *St Dominic with Virgin and Child Enthroned with Saints* in the Chiesa di San Domenico. Ask the driver to let you off at the Chiesa before you reach the town. Afterwards, it is well worthwhile to continue on into Fiesole, an ancient Etruscan center with a Roman theater.

Fra Angelico
St Dominic with Virgin and Child Enthroned with Saints, 1424–1430

A grave-faced Virgin and her Child, framed by exquisitely detailed architecture, sit under a small *baldocchino* backed by a cloth of honor. (The artist – then in his 20s – was an innovator: notice the slight angle of the Virgin to the viewer and the natural fall of her garments around her knees.) The naked infant, balanced on her left arm, reaches for the flowers in her right hand. The saints who are part of the scene are, from left, Thomas Aquinas, Barbara, Dominic, and Peter Martyr. However, they are somewhat separated from the holy pair by a semi-circle of multi-colored winged angels. Four of these genuflect and bow to the Holy Child, while others, registering a variety of facial expressions, comment on the scene from behind the cloth of honor. Their presence imparts a mystical quality to the setting.

Return to Florence

If you decide not to take the Fiesole side trip, diagonally across the Piazza of San Marco and about 100 yards down Via Ricasoli is the Galleria dell'Accademia.

Galleria dell'Accademia

The Accademia's chief claim to fame is that it is now the home of the famous Michelangelo sculpture of David – the original, not the copy now in the Piazza Signoria. This is the major Accademia work described in this Trail. There are also numerous other Michelangelo statues, several all the more instructive because of their unfinished state. (The authorship of a couple of these is now disputed.) But it also houses a fine collection of pre-Renaissance Tuscan art.

> **Location:** Via Ricasoli 60
> **Contact details:** Tel. 055 2388 609. Reservations: 055 294 883
> **Opening hours:** 8:15 am–6:50 pm Tues.–Sun., closed Mon.
> **Admission:** Euro 8.50

The *David* is located at the end of the long gallery at the entrance, past a line of unfinished sculptures attributed to Michelangelo.

Michelangelo
David, 1501–1504

Irrespective of the thousands of miniature plaster-of-Paris Davids that routinely fill the souvenir shop windows and market stalls of Florence and Rome, the sight of Michelangelo's 13-foot high giant in the tribune of the Accademia never fails to excite and to move. The combined effect of grandeur of scale, stunning physical beauty, gleaming white marble flesh, and explosive psychological tension ensures that each viewing of the *David* is a memorable experience. Created under wraps in a private chapel, the *David* created a sensation when it was unveiled in the Piazza della Signoria. It was the largest monumental sculpture since antiquity. From the moment it was unveiled, Florentines understood that a new era in sculpture had begun.

In contrast to the *Davids* of Donatello and Verrocchio, this is no victor with his foot resting on the head of the vanquished giant. Goliath is still very much alive: David fixes his fearsome opponent with a vigilant gaze – but one that is full of frowning apprehension. His left hand slowly draws the sling across his shoulder while he sizes up the aggressor. Can he win? Or should he flee? One leg is firm, braced ready for action. So is his right hand, cradling the missile with which he could instantly load his sling. But his left arm and leg remains flexible – ready for flight. In this way, Michelangelo has created dramatic tension between the two possibilities. David's dilemma is poignant, but his stand is courageous. It is not hard to understand why the Florentines have historically believed that David symbolizes liberty and the civic strength of Florence itself.

Irving Stone, author of *The Agony and the Ecstasy*, popularized the notion of the young artist personally selecting his own rock of marble from the mines at Carrarra. In fact, the block had been gathering dust in a Florentine cellar since before Michelangelo was born! It had been thought to have been spoiled by Agostino di Duccio, who started chiselling a human form into it 40 years before. But the figure that subsequently emerged was not some second-hand form that had been trapped in the old marble. It was the fresh, vigorous – even revolutionary – hero of the young Michelangelo's genius.

On the right of the main entrance hall is the Sala del Quattrocento.

Ghirlandaio
St Stephen between Sts James and Peter (Santo Stefano tra i Santi Jacopo e Pietro), 1467–70

The principal interest in this rather stilted painting lies in its vicissitudes. In the 16th century, St Stephen apparently fell out of favor, so Fra Bartolomeo was entrusted with the task of painting him out, and replacing him with St Jerome. Apparently, the Accademia approves this act of vandalism, for it now claims that it was unfortunate that the original was restored in the 19th century.

The next room is the Salone del Primo Cinquecento.

Botticelli
Madonna with the Christ Child, St John the Baptist and two Angels (Madonna con Bambino, San Giovannino e due Angeli), c.1497

In this late Botticelli, the use of intertwining arms and legs to frame the infant is the most striking design feature.

FLORENCE AND SURROUNDS

When you leave the Accademia, walk about 100 yards to the southeast to reach the Piazza SS Annunziata and the Spedale degli Innocenti.

Spedale degli Innocenti

Location: Piazza della Santissima Annunziata 12
Contact details: Tel. 055 2477952
Opening hours: 8:30 am–2:00 pm – Thur.–Tues., closed Wed.
Admission: Euro 2.60

Ghirlandaio
Adoration of the Magi 1488

With its tonal subtlety and rich gilding, this treatment of a popular Renaissance theme has impressed many critics as one of Ghirlandaio's finest works. It is distinguished by the presence front stage of two of the *Innocenti* – orphaned children housed in the Ospedale. This institution provides an unusual link with Prato (which is discussed below), for the Ospedale was founded in 1419 from a bequest from Francesco Datini, 'the Merchant of Prato', who as we shall see when we get to Prato, was painted by Fra Lippo Lippi. The man in black behind the staff of John the Baptist is believed to be Ghirlandaio himself.

The Spedale also boasts a Botticelli *Madonna and Child with Angel* (c.1464–5) which he painted while apprenticed to Filippo Lippi. You'll notice that in the early part of his career, the faces painted by Botticelli resembled those of Lippi.

Walk about 400 yards to the southwest to Florence's spiritual center, the Piazza del Duomo crowned by Filippo Brunelleschi's imposing dome – still regarded as an amazing architectural feat. (If you have the energy, you can walk up inside its two 'skins'.) The real name of the Duomo is **Santa Maria dei Fiori**. Entrance to the cathedral is free. Don't be put off by the long lines – they move fairly swiftly. Visitors need to wear sleeves, or consent to wearing a stole that will be provided. One of the most unexpected features is a stained glass window designed by the sculptor, Donatello, for the drum of the great dome. Depicting the *Coronation of the Virgin*, much of the detail is faded.

On its eastern boundary is the Museo dell'Opera del Duomo, a treasure house of works associated with the building and decoration of the Cathedral. Indefatigible climbers might also wish to scale the

Campanile for the views. On the **Baptistery** doors, view copies of Ghiberti's famous doors, especially the 'Gates of Paradise' doors, depicting scenes from the Bible.

There are plenty of signs to the Museo dell'Opera del Duomo (the Cathedral Museum), worth visiting for its architecture alone: a symphony of green, white and pink marble. Walk across the square to the shops and offices on the Campanile side of the Cathedral. The Museo dell'Opera del Duomo was once a private chapel – the one to which the young Michelangelo was given access so he could create the David in complete privacy. Look for ceramics and sculptures by Andrea and Luca della Robbia and Arnolfo di Cambio. Some of the original panels of Ghiberti's Baptistery (Gates of Paradise) doors are there, as is Donatello's remarkable, haggard, tragic *Maddalena*.

Baptistery, detail of Ghiberti's **East Doors**

Museo dell'Opera del Duomo

Location: Piazza Duomo 9
Contact details: Tel. 055 230 2885
Opening hours: 9:00 am–7:30 pm Mon.–Sat., 9:00 am–1:40 pm Sun.
Admission: Euro 6

One of the purposes of the Museo is to commemorate the work of the architect of the Duomo, Filippo Brunelleschi. In the vestibule, you'll find his marble bust (attributed to Buggiano) and in other ground floor rooms, you will be able to see his death mask, his model for the dome, and also several of the tools and pulleys used in its construction. The Museum also gives you an unusually good opportunity to compare the work of two remarkable sculptors of the Italian Renaissance: Ghiberti and Donatello. The received wisdom is that Ghiberti, following on in the tradition of Gentile da Fabriano, continued, in sculpture, the symmetry, grace, and linear rhythm of the International Gothic painters – increasingly adding realistic features and other Renaissance developments (such as perspective) as his career matured. Donatello, on the other hand, is regarded as the great innovator. An admirer of Masaccio and of classic architecture and sculpture, he was less intent on decorative naturalism and more interested in depicting raw realism, drama, and emotion.

Donatello
St John the Evangelist, 1408–15

Donatello's *St John* knits his brows and fixes you with a penetrating gaze. The power of this figure may well have been an inspiration for Michelangelo's *St Peter* in St Pietro in Vincoli in Rome, produced more than a century later. The realism achieved by the sculptor is very evident in St John's relaxed hands and the drape of his garments around his knees.

More wonderful Donatello sculptures are in Room 10, room of *Le Cantorie (Choir Lofts)*.

Donatello
The Bearded Prophet, 1418–20

This and the following two sculptures were made for the

Campanile alongside the Cathedral. *The Bearded Prophet* is a further example of Donatello's remarkable ability to capture a realistic figure – and pose – in stone. The old man is deep in thought; his right foot is braced to support his weight, while the toes of his left foot, cloak ruched around them, splay over his platform into our space.

Donatello
The Prophet with Scroll, 1416–18

The Prophet has unrolled his scroll to display its message, which he indicates with his right forefinger, all the while seeming to be seriously burdened by its import. The expressiveness of the face conveys great feeling.

Donatello
Abraham and Isaac, 1421

His face wearing an expression of great sorrow, Isaac looks up from his horrible task to hear from the angel who will stay his hand.

Donatello
The Prophet Habakkuk, 1423–26

The unkind but popular name for Donatello's prophet is *Lo Zuccone* or Pumpkin Head and is a good example of how Donatello was prepared to use even ugliness to convey expression. Habakkuk's body is in motion: he is 'caught' in intense discussion.

Donatello
The Prophet Jeremiah, 1423–26

Jeremiah has set his bottom lip, but manages nevertheless to deliver a reproving look to his audience.

Donatello
The Cantoria (Choir Loft), 1433–38

Against a mosaic background of tiny glass mirror tiles that glisten in the light, Donatello's little *putti* are running, jumping, dancing and merry-making in a double row around the *cantoria*. Unlike those of Luca della Robbia's twin *cantoria* opposite, (which we find equally beautiful), they are not separated by panels; they therefore seem to be frolicking in a continuous riot. Don't you find it amazing that they come from the hand of the maker of *Habbakkuk*?

In an adjoining room – the Room of the Silver Altars – you will find Donatello's most expressive sculpture:

Donatello
St Mary Magdalene, 1455

Donatello's wooden sculpture of the Magdalene is a shocking portrayal of psychological anguish and physical suffering. Mary's struggle in the wilderness to gain spiritual perfection through self-abnegation and the mortification of the flesh was a subject selected by several Renaissance artists. No one has succeeded more than Donatello.

Donatello's **St Mary Magdalene**

The Pietà was a subject that continued to inspire Michelangelo throughout his life. If you have visited Rome or are intending to do so, you will be able to compare this work with the artist's most famous rendition in St Peter's.

Michelangelo
Pietà c.1554

This work has been surrounded by controversy – even as to its authorship. Nevertheless, the Museum attributes it to the master, though we know that the figure of Mary Magdalene is the work of a student who tried to restore the sculpture after Michelangelo – before it was even finished – tried to smash it with a hammer! Some believe that Michelangelo intended the work for his own tomb. Despite the sculptor's problems with the hardness of the marble and the imperfections it contained, the work is generally regarded as one that conveys a serene acceptance of death. The serpentine line of the figure of Christ certainly imbues the work with great pathos. According to Vasari, the face of Nicodemus – the dominant figure – was that of Michelangelo himself. (In *The Last Judgment* in the Sistine Chapel, Michelangelo inserted his own face in the flayed pelt held up by St Bartholomew.) This and the *Rondanini Pietà* in Milan, are Michelangelo's last extant sculptures.

One hundred yards north of the Duomo is the Medici Palace. Begun in the mid-15th-century as a house for the family of Cosimo de'Medici, this is considered to be the first Renaissance palace in Florence.

Museo di Palazzo Medici-Riccardi
(The Medici Palace)

Location: Via Camillo Cavour 1 (at Via dei Gori)
Contact details: Tel. 055 27601
Opening hours: 9:00 am–7:00 pm. Thurs.–Tues., closed Wed.
Admission: Euro 4

A major reason for visiting the Medici Palace is to see the splendid Lippi *Madonna and Child* that is displayed there. Mind you, because of the focus on the fabulous frescoes of the Benozzo Gozzoli Chapel, the picture – which gets moved about – might take some finding: ask the staff. If it is in the glass case you'll be able to see the drawing on the verso of the painting: an attractive head, sad-faced, looking upward in the manner of Magdalene at the foot of the cross. And don't miss the Gozzoli frescoes: they depict the entire Medici family accompanying the Magi in·resplendent procession to see the newborn Christ Child.

Filippo Lippi
Madonna and Child, late 1460s

The Palazzo Medici Madonna is one of Fra Filippo's last and most notable renditions of this theme. The arrangement of Madonna and Child is fairly standard for the period: from the 13th century, Mary and the Child are often depicted with their cheeks lovingly touching, and even the lively stance of the baby is to be found in other paintings of the time. Fra Filippo's version is at once very tender, and richly decorative. The Madonna supports her baby's head against her cheek and his left arm encircles her neck. Her right arm gently supports him as he tries the strength of his baby legs on the parapet. (Who has not held a little child, not yet able to walk, in just this way?) The expression on his face is beatific, contrasting with the wistful sadness in his mother's face. Filippo's interest in the new chiaroscuro is demonstrated by the variations of light and shade across the two faces.

The Virgin's dress appears to be gold-embossed velvet; her cowl is edged with gray pearls, and her headdress is caught with gold and pearl pins. The folds of the sheer fabric of her cowl and of the baby's chemise are very characteristic of Filippo. So is the splendid architectural niche that frames the figures and contributes to the three-dimensional feel of the picture.

A few yards to the southwest is the Medici family church, the Chiesa di San Lorenzo, believed to be the oldest church in Florence. (It dates from the 4th century CE.) In the same complex (at the rear of the church) are the Medici Chapels – the family's burial place.

Church of St Lawrence (Chiesa di San Lorenzo)

Location: Piazza San Lorenzo
Contact details:: 055 216634
Opening hours: 10:00 am–5:00 pm, Mon.–Sat., closed Sun. (also closed to tourists during frequent religious services)
Admission: Euro 2.50

There are many reasons for visiting this historic church. San Lorenzo is a treasure house of art. But your persistence in waiting to gain access in between San Lorenzo's frequent religious services will be repaid with a single visit to the Cappella Martelli (a small chapel in the left transept, diagonally opposite the main altar). Here, you will have an unencumbered (if not very well-lit) view of a splendid painting by Fra Filippo Lippi.

Filippo Lippi
Annunciation, late 1430s – 1440

Lippi's ingenious painting embodies three greatly admired principles of Italian Renaissance art: symmetry (the scene is cleanly sliced into two half-pictures by the uncompromising central pillar); proportion (the vehicle for which is the architectural structure framing the figures), and perspective, through which the two lines of buildings converge on what became known as Alberti's vanishing point. (Leon Battista Alberti, an architect and writer, was a contemporary of Lippi.) The angels in the left half-picture are having their own discussion, though one glances over his shoulder as if interrupted by the viewer. In the right-hand picture, however, the Virgin and the Archangel are completely absorbed with each other. In the foreground, a glass flask of pure water stands in its specially designed niche. This flask is the most intensely studied single object in Fra Filippo's *oeuvre*. It may symbolize Mary's purity; the water that flowed from the side of the crucified Christ; or that which accompanied the wine of the Eucharist. Standing, as it does, between the viewer and the event depicted in the painting, it draws our gaze inexorably upwards to the Virgin, thence through the brightly lit arch and along the line of buildings at the rear; finally, round again to the shaded, but red-cloaked angel who seems momentarily distracted by our reaction to the scene. This much discussed carafe is a device that was rare in Italy but common in Flemish paintings, and so gives testimony to the early influence of northern painters on Lippi.

Lovers of sculpture – especially that of Donatello – will find many works to captivate them. Start with the wondrous bronze pulpits in the nave of the church:

Donatello
The Pulpits, 1460–67

The two pulpits were probably commissioned by the Medici family. The one on the left of the nave (as you face the Altar) depicts the Passion; that on the right, the Resurrection, Ascension of Christ, and the Pentecost. These were works from the end of Donatello's career and they well repay a leisurely viewing. You will marvel at the individual characterizations, the movement, the wide range of emotions, the sheer drama that Donatello has been able to reproduce in this difficult medium. Other things to look for include the use of perspective and architecture to create incredible depth and to unite two consecutive episodes in a single frame (the Crucifixion/Lamentation; the burial/the women at the tomb); the use of classical models for his figures (the grief-stricken woman with arms raised in *The Lamentation* is a copy of the Greek maenad); and the innovations (a resurrected Christ who is more ravaged by his torment than triumphant). Each pulpit stands on four marble pillars, unfortunately, above eye level: take your medium-range binoculars.

Next, walk into the Old Sacristy: the Medicis commissioned Donatello to decorate it with scenes from the life of St John. You will easily identify the following episodes, depicted in the stucco tondos that adorn the pendentives of the chapel roof:

Ascension of St John, 1434–1443
The Raising of Drusiana, 1434–1443
Martyrdom of St John, 1434–1443
St John on Patmos, 1434–1443

You will also see the white and blue (now gray) stucco tondos depicting the *Four Evangelists* and the polychrome stucco reliefs of *Sts Stephen and Lawrence*, and *Sts Cosmas and Damian*. Finally, see the two 10-panel bronze doors of the Old Sacristy, which depict martyrs, saints and apostles in low relief. Unlike the panels in the pulpits, these contain no background architecture or landscapes. Remarkably, Donatello has still been able to achieve depth and perspective by having the toes of some of the figures step out towards us over their frames, or their bodies leaning against the frames in our direction.

The Medici Chapels (Cappelle Medici)

Location: Piazzale degli Aldobrandini
Contact details: Tel. 055 2388602
Opening hours: 8:15 am–5:00 pm daily, except closed 1st, 3rd and 5th
Mon. and 2nd and 4th Sun. of the month.
Admission: Euro 6

You enter the Medici Chapels from the Piazza di Madonna degli Aldobrandini (behind the church). The chapel of greatest interest is the New Sacristy (Sagrestia Nuova), which is actually the crypt of the Chapel of Princes (Cappella dei Principi). In order to reach it, you have to pass through the massively ornate, octagonal Cappella – the resting-place of many Medici nobles. Close by is Michelangelo's unfinished statue of a tender Madonna and Child.

The New Sacristy, which was designed and decorated by Michelangelo, contains the tombs of two of the more notable of the Medici: Giuliano, who was killed in the Pazzi Conspiracy, and his brother, Lorenzo the Magnificent, are buried within the entrance wall, with only inscriptions to mark their location. But the most splendid tombs in the Chapel – adorned by the works of Michelangelo – are for younger generations of Medicis: Lorenzo's third son (the Duke of Nemours) and Lorenzo's grandson (the Duke of Urbino), both young soldiers struck down in their prime. Each of these latter tombs boasts two allegorical figures: a male and a female – the only female nudes ever sculpted by Michelangelo. On Lorenzo's tomb, alongside the male *Dusk* is *Aurora* (the Dawn) and on Giuliano's, reclining with the male *Day*, is *Night,* asleep with her mask at her feet.

In the same chapel, on the wall that lacks the decorative marble facing you will find the tomb of Lorenzo the Magnificent. This is the site for Michelangelo's *Virgin and Child.*

Michelangelo
Virgin and Child

The Infant sits on his mother's knee with his body towards the viewer, but he has turned his head away from our gaze to nestle against his mother's breast, as if for nourishment but perhaps also for protection from the terrible fate that awaits him. To facilitate this complex configuration, Michelangelo depicts the Madonna with legs crossed – apparently a highly controversial posture for the Virgin! Yet the sculptor was also experimenting with the *contropposto* movement that so interested Renaissance artists: the crossed legs balance her shoulders which have swivelled around to accommodate her nestling Child. Her face suffused with love, she adjusts her position on her seat with her right hand while her left protectively encircles the baby's turned shoulder: the effect is one of great tenderness.

About 200 yards to the west is Santa Maria Novella, the major Dominican church in Florence, dating from the 13th century.

The Chiesa di Santa Maria Novella

Location: Piazza Santa Maria Novella
Contact details: Tel. 055 282187
Opening hours: 9:00 am–2:00 pm. Sat.–Thurs., closed Fri.
Admission: Euro 2.50

You enter Santa Maria Novella via the former cemetery – through a side door that places you about halfway along the nave. On the wall of the nave (facing you just off to the left as you enter the church), you will find the extraordinary *Trinity* of Masaccio.

Masaccio
Trinity (Trinita'), 1427–28

This massive fresco was obscured for centuries, before being restored to its rightful prominence only 50 years ago. It's a little hard to pick up the symbol of the third member of the Trinity – the Holy Ghost – who is portrayed as a dove linking God the Father and his crucified son. An older, resigned Virgin draws our attention to her son. Joseph's robes reflect the mainly pink and rose tones of the picture. Over the heads of the figures, note the beautifully rendered barrel vault, whose foreshortening gives great depth to the scene. This is the last surviving work of Masaccio, and is often interpreted as a brooding premonition by the artist of his own impending (and untimely) demise, perhaps because of the skeleton and the morbid reminder in the Latin inscription on the plinth: "I once was as you are now …"

Hanging in the center of the nave is the largest – and some say, the earliest – of several painted wooden crucifixes that Giotto produced.

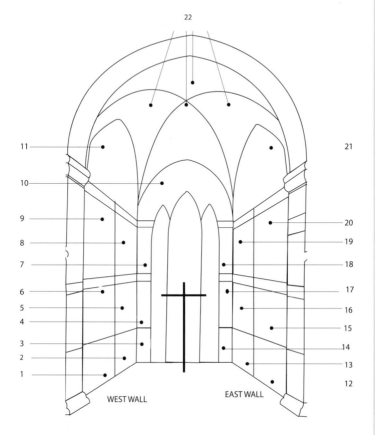

Scenes from the Lives of the Virgin and John the Baptist, Santa Maria Novella

Ghirlandaio's frescoes need to be viewed from four perspectives: the ceiling vault contains pictures of the four Evangelists; the west wall, scenes from the life of the Virgin; the east wall, scenes from the life of John the Baptist and, the rear, the Coronation of the Virgin.

Legend: *1. Portrait of Giovanni Tornabuoni. 2. Birth of the Virgin. 3. Expulsion of Joachim from the Temple. 4. Annunciation. 5. Marriage of the Virgin. 6. Presentation of the Virgin. 7. St Dominic Burning the Heretical Books. 8. Massacre of the Innocents. 9. Adoration of the Magi. 10. Coronation of the Virgin. 11. Death and Assumption of the Virgin. 12. Annunciation to Zacharias. 13. Visitation. 14. Portrait of Francis Tornabuoni. 15. Birth of the Baptist. 16. Naming of John the Baptist. 17. St John in the Desert. 18. Death of St Peter Martyr. 19. Baptism of Christ. 20. Preaching of the Baptist. 21. Feast of Herod. 22. Four Evangelists.*

Giotto
Crucifixion, c.1300

The body of Christ hangs heavily from the cross, blood and water gushing from the spear-wound inflicted in his chest and from the wounds in his feet: this is a man suffering a slow, agonizing death. The work is a further illustration of Giotto's position between the art of the Gothic/Byzantine period and that of the early Renaissance. The figure of Christ is slightly elongated, as in the iconic forms, but its twisted posture and slackened stomach muscles reveal the new interest in physical form and naturalism. Some say this is the first modern Christ to be painted. At either end of the horizontal arm of the crucifix are the figures of the Madonna and St John: note the naturalistic folds of their garments.

In the chapel on the left of the great altar – just to remind you of how amazingly well-rounded the Renaissance artists were – you will find Filippo Brunelleschi's crucifix. In the Cappella Tornabuoni (or Cappella Maggiore) you'll find Ghirlandaio's cycles of the lives of the Virgin and John the Baptist.

Ghirlandaio
Scenes from the Lives of the Virgin and John the Baptist, 1485–90

This massive fresco was restored for the Year 2000 Jubilee. It can be examined in four sections. (Refer to the chart.) In the ceiling vault is a representation of the authors of the Gospels: Matthew, Mark, Luke and John. On the west wall are seven scenes from the life of the Virgin, including a gory Slaughter of the Innocents with babies' heads everywhere. On the east wall are seven scenes from the life of John the Baptist. On the rear wall (in the lunette above the stained glass windows), Ghirlandaio has depicted the Coronation of the Virgin. On the left of the same wall (reading from top to bottom and alongside the stained glass), you will find St Dominic burning the heretical books; the Annunciation; and a portrait of Giovanni Tornabuoni, the donor of the chapel. On the right side are the death of St Peter Martyr; St John the Baptist in the desert, and the wife of the donor.

Confusingly, there are two Strozzi Chapels in Santa Maria Novella. The one that contains the frescoes by Filippino Lippi (son of Filippo) is to the right of the main altar. You will find a typically gruesome (though faded) *Last Judgment*, and *Christ and Mary in Maestá*. Before leaving

Santa Maria Novella, look in the lunette on the inner side of the main doorway (at the beginning of the nave) where you will find a rare early *Nativity* by Botticelli. (You will need your binoculars: it is a little difficult to see from the floor.)

Botticelli
Nativity, c.1476

The ox and the ass are in the upper center of the painting in a stall made of square stones. Below is the Holy Infant resting on a white cloth and seemingly uncomfortably propped up against two blocks of stone. The Virgin, kneeling to the left, has her hands clasped in prayer, and the infant Jesus reaches out to her. The young St John, dressed in a goatskin, sits behind the Virgin, and St Joseph, holding a staff in his left hand, rests his sleepy head on his right.

A further 300 yards to the southwest is the Chiesa di Ognissanti, a Benedictine church that was also begun during the 13th century.

Ognissanti

Location: Borgo Ognissanti 42
Contact details: Tel. 055 2398700
Opening hours: Daily from 7:00 am–12:00 pm and 4:00 pm–6:00 pm

Ognissanti is Botticelli's burial place. The precise location of his tomb is not known, though it's believed to be somewhere in the right transept. Halfway down the nave, over the confessional on the right, is Botticelli's first surviving fresco: *St Augustine's Vision of St Jerome*. On the opposite side of the nave is Ghirlandaio's corresponding fresco of *St Jerome in his Study*. The two pictures need to be viewed in conjunction because they depict different parts of the same narrative.

Domenico Ghirlandaio
St Jerome in his Study, (1480)

The white-bearded St Jerome is pictured in his study, translating the scriptures into Latin. (His translation became known as the Vulgate.) Here as elsewhere (the Uffizi, the Sistine Chapel), Ghirlandaio suffers from close comparisons with the nearby work of his more gifted contemporary, Botticelli. In contrast with the simple, expressive study of Botticelli's Augustine, Ghirlandaio's Jerome seems almost overpowered by the elaborateness of his study and its furnishings – evidence of Ghirlandaio's admiration for the northern European art.

Botticelli
St Augustine's Vision of St Jerome, 1480–90

St Augustine, having taken up his pen to write of Jerome, instead receives a vision of the latter, telling Augustine that in death, he has achieved perfect happiness. Augustine, his face a study in concentration, is overcome by the vision, and moves his right hand to his heart. Botticelli's success in depicting a particular moment in time can be contrasted with Ghirlandaio's, flatter, more descriptive treatment of St Jerome. But, notwithstanding the pious subject, the picture also contains a hidden joke. For those with terrific eyesight and unusually good translation skills, hidden among the lines of scribble on the pages of the open book behind the clock on Augustine's shelf, Botticelli has written an imaginary conversation between two Ognissanti monks, poking fun at their order's reputation for a lack of studiousness. Under the figure of St Augustine is a clock with the hand standing between I and XXIV, ie, the hour of sunset and the hour of St Jerome's death.

Near Botticelli's St Augustine, you will find, in the Vespucci Chapel, a double fresco by Ghirlandaio: in the lunette is a graceful *Madonna della Misericordia* and underneath the lunette, a picture that Ognissanti calls the *Deposition* and which others refer to as a *Pietà*.

Ghirlandaio
Madonna della Misericordia, c.1471

This fresco was completed a few years after the monumental treatment of the same theme by Piero della Francesca in Sansepolcro. While it lacks the metaphysical impact of the Piero altarpiece, this early work –with its pleasing composition and deft foreshortening – gives evidence of the promise of the young Ghirlandaio. The greatest controversy to have surrounded this fresco concerns not the Madonna but the dark-haired young man whose face is squeezed in on the Virgin's left. Following the lead of the often unreliable Vasari, some scholars have speculated that this may have been the grandson of the chapel's patron, the navigator, Amerigo Vespucci, after whom America was named.

Ghirlandaio
Pieta, c.1475

This fresco compares unfavorably with the *Madonna della Misericordia* immediately above it. However, some critics attribute the awkwardness of the design to the readiness of the young painter to experiment in the northern European style that was coming into vogue in the Florence of the day. It will certainly interest admirers of the works of Cosme' Tura.

For a very special experience at Ognissanti, schedule your visit for a Monday, Tuesday or Saturday morning. If you do, you will then be able to walk out of the church, then turn right under the portico on the left of the entrance to the church. Walk through the colonnades to the former monks' refectory, or dining-hall (*cenacola*). You'll find the fresco on the far wall. Stools have been placed in front of the picture; Gregorian music may be playing; you may even have this delightful experience all to yourself!

Ghirlandaio
Last Supper (Cenacola di Ghirlandaio), 1480

As in the case of the famous *Last Supper* of Leonardo da Vinci, (which is discussed in Trail 6), Ghirlandaio's fresco occupies the entire rear wall of the Ognissanti refectory. And, as in Leonardo's version, Christ (golden halo) and 11 of his apostles are seated behind an elongated table, facing the viewer. The 12th apostle, Judas, sits alone on the viewer's side of the table: he appears to be engaged in a vigorous defense of his innocence in response to questioning by the long-bearded Peter. This is a somewhat sleepier version of the subject that Leonardo charged with such emotional intensity. Ghirlandaio has nevertheless imbued the scene with beauty: the painter has set his figures in a *trompe l'oeil* extension of the actual room, incorporating actual architectural features – like the lunettes and vaults of the wall and ceiling – into his picture. Under these arches can be seen a misty sky with flying swifts, ducks and partridges, and a grove of lovely citrus trees.

When you emerge from Ognissanti, if you have not yet had your fill of Ghirlandaio, reverse direction, and walk about 500 yards to the southeast to the Chiesa di Santa Trinita', where you'll find his *Scenes from the Life of St. Francis* in the Maggiore Chapel and an *Adoration of the Shepherds* in the Sassetti Chapel. About 300 yards east of Santa Trinita' is

Ghirlandaio's Last Supper

the church of Orsanmichele, on Via Calzaiuoli (which used to be a food market). It is well worth a visit. Its external wall is punctuated by 14 aedicules (niches) which once contained sculptured figures by Donatello, Nanni di Bianco, Giambologna, Ghiberti and Verrocchio, thus providing a unique open-air gallery demonstrating the development of Renaissance sculpture over two centuries, from the end of the 14th to the beginning of the 17th. Several of the sculptures have been removed for conservation purposes, some of them being replaced by substitutes. Inside the church is a fabulous altar designed by Andrea Orcagna, a sculpture of the *Madonna and Child with St Anne* by Francesco da Sangallo (1522) and Bernardo Daddi's *Virgin and Child* (1348).

A further 200 yards to the east will bring you to the Bargello.

The Bargello

Location: Via del Proconsolo 4
Contact details: Tel. 055 2388 606
Opening hours: 8:15 am–1:50 pm Tues.–Sun., closed 2nd and 4th Mon., and 1st, 3rd and 5th Sun.
Admission: Euro 4

This 14th-century palace was Florence's first town hall. It later became the residence of the Chief of Police and, in Renaissance times, the site of public executions. At least one of the Pazzi conspirators who, on Easter Sunday,

1478, attempted to assassinate Lorenzo the Magnificent (and who did succeed in killing Giuliano, his brother) was hanged from its battlements. His hanging corpse was famously sketched by Leonardo da Vinci.

The Bargello does for lovers of sculpture what the Uffizi does for lovers of painting. Apart from four works by Michelangelo, its magnificent collection includes sculptures and wax and bronze models by Sansovino, Bandinelli, Ammannati, Cellini (including the sculptor/jeweller's *Perseus*), Giambologna, Vicenzo de Rossi and Vincenzo Danti. You can also see many fine works in wood and ivory by anonymous medieval and Renaissance artists, Florentine ceramics (particularly Majolica), and, in the loggia at the head of the courtyard stairs, Giambologna's marvellous bronze menagerie of animals and birds, as well as two *putti*, fishing.

Ground floor

As you line up for tickets (not nearly as long a wait as for the Uffizi) you will be able to look to your right through a doorway (cordoned off) into the Michelangelo and 16th Century Sculpture Room. You have to walk out of the *Biglietteria* into the courtyard to gain access to this room.

Placed in a somewhat higgledy-piggledy fashion around this ground floor gallery are some works that sculpture-lovers will find very familiar:

Michelangelo
Bacchus, 1496–97

A work from Michelangelo's youth, Bacchus is depicted as a decidedly tipsy and youthful god, accompanied by a playful – and even younger – satyr. Clearly designed to be viewed in the round, the satyr munches on grapes from his position behind Bacchus, appearing to justify an audience of his own. The larger figure wears a grape-festooned helmet and offers a chalice of wine in a toast. This was the first life-sized marble figure of a naked classical deity to be sculpted in the Christian era.

Michelangelo
Brutus, c.1538

The identity of this larger-than-life marble bust is a little uncertain: he is either the local hero who despatched the last Roman king or Julius Caesar's assassin. His head is turned over his left shoulder, presenting a view from the front like the head on a Roman coin.

The patron who commissioned the work has inscribed on the plinth his explanation of why Michelangelo ceased to work on it: the artist had a sudden flash about the crimes committed by his subject and was unable to go on. A more likely explanation is that it became politically dangerous: "Brutus" was the nick-name applied to Lorenzino de' Medici when he murdered his cousin Alessandro in 1537.

Michelangelo
Virgin and Child with St John (Tondo Pitti), c.1503

In this circular, unfinished bas relief, the Virgin turns her elegant head over her right shoulder, her troubled gaze perhaps indicating that she has sensed impending danger. Her infant son, who has mischievously put his elbow on her book, leans comfortably into his mother. The young St John stands behind, his low-relief image almost disappearing back into the marble.

Michelangelo
David-Apollo, c.1525–1530

According to the historian Vasari, this sculpture – commissioned by the Medici governor – depicted Apollo extracting an arrow from his quiver, and it was to be Michelangelo's means of "making peace with the pope and with the house of the Medici, which had been greatly offended by him." With the fall in 1530 of a free Florence, Michelangelo could survive only by working for its imperial oppressors. The Medici inventories described it as a *David*, however: hence its double-barreled name. The figure is certainly ambiguous: Is that a bow he carries on his back? Is that a stone in his right hand? Is his right foot resting on the head of a vanquished foe? If, indeed, this is *David*, he has a strangely dreamy demeanor. He is no longer the symbol of defiant Florentine strength that the artist had created a quarter of a century earlier. Perhaps Michelangelo had intended to produce a new *David*, more suited to the troubled times of his late middle age. Whatever its true identity, Michelangelo's genius in representing the human form is very much in evidence. You will find a more finished version of this pose – straightened, weight-bearing leg; other knee bent; one arm raised and bent, swivelling the upper body; head turned over a shoulder – in the Palazzo Vecchio, when you view the master's *Victory*.

As its name suggests, the Donatello Room (take the stairs from the courtyard) houses many of the sculptor's most famous works. In the Donatello Room, too, you can also see the two gilded bronze panels of *Abraham's Sacrifice* submitted by Brunelleschi and Ghiberti in competition for the contract to make the main Baptistery doors. Which one would you have selected?

The Donatello Room

Donatello
David, 1408–09

Donatello's white marble David is a long-necked young hero, standing victoriously astride the severed head of his foe. The stone that felled Goliath is still embedded in the tyrant's forehead; a second stone, sitting at-the-ready in David's sling, hangs from the hero's hand, coming to rest just over the tyrant's head.

Donatello
The Marzocco, 1419–20

This is the original of the heraldic lion of Florence that you saw in the Piazza della Signoria. In his paw, he holds the city's coat of arms – the lily. Look high up on the right rear wall of the room to see the (now brilliantly painted) red and gold *Stemma Martelli*, the coat of arms made by Donatello for the Casa Martelli.

Donatello
St George, and *St George and the Dragon*, c.1417

The copy of *St George* that now stands in the original niche in one of the external walls of *Orsanmichele* looks pretty good – until you see the original, now fixed on the wall of the Donatello Room here in the Bargello. The real work has a much more dramatic impact on the viewer. Such regal bearing! Such determined concentration! This is the image of Renaissance man: a balance of physical courage and energy (*vita activa*) with inner strength (*vita contemplativa*).

On the plinth below the *St George* is Donatello's remarkable bas-relief of the saint defending the Princess of Cappadocia from the dragon. The

FLORENCE AND SURROUNDS

revolutionary technique he used was called *rilievo schiacciato* – a way of achieving great depth from a shallow ground by finely grading a series of surfaces. The entrance to the cave of the winged dragon looks deep enough to walk through. There is great drama in this little bas-relief: the dragon rears, wings flaring, just in time to receive the mortal thrust of St George's sword.

Donatello
David, 1430

This is Donatello's celebrated bronze version of David – the historic symbol of Florentine freedom and liberal thinking – and the first, life-sized, free-standing nude of the post-classical age. But the work can be read in two ways. The conventional interpretation is the more obvious: David the giant-killer stands over his vanquished foe. A different interpretation (in part stimulated by the victor's winged helmet) has an allegorical meaning. This is not David standing over Goliath, but Mercury (symbolizing truth) standing over the decapitated head of Argus (symbolizing envy). But the elegant young hero – whatever his identity – is modest in his victory. He lowers his head in thought, and rests his leather-sandalled foot – ever-so-lightly – on the severed head. Again, Donatello has balanced physical courage with grace, gentle virtue and intellectual strength.

Resting his foot almost casually on the head of Goliath, Donatello's David *appears to have drifted into a private, spiritual reverie.* Illustration Matt Morrow.

Donatello
Attis, (c.1440)

The identity of this strangely dressed but very appealing small figure is much debated. We think it is one of Donatello's playful *putti* who has escaped from the *Cantoria* in the Cathedral Museum, donned leather chaps, and flown into the Bargello to pose as Cupid!

The Magdalene's Chapel (Cappella di Maria Maddalena e Sagrestia), up the stairs, contains – though in very bad condition – works that are attributed to Giotto and his workshop: Benvenuto Cellini's beautiful hatpin, decorated with Leda and the Swan, is in the Carrand Room on this floor. In the Verrocchio Room (up another flight of stairs), you'll see Andrea Verrocchio's bronze *David*, who also stands victorious over the decapitated Goliath's head, but who lacks a helmet. The fabulous collection of ceramics by Giovanni and Andrea della Robbia is also here.

If you wish to remain in pursuit of Michelangelo a little longer, walk about 200 yards further east to the Casa Buonarroti.

Casa Buonarroti

Location: Via Ghibellina 70
Contact details: Tel. 055 241 752
Opening hours: 9:30 am–4:00 pm Wed.–Mon., closed Tues.
Admission: Euro 6.50

We cannot be sure that Michelangelo ever actually lived in this house but he did buy the land for his nephew, Leonardo, who built the house, after which it remained in the possession of the family for 300 years. (You can see the house of his boyhood on the corner of Via dell'Anguillara and Via Bentacordi, west of Santa Croce.) Casa Buonarroti is now a fine museum containing a significant record of the artist's life and work. Make sure you do not miss these three famous works.

Michelangelo
Battle of the Centaurs (Battaglia dei Centauri), 1490–2

Michelangelo never finished this marble bas-relief; yet the naked, fighting figures pulsate with energy. Captured in the frenzy of battle, they display fear, pain, and violent intent. On the left, two powerful warriors prepare to hurl rocks at their foe. The massive rump of a vanquished centaur protrudes from the bottom edge of the marble, his hoof horribly twisted, his luxuriant tail no longer thrashing. The young Michelangelo, inspired by the reliefs from the Roman Imperial period, used this vicious battle to experiment with composition, placing the foreground figures on several different planes to ensure that each is clearly visible. The Buonarroti family obviously loved this work: it remained in their possession long after Michelangelo's death.

Michelangelo
The Virgin of the Stairs (Madonna della Scala), c.1490

The Madonna lifts the fold of her shift so her baby can nurse. The infant's little arm and upturned palm are thrust behind him, the closer to nestle to his mother's breast. Encircled by his mother's protective arm, his well-muscled baby's back shuts out the world. Michelangelo has achieved the most tightly integrated mother and child. Mary turns her face towards three children playing on the stairs in the top left hand corner of the scene. Her profile displays an aquiline nose. Elegant, soft drapery flows over her hair and shoulder, her knees, her crossed ankles, the block on which she sits. This is one of Michelangelo's earliest works, executed in his middle teens. But we can already note some elements of his style that we now recognize as characteristic: his respect for the features of the medium in which he's working, for example. He leaves the borders of the marble untreated, so we can see the differing levels he has employed in the construction of the bas-relief.

Michelangelo (?)
Santo Spirito Crucifix, c.1492

The authorship of this crucifix continues to be disputed, one theory being that it is the work of a pupil, Taddeo Curradi. Christ is represented with a smooth, lightly muscled torso and a fluidity of line. Some believe that the Santo Spirito figure was modelled on that of a young man who had died in the Santo Spirito monastery. It seems that this early work exerted considerable influence over subsequent sculptural treatments of Christ on the cross throughout the ensuing 16th century.

Two hundred yards south, walking towards the Arno, is one of the most famous churches in Florence. Santa Croce is the place of burial of many famous Italians, from Michelangelo to Marconi, including Galileo, whose daughter is now thought to have been secretly buried beside him.

Chiesa di Santa Croce

Location: Piazza Santa Croce
Contact details: Tel. 055 244 619
Opening hours: 9:30 am–5:00 pm Mon.–Sat., 1:30 pm–5:00 pm Sun.
Admission: Euro 3 includes admission to the Museo dell' Opera

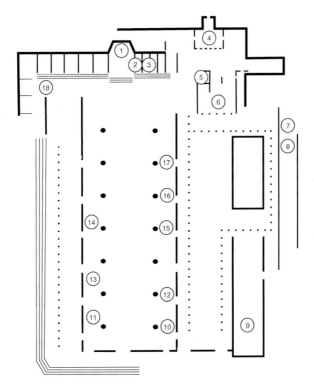

A diagram of the Chiesa di Santa Croce

Legend: 1. The Main Chapel. 2. Bardi Chapel 2. 3. Peruzzi Chapel. 4. Sacristy Taddeo Gaddi. 5. Baroncelli Chapel. 6. Pazzi Chapel. 7. Lucca Della Robbia Cupola. 8. Della Robbia Tondo – Evangelists and 12 Apostles. 9. Museum (Cimabue's Painted Crucifix, Taddeo Gaddi's Tree of Life.). 10. Tomb of Michelangelo. 11. Tomb of Galileo. 12. Cenotaph of Dante. 13. Memorial of Leonardo Da Vinci. 14. Tomb Slab of the Ghibertis. 15. Tomb of Machiavelli. 16. Donatello's Annunciation. 17. Monument to Rossini. 18. Bardi Chapel 1: Donatello Crucifix.

The Giotto Frescoes

In his later career, from about 1320, Giotto painted frescoes in the Bardi and Peruzzi Chapels of Santa Croce, to the right of the main altar. These depict the stories from the life of St Francis in the Bardi

Chapel (a shorter Franciscan cycle than that in Assisi), and twin cycles of St John the Baptist and St John the Evangelist in the Peruzzi Chapel. These pictures will undoubtedly move you, but they are not charged with the same dramatic or psychological intensity as are the Scrovegni frescoes in Padua. Unfortunately, these frescoes are badly deteriorated. Not only did Giotto decide to experiment – unsuccessfully, as it turns out – with a new dry plaster fresco method: subsequent generations of Florentines allowed the pictures to be covered in plaster, and even to have funeral monuments erected over them!

The Bardi Chapel

The chapel closest to the altar (on the right) is the Bardi Chapel. Note that Santa Croce has a second Bardi Chapel – over in the left transept – where Donatello's wooden crucifix is displayed; not to mention a Bardi di Vernio Chapel – the one on the extreme left of the altar – which contains a *Deposition* by Taddeo Gaddi, Giotto's pupil.

Giotto
Franciscan Life Cycle and *Stories of St John the Baptist* and *St John the Evangelist*, 1325
Florence, Santa Croce, Bardi Chapel.

LEFT WALL (from lunette in the top tier)
   St Francis Renounces his Worldly Goods: Against the backdrop of a Romanesque-Gothic building, Francis divests himself of all his possessions, save that of a simple cloth.
   The Sermon at Arles: The friars huddle around a table listening to an obviously inspired St Francis recount his vision.
   Funeral of St Francis and Confirmation of the Stigmata: The sorrowing friars grieve at St Francis' death-bed. One raises his hands in astonishment at the sight of the stigmata: others kiss the wounded feet and hands of the saint. Notwithstanding the anguish of the monks, the mood is one of serenity and calm.

RIGHT WALL (from lunette in the top tier)
   Approval of the Franciscan Rule: Rows of friars kneel before the enthroned pope on a solemn, formal occasion.
   St Francis's Trial by Fire before the Sultan: A colorful version of one of the Franciscan stories. The clothing of the figures falls into

BARDI CHAPEL		PERUZZI CHAPEL	
Left Wall: LIFE CYCLE OF ST. FRANCIS	Right Wall: LIFE CYCLE OF ST. FRANCIS	Left Wall: STORIES OF ST. JOHN THE BAPTIST	Right Wall: STORIES OF ST. JOHN THE EVANGELIST
St. Francis Renounces his Worldly Goods	The Pope Approves the Franciscan rule	The Announcement to Zaccaria	St. John the Evangelist at Patmos
The Sermon at Arles	Trial by Fire before the Sultan	The Birth of St.John the Baptist	St. John the Evangelist Revives Drusiana
Funeral of St. Francis and Confirmation of the Stigmata	The Vision of Bro. Augustine and of Bishop Guido at Assisi	Herod's Banquet	St. John the Evangelist is Assumed into Heaven

This diagram shows the layout of works in the Bardi and Peruzzi Chapels in the Chiesa di Santa Croce.

naturalistic folds: note the white mantle of the servant, and the voluminous golden cloak of the bearded figure next to him.

The Vision of Brother Augustine and of Bishop Guido of Assisi: In characteristic fashion, Giotto arranges groups of figures around a space in which occurs the central action of the picture.

Just to the right of the Bardi Chapel is the Peruzzi Chapel.

The Peruzzi Chapel

Giotto
Stories of St John the Baptist and *St John the Evangelist,* 1315–20
LEFT WALL (from lunette in the top tier)

Announcement to Zacharias: The angel prophesizes to Zacharias that he will have a son – a prophecy from which the old man shrinks in disbelief

Birth of St. John the Baptist: The picture contains two episodes. On the right, Elizabeth is about to give birth to John the Baptist. On the left, John's father, Zacharias, having temporarily been struck dumb by God for disbelieving the prophecy that he would have a son, now writes his new son's name on a tablet (whereupon his speech was restored).

Herod's Banquet: While the musicians play and the guests dine, a soldier offers the head of John the Baptist to Herod – as though it were simply another dish. In a second episode on the right, Salome offers the head to Herodias.

RIGHT WALL (from lunette in the top tier).

St John the Evangelist at Patmos: John sits, head resting on his right hand, experiencing a vision of the end of the world (the dragon) and the second coming of Christ (with the sickle).

St John the Evangelist Revives Drusiana: Against the backdrop of the walls and domes of Padua, St John performs a miracle.

St John the Evangelist is Assumed into Heaven: Two groups of astonished spectators witness the assumption of the saint into heaven. One man shields his eyes from the heavenly radiance.

The Baroncelli Chapel

The Baroncelli Chapel is in the right transept. It is worth a visit to view more frescoes by Taddeo Gaddi, (1332–38), and Giotto's *Baroncelli Altarpiece*, or *Polyptych*.

Giotto
Baroncelli Polyptych, 1310–1320

The central panel of this polyptych, executed by Giotto's workshop, features the Coronation of the Virgin in a scene suffused with golden light and sound. The four lateral panels depict the glory of the angels and saints: it's a very musical occasion, with angels playing violins, harps, zithers and bugles. The golden haloes around the heads of each shine with such Byzantine radiance that they sometimes obscure the faces of their colleagues. Remarkably, the division of the scene into five separate panels does not destroy its unity: the viewer surveys the scene as a whole, not as a series of five individual pictures. The predella carries pictures of the dead Christ (under the Coronation), St John the Baptist, St Francis and St Onophrius. Art historians are more confident of Giotto's authorship of the decorative borders than of the actual figures of Christ and the Madonna.

The Pazzi Chapel

The freestanding chapel of the Pazzi family (those who conspired against the Medicis) is outside the main cathedral, on the right of the building. An architectural gem of Brunelleschi, the chapel was decorated by Luca della Robbia with 12 blue and white glazed terracotta tondos of the apostles. The four tondos of the Evangelists may have been made by Brunelleschi. Go into the museum, where you'll see the great *Crucifix* of Cimabue (1280): it was badly damaged in the 1966 flood, but has since been restored.

Another 200 yards or so to the south west will bring you to the charming Museo Horne, on Via de' Benci. There you can see a fragment of a polyptych by Giotto and a badly damaged Masaccio.

About 400 yards north west is the Palazzo Vecchio (see page 120). We are now virtually back at the starting point of this Trail. In the Palazzo, Donatello enthusiasts may want to walk up to the third floor (Sala dei Gigli) to see *Judith and Holofernes*. Be warned: the sculpture has been erected on the tall column on which it stood in one of its previous locations– not at all suitable for gallery viewing – so it's very high in the air.

Otherwise, cross to the southern bank of the Arno on the famous Ponte Vecchio. About 200 yards from the bridge is the Pitti Palace.

Palazzo Pitti (Galleria Palatina)

Location: Piazza Pitti
Contact details: Tel. 055 2388614
Opening hours: 8:15 am–6:50 pm Tues.–Sun., closed Mon.
Admission: Euro 8.50

In the mid-15th century, Luca Pitti, a cloth merchant, tried to outdo the Strozzi and Medici families by building his grand palace of golden *pietra dura* from the quarry which is now the Boboli Gardens. When the Pitti heirs fell on hard times in the mid-16th century, Eleanora di Toledo, the wife of Cosimo dei Medici, acquired the palace. In the 19th century, at a time when Florence was the capital of Italy, the Pitti was the royal residence until King Victor Emmanuel III presented it to the state.

The Renaissance paintings are displayed in the Palatine Gallery (Galleria Palatina): walk up the splendid Ammannati staircase. Its rooms are named after characters from classical mythology. In several of the rooms, ceiling frescoes by Pietro da Cortona tell the stories of these

FLORENCE AND SURROUNDS

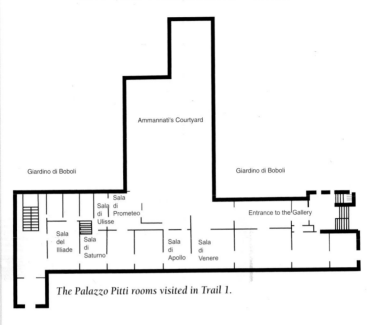

The Palazzo Pitti rooms visited in Trail 1.

classical heroes.

When compared with the Uffizi, the Pitti collection is much stronger in late, rather than early, Renaissance. In addition to the Palatine Gallery, the Pitti also has galleries for modern (18th- to 20th-century) painting and for jewelry.

Sala di Prometeo (Prometheus Room)

Head for the Sala di Prometeo with its green silk brocade-covered walls. Although the Pitti cannot match the Uffizi in its holdings of the works of Fra Lippo Lippi, it does boast one of the later, more complex of his renderings of the Madonna.

Filippo Lippi
Madonna and Child with the *Birth of the Virgin* and the *Meeting of Joachim and Anna*, (*Madonna con Gesu' Bambino*), mid to late 1460s

This large tondo offers three paintings in one. In the foreground, the Madonna and Child sit on an unusual carved throne. They are sharing a ripe pomegranate, a symbol of Christ's Passion, and Jesus is offering a seed to his mother. Behind the Madonna and Child, the

scene of the birth of the Virgin stretches across the canvas, with visitors walking from the right towards the bedroom on the left. On the stairs, Mary's mother, the pregnant Anna, greets Joachim, her father. There is much to captivate us in this complex Madonna. The color scheme of soft gray-greens and apricot tones is subtly harmonious. The architecture illustrates Filippo's love of mathematically precise perspective. The clean lines of this late work represent a departure from Lippi's earlier decorativeness. The two background scenes illustrate an interesting, if esoteric theological debate on the matter of the precise moment at which Mary became purified, or freed from original sin. The scene of her birth acknowledges the view of the Maculists (among them, the Dominicans), who argued that only Christ was completely free of original sin, and that Mary's purity occurred at her birth, when her soul joined her body. The meeting between Joachim and Anna, however, was a favorite theme of the Immaculists (among them the Franciscans), who believed that Mary's immaculate status dated from her conception.

Sala di Ulisse (Ulysses Room)

The Sala di Ulisse has dusky pink silk-covered walls. It also has Raphael's *Madonna dell'Impannata* – on the wall to your left as you walk through the door.

Raphael
Virgin and Child with St Elisabeth, St Catherine and the Young St John the Baptist (Madonna dell'Impannata), 1511–1517

This painting takes its name from the half-drawn curtain (*impannata*) over the background window. Discussion continues about which parts of the painting were executed by Raphael, and which by colleagues from his studio, but the beautifully inclined head of St Elizabeth is almost certainly his work. The painting exudes great warmth, and has as its central focus a delightfully animated Christ Child. The affectionate interaction between the figures is also very appealing. In the bottom right-hand corner of the painting, a wide-eyed St John gazes out of the painting, his hand raised in the characteristic pose of the precursor of Christ.

Sala dell'Iliade (Iliad Room)

Stop to look at Titian's *Portrait of a Gentleman* (*Ritratto di un Gentiluomo*) and Raphael's interesting portrait of a pregnant woman. The Iliad Room also has Artemisia Gentileschi's dramatic picture of *Judith* (*Giuditta*) (c.1614–20).

Sala di Saturno (Saturn Room)

At last count, there were seven Raphaels in this room.

Raphael
The Granduca Madonna, c.1506

Perhaps it is the dark background and absence of the characteristic distant Renaissance landscape that renders the Granduca Madonna such a monumental image. The fullness of the human figures – especially that of the deliciously plump infant – also helps to give the painting a strong sculptural feel. Notwithstanding the substance of the actual figures, the edges shade subtly into the dark space that surrounds them: Raphael's admiration for both Michelangelo and Leonardo is obvious in this work. The fair-haired, oval-faced Madonna holds her baby lightly and gazes at him with great tenderness. The infant has turned to look out at us – an expression of sad awareness in his eyes.

Raphael
The Baldachin Madonna (*Madonna del Baldacchino*), c.1508

In 1508, Raphael went to Rome to work in the Vatican, leaving others to complete this large altarpiece that he had painted for a chapel in the Church of Santa Spirito, so the architectural surrounds and the two angels aloft may not have been painted by him. The composition of the painting is a *sacra conversazione*, which is rather conventional by Raphael's standards – possibly because of his client's requirements. The

Raphael's Madonna and Child sit under a splendid canopy (baldachin) with angels aloft. Illustration Matt Morrow

pale-skinned Madonna and Child enthroned are flanked by a symmetrical arrangement of saints: Sts Peter and Bruno on the left and Sts James and Augustine on the right. Two equally pale-skinned cherubim perch at the foot of the throne

Raphael
Madonna of the Chair (Madonna della Seggiola), c.1512

This is possibly the most famous of all Raphael's Madonnas, having become a universal symbol of tender maternity. The tondo format – which Raphael liked so well – is a perfect space for the depiction of the love encircling the infant. Wrapped securely in his mother's protective arms, the baby nestles against her cheek, his fretful expression suggesting that he recently has had to be comforted. His baby arms bury beneath his mother's shawl, searching for her breast, and, over his shoulder, John, his young cousin, completes the circle of love. The expressiveness of the Virgin's somewhat reproachful eyes is enhanced by the rich vermilion of her blouse and the velvety texture of her shawl. Raphael was concerned in this picture to create an almost secular image of natural affection and human warmth. It is as though he has captured a private, intensely personal moment between mother and child. The sacred symbols – the haloes, and the crucifix held by the young John the Baptist – are de-emphasized – allowing the religious theme of the impending Passion to be overwhelmed by the sanctity of motherhood.

The next room is the Sala di Giove. As you pass through it, stop to look at Titian's *La Velata (Ritratto di Donna)* in her beautiful gold and white silken dress, on the wall to the left of the exit door. You will then arrive at the Sala di Marte (Mars Room), which contains a Tintoretto portrait and several pictures by Rubens.

Sala di Apollo (Apollo Room)

The Sala di Apollo has scarlet brocaded walls – and lovely Titians and Tintorettos. Look for Tintoretto's *Portrait of Vincenzo Zeno (Ritratto di Vincenzo Zeno)* and Titian's *Man with Gray Eyes (L'Uomo Dagli Occhi Grigi)*. They are both on your right as you pass through the doorway (that's if the latter is no longer in restoration). But the *piece de resistance* is Titian's *Magdalene*.

Titian
St Mary Magdalene in Penitence (La Maddalena), c.1530

In this painting, Titian's objective of reconciling the voluptuous with the sacred is most daringly executed. The saint's golden tresses – luxuriant as they are, do not quite cover her naked body. The sensuousness of the figure is evident: Titian's Magdalene is equal in natural endowments to any Venus that he has painted elsewhere. But he has also succeeded in portraying her as a genuine penitent. Her soulful eyes are uplifted to the divine; on her face is an expression of piety rather than lasciviousness. (Just what it is that the Magdalene repents remains in dispute. Magdala was a Biblical town once noted for its harlots, but this in itself does not justify drawing conclusions about the nature of the Magdalene's sins before she met Christ.)

Sala di Venere (Venus Room)

The Sala di Venere has rose-red brocaded walls and a number of Titian portraits. The best of these (on the left of the doorway through which you enter the room) is *La Bella* (1536) – with her sumptuous velvet sleeves, her chestnut hair, and her big, dark eyes – the same woman he painted, two years later, as the Venus of Urbino. High on the right-hand wall to the right of the full-length windows towards the end of the room is Titian's rendition of *Ecce Homo* (Man of Sorrows).

When you leave the Pitti, you may care to take a short walk a little way along the street on your left to the Piazza San Felice. In the square is a 13th-century church – San Felice – whose 15th-century facade may have been designed by Michelozzo. Inside are various frescoes from the Giotto workshop, and a crucifix: However, the church is often closed.

About half a mile to the west of the Pitti is the church of Santa Maria del Carmine and its celebrated Brancacci Chapel. This is a treasure-house of works by Masaccio, Masolino, and Filippino Lippi.

The Brancacci Chapel (in the Church of Santa Maria del Carmine)

Location: Piazza del Carmine
Contact details: Tel. 055 2382195
Opening hours: 10:00 am–5:00 pm, Mon., Wed–Sat., 1:00 pm–5:00 pm Sun., closed Tues.
Admission: Euro 3.10

The numbers on the chart correspond to the numbers of the descriptions on p. 115–117.

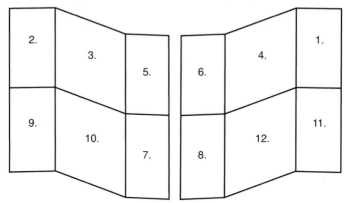

The layout of the frescoes of Masaccio and Masolino in the Brancacci Chapel, Santa Maria del Carmine, Florence.

1. Masolino
The Temptation of Adam and Eve

Note that the Serpent has a woman's head! And a blonde one, to boot!

2. Masaccio
Expulsion of Adam and Eve, 1426–27

A visit to the Brancacci Chapel is justified if for no other reason than to take in Masaccio's most famous scene – the expulsion of Adam and Eve from the Garden of Eden. No painter before Masaccio – not even the great Giotto – had captured intense anguish so powerfully. The picture – which was painted when Masaccio was in his mid twenties – shows great emotional maturity.

3. Masaccio
The Tribute Money, 1425–26

All the frescoes on which Masaccio and Masolino collaborated were concerned with scenes from the life of St Peter. *The Tribute Money*, depicting a scene from Matthew's Gospel, is the critics' favorite among these collaborative pictures. When a tax collector approached the impoverished Jesus and his Apostles to collect a

FLORENCE AND SURROUNDS

Masaccio's Expulsion of Adam and Eve

capitation tax. Jesus had to perform a miracle to find the money. He instructed Peter (center, in the yellow cloak) to catch a fish in the sea (on the left of the picture) and to pay the tax (on the right) with the coin he would find in the fish's mouth.

4. Masolino
St Peter Healing a Lame Man and the Raising of Tabitha, 1424–25

5. Masolino
St Peter's Sermon, 1424–25

6. Masaccio
St Peter Baptizing the Neophytes, 1424–25

Notice the shivering man waiting to be baptized.

7. Masaccio
St Peter, Followed by St John, Heals the Sick with his Shadow, 1424–25

8. Masaccio
St Peter Distributing Alms, and the Death of Ananias, 1424–25

9. Filippino Lippi
St Peter in Prison Visited by St Paul

10. Masaccio and Filippino Lippi
The Resurrection of the Son of Theophilus, and St Peter Enthroned

11. Filippino Lippi
The Angel Freeing St Peter from Prison

12. Filippino Lippi
The Disputation of Peter and Paul with Simon Magus in Front of the Emperor (on the right) and The Crucifixion of St Peter (on the left)

For Lippi enthusiasts (and who is not one by now?), we conclude this Trail with a 15-mile trip to Prato, northwest of Florence, and Empoli, another 15 miles to the southwest of Prato. Both places are easily reached by train. However, you cannot go from Prato to Empoli by direct train; you must return to Florence first.

Prato

As far as the exhibition of its paintings is concerned, Prato has been in a long transitionary period. Since 1998, the four major Lippi panel paintings have been held in a temporary exhibition, "The Treasures of the City" (*I Tesori della Città*) in the Museum of Mural Painting (Museo di Pittura Murale) which is attached to the Church of San Domenico. The temporary exhibition is scheduled to continue until the refurbishment of the city's main museum, the Galleria Comunale di Palazzo Pretorio, is completed. There are signs to this exhibition all over Prato. It is a collection not-to-be-missed: besides the pictures by Lippi and his son Filippino, it boasts works by Daddi, Uccello, Signorelli, Gaddi, and Monaco.

The Lippi murals in the Duomo (Cattedrale di San Stefano) are in the process of being restored. To see them, you must book a tour – the information is under the Duomo heading.

Start your visit in the Museo dell'Opera del Duomo, which is in the center of the old town.

Museo dell'Opera del Duomo

Location: Piazza del Duomo.
Opening hours: 9:30 am–12:30 pm; 3:00 pm–6:30 pm. Wed.–Sat.,
9:30 am–12:30 pm Sun., closed Tues.
Admission: A composite ticket, costing Euro 5, gains entry here as well as to the Museo di Pittura Murale and the Castello dell'Imperatore.

Donatello
Panels for the External Pulpit of the Duomo, 1428–38

Donatello's plump little *putti* leap and laugh and sing and dance to the unheard music of the instruments they are playing (a different one in each panel). Everything is movement – the swirl of their garments, the flutter of their little wings, their dancing feet (which often kick out of their frames into "mid-air").

Lippi
Madonna and Child, c.1436

This panel (in poor condition) portrays a downcast Madonna with touches of gold in her halo framed by an orchid pink aedicule. The infant, it has to be said, has a curiously aged visage but the pose – with the child gently fondling his mother's chin – is very tender.

Giovanni Bellini
Crucifixion, c.1505

This is the only rendering in Tuscany of one of Bellini's favorite themes. This late painting is appropriately desolate, with its bare branches on the trees and its skulls on the ground.

Caravaggio
The Crowning with Thorns, c.1605

In almost total darkness, a large red-robed man steadies the torso of Christ to make it easier for his soldier partner to lever the crown of thorns into their victim's scalp. The dark fingers of the first assailant press into his naked flesh, reminding us of his human vulnerability. Light entering from the bottom left of the picture illuminates the naked back of a fourth, seated figure whom we then see is jerking the rope to control Christ's bound wrists as his fingers splay in an involuntary spasm of pain. The light then leads your eye to the flexed shoulder and chest of Christ being tortured, and finally to the wide-eyed suffering but resolute expression on his face.

Proceed next door to the Duomo, noting on the way the famous exterior pulpit of Donatello, now adorned with copies of the panels you have just inspected.

Duomo (Cattedrale di San Stefano)

Location: Piazza del Duomo
Contact details: While the Lippi frescoes are being restored, your only chance to view them comes on weekends, when special tours of the scaffolding are organized. You must book beforehand through Agenzia per il Turismo, 0574 24112, Mon.–Sat. 9:00 am–1:00 pm.
Opening hours: Between services, as with other churches. Tours of the scaffolding occur from 10:00 am–11:00 am and 4:00 pm–5:00 pm Sat. and Sun. 10:00 am–11:00 am. Sun.
Admission (for the tour): Euro 8

Filippo Lippi
Life Cycles of St Stephen and St John the Baptist, 1453–mid 1460s

Fra Filippo Lippi began painting his frescoes on the walls of this

FLORENCE AND SURROUNDS

Palazzo Vecchio

cathedral in 1453. It was a monumental task that was to take him about a decade and a half to complete. The work consists of parallel life cycles of St Stephen (on the north wall) and St John the Baptist (on the south wall) – with corresponding treatments of major events in each saint's life. The work progressed from the lower tiers (which belong in Lippi's middle period) to the higher tiers (which strongly resemble the Spoleto frescoes of his later period).

Look up into the vault of the choir to see the enormous figures of the Evangelists:

Filippo Lippi
Four Evangelists, 1450–1460

In common with many other churches since the Byzantine era, the four segments of the vault of Santo Stefano are illustrated with *The Four Evangelists*. Each is seated on a bank of clouds, in front of an aureole and a further arc of (much faded) winged cherub heads. These were probably completed in the 1460s and so are close to the Spoleto frescoes in both time and style: the rainbows and sunbursts of golden rays are common to both. Matthew, in green cloak, holds a rolled parchment in his hands; the white-bearded Mark wears loose flowing pantaloons and holds a book; Luke is golden-haired and saffron-cloaked, and a troubled, gray-bearded St John the Evangelist has quill in hand, his evangelical symbol, the eagle, still visible above his head.

About 200 yards to the southwest is the Piazza San Domenico and the Museum of Mural Painting (Museo di Pittura Murale).

Museum of Mural Painting (Museo di Pittura Murale)

Location: Behind the Church of San Domenico

Contact details: Tel. 057 4616498

Opening hours: 10:00 am–1:00 pm, 3:30 pm–7:00 pm, Mon., & Wed.-Sat. 10:00 am–1:00 pm. Sun., closed Tues.

Admission: A composite ticket, costing Euro 5, gains entry here as well as to the Museo dell'Opera del Duomo and the Castello dell'Imperatore.

Filippo Lippi
Adoration of the Infant Jesus (*Nativita con I Santi Giorgio e Vincenzo Ferrer'*), 1460s

This Adoration is another example of a wilderness Adoration, combining the stable, ox and donkey themes of narrative Nativity paintings with the customary adoring saints and rocky hillside setting of the penitential treatments of this theme. Joseph's active participation in the Adoration is unusual. The saints – St George on the left and the Dominican preacher, St Vincent Ferrer, on the right, are there to draw attention to the Incarnation – the human suffering of Christ, rather than to the narrative of sacred history. The figures are arranged as an inverted triangle, with the Christ Child at its lower apex. The folds of the garments are more fluid than in some of Filippo's earlier works. Some scholars believe that the beautiful hands of Joseph were painted by Filippo's son, Filippino, while others have speculated that the young Botticelli may have been responsible.

Filippo Lippi
Madonna and Child Enthroned with Saints (*Madonna del Ceppo*), 1452–3

The *ceppo* was a wooden collection box – the forerunner of charitable trusts or chests. Prato's *ceppi*, one of which was founded by the merchant, Datini, helped pay for the work Filippo executed in that city. As the major donor of the painting, he is pictured as the large figure in red, kneeling behind four other *buonomini* (rectors). (You will see his statue, holding the *ceppo*, in the *piazza* of the Palazzo Comunale.) A quietly assured Virgin (who could well have been modelled on Lucrezia Buti, the Prato nun who became Lippi's lover and the mother of Filippino) sits with her blessing Child in *sacra conversazione* with attendant saints.

In Lippi's Madonna del Ceppo, *the red-cloaked kneeling figure in the bottom left of the picture is Francesco Datini, the Merchant of Prato, founder of one of the very first charitable trusts.* Illustration by Matt Morrow.

St Stephen wears, on his head, some of the stones with which he was martyred. He carries the banner of the republic of Prato – a red cross on a white ground signifying martyrdom and the Resurrection. St John wears his camel-skin robe, carries his reed cross and a banderole inscribed with the words, "Behold, the Lamb of God."

Filippo Lippi, with Fra Diamante
Madonna of the Girdle (Madonna della Cintola), c.1456

After the Virgin's death, Doubting Thomas could not resist looking into her tomb to see if she had truly been assumed into heaven, and discovered that the tomb was filled with roses. To strengthen this proof, moreover, as Mary ascended, she handed him her girdle (belt). Twelve hundred years later, a merchant of Prato (though not Datini) obtained the same *cintola* as part of his Palestinian wife's dowry. He brought it back to Prato, and ever since, it has been venerated in San Stefano. Thomas kneels at the sarcophagus and prepares to receive the *cintola* from her hands.

Filippo Lippi
Death of St. Jerome and Stories from his Life (Esequie di San Girolamo e Storie della sua Vita), c.1453

The top of the picture, whose celestial scene recedes both upwards and into the background, is almost Gothic in its strictly symmetrical arrangement of angels and disembodied cherubs framing God the Father, the dove of the Holy Ghost, and Christ. Much of this work was probably painted by assistants. Below this representation of the Trinity is a set of four scenes that become increasingly naturalistic, the closer they are to the foreground of the painting. In the middle distance is the Nativity, a reminder that St Jerome founded a monastery near Bethlehem, and two versions of his ascending soul. The first of these is illuminated by heavenly rays, and the second appears before St Augustine, who was writing to Jerome as he lay dying. Jerome, dignified in death, is surrounded by mourners.

For many travellers, this will be the end of this Trail. However, if you are prepared to go a few extra miles, you can catch one last Lippi painting in Tuscany – in a small but charming museum of Empoli. If you are travelling by car, you may wish to stop off on the way in the village of Vinci – birthplace of Leonardo.

FLORENCE AND SURROUNDS

Empoli

Although Empoli is only about 12 miles southwest of Prato, it can be reached by train only via Florence. Train travellers from Florence to Siena pass through Empoli, which dates back to the 12th century. Although the town prides itself on the fine glassware produced by its craftsmen, it is most famous in modern times as the hometown of the distinguished musician and arranger, Ferruccio Busoni. His memory is marked by a museum in the center of town. Further back, and further out, the village of Pontormo achieved fame as the birthplace of the famous Renaissance painter known by that name.

Museo della Collegiata

Location: Piazza della Propositura
Contact details: Tel. 0571 76284
Opening hours: 10:00 am–noon Tues.–Sun., closed Mon.
Admission: Euro 5

Filippo Lippi
Madonna and Child Enthroned, 1420s

This very early Madonna of Fra Filippo follows the relatively new fashion of surrounding the enthroned Madonna with a rising circle of saints. Who are they? St Michael (on the viewer's left) has wings and carries a sword. St Bartholomew, is the one on the right with the knife – signifying his martyrdom. (He was traditionally thought to have been flayed alive, though some thought he was crucified or beheaded.) The third saint, standing behind Michael, wears a white cloak, has a tonsure, and carries a spray of lilies. He may be the Carmelite, Albert of Trapano, Sicily. The picture reveals Filippo's debt to other Renaissance artists: to Masaccio for the facial expressions, to Donatello and Masaccio, Michelozzo and Gentile da Fabriano for the foreshortenings. Donatello, the sculptor/painter, had also used this kind of alternating flat and tightly gathered drapery, (though usually to reveal the anatomy of the wearer rather than to conceal it as in the Empoli Madonna). It seems this little chopped-off panel came from a small tabernacle in the Carmelite Convent (delle Selve) between Florence and Empoli.

If you would like a further sample of the work of Tintoretto before deciding whether to take the Venice Trail (Trail 3), you may care to travel the 40 miles to the west to visit the beautiful walled city of Lucca, a medieval capital of Tuscany. The Venetian painter, Tintoretto's *Last Supper* is in the Duomo (*Cattedrale di San Martino*). If you do decide to visit San Martino, there are two very good reasons for paying the small charge to visit the Sacristy. One is to have a really close-up view of Jacopo della Quercia's sublime marble sarcophagus for Ilaria del Carretto (with her little dog nestling sadly at her feet). The other is to see Ghirlandaio's exquisite *Virgin and Child with Saints*. However, we don't provide detailed coverage of this city. Another interesting city is Pisa, where you could visit the Museo Nazionale di San Matteo to see a Donatello, a Masaccio, and a couple of Ghirlandaios.

The end of the 15th century was also the end of the Florentine dominance of Renaissance painting. With the accession to office of the Della Rovere popes – Sixtus IV (1471–1484) and Julius II (1503–1513) – it was Rome that became the site of artistic patronage for a generation. By the time Rome fell to, and was sacked by, the French in 1527, it seemed too late for Florence to recover the lost ground. Raphael and Leonardo were lost to Florence forever, and a new northern rival – Venice – was soon to assume leadership through such painters as Titian, Tintoretto, and Veronese.

Bernini's Fountain of the Four Rivers *at Piazza Navona*

TRAIL 2:
Rome and Surrounds

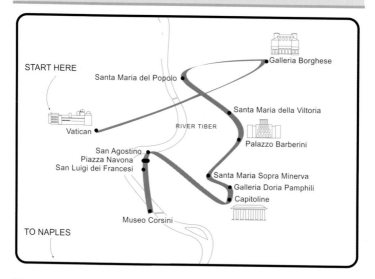

START HERE

Santa Maria del Popolo

Galleria Borghese

Santa Maria della Viltoria

Vatican

RIVER TIBER

Palazzo Barberini

San Agostino
Piazza Navona
San Luigi dei Francesi

Santa Maria Sopra Minerva

Galleria Doria Pamphili

Capitoline

Museo Corsini

TO NAPLES

Rome

Rome, though it declined in importance during the Middle Ages, rose to prominence again in the 15th century. As the center of the papacy, and thus of enormous power and wealth, it was transformed over the Renaissance period, during which it was bejewelled by churches, palaces and some of the most famous artworks ever executed. Many of these are found within the small sovereign state of the Vatican.

Much later – in the middle of the 17th century – another artist working under papal patronage was to leave his distinctive mark on Rome. This was Gian Lorenzo Bernini – the greatest of the Baroque sculptors and architects. Because he falls well outside the Renaissance, on this Trail we have focused only on four places – St Peters, the Museo Borghese, the Palazzo Barberini and the Piazza Navona – where his presence is most palpable. If you choose to approach the Vatican via the Ponte Sant'Angelo, for example, your celestial guard of honor will be the white angels that flank the bridge. They were made by Bernini and his workshop in the late 1660s: angels flying all over Rome were among Bernini's many legacies to the Eternal City!

The Vatican

Location: The Vatican Museums are to be found nearly two and a half miles west of Stazione Termini. You can catch the metro (underground) from Termini to Ottaviano, then follow the (abundant) signs.

Contact details: Tel. 06 69883333

Opening hours: 8:45 am–2:20 pm daily

Admission: Euro 10

The Vatican Museums do not offer the same comprehensive coverage of the Renaissance as does the Uffizi in Florence. This simply reflects their history: the Vatican Museums were originally founded in the early 18th century to house numerous works from antiquity – which they continue to do to the present day. The art gallery was not established until the end of that century, so the Vatican has had to rely heavily on works that were commissioned in the High Renaissance, when the papacy had become the dominant patron of the arts in Italy. This explains why the Vatican has so many frescoes on its walls: by the 16th century only the church had the resources to commission major works for its buildings.

Visiting the Vatican may take up to one day, especially if you wish to see some of the other collections which are not covered in this Trail.

Once you have climbed the grand circular stairs to the entrance of the museums, turn sharply to the right to enter the Vatican Gallery (Pinacoteca Vaticana) and go to Room 2.

Pinacoteca Vaticana

Room 2

Giotto
Stefaneschi Polyptych, 1313

Cardinal Stefaneschi, who commissioned this glowing, two-sided altarpiece, was a leading figure in the move to return the papacy from Avignon. The polyptych, which was to stand on the high altar of

St Peter's basilica, therefore had a political purpose. That is why, on one of its painted sides, Giotto represents the enthroned St Peter, the symbol of the church in Rome, as almost the equal of Christ himself. The central panel on the front of the altarpiece shows Christ in majesty. He is flanked by two saints undergoing martyrdom – St Peter in the left panel, and St Paul in the right. In the predella are the Virgin and Child, surrounded by the 12 apostles. On the back, (the verso), St Peter has taken center stage. On his left are the apostles James and Paul, and on his right, the apostles Andrew and John.

Room 3

Fra Angelico
Madonna and Child with St Dominic, St Catherine and Angels, c.1435

This is Fra Angelico's smallest altarpiece. The ornate gold-patterned background and the haloes show the continuing Byzantine influence in Fra Angelico's time, although this kind of elaborate ornamentation was also pretty popular with Italian artists of the late medieval period. The different scale of the three sets of figures is an innovation: a large Madonna and Child, angels who are half the size of the Virgin, and the even smaller figures of the two saints in the foreground.

Filippo Lippi
Marsuppini Coronation of the Virgin, mid 1440s

Despite the long, thin physiques of the figures in this rendition of the Coronation of the Virgin, Fra Filippo has achieved a naturalistic effect by giving them an overall uniform height, and an interesting range of (somewhat grave) facial expressions. As with the same painter's *Maringhi Coronation* in the Uffizi, Mary kneels to be crowned by her son. (The most common arrangement was for the crowned Queen of Heaven to be seated next to Christ.) The cardinal-red robed figure staring out at the viewer in the left section of the triptych is St Gregory the Great. The other monk-like figures are saints from the Olivetan and Camaldolensian Orders. Once again, Lippi has framed his picture in elaborate, ornamental architecture, the main feature of which is the multi-tiered throne. The realistic sky that can be seen behind the architecture gives the picture a spaciousness, despite the crowded left and right panels.

Giovanni Bellini
Pietà (Pala di Pesaro or Il Seppellimento di Cristo'), 1471–4

This is the painting that once appeared in the tympanum above the Coronation of the Virgin in Bellini's *Pala di Pesaro* (Trail 5). Christ's body rests on the edge of the sarcophagus into which he will be lowered. Joseph of Arimathea, owner of the tomb, supports the body from behind while wrapping it in the burial shroud. The tall, solemn, bearded man holding the metal jar of ointment is Nicodemus. A swollen-faced, weeping Magdalene gently applies the ointment to Christ's wounded hands, the curls of her hair catching the golden afternoon light. Christ's noble face is almost in profile, his eyes and mouth peacefully closed.

Leonardo da Vinci
St Jerome, c.1483

In a stark, stony environment – in which the lion in the foreground is the only other living object – the emaciated saint exudes strength of will. The suffering, which is so clearly visible in his face has been freely chosen by him, and he will continue on this path of suffering until he meets his God.

Room 8

Raphael
Oddi Altarpiece 1503–04

The *Oddi Altarpiece* is generally regarded as Raphael's first masterpiece. Later in his all-too-short life, Raphael was to shift to wider historical themes, as you can see for yourself if you proceed from the Oddi Altarpiece to the celebrated Raphael Rooms elsewhere in the Vatican Museum.

The Coronation of the Virgin: The main panel of this altarpiece carries a magnificent, two-part rendition of the Coronation of the Virgin. In the lower section, the Apostles stand around the sarcophagus of the Virgin which no longer contains her body. But from which sprout fresh flowers. In the center is the ever-doubting St Thomas, this time holding the Virgin's sash (or girdle) which she has dropped on her ascent into heaven, no doubt as proof of her elevation. In the upper half of the picture, the Virgin sits next to her son, who crowns her to the accompaniment of celestial music and the fluttering wings of the little *putti* overhead.

Predella: Annunciation: Raphael's jewel-like little paintings in the predella under the *Oddi Altarpiece* are worthy of a visit in their own right. In the Annunciation, the swishing robes of the angel contrast with the stillness of the Virgin, emphasizing her air of acceptance, even resignation. The 20-year-old Raphael displays mature skill as a colorist: the soft brown and terracotta tones of the architecture and the rose tints of the clothing are gently lit from behind the viewer. The perspective of the picture draws our gaze beyond the figures of the archangel and the Virgin, through the double archway and above the landscape to the flying dove of the Holy Spirit and the figure of God the Father, hovering in a sky of smoky blue that the rising sun is lightening on the horizon.

Raphael
The Foligno Madonna, c.1512

So great is Raphael's reputation as a draftsman that his supreme mastery of color is often overlooked. *The Foligno Madonna* provides ample evidence of his expertise in this area: it is a symphony of blue (the sky with its sublime angels), sunny gold (the aureole framing the Virgin and Child) and brilliant red (the robes of the Virgin and St Jerome, kneeling in the foreground). The whole effect is of a countryside sparkling in the aftermath of a sunshower. The Virgin sits on her throne of clouds, her left arm encircling a very human, wriggling infant Jesus who seems only too keen to escape back to earth. On her left are the adult St John the Baptist and St Francis; the second figure on the right is that of the donor, Sigismondo dei Conti, who commissioned the altarpiece to give thanks for his home's lucky escape when it was hit by lightning. Below the Virgin is a little angel, gazing upwards at the celestial scene. Despite their symmetrical arrangement, there is nothing stiff or formal in the six figures. Their robes fold and flow naturalistically around their relaxed limbs and their faces radiate warmth. Of particular interest is the figure of St John the Baptist. As is often the case, he is clothed in the characteristic camel-skin of his period as a hermit in the desert, he carries his crucifix-shaped staff, and his gesture portends the fate of the infant Jesus. But his face, framed by thick, unkempt hair, is extraordinarily beautiful. Its refined features, its intelligence, and its great sensitivity seem to embody the best of Renaissance ideals – truth, wisdom, and goodness.

ROME AND SURROUNDS

Raphael
The Transfiguration, 1520

Raphael was completing this picture when he suddenly died, and it was carried in the funeral procession that took his body to its final resting place in the Pantheon. The painting serves beautifully as a bridge between the High and the Late Renaissance. In its chiaroscuro treatment of somber but luminous colors, Raphael is anticipating the

style of Tintoretto (who had been born only a few months before Raphael's death). The dual space composition so typical of Raphael is treated with an unequalled force, geometrical rigor, and dynamism. Down below, where the light of the dawn has yet to arrive, the central figure is the apparently epileptic boy, whose vision of the transfigured Christ may have reached an unbearable intensity. Up above, the soaring Christ with his shining raiment has been joined by the prophets Elias and Moses, his glory stunning the three apostles he had chosen to accompany him (including, inevitably, Peter).

Raphael's Transfiguration *shows three apostles, overcome by fear and blinding light as Christ, in the company of Moses and Elias, is transfigured to reveal his divinity.* Illustration by Matt Morrow.

Room 10

Titian
Madonna with Six Saints (Madonna di San Nicolo dei Frari), c.1520

Critics of this picture claim that it lacks balance: St Nicholas certainly seems to be taking up a great deal of room in the lower space – which is crowded further by the apparently obligatory presence of Sts Francis and Anthony (no doubt because the work was commissioned originally for Venice's Franciscan Church of St Nicholas). The celestial upper space also seems crowded but we can't blame the patrons for that. This damage was done in the 18th century, when the topmost figure – the Dove of the Holy Ghost – was removed to be used as a pendant to Raphael's *Transfiguration*.

Room 12

Caravaggio
The Entombment (La Deposizione dalla Croce), 1602–04

Is this the most realistic depiction of the Entombment ever produced? Caravaggio's Christ is a well-built man who has become a heavy, dead weight in the arms of John and Nicodemus. Three women are there, too. A realistically aged Mary, her mother's face set against her grief – stretches out her right arm (and, for all we know in the darkness, her left) to embrace her loved ones. A second woman (Magdalene?) weeps quietly, while a third throws up her arms to express her uncontrollable grief. John, cradling Christ with his right arm, touches the wound in Christ's side with his left hand.

The Chapel of Nicholas V (Cappella di Niccolo V)

When visiting the Vatican Museums, it is worth taking the short detour en route to the Sistine Chapel in order to see Fra Angelico's remarkable frescoes in the Chapel of Nicholas V. They cover three walls of a small room and contain scenes from the lives of St Stephen and St Lawrence. It is fascinating to compare these cycles with the frescoes in San Marco, Florence. They are busier and more ornate than those on the walls of San Marco; the richness of their decoration and their sublime architectural detail provide a feast of color and theological narrative.

A detail from Fra Angelico's depiction of St Lawrence distributing alms, one of the works you may see in the Chapel of Nicholas V. Illustration by Erin Round.

The Raphael Rooms (Stanze di Raffaello)

In 1508, Pope Julius II commissioned Raphael to paint frescoes to cover four rooms in the papal apartment. This project was to be Raphael's major preoccupation for the rest of his short life. There are four rooms: the frescoes within them firmly established Raphael's reputation in Rome. The Hall of Constantinople is the room one enters first, but the frescoes in this room were the last to be completed and it is thought that Raphael himself had little to do with them. The frescoes show scenes from the life of Constantine: *The Battle of Milvian Bridge* was completed from a preparatory sketch by Raphael. Proceed to the next room, the Room of Heliodorus. Heliodorus, according to Jewish history, was a thief who is smote by a horseman as he leaves with treasure from the Temple of Jerusalem: this incident is the subject of one of the frescoes. In *The Meeting of Leo I and Attila*, the portrait of Leo I was originally given the features of Julius II, but after he died, Raphael prudently painted over it the features of his successor, Leo X. *The Mass at Bolsena* shows an incident in which a doubting priest saw the bread (host) began to bleed while he was celebrating mass. *The Deliverance of St Peter*, a dramatic fresco, is worth a closer look.

Raphael
The Deliverance of St Peter, 1512–14

The odd shapes of walls – punctured by arches, doorways and windows – often caused great difficulties for the fresco painter. Raphael has not completely overcome the architectural problems of the space in which he has painted *The Deliverance*, but the work is interesting because of the way he has used different sources of light in an otherwise nocturnal, gloomy environment. In the center, the awakening Peter is illuminated by the celestial glow surrounding the delivering angel. To the right, the more localized aureole of the angel reflects gently from the armor of the guards as he leads the saint to freedom. To the left, other guards are awakening in the silvery moonlight of a cloudy night. The modern writer, André Malraux, said this is the greatest image of freedom ever created by a painter. Peter was the favorite saint of the pope who had brought Raphael to Rome – Julius II – and Raphael has given the saint the face of the pope. *The Deliverance* is the only painting in which Raphael has made Peter the central focus, although he figures prominently in several of the tapestries that Raphael designed for the Sistine Chapel. Look for these in the Pinacoteca of the Vatican Museum. With the departure of the tapestries, there is now no work by Raphael in the Sistine Chapel. But you can look at a picture that helps fill this gap – a splendid treatment of the Baptism of Christ by Raphael's master, Perugino, in collaboration with Pinturicchio.

The spirit of the Dominicans – and especially of their most famous philosopher St Thomas Aquinas – pervades the Room of the Segnatura. The four walls portray four dimensions of Christian truth: classical thought, the arts, the virtues and religion. Above each of these is the appropriate allegorical figure – Philosophy, Poetry, Justice and Theology. Two of the frescoes are particularly noteworthy:

Raphael
The Dispute over the Holy Sacrament (Disputa'), 1509

It is in this broader context that *The Dispute* (whose title many claim to be a misnomer) must be appreciated. In heaven, Christ sits at the center of the Holy Trinity, flanked by the Virgin and John the Baptist and a row of other saints from antiquity, of whom Peter and Paul are the most prominent. Beneath this heavily populated celestial space stands the Eucharist, surrounded by several fathers of the church (including Aquinas) and others (including, controversially, the Dominican Savanarola) engaged in vigorous dialogue. You will find it interesting to compare this treatment of a theological subject with a second work by Raphael, below.

Raphael
The School of Athens, 1509

In *The School,* the discourse is also lively, interesting because several of Raphael's fellow artists appear – Leonardo as Plato; Michelangelo in the center foreground, head resting on his left hand; the architect Bramante as Euclid; Sodoma in the right foreground in the white beret; and next to him in the black beret, Raphael himself. In his depiction of a grand architectural setting for the Athenians, Raphael may well have been influenced by Fra Angelico, who, a century earlier, had used a similar antique setting in his treatment of themes connected with Sts Stephen and Lawrence in the nearby Chapel of Nicholas V.

The final room is the Room of the Fire in the Borgo. The principal fresco in this room is *The Fire in the Borgo*, but although Raphael designed the work, his assistants completed it, and not always perfectly. It portrays a miracle in which Pope Leo IV extinguished a fire by making the sign of the cross. After your long walk through the labyrinthine corridors of the Vatican Museum, you come to the Mecca for most tourists in the Vatican: the Sistine Chapel.

The Sistine Chapel

Of the several painters who contributed to the frescoes on the walls of the Sistine Chapel, one of the most important is Botticelli.

Botticelli
The Sistine Chapel Frescoes, 1481

Botticelli executed his three paintings in the Sistine Chapel (including the portraits of popes above them and the drapery beneath) within just 11 months. They comprise *Scenes from the Life of Moses*, *The Rebellion Against the Laws of Moses*, and *The Jewish Sacrifice and the Temptation of Christ*. The several episodes of the narrative of Christ's joust with the Devil are represented in *The Temptation of Christ*, which stretches like a tableau across the background of the foreground picture of *The Jewish Sacrifice*. In a wooded forest in the top left-hand corner of the picture, the Devil, disguised as a hermit, tempts the fasting Christ to turn stones into loaves of bread. In the center he invites Christ to survey the riches of the world over which he can declare himself master and to display his power by casting himself off the building. In the top right-hand corner, in front of a communion table laid by angels, Christ drives off the Devil, who is then forced to reveal his true identity. In the foreground of this remarkable chronicle, the Jewish high priest officiates at the pre-Christian sacrificial rite – a reference, evidently, to Christ's own sacrifice in the crucifixion. In the middle ground on the left of the painting, Christ explains to a group of angels the relationship between the two events.

Understanding Botticelli's *Rebellion Against the Laws of Moses* will help you understand the Sistine Chapel as a whole, for it contains a dire warning from Pope Sixtus IV – the builder of the Chapel – to those who were continually challenging his papal authority. In designing the program for the chapel, Sixtus wanted to trace the line

Resurrection
(Paludano)

EAST WALL

Disputation over Body of Moses
(Da Lecce)

Jacob
and Joseph

Eleazar and Matthan

Last Supper and Scenes
from the Passion (Rosselli)

Achim and
Eliud

David and
Goliath

Prophet
Zechariah

Judith and
Holofernes

Azor and
Sadok

Testament of Moses (Signorelli)

Handing over
the Keys
(Perugino)

Prophet
Joel

Drunkenness
of Noah

Delphic
Sibyl

Zerabbabel with
Parents

The Flood

Josiah with
Parents

Stoning of
Moses
(Botticelli)

Sermon on
the Mount
(Rosselli)

Erithraen
Sibyl

Noah's
Sacrifice

Prophet
Isaiah

Uzziah with
Parents

The Fall

Hezekias with
Parents

Moses and
the Tablets
(Rosselli)

NORTH WALL

Prophet
Ezekiel

Creation
of Eve

Cumaean
Sibyl

SOUTH WALL

Calling of the
Apostles
(Ghirlandaio)

Rehoboam with
his Mother

Creation
of Adam

Asa with
Parents

Crossing the
Red Sea
(Rosselli)

Persian
Sibyl

Dividing Land
& Waters

Prophet
Daniel

Temptation
of Christ
(Botticelli)

Solomon with
his Mother

Creation of
the Heavens

Jesse with
Parents

Life of Moses
(Botticelli)

Prophet
Jeremiah

Creating Day
& Night

Libyan
Sibyl

Baptism of Christ (Perugino)

The
Punishment
of Haman

Jonah

Moses and
the Brazen
Serpent

Journey of Moses (Perugino)

WEST WALL
ALTAR AND LAST JUDGMENT

Walls and ceilings of the Sistine Chapel

of his authority back through the previous popes to St Peter, the first pope – even to Christ, who had anointed St Peter, and Moses, who had been chosen by God. The Sistine Chapel had a clear political purpose. Most of its paintings can be related back to this purpose.

Two rebellions against God's Old Testament leaders, Moses and Aaron, are featured. Moses, shown as an old man with a long white beard is protected by Joshua, while on the right the Jews, tired of their privations in the desert, are demanding a new leader. In the center of the picture, the sons of Aaron and a group of Levites led by Korah have opposed the authority of the blue-robed high priest, Aaron, who now aims his censer in their direction. The group on the left illustrates the punishment that awaits the rebels – the ground opens up to swallow them. The faithful can expect salvation, however: Korah's two innocent sons are lifted up on a cloud. Above the triumphal arch, writ large for those who fail to understand the symbolism are the words: "Let no man take the honor to himself except that he is called by God, as Aaron was."

Scenes from the Life of Moses consists of a series of episodes from different points in time, including Moses in the wilderness (taking off his sandals as instructed by the voice in the Burning Bush), Moses on the mount speaking directly to God, Moses driving off the shepherds who molested Jethro's two daughters, and Moses giving water to their sheep. Jethro's daughters are painted as beautiful young Florentines. (Moses married Zipporah, the girl on the left, and Botticelli's depiction of her inspired Marcel Proust's description of Odette.)

Ghirlandaio
The Calling of Peter and Andrew (Le Vocazioni di San Pietro e San Andrea), 1481

Ghirlandaio's narrative painting – the only such picture that Ghirlandaio is known to have produced – depicts not only the calling of Peter and Andrew, but also of James and John. In fact, three separate incidents are shown in the one frame. First, (on the left, behind the group of figures in the front of the picture), Christ calls Peter and Andrew away from their boats and the nets they are casting into the sea. On the opposite bank, Christ sees James and John fishing with their father Zebedee, and calls them as well. Third, in center stage, Peter (in the yellow robe, next to Christ) and Andrew – no longer dressed as fishermen – kneel before their new master. Behind these figures, and uniting all three incidents, a bay stretches back into the distance. The 'V'-shaped space between the two shores, accentuated by the line of the twin landscapes and even the direction of the flight of the birds, focuses our attention on Christ and Peter and Andrew – but especially on Christ and the yellow-robed Peter, which after all, was the intention.

It is Michelangelo who dominates the Sistine, with his massive works on the Chapel's ceiling and back wall. No video, no coffee-table representation, no one's verbal account can possibly prepare you for the impact of what you will see when you enter this famous chapel. And the contrast between the cool tones and idealistic Renaissance figures of the ceiling with the dark terror of the Judgment – now admittedly lightened somewhat by the Chapel's restoration – can be easily explained: Michelangelo painted the ceiling at the height of the Renaissance, between 1508 and 1512; he started painting the Last Judgment 23 years later – and just eight years after the terrible sack of Rome in 1527.

Michelangelo
The Ceiling of the Sistine Chapel 1508–12

The themes of this famous ceiling are all to do with the Old Testament and ancient mythology: 54 scenes in total. These can best be examined in five groups: the nine central narratives running down the middle of the chapel; the ten medallions which shrink some of the central narrative scenes; the 12 prophets and sybils which frame the narratives and medallions; and around the outer perimeter, 24 portrayals of the ancestors of Christ, and four pendentives (triangular sections in the corners) showing Old Testament episodes. Of these groups, the most important is made up of the nine central narratives, themselves organized into three triads. Use the diagram to help you locate the pictures.

Start with the triad over the altar – all concerned with the creation of the universe by a titanic, whirling God – a God of awesome power, of flowing beard and hair, gesturing dynamically to effect his acts of creation: *The Separation of Light and Dark; The Creation of the Sun, Moon and Planets; The Separation of Water from Firmament – Water Brings Forth Life*.

The middle triad – which contains Michelangelo's most famous painted image, of God creating Adam, deal with Adam and Eve: the flowing *Creation of Adam*; the ingenious *Creation of Eve*; and the poignant *Temptation and Expulsion*.

Michelangelo's ceiling of the Sistine Chapel detail (Creation of Adam)

The third triad deals with Noah, who was particularly important for this project: Noah's ark was commonly held to be a symbol of the church, and Julius II, the Pontiff who had commissioned the work, made it a central part of Michelangelo's brief to strengthen his papacy's claims to legitimacy. This triad consists of *The Sacrifice of Noah*, *The Flood*, and *The Drunkenness of Noah*.

Michelangelo
The Last Judgment, 1535–41

This fresco is generally regarded as a highpoint of the Renaissance – the greatest painting by its supreme genius (albeit one whose talent was more suited to the three-dimensional work of sculpture and architecture). It was unveiled on 31 October, 1541 – 29 years to the day after the unveiling of the ceiling frescoes.

Many people viewing *The Last Judgment* for the first time experience vertiginous awe. The sheer drama of the subject and the dynamic of vigorous movement in a universe with no frame dramatically combine to convey the terror of this apocalypse. The best way to explore the massive fresco is to work your way around the clock. Start at the center – with the mighty figure of Jesus, knees flexed, right arm up-raised in righteous wrath, ready for action. He is flanked, on his right,

1. Angels, including Gabriel, carry the symbols of the Passion
2. Eve
3. John the Baptist
4. St Andrew with his cross
5. Mary averts her head in pity
6. Christ, the Judge
7. St Peter with the keys of heaven

8. St Lawrence with the gridiron on which he was roasted to death
9. St Bartholomew with his human skin: Michelangelo's self-portrait is in the face of the skin
10. Simon Zelotes with his saw
11. St Catherine with her wheel (the instrument of her torture) and St Sebastian holding arrows (he was shot with arrows)
12. Redeemed souls hanging by a rosary
13. Trumpeting angels
14. Charon ferrying the damned to hell

Michelangelo's dramatic **Last Judgment**. *The diagram shows a few of the characters you can see in this fresco.* Illustration by Matt Morrow.

by Mary, who seems to shrink from the horror of the scenes below her, and by St John the Baptist, his brown-bearded face turned over his left shoulder to stare fixedly at his Savior. On his left, standing behind other saints, is the impressive white-bearded figure of St Peter. At their feet are other saints, including Bartholomew, carrying the flayed skin of his own martyrdom (whose collapsed face is a self-portrait of the anguished artist).

Move down the vertical axis through the trumpeting angels until you reach the mouth of hell at 6 o'clock. Then, adopting a clockwise path, proceed through the elect ascending into heaven, until you reach – at 10 o'clock – the lunette showing the angels bearing the crucifix aloft. Pass through 12 o'clock to reach the corresponding lunette at two o'clock showing more angels borne down by the pillar to which Jesus had been tied during the flagellation. Drop down with the damned heading towards eternal suffering, until you reach 5 o'clock – where the Boat of Charon is already conveying some of them to hell. (Compared with their counterparts in earlier versions, such as Giotto's, the devils here seem much more human. Michelangelo may be making a point about modernization – as we move away from the Middle Ages, the boundaries between devils and men become progressively more blurred.)

This completes your Vatican Museum visit, unless you wish to view the many splendid antiquities or the Vatican's collection of modern art. From here, you may wish to walk to St Peter's Basilica.

St Peter's

Location: Piazza San Pietro
Contact details: Tel. 6988 4466 or 6988 4866
Opening hours: 7:00 am–7:00 pm

St Peter's is the most famous Catholic church in the world. In its opulent interior, there are many splendid sculptural and architectural features. The spectacular dome was designed by Michelangelo. Also within its walls, you will find one of Michelangelo's best-loved sculptures:

Michelangelo
Pietà 1498–99

This is justly the most celebrated of Michelangelo's early sculptures, completed when he was in his early twenties. In luminous white marble, he created a profoundly moving work. The Madonna holds in her lap the son whom she had once nursed. Through the exquisite integration of the two figures, Michelangelo was able to preserve a perfect balance, notwithstanding the adult proportions of the dead Christ. He did this by endowing Mary with a lap capacious enough to accommodate the body of the 33-year-old Jesus, and by rendering his body along graceful flowing lines that curve around the figure of the mother. As you will see, this was a theme to which Michelangelo returned at the end of his life, nearly six decades later.

In the Sacristy of the Basilica (the Beneficiati Sacristy) there is a tabernacle that had work done on it by Donatello and Michelozzo – his long-time collaborator with whom he lived in Rome sometime in the early 1430s. The tabernacle contains a relief of the *Burial of Christ,* the upper half of which is Donatello's work.

As you move around St Peter's and its environs, you are surrounded by Bernini. Inside the Basilica, you can't miss the famous hundred-feet high *baldacchino* (canopy) with its barley-sugar columns, made from bronze taken from the Pantheon. However, Bernini's influence as an architect is even more significant, for he was responsible for integrating the earlier designs of Michelangelo and Maderna into a coherent whole. And outside the Basilica, it was Bernini who created the grand design of the Piazza, which has been called "the noblest setting of any church in all Christendom."

The post-Vatican Trail has the shape of an "S", with the bottom loop being much larger than the top one. If you take the Trail on foot, you will end up walking more than six miles, so it's best to allow two leisurely days to complete it.

There are many good reasons to start your exploration of the art of Rome beyond the Vatican in the beautiful Villa Borghese and its expansive gardens, to the northeast of the city center. There is much to enjoy there: a lake, small temples, rowing boats and sculptures.

There you will also find the Museo (and Galleria) Borghese. People often get lost in the vast gardens of the 17th century Villa Borghese, trying to find the Picture Gallery (*Galleria*). (The confusion arises from the fact that many maps use the label Villa Borghese to refer to the gardens *plus* the building that houses the Galleria) You'll find the Gallery on the second and third floors of the Museo Borghese.

ROME AND SURROUNDS

Galleria Borghese

Location: Villa Borghese, Piazzale Scipione Borghese. Take the Metro to
Spagna, then walk through the tunnel that leads straight from the station into
the Gardens. Once out of the tunnel, walk up the hill and follow the signs to
the Museo.
Contact details: Tel. 06 8417645. Pre-bookings: 06 32810
Opening hours: Closed 9:00 am–9:00 pm Tues.–Fri., 9:00 am–midnight
Sat., 9:00 am–8:00 pm Sun., closed Mon.
Admission: Euro 8

These days, most travellers seem to visit the Galleria Borghese
principally to view its fine collection of paintings by Caravaggio, which
are the works we focus on. But the fabulous art treasures it holds – most
of them collected by Cardinal Scipione Borghese, the shrewd nephew of
Pope Paul V (1605–21) – are many and varied, ranging from antique
sculpture to 18th-century painting. The *biglietteria* (ticket office),
cafeteria, cloakroom and shop take up what the authorities call the
Services and Amenities level. You ascend stairs to reach what they call
the Ground Floor, which contains the statues and the Caravaggio
paintings. To get to the First Floor, you usually have to go back outside
before climbing up again.

Ground Floor

On entering the upstairs Ground Floor Gallery, stop for a moment
to look at the Roman floor mosaics (which contain depictions of
gladiators at their gory work) and at the classical Roman sculptures
that provided such inspiration to the sculptors of Renaissance and
Baroque Italy. Room I contains Antonio Canova's captivating
sculpture of the reclining *Paolina Borghese Bonaparte* 1805. In the
next two rooms, you will find two of Bernini's damsels in serious
distress: in Room III, Daphne is turning into a tree to avoid Apollo's
clutches: *Apollo and Daphne* (*Apollo e Dafne*) 1622–25; and in Room
IV, the tearful Proserpine is being carried off by Pluto: *Rape of
Proserpine* (*Ratto di Proserpina*),1621–22. These life-sized sculptural
groups ushered in a new era of European sculpture. Equally
revolutionary was his grim-faced *David*, 1624, (Room II). Room VI
displays his *Aeneas and Anchises,* 1618–20 and his larger-than-life-
sized allegorical statue of *Truth Unveiled* (*La Verita'*) (1646–52).
Although this floor is primarily devoted to sculpture, it also

contains a single room that boasts no fewer than six paintings by Caravaggio. If you walk around Room VIII in a clockwise direction (as most people seem to do) you will see these works in the following order:

Caravaggio
Boy with a Basket of Fruit (Fanciullo con Canestro di Frutta), 1593

The picture is half portrait (*self*-portrait?) and half still life. The expression on the boy's face is hard to read: is he trying to be alluring with his softly parted lips, and his shirt falling off one shoulder? Or is that a look of mockery on his face? The still-life is perhaps more satisfying: it is one of Caravaggio's marvellously observed baskets of over-ripe fruit. (You'll have to dodge around because the glass over the picture catches the light, but you'll agree that the original is more mysteriously compelling than any reproduction can ever convey.)

Caravaggio's Boy with a Basket of Fruit

Caravaggio
St John the Baptist (San Giovanni Battista), c.1610

Caravaggio paints John in the wilderness as a near nude adolescent – one of several similar versions of this theme. He sits on a brilliant red blanket, loosely holding his shepherd's staff, a ram at his side. He appears to be downcast, or bored and stiff in his uncomfortable pose.

Caravaggio
St Jerome, Writing (San Girolamo Scrivente), 1605

Jerome is pictured as the elderly hermit, sitting in his cave, painstakingly translating the Bible from Hebrew to Latin. He is naked except for a red blanket thrown loosely over his thin shoulders. With his left hand, he holds the pages of the Hebrew text he is translating. Caravaggio has produced an image of intense concentration. The saint's right arm reaches out to dip his pen, but his eyes remain riveted to the page. The light from over the viewer's left shoulder picks up the bony skull of the *memento mori* and Jerome's own, remarkably similar, shiny pate, a reminder, perhaps, that his own death was near.

Caravaggio
Madonna of the Grooms (Madonna dei Palafrenieri), 1606

It's not hard to see why this *Madonna and Child* was controversial. The courtyard is in darkness, except for a misty haze coming from over the wall: even the figure of the aging St Anne is in semidarkness. The main purpose of the golden light that has begun to filter through from the bottom left seems to be to emphasize the nakedness of the Child, highlighted by the shadow of his penis on his thigh, and the attractively buxom form of the mother. Caravaggio has captured a very human interaction between mother and child, as well as conveying a moment of drama and beauty. The painter was presented with a design problem following Pope Pius V's settlement of a dispute about whether it was the Virgin or the Child who crushed the head of the serpent. The pope decided that *both* had done so: hence Christ's foot on top of that of his mother.

Caravaggio
David with the Head of Goliath (Davide con la Testa di Golia), 1606

This is no triumphant David: the boy looks almost regretful for the deed he has had to commit. He holds up the head of the tyrant by its dark hair, revealing the even darker wound in the forehead. You can just make out the gouts of blood issuing from the severed neck. Notwithstanding, the young hero appears still vulnerable in his baggy pants, his lean, pale torso showing through the voile shirt. David is a portrait of Cecco (Francesco Boneri, Caravaggio's young lover) whereas he painted himself into Goliath. As the picture hangs right next to the *Sick Bacchus*, you have the opportunity to compare two of the artist's most unflattering self-portraits (13 years apart).

Caravaggio
Sick Bacchus (Autoritratto in veste di Baco), 1593

Despite the (somewhat modern) name of the painting, we're not at all sure that it was Bacchus that Caravaggio had in mind when he decided to paint himself in the grip of some awful illness. He's certainly sick: his face has a ghastly, gray-green pallor; his eyelids appear swollen and inflamed; his lips are dry. But those are ivy leaves, not grape vines, in his hair, and where is the glass of wine offered to the viewer by his Uffizi *Bacchus*? Perhaps the grapes are meant to be a substitute for the wine: in his dirty right hand a bunch of green ones, well past their prime; and, accompanying the bruised yellow peaches on the slab in front of the viewer, a bunch of glistening black ones. It's interesting, though, that an earlier name for the picture was *Satyr with Grapes*.

The Picture Gallery containing most of the other paintings is on what is called the First Floor. To gain access, you will have to exit and re-enter the building via the stairs.

First Floor Picture Gallery

On a table by the wall on the left of the entrance, in Room XIV, there is Caravaggio's *Portrait of Paul V*, c.1605, an unflattering representation of a not very attractive pope. Above the next table on the same wall (flanked by two more Bernini busts of Cardinal Scipione Borghese) are three portraits in oils by this sculptor. They are: *Portrait of a Boy*, (c.1638); a *Self-portrait* from 1630–5, and *Self-portrait as a Young Man* (1623). Nearby are two celebrated paintings by Peter Paul Rubens: *Susanna and the Elders* (1605–7) and *The*

Entombment (1602). Further around on this floor, in Room XX, is a rarity – a Bellini painting in Rome!

Giovanni Bellini
Madonna and Child, c.1510

Although this painting has been apparently signed by Bellini and has the vibrant colors of the artist's last period, it has not attracted the approval of the critics. Many believe that this was a product of Bellini's studio, and is modelled on the finer *Madonna and Child*, with St John the Baptist and a saint, which was painted at about the same time and now hangs in the Accademia in Venice. Yet the trademark green cloth of honor is there, as is a Bellini spindly tree and distant landscape. So is the barrier between the child and the viewer. The Virgin plays with her child's foot – a very human interaction also characteristic of Bellini.

This Room also contains four Titians: *Sacred and Profane Love,* c.1514; *St Dominic*, 1565; *The Flagellation*, 1560 (an unusual rendition that shows only Christ's head and torso with visible scourge wounds), and *Venus and Eros*, c.1560 (in which, under a hazy, rosy sunset, Venus is tying a blindfold around the eyes of Cupid). The big reward on this floor is in Room IX, which contains three paintings by Raphael: *The Entombment of Christ* (1507); *Portrait of a Young Woman with a Unicorn* (1506) and his well-known *Portrait of a Man* (1502–4). On the same wall as the latter, is a 'chocolate box' version of the *Madonna and Child, with Saint John and Angels* c.1488, painted by Botticelli and his assistants.

Raphael
The Entombment of Christ, 1507

This is generally regarded as the greatest painting from the Florentine period of the still youthful Raphael. To view this picture is to be deeply moved by the anguish of Mary and the profound distress of her companions. Even in death, Christ himself seems not yet to have escaped his agonies. If anything, the emotional intensity is heightened by the strong sense of movement, for the dead Christ is not prone in the arms of his mother (as in most conventional treatments of the Pietà theme), but is being carried along while she swoons away from him. Evidently, Raphael himself experienced great emotional stress in completing this painting – never again did he return to any of the themes associated with the agony and death of Christ.

Piazza del Popolo

If you are a Caravaggio enthusiast you will not mind taking a leisurely walk of half a mile or so through the gardens to the west in order to see two more of his most dramatic pictures.

Chiesa di Santa Maria del Popolo

Location: Piazza del Popolo 12
Contact details: Tel. 361 0836
Opening hours: 7:00 am–noon, then 4:00 pm–7:00 pm daily

Within the Church, there are a number of chapels endowed by famous Roman families. Within the Della Rovere Chapel are Pinturicchio frescos, and the admirable Chigi Chapel was designed by Raphael. It contains a fine mosaic, *God and the Planets*, executed by de Pace in 1516 to a design by Raphael. But the main reason for visiting this church is to view the two spectacular paintings by Caravaggio: the *Conversion of St Paul*, and the *Crucifixion of St Peter* (on either side of the altar). Take plenty of coins with you to feed the user-pays lighting – otherwise you will have to view the Caravaggio works in complete darkness!

Caravaggio
Conversion of St Paul (Conversione di Saulo), 1601

Such drama! Struck blind at the moment of his conversion – as if by lightning – Saul, the senior Roman official, has fallen from his horse, and now stretches his arms heavenwards in a gesture of eager acceptance. His elderly attendant gently leads the horse away from the prostrate form of his now sightless master. Piercing the inky darkness, the light finds the horse's blonde flanks, the helpless soldier, his red cloak, and his sword and helmet which have fallen to the ground. The composition is masterful, helped by the radically foreshortened Saul/St Paul and horse.

Caravaggio
Crucifixion of St Peter (Crocifissione di San Pietro)

Here Caravaggio demonstrates his unerring knowledge of anatomy and his capacity to portray physical and psychological suffering. Peter has had his hands and feet nailed to the cross. But his ordeal has not ended with this unspeakable agony. Deciding that he is not fit to die in the same manner as his master, he has requested that he be crucified upside down. Tendons strain in his forehead and neck. Yet his expression reveals his acceptance of the pain and of the indignity of his end.

In the Chigi Chapel, (when it is lit) you'll also find Bernini's two marble statues of the Old Testament figures, *Daniel* (with the lion) and *Habakkuk* (with an angel).

Your next destination is not far away: proceed in a southeasterly direction for about half a mile or so to the Piazza Barberini. Along the way, you may care to visit the Chiesa di San Lorenzo in Lucina which contains the celebrated Fonseca Chapel designed by Bernini. Bernini also sculpted the realistic *Bust of Gabriele Fonseca*, earnestly leaning way out of his marble frame in the grip of a spiritual experience.

A little further on is the Bernini-designed Piazza Montecitorio. If you are prepared to tale a short detour of 100 yards or so before your next important visit – to the Barberini Palace – you can also visit the famous Cornaro Chapel – also designed by Bernini – in the Chiesa di Santa Maria della Vittoria. Steel yourself. Bernini's sculpture of the Carmelite Saint Teresa, *St Teresa in Ecstasy* (1644–52), will blow your socks off! Bernini's inspiration for this remarkable work was Teresa's own account of her dramatic spiritual experience. She describes a small angel repeatedly piercing her heart with a golden arrow. "The pain was so great," she said, "that I screamed aloud; but simultaneously I felt such infinite sweetness that I wished the pain to last eternally. It was not a physical pain, but a spiritual one, although it affected to a certain extent also the body. It was the sweetest caressing of the soul by God." Look at the "boxes" on either side of the central group: they contain eight members of the Cornaro family who, understandably, are exhibiting a lively interest in Teresa's passion. (Is there no privacy?)

A short walk to the west brings you to the Piazza Barberini with its famous Bernini *Triton Fountain (Fontana del Tritone)* at its center. On the eastern side of the Piazza is the Barberini Palace, much of which – especially the Grand Staircase – was designed by the ubiquitous Bernini.

National Gallery of the Barberini Palace (Galleria d'Arte Antica al Palazzo Barberini)

Location: Via delle Quattro Fontane 13
Contact details: Bookings 06 32810
Opening hours: 8:30 am–7:30 pm, Tues.–Sun., closed Mon.
Admission: Euro 6

This palace was erected by Pope Urban VIII, a member of the prominent Barberini family. It contains paintings from the 13th to the 16th centuries. Don't miss the glorious illusionist ceiling fresco in the Gran Salone. In the Room 3, two Filippo Lippi paintings hang side-by-side.

Room 3

Filippo Lippi
Annunciation (Annunciazione e due Devoti), early 1440s

This is Fra Filippo's most opulent Annunciation – an excellent example of the *ornazio* that so greatly impressed his contemporaries. *Ornazio* referred not only, or even mainly, to ornamentation, but rather to the depiction of movement that reveals the character of the subject, and was a quality praised by the ancients. The archangel in this painting is 'ornate' in all senses. The delicacy of his movements is matched only by that of his exquisite floral crown. The Holy Ghost unobtrusively wings in from an open window on the left of the picture … The Virgin Mary stands on a richly inlaid platform, framed by ornate marble columns and elaborate furniture. The red-brocaded bed and the rosy hues of the angel's robes on the left of the painting contrast with the less-cluttered space and cooler tones on the right. Beyond the central arch is the customary Renaissance garden and distant mountains. The Virgin resignedly accepts, from the hand of the angel, a lily signifying her divine fate. Two young women discuss the scene from their vantage point on the stairs. The presence of the two donors in the right-hand foreground is an innovation. Donors were often painted in as pious worshippers in celestial scenes such as the Virgin Enthroned. Rarely had they been depicted, as Fra Filippo has done in this work, as active participants in a sacred event.

Filippo Lippi
Tarquinia Madonna, 1437

The Tarquinia Madonna is one of Fra Filippo's earliest dated works and one of his most innovative paintings. Instead of being seated on a golden throne with the usual heavenly accoutrements, Mary and her Child are pictured – Flemish style – in an earthly bedroom with a sunny courtyard in the background and a garden visible through the open window. The arrangement of the figures of Mother and Child originated in Byzantine art and was fairly standard in 13th- and 14th-century Italian painting. But within this traditional format, Fra Filippo has achieved an appealing softness. The infant, it has to be admitted, is less than attractive. But Lippi has captured the Madonna and Child in an intimate moment: in a loving embrace, the baby's right arm encircles the Madonna's neck while the tiny left hand gently pats her throat. A series of arcs frames the figures. The rounded, low arms of the throne enclose the two figures; this semi-circle is mirrored by the reverse arc of the platform which also encloses the folds of the Madonna's robes. This arrangement suggests, perhaps, that the original panel might have been an early tondo, like Fra Filippo's much later tondo in the Pitti Palace in Florence.

Room 10

For those who are interested in the multi-faceted genius of Bernini, this room contains two of his paintings: a *Portrait of Urban VIII* and *David and Goliath* (*Davide con la Testa di Golia*).

Room 13

Caravaggio
Judith and Holofernes (Giuditta e Oloferne), 1599

The book of *Judith* in the Bible relates the story of the heroine causing Holofernes' army to flee Bethulia by displaying the head of their Commander on the battlements. Grabbing a tuft of thick, black hair, Judith pulls the not-quite severed head of the tyrant away from his not-quite dead body, while blood spurts from the site of her terrible knife. Holofernes seems to have woken from his drunken slumber just long enough to realize he is being murdered. Shrinking back ever-so-slightly from the gore (and admirably pristine in her white muslin), Judith's expression is an unforgettable mixture of determination and disgust. Beside her, her grim-faced maid waits to receive the horrid product of the decapitation. The event takes place in darkness – except for the brilliant illumination of the upper bodies and heads of the three figures. This is one of the pictures for which Caravaggio used the beautiful courtesan, Fillide Melandroni, as his model.

Caravaggio
Narcissus (Narciso), 1599

Angry because Narcissus rejected the love of the nymph, Echo, Nemesis, (the God) condemned him to drown while admiring his own reflection. It is as though Caravaggio has been lying in wait with a camera to capture the exact moment when Narcissus will catch sight of himself in the pond. There is the young man's left hand, just about to cup the water for drinking – but this action is suspended, almost before it has begun: instantly captivated by his reflection, Narcissus is instead slowly lowering his head to kiss his watery image. Again, the scene takes place in almost total darkness, except for the light that illumines his limbs and the white satin of his sleeves. At center stage is that remarkable knee. If a student were to draw its outline, it would resemble a mildly misshapen potato. But Caravaggio's extraordinary mastery of chiaroscuro has invested it with such substance – with a strong kneecap, with muscular flexibility, with movement and stress, with flesh that glows in the half-light.

Caravaggio's Narcissus

Caravaggio
St Francis (San Francesco), c.1605

This is, without doubt, a *poor* friar: his cassock is worn and fraying; his hair is roughly cropped; his hands grimy. This time, the Caravaggo light finds no gleaming satin sleeves, no fall of velvet. Instead, it picks up the pale flesh of Francis's shoulder showing through the hole above his sleeve, the dust of his travels in the wilderness, a raw timber crucifix in place of the gilt of many altars. It is a meditative picture: Francis holds the *memento mori* in his hand, contemplating the brevity of human life.

About 200 yards to the south is the noted Bernini-designed Chiesa di Sant' Andrea al Quirinale (Via del Quirinale 29). You then have a longish walk of about 1000 yards to the west to reach the Piazza della Minerva, containing Bernini's obelisk-bearing elephant. On the eastern side of the Piazza is Santa Maria Sopra Minerva – the burial place of Fra Angelico, in front of whose tomb stands one of the less well regarded of Michelangelo's sculptures.

Santa Maria Sopra Minerva

Location: Piazza della Minerva
Contact details: Tel. 06 6793926
Opening hours: 7:00 am–noon, 4:00 pm–7:00 pm daily
except when services are taking place.

Michelangelo
Risen Christ, 1518–20

Close by the tomb of Fra Angelico is this piece of sculpture –
probably the one held in the lowest regard by the critics. An
overworked Michelangelo had it executed by his assistants in
Florence – much to the dissatisfaction of his patron when it finally
arrived in Rome. So unhappy was the patron that he politely
declined an offer from Michelangelo to have another go at the
theme!

Walk to the east for a short distance, and you'll find a palazzo with an
amazing concentration of fine works.

Doria Pamphili Gallery (Galleria Doria Pamphili – often spelled Pamphilj)

Location: Piazza del Collegio Romano 2
Contact details: Tel. 06 6797323
Opening hours: 10:00 am–5:00 pm Fri.–Wed., closed Thur.
Admission: Euro 7:30 (audio guide included in ticket price)

Four important Renaissance painters are the focus of the visit here;
Bellini, Lippi, Titian and Caravaggio.

Giovanni Bellini
Madonna Adoring the Child with St John the Baptist, 1480–90

Yet another Bellini Madonna, and one deemed by the critics to be a
studio version of the famous *Madonna with the Baptist and a Female
Saint* in the Accademia in Venice. Once again, we have the Virgin
praying over the Infant in her lap. The Christ Child is stretched
across her knees as a portent of the Pietà, his large size
emphasizing this reference.

Filippo Lippi
Annunciation, mid to late 1440s

This is another example of the medieval narrative practice of putting events from different moments into the one scene. Mary has been interrupted at prayer by the arrival of the Archangel. The hands of God the Father have released the dove of the Holy Spirit, which, in turn, impregnates her with divine grace. The angel has announced that the Holy Ghost will cause her to conceive; Mary protests that she is a virgin, but the outer edges of her cloak part to reveal that she is already pregnant. She accepts her fate, knowing that, once her son is born, she will lose him. An urn containing white lilies punctuates the space between Mary and the Angel, who is yet to hand her his own stem of lilies – a symbol of the bittersweet fate that awaits her. The ornamentation is both decorative and stark, and helps to emphasize the long narrative story being told. This way of telling the story distinguishes Lippi from several other Renaissance painters right up to Titian who liked to portray the single, dramatic moment. Though not as ornate as some other representations of this theme by Fra Filippo, the *Doria Annunciation* is full of color. The gold of the brocade that shimmers behind Mary's head is repeated in the embroidered hem of her robe and in the inlaid furniture. Rose tones light the foreground, providing a contrast with the brooding sky and the darker, more mysterious earthiness of the distant landscape beyond the archway.

Titian
Salome with the Head of John the Baptist, c.1515

Better than any other, this early painting illustrates Titian's unwillingness – perhaps unconscious inability – to eroticize death in the manner soon to be displayed by Caravaggio. Here we have the famously seductive dancer at the moment of her capital triumph, but she is one of the least voluptuous of all Titian's women. Her serene gaze – and the richly textured costume that has replaced the veils – are difficult to relate to the daring dance she has just completed. So calm is her demeanor, in fact, that some have suggested that this may not, after all, be the villainous Salome, but Judith, the heroine who despatched the tyrannical Holofernes. The incongruity between the lyrically calm feel of the painting and the recently severed head on the platter may be explained by the influence of Giorgione on the then young Titian. Certainly, several of the distinctive Giorgionesque elements are present: the red and green palette, for example, and the glimpse of sky under the background arch.

Caravaggio
Penitent Magdalene (Maddalena Penitente), 1597

This is a very different image of the repentant Magdalene, who conventionally was shown in the wilderness dressed in animal skins. This is a city woman, dressed in the rich fashion of the well-off young woman of the Renaissance. Caravaggio has painted her drying her hair. But she is such a sad young woman! Her head is bowed and a tear courses down her nose. Her jewelry, as though ripped from her neck in a fit of passion, lies in pieces on the floor. Next to her is a small glass carafe of oil – a reminder of the precious unguent with which she anointed the feet of her Lord.

Caravaggio
The Rest on the Flight into Egypt (Riposo nella Fuga in Egitto), 1597

Against the background of a (Lombard) landscape, the weary Holy Family pauses on their long journey to Egypt. An exquisite, red-haired angel, whose wings protrude practically into the face of the viewer, has been sent to lull them to sleep with a soothing violin music: Joseph helpfully holds the manuscript. But the Virgin is already asleep, her exhausted head drooping onto that of her infant who sleeps peacefully in his mother's arms.

Caravaggio
St John the Baptist (San Giovanni Battista), 1602

Caravaggio admired Michelangelo. This is his second representation of one of the *ignudi* in the Sistine Chapel – the one on the left just above the Eritrean Sybil – as John the Baptist. John is pictured as a young shepherd, frolicking with a ram that has thrust its head against his cheek. The light illumines the youth's strong back and the continuing line of his right thigh, highlighting the reverse Z configuration of the body. It also picks up the left thigh – and even the left foot (hidden in Michelangelo's version). A further trademark of Caravaggio is the swathe of red fabric.

If you now walk a little over another half a mile to the south you will be able to compare the Doria Pamphili *ignudo/John the Baptist* with Caravaggio's second version of the same theme, which is in the Capitoline Museums.

Capitoline Museums (Musei Capitolini)

Location: Piazza del Campidoglio
Contact details: Tel. 67 103069
Opening hours: Tues.–Sun. 9:00 am–8:00 pm, closed Mon.
Admission: Euro 7.75 (plus Euro 1.03 if reservation made)

Michelangelo designed the paving as well as the facades of both palazzos in this piazza, but died before his design was completed. Palazzo Nuovo houses mostly classical sculptures; Palazzo dei Conservatori contains sculptures and, on the second floor, paintings. It is on two works on the second floor that this visit concentrates. However, you may also wish to view the works by Veronese, Rubens and others while you are here.

View on a section of Forum

Titian
Baptism of Christ, c.1516

This is an early treatment of one of the most venerable Christian themes. The influence of Giorgione is clearly visible in the mysterious landscape and the ultramarine sky. The predominantly red-green palette is also Giorgionesque. From Ravenna onwards, artists along the Adriatic were inclined to emphasize the water in which the baptism was occurring. Titian's Christ is shown partially immersed in the river. The pious onlooker is Giovanni Ram, the Venetian collector who was to own the painting.

Caravaggio
St John the Baptist (Giovanni Battista), c.1600

Here is Caravaggio's second adolescent St John, modelled on Michelangelo's *ignudo* in the Sistine Chapel. The shepherd's rest has been disturbed by a (different) ram and he smilingly looks over his shoulder at the viewer. Caravaggio, though an admirer of Michelangelo, was not as interested in musculature as was the great sculptor, but the fine body of the boy reveals carefully detailed ribs and hip-bones. Does anyone paint skin tones as well as Caravaggio?

Caravaggio
The Fortune Teller (Buona Ventura), 1595–1600

This picture of a young dandy having his palm read by a gypsy girl is the second Caravaggesque painting on this theme (the other is in the Louvre). The models and their clothing appear to be the same in both paintings but some dispute the authorship of the Capitoline version. Admirers of the picture point to its subtle eroticism. Does the foppish young man realize that, as the gypsy traces his palm with her finger, she is simultaneously removing the ring from *his* finger?

While you are in the vicinity, Donatello admirers may like to visit nearby Santa Maria in Aracoeli (which backs onto the Campidoglio to see the tombstone he made for Archbishop Giovanni Crevelli).

If you are taking a walk through the Forum, you may care to continue beyond the Colosseum – about 400 yards to the north – to the church of San Pietro in Vincoli (St Peter in Chains) in order to see Michelangelo's powerful representation of Moses.

About a mile to the north west of the Colosseum is the Piazza

Navona, containing Bernini's most spectacular fountain – the *Fountain of the Four Rivers (Fontana dei Fiumi)*. In the same Piazza is the *Fountain of the Moor (Fontana del Moro)* which was redesigned by Bernini.

Admirers of Caravaggio are well-advised to negotiate the side street to the east of the Piazza Navona, about 100 yards or so to find the Chiesa di San Luigi dei Francesi. A great treat lies in store for you: its Contarelli Chapel contains Caravaggio's great Matthew trilogy.

Chiesa di San Luigi dei Francesi

Location: Via Santa Giovanna d'Arco
Contact details: Tel. 688 271

Caravaggio
Calling of St Matthew (Vocazione di Sàm Matteo), 1599–1600

Levi, the tax collector and four of his colleagues sit in the half-gloom, counting money. The three closest to the window are suddenly interrupted by the appearance of two mysterious strangers, one of whom points at the red-bearded Matthew and commands him to follow. "Who, me?" says red-beard, even before the two companions on his right are aware of this intervention. The episode – dramatic in terms of its liturgical significance – is nevertheless depicted as a low-key exchange between ordinary people – right down to their contemporary Renaissance dress. Even the figure of Christ is almost totally obscured by that of St Peter, gesticulating to ensure that Matthew has heard his master's command. Two subtle clues attest to its religious meaning – the fine halo above Jesus' head and the cross formed by the frame of the window.

Caravaggio
Martyrdom of St Matthew (Martirio di San Matteo), 1599–1600

The precise nature of the environment of this tumultuous scene is not at all clear. The conventional interpretation is that it is taking place in a church and that the semi-naked figures are penitents or candidates for baptism. Others believe it could be a bathhouse (see the steam rising from behind, and those figures in loin-cloths would be bathers). All agree, however, that the central figure in the picture is not St Matthew, being murdered, but his assassin, who stands astride the saint, gripping his wrist violently and shouting abuse. A young boy (altar-boy or bath-house attendant)

runs screaming in fright from the scene. None of the other penitents, bathers or candidates for baptism try to help the beleagured saint, but an angel reaches down to place the Martyr's Palm in his hand.

Caravaggio
St Matthew and the Angel (San Matteo e Angelo), 1602

This is Caravaggio's substitute picture for an earlier version that had proven unacceptable to the church because it was perceived to depict Matthew as a plodding, ignorant peasant. Looking at this version (the first was destroyed during the War) one wonders just what concessions the painter has made to his sensitive patrons: there is the angel, still ticking off the items that the Evangelist must include in his gospel, and there is the then old Matthew, seemingly struggling to keep up. One knee perches awkwardly on his stool, which has begun to overbalance onto our heads, with the book in which the saint is writing likely to follow. Caravaggio's use of perspective – as well as chiaroscuro – is unerring. If you follow Matthew's gaze, you see that the painter has the angel hovering *between* Matthew and us, the viewers.

If you have not yet had your fill of Caravaggio, then proceed another 100 yards to the north to the Chiesa di San Agostino, the site of yet another St John the Baptist. We, however, focus on his wonderful *Madonna of Loreto.*

Chiesa di San Agostino

Location: Piazza di San Agostino

Caravaggio
Madonna of Loreto (Madonna dei Pellegrini), 1604

It has been said that this Madonna is at once Caravaggio's most ordinary and most beautiful. Mary is depicted as everywoman (albeit an elegant, long-necked everywoman) standing at the door of her house, feet crossed to help her bear the considerable weight of her infant on her thigh. She inclines her lovely head towards the two careworn pilgrims who now kneel, praying fervently, at her step, the man displaying another pair of Caravaggio's keenly observed, dusty, calloused feet.

The Trail now takes you another half a mile or so to the west – over the Tiber to Janiculum – to the Palazzo Corsini, which contains much of interest to art lovers.

Corsini Gallery (Galleria Nazionale d'Arte Antica a Palazzo Corsini)

Location: Via della Lungara
Contact details: Tel. 6880 2323
Opening hours: 9:00 am–7:00 pm, Tues–Fri; 9:00 am–1:00 pm, Sat.; 9:00 am–1:00 pm, Sun., closed Mon.
Admission: About Euro 7

Fra Angelico
Triptych 1447

For those who have experienced the glory of Fra Angelico in San Marco in Florence, it will probably not be worthwhile to make the trip across the Tiber to see this tiny work. The three panels in the triptych portray the Ascension, Universal Justice and the Pentecost.

Caravaggio
St John the Baptist (San Giovannino), 1604

This is an odd representation of one of Caravaggio's favorite themes. The model was probably a Roman street boy, and, as there are few clues, the figure could be anybody. The light reveals a fairly undistinguished torso and a brilliant red blanket, but his face is still in semi-darkness. Yet, is that a shepherd's staff that the young boy is reaching for with his right hand? And what has startled him? A wild animal padding about on dry leaves? Or the voice of his Lord, perhaps?

Your visit to the Corsini concludes your Renaissance Trail in Rome. However, a trip from Rome to Naples (you can go by train from Stazione Termini), although it will easily consume a full day, is a memorable experience for all travellers. Pompeii is close by, and the great city of Naples has many attractions, such as the once-elegant and still fascinating 19th-century arcade complex – the Galleria Umberto I – the huge Teatro San Carlo (Italy's largest opera house) and, of course, the great National Archeological Museum. For all that, it's almost worth

taking the trip just to spend a few hours in the extraordinary – and vast – Capodimonte Museum.

Naples

Our first stop in Naples is at the Capodimonte Museum, which you will find in the hills to the north of the city center – about four miles out. When the Farnese transferred from Parma to Naples, they brought with them their extensive art collection, which is now housed in the Capodimonte.

Royal Palace of Capodimonte (Palazzo Reale di Capodimonte)

Location: Via Capodimonte
Contact details: Tel. 081 7499111
Opening hours: 10:00 am–7:00 pm Tues.–Sat.,
9:00 am–2:00 pm Sun., closed Mon.
Admission: About Euro 6.

Masaccio
Crucifixion 1426

This is a major panel from the dismembered Pisa Altarpiece. It strikingly demonstrates Masaccio's great debt to his sculptor contemporaries. Jesus has died, his head sinking into his collarbone. (This is possibly an experiment in foreshortening to compensate for the picture being viewed from below.) The torso of Christ, however, is treated in a fully three-dimensional manner. The whole composition dynamically conveys the interactions and intense emotions of the mourners – captured in the outflung arms of the grief-stricken Mary Magdalene.

Botticelli
Madonna with Child and Angels (Madonna con Bambino e Angeli)

With her baby son, an angel and St John, Mary sits in a corner formed by two garden walls, protected for now by her closed courtyard.

Three pairs of worried eyes search the Madonna's face for a sign of interaction, but she is lost in thought. Almost absentmindedly, she lightly holds her Child's baby feet, perhaps already envisioning the stigmata they will bear following his crucifixion.

Titian
Annunciation (Annunciazione), c.1557

Titian's use of impasto gives great vibrancy to this large painting. On hearing the angel's message, the Virgin crosses her hands in a gesture of submission to God's will. Her sheer veil and bright red dress contrast vividly with the dark pillar behind her.

Titian
St Mary Magdalene in Penitence (Maddalena Penitente), 1567

Titan loved the subject of *Maddalena Penitente* – not least of all because it gave him the opportunity to paint beautiful women – and he painted several versions. This Magdalene is not as sensational as her bare-breasted sister in the Pitti, but she has taken her hand to her heart in the same way, and gazes imploringly to heaven. She also has a similar fall of stunning, golden-red curls.

Caravaggio
Flagellation (Flagellazione)

You approach this picture via a long corridor. By the time you reach the terrible scene, you feel you are part of it. Christ, his flesh bare and vulnerable, is tied to a pillar: one of his torturers is tightening the cords that bind his arms and wrists. A second figure, kneeling in front of Christ with his head turned away from the viewer, is hastily tying together a bunch of sticks so that he might join in the flagellation. But the truly terrifying figure is that of the thug on the left. Having just hit Christ's head sideways, he readies his own bunch of sticks. Under the force of the blow, Christ's body has slewed to the left as his head was punched to the right. He has been abandoned. In the semi-darkness, he is alone with his tormentors.

We suggest you visit the a church in the famous Neapolitan district of Spaccanapoli to see one more Caravaggio. Travel back towards the city about three miles in a southwards direction to come to:

Chiesa del Pio Monte della Misericordia

Location: *Via Tribunali 253*

Caravaggio
Seven Acts of Mercy (Sette Opere di Misericordia), 1606

This is an uncharacteristically crowded picture for Caravaggio, and confusing, to boot! In the lower section of the painting, nine figures from entirely different historical periods are thrown together in a dynamic representation of the acts of mercy described by Christ and reported in St Matthew's Gospel (though, in reality, it is difficult to identify precisely all of them in Caravaggio's picture).

View the scenes from left to right. First, the host of the inn indicates that he can find a room for the red-bearded pilgrim: "I was a stranger and you took me in." Behind them (appearing between their two heads), Samson lustily drinks water from the jawbone of an ass: "I was thirsty and you gave me to drink," (though exactly who is responsible for the merciful act of quenching Samson's thirst is not clear). Slightly in front of the red-bearded pilgrim, the man with the compassionate expression on his face is St Martin of Tours. He has removed his sword from its scabbard and prepares to cut his cloak in half to share it with the almost nude beggar, half-sitting, half-lying with his back to the viewer: "I was naked and you clothed me." (This figure may represent the group of young Neapolitan nobles who commissioned the painting and who had founded a charitable organization around 1600). In the middle of the picture, a man helps remove a corpse from the prison. (The burial of the dead was a significant public health issue in Naples at a time when prisoners' corpses were just heaped outside the city's jail to be gnawed by roving dogs.) The woman with her orange skirts caught up visits the jail and (somewhat diffidently) offers her breast to the old man in the jail: "I was in prison and you visited me; I was hungry and you gave me to eat." Embodying a familiar theme, she symbolizes the *Caritas Romana.*

In the upper section of the painting, the Madonna and her very appealing Child (seen through the flailing wings of angels) look down on the flurry of activity below, just like any curious neighbors leaning out over their laundered sheets drying in the wind.

Although the Renaissance is only lightly represented in Naples, the few Titians we've seen may have whetted your appetite sufficiently for you to decide to venture on to his stronghold – Venice.

Panoramic view of Venice

TRAIL 3:
Venice and Surrounds

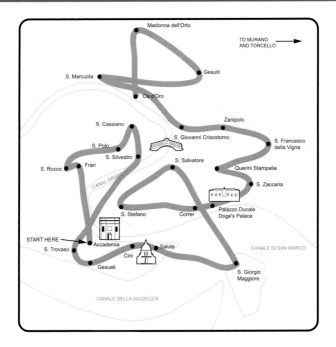

Venice

This Trail can be covered in two very demanding days. Much of the first day will be spent in the major Venetian museum – the superb Accademia Galleries. One could easily spend an enjoyable two days in these great galleries alone, so we have had to be ruthless in the choice of the paintings we have selected for your attention. The Trail seeks out the works of the three most famous Renaissance painters who were based in Venice – Bellini, Titian, and Tintoretto.

VENICE AND SURROUNDS

Venice is divided into five communities – or sestieri. After a start in the southwestern sestiere of Dorsoduro – visiting the famous Accademia – the Trail moves on northwards to where Titian has his most important early works and where you will come across the entire spectrum of Tintoretto's *oeuvre* in the sestiere of San Polo e Santa Croce. The Trail then moves southwards back to Dorsoduro.

We then cross the Grand Canal to the sestiere of San Marco. It proceeds to the bottom of the less fashionable sestiere of Castello and then northwest until it finishes in the equally unglamorous sestiere of Cannaregio. With a few deviations, the overall trajectory of the grand tour is in an counterclockwise direction, starting at 9 o'clock and finishing at 12 o'clock.

Unless otherwise specified, most churches are open to tourists (at a minimum) from about 10 am to noon and from 4 pm to 6pm (unless there is a service underway), and many do not charge for admission – although donations are of course welcome and appropriate. Most galleries charge between Euro 2 and 9 and some offer reductions to seniors. The Monday closing, so common around Italy, is less in evidence in Venice.

The Accademia

Location: Campo della Carita'
Contact details: Tel. 041 5222247
Opening hours: 9:00 am–7:00 pm, daily except public holidays –
9:00 am–2:00 pm.
Admission: Euro 6.50

The Accademia, like such other great galleries as the Brera in Milan and the National Gallery in Bologna, was begun in the Napoleonic era. By 1811, the present complex was largely in place – being composed of several adjacent buildings, including a Renaissance church, a Palladio convent, and the premises of the most ancient of the Grand Schools. Because it was established so late, it has had to concentrate heavily on the works of the local Renaissance painters – Giovanni Bellini, Titian and Tintoretto. But as Venice's age of glory lasted from the late Renaissance to the Baroque, the Accademia's holdings of 17th-century Italian painting are superior to those of both the Uffizi and the Vatican.

Sala 2

Giovanni Bellini

Pala di San Giobbe (Madonna and Child Enthroned with Angel Musicians, among Saints Francis, John the Baptist, Job, Dominic, Sebastian and Louis of Toulouse),1487

Bellini places his 11 figures under a monumental Byzantine mosaic apse, thereby connecting Venetian Renaissance painting with the city's Byzantine history. But in other ways, this picture breaks with tradition. For example, instead of being confined each to his own separate panel, the saintly figures around the Madonna and Child are arranged in two naturalistic groupings on either side of the throne. On the left of the picture is St Francis with his arm extended. Next to him is John the Baptist. Standing in the place of honor nearest the Holy Child is St Job (San Giobbe). On the right are Sts Dominic, Sebastian, and the Franciscan Bishop, Louis of Toulouse. Perched on the steps of the dais below, the heavenly musicians play their fine instruments – the lute and the *lira da braccio* – perhaps in honor of Job who was a patron saint of music. There is wonderful variety in the poses and individual responses of the figures. The Madonna, too, is magnificently contemporary. Strong and straight-backed, she projects from the painting with an assertive force. Her left hand is raised – almost as a priest would raise his hand to bless his flock. The scene is suffused with a mellow, golden light, reminiscent of the golden glow of the interior of St Mark's. The seraphim flying in an arc around the painted mosaic vault each carry the message: *Ave Gratia Plena* (Hail, full of Grace), Gabriel's greeting to the Virgin on the Annunciation. The message above them says, "Hail, undefiled flower of virgin modesty."

Giovanni Bellini

Mourning the Dead Christ at the Foot of the Cross, c.1510

Although the Accademia is happy to claim this as a work executed by "Giovanni Bellini and assistants," others claim that Bellini was doing no more than helping out his colleague Rocco Marconi. While the elaborateness of the background was characteristic of Bellini's work at the end of his career, by 1510, he was 80 years old, so it would seem prudent to be cautious about attribution.

Sala 3

Giovanni Bellini
The Herald Angel and The Annunciation: part of the organ doors for the Church of St Mary of the Miracles, 1500

When we look at these two panels, it is easy to believe that the influence of Flemish painters like Rogier Van der Weyden and Jan Van Eyck was strong in Venice. Bellini's *Annunciation* presents a brilliantly colored interior with wonderfully precise and decorative detail, an external landscape seen through an open door, and two figures drawn with photo-real clarity. The Virgin is meditating at her *prie-dieu*: her left hand still marks her devotional book. Her right hand, however, indicates her compliance with God's decision to make her the mother of God: "Behold the handmaid of the Lord." The Archangel, carrying the lily of purity, has rushed through the open doorway. His amber hair flies out behind, as do his garments: in contrast to the stillness of the Virgin, Gabriel is all movement. The folds of his robes are angular and full of light and shade, suggesting a "crackly" material, (taffeta?) and contrasting with the satiny drape of the Virgin's green robe.

Sale (Rooms) 4–5

Giovanni Bellini
Madonna with Child with Saints Paul and George, 1490–1500

Bellini has used the horizontal format he often chose for the subject of the Madonna and Child when they were to be flanked by saints. Certainly, the rectangle enables him to achieve a sense of spaciousness – especially when it encloses portrait-style, half-length figures, as it does in this picture. St George, it must be said, has an ordinary-looking, if kindly, face – quite different from his characteristic swashbuckling image. Perhaps this an actual portrait of a worthy citizen who required a presence in the painting?

Giovanni Bellini
Virgin with Child (The Camerlenghi Madonna), 1470s

This is the probably the earliest of the eight Bellini Madonna paintings in this room, and the simplest. The Mother and Child emerge from a night-black background, the parapet being the only visible element in their environment. The infant thrusts his feet forward, ready to enter our domain. His hand is raised in a resigned blessing, even as he accepts his human fate. But the sad-faced Madonna restrains him, seemingly to postpone his destiny for as long as possible. Possibly because of its simplicity and accessibility, this image was more frequently copied than any other of Bellini's Madonnas. Like Titian's *Madonna* in Sala 11, it was painted for the Camerlenghi family.

Giovanni Bellini
Enthroned Madonna Cherishing Sleeping Child, 1475

Not for Bellini the golden grandeur of a heavenly queen on a glittering throne. Bellini's treatments of the Madonna are always modest, and this is no exception. Simplicity triumphs over grandeur, for the solid, carved wooden chair on which she is seated, and the framed space behind her would not have been out of place in any moderately prosperous Venetian abode. The long-limbed child stretched somewhat improbably across her knees is older than is usual in such pictures, suggesting that Bellini was perhaps trying to evoke the Pietà, in which the Virgin holds her adult, crucified son.

Giovanni Bellini
Madonna with Blessing Child (Contarini Madonna), 1475–80

Here, the Madonna and her Child are rather more assertive than in many other treatments of this theme by Giovanni Bellini. The Virgin, looking out of the picture, wears a subtle expression – of admonition, perhaps? Her son stands upright on the parapet, directly blessing the worshipper. Behind the two stretches a landscape – on the left of the picture, above the Christ Child's blessing hand, a city, and on the right, the countryside with hilltop village and campanile. The horizon is set low to reveal a sweeping sky. On the right of the picture is the countryside; on the left, is a city. This configuration of buildings and fingers held up in blessing has sometimes been interpreted as symbolizing divine approval for human endeavor. Bellini has not bothered to use perspective to relate the background scene to the figures in the foreground – but this hardly matters, as the whole picture reveals Bellini's unified vision. Mary stares thoughtfully out of the picture, her hands clasped protectively around her child, though barely able to conceal his naked, human vulnerability. Her eyes are puffy – she appears to have been weeping. Her child looks directly at the worshipper to bestow his blessing, but it is a blessing full of gravitas.

Giovanni Bellini
Madonna of the Trees (Madonna degli Alberetti), 1487

This is one of Bellini's naked Holy Infants, in which the painter wishes to symbolize the Incarnation – Christ's assumption of human form so as to sacrifice himself in expiation for the sins of the world. The child's head casts a shadow on his mother's neck and the shadow of her own head can be seen on the green cloth behind. These details reinforce the humanity of the figures. The infant parts his lips, as if to speak to us – his mother waits expectantly. The little feet are placed one on top of the other – just as they will be placed to receive the nail that will fix them to the cross. Bellini locates his Madonna and Child between a cloth of honor (like those hung for visiting monarchs), and a parapet, which separates the pair from the viewer. The infant seems to point with the toes of his left foot at Bellini's signature engraved on the face of the marble wall. Behind the banner, standing like sentinels, are the spindly trees from which the painting derives its name. Bellini has softened the outlines of the figures and the mountains low on the horizon are enveloped in haze. Despite the confined space occupied by the mother and child, the effect is one of light, airy space.

Giovanni Bellini
Madonna with Child and Red Cherubim, 1480–90

Like infra-red photographic negatives about to reveal their final contours, Bellini's strange cherubim fly about the Virgin's head, imparting a surrealistic glow to an otherwise darkening sky. In contrast to many of his other Madonnas, the Virgin and her Child are interacting. The infant's mouth has opened – one is tempted to think, to ask the inevitable question about those flying red angels! However, it is more probably to seek maternal reassurance in dealing with his destiny. This he receives: the Madonna clasps him firmly in her two hands and calmly returns his gaze.

Giovanni Bellini
Madonna and Child with Two Female Saints (Catherine and Mary), c.1500

Using a spacious, horizontal rectangle as his field, Bellini has set

Bellini's **Madonna of the Trees** (*Madonna degli Alberetti*)

four half-length, portrait figures against a dark ground, then bathed them in a luminous, rose-golden glow. The result is dramatically beautiful. The pearls and rubies of the saints' jewelry gleam. Their very flesh glows – from within or without, it is difficult to tell. Confining himself largely to the reds in his palette, Bellini nevertheless has created a symphony in color. The light amber of the Magdalene's flowing tresses is stunning. The child's hair is a softer, blonder variation, and St Catherine's

VENICE AND SURROUNDS

coiffured locks are almost burgundy. A similar pattern of variation appears in the women's robes, the pink-rose of the Madonna's dress picked up in deeper tones and different fabrics worn by Catherine and Mary Magdalene. On closer inspection, even the burnt sienna background is flecked with hints of red. Interestingly, the figures do not interact. Look at the expression on the four faces: each one is different, each figure is lost in a personal reverie.

Giovanni Bellini
Pietà, c.1505

An aging, world-weary Madonna sits on the ground once more to cradle her son in her arms as she did when he was an infant. In the background, under a glowering sky, stretches the city of Jerusalem. Beside her, a tree has been lopped – perhaps to provide her son's cross?

Giovanni Bellini
Madonna and Child, St John the Baptist and a Saint, 1500–04

This sunny picture presents a half-length, portrait style image of the Madonna, holding her child in the Pietà pose, his baby feet already crossed one on the other as if to receive the nail for the cross. Painted in Bellini's 70th year, the work demonstrates his late-career preoccupation with the depiction of space. Free of architectural impedimenta, the figures sit in the open air, with only a narrow strip of water, a township, and a distant row of hills separating them from the sky. The figure of John the Baptist is easily recognizable, but we can't be certain of the identity of the female saint. She could be St Catherine: the year before, Bellini painted a very similar-looking John the Baptist in his *Marriage of St Catherine,* now in the National Gallery of London.

Piero della Francesca
St Jerome and a Donor (San Girolamo), 1440–50

It was very unusual for 15th-century painters to depict donors and saints as equals, which is what Piero has done in his picture of St Jerome and Girolamo Amadi. Another unusual feature of the picture is the way in which St Jerome is portrayed – not as the conventional emaciated hermit, but rather as a Christian scholar engaged in civilized discourse with a fellow believer. The urban settlement in the background is believed to be Piero's hometown of

Sansepolcro, where he demonstrated his commitment to civic values by serving for many years as a municipal councillor.

Mantegna
Saint George, c.1446

St George stands, in full armor, against a minutely detailed landscape whose road disappears into a distant walled city. His is a pose of victory: the dragon lies dead at his feet, its jaw pierced by a section of the Saint's wooden lance, the remainder of which, George holds in his right hand. Above the knight, punctuating the cloudy, azure blue sky, hangs one of Mantegna's celebrated fruited garlands. Both the dragon's snout and George's right arm protrude beyond the *trompe l'oeil* marble frame of their niche, creating the impression that they are in our space. The saint's orientation toward his left suggests that the panel may have been the left wing of an altarpiece

Sala 6

Titian
St John the Baptist, 1545–60

In this picture, Titian demonstrates his capacity to treat a well-worked theme with great force, for the figure of the Baptist has been invested with unusual authority. But much of the treatment is quite conventional, from the gesture of St John's hand to the all-too-familiar accoutrements – the lamb, the reed cross, and the animal-skin cloak. That is why some early commentators criticised the work for its academicism, in other words, for its reliance on these stereotypical symbols. The trees in the background landscape thrash against a big, billowing sky – contrasted in the left foreground by the peacefully sleeping lamb.

Tintoretto
Assumption of the Virgin, c.1550

It's interesting to compare this picture with its famous Venetian predecessor – Titian's *Assumption of the Virgin*, painted a generation earlier, which you will find in the Church of Santa Maria Gloriosa dei Frari on the next leg of your Venetian Trail. Tintoretto has learned from the master how to invest his painting with a giddying sense of elevation, but the figures – characteristically colored and illuminated – are too solid to achieve the exhilarating dynamism of the Titian work.

Sala 10

Titian
Pietà, 1576

This shadowy picture was one of Titian's last paintings. It was finished, after his death, by Palma il Giovane and was intended to hang over the painter's tomb in the Church of Santa Maria Gloriosa dei Frari – the site of his first great triumph: the Assumption of the Virgin – six decades earlier. The stone figures of Moses and a cross-carrying Sybil on either side of the imposing sepulcher suggest funerary pomp. But the four central figures are movingly portrayed. Mary, her dead son across her lap, is all sadness and tenderness. Some believe that the grieving St Joseph on her left is a suitably impoverished version of the famous painter himself. The protesting posture of Mary Magdalene has been interpreted as a response to the plague that was sweeping Venice at the time

Tintoretto
Virgin with Child with Saints Cecilia, Marina, Cosmas, and Damian, c.1550

This *Virgin with Child* once sat on light, billowing clouds. Unfortunately, they have suffered irreparable damage. As it was painted for the high altar of a Dominican church, Tintoretto was paid 220 ducats for the picture – a very high price.

Sala 11

Tintoretto
Crucifixion, 1554–5

Christ's own ordeal is nearly at an end. At the foot of the cross, Mary Magdalene has collapsed under the weight of her grief. The two thieves writhe on their own crosses, and, in the bottom right-hand corner of the picture, soldiers toss for the Savior's cloak. It seems that, in painting this picture, Tintoretto reached a half-way point between the Titianesque volup-tuousness which influenced him in his youth, and the tenebrist light and shade to which he was committed in his later years. While the painting is enveloped in the gloom befitting its subject, it is punctuated by the vivid reds of the garments and the rose-colored banners that swirl to the left of the scene.

Tintoretto
Madonna dei Camerlenghi, 1567

This painting helps us understand why the theme of the Madonna did not attract Tintoretto. Were it not for the lack of a crown and the large Christ Child sprawled (somewhat awkwardly) in her arms, Mary could be a queen holding court. The formality of the poses of the courtiers, who seem largely oblivious to the sagging St Sebastian, suggest that the picture was the result of a tightly defined commission – one which failed to stimulate Tintoretto's customary energy and spirit.

Sala 13

Titian
Virgin with Child, c.1560

Although he was such a superb painter of women, or perhaps because of it, (his women were mostly voluptuous!) Titian produced relatively few pictures of the Madonna. Despite the background image of the burning bush – symbol of Mary's virginity – the picture presents a secular representation of young motherhood. The history of this painting reads like Chekhov's *The Cherry Orchard:* it was in the possession of a noble Milanese family for three centuries, but at the end of the 19th century it was sold – presumably under financial duress – to a family in nearby, prosperous Bergamo.

Sala 23

Room 23 in the Accademia is actually the former church of Santa Maria della Carita', founded around the beginning of the 12th century. Here, you will find works by many painters of the Venetian Renaissance: Alvese and Bartolomeo Vivarini, for example, Andrea da Murano and Paris Bordon (including the dramatic *Sea Storm* that the latter painted with Jacopo Palma il Vecchio). You will also find a series of four lunettes under which sit four triptychs painted for the apse of La Carita' by the Bellini family. Interestingly, the Bellinis for the most part have reverted to the unadorned golden backgrounds of the Byzantine and very early Renaissance – perhaps to meet the requirements of those who commissioned the work.

Jacopo, Gentile and Giovanni Bellini, and collaborators
The Apse Triptychs, c.1460
Saint Lawrence between Saint John the Baptist and Saint Anthony of Padua
Madonna and Child with Angels in the lunette
The Nativity between Saints Francis and Victor
The Trinity between Saints Dominic and Ubaldo in the lunette.
Saint Sebastian between Saint John the Baptist and Saint Anthony, the Abbot
Christ in Pietà and two Angels in the lunette.
Virgin with Child and Saint Jerome and Saint Ludovic
Eternity and the Assumption in the lunette.

These paintings, in the composition of which Giovanni Bellini may have played a relatively minor part, were originally located in the Chiesa della Carita'.

Sala 24

Titian
Presentation of Mary in the Temple, 1534–9

Titian has depicted Mary as a young girl, dressed in light blue, bravely approaching the priests who tower over her at the head of the stairway. In the crowd of onlookers are portraits of leading members of Venice's Confraternity of Charity – owners of the Scuola della Carita' who commissioned the painting. It seems they also instructed him to incorporate a real doorway in the design of the picture (bottom right). The bottom left of the canvas was subsequently sacrificed for a second doorway. Titian has beautifully balanced the picture with interesting figures that contrast with the more self-important members of the crowd: a begging gypsy mother on the viewer's left; a white-bearded St Joachim who has turned his back to the viewer in a gesture of affection towards St Anne; a pair of elegantly attired ladies at the foot of the steps, and a large peasant woman hoping to sell her eggs, chickens, and a black pig. Under a magnificent sky, the mountainous crags of Titian's beloved Cadore can be seen in the distance. While this is very much a painting in the traditional Venetian processional style – large and architecturally expansive – it is not characteristic of the *oeuvre* of Venice's most famous painter. However, the handling of light and color is distinctively Titianesque, and sets this painting apart from the work of such artists as Titian's contemporary, Paris Bordon, who commonly favored this style of composition.

From the Accademia, you must walk about 700 yards a little west of north in order to reach the two other major sites on the western side of the Grand Canal. The first of these is the Frari – the Franciscan Chiesa di Santa Maria dei Frari.

Chiesa di Santa Maria dei Frari

Location: Campo dei Frari
Contact details: Tel. 041 5222637
Opening hours: 9:00 am–6:00 pm Mon.–Sat., 1:00 pm–6:00 pm Sun.
Admission: Euro 2

Now go to the Pesaro Chapel.

Giovanni Bellini
Frari Triptych (Madonna and Child with Sts Peter, Nicholas, Benedict and Mark), 1488

According to Ruskin, this is one of the two greatest paintings ever executed. It is, indeed, very beautiful – but also intriguing. As he did in the *San Giobbe Altarpiece* in the Accademia, Bellini has framed his figures in magnificently ornamental architecture. The Virgin and her Child – standing stiff-kneed on her lap – occupy the central aedicule. In the alcove on the left of the painting are Sts Nicholas and Peter, and in the right, Sts Benedict and Mark. The inscription in the mosaic of the vault above the Virgin's head reads: "Sure Gate of Heaven, lead my mind, direct my life, may all that I do be committed to thy care." The text is carried by St Benedict, and with his stern stare, he challenges us to acknowledge it. It is Ecclesiastes 24, which refers to the Madonna's Immaculate Conception. Like the *San Giobbe Altarpiece*, the gold mosaics and the light on the Corinthian columns inside the side alcoves strongly evoke the Byzantine glow of St Mark's. Again, the architectural space resembles the apse of a church.

Bellini's Triptych, Church of the Frari

This format has been interpreted, sometimes, as Mary representing the priest and the high altar, and her infant, the Eucharistic offering or sacrifice. The alcoves are open sufficiently to allow late afternoon light to enter. Not only is the picture flooded with a glorious golden glow: with its countervailing shadow the light also unites the three separate parts of the triptych.

Titian
Assumption of the Virgin, 1518

This was the painting that established Titian as the leading painter in Venice. The great 18th-century sculptor, Canova, was reported to have considered Titian's *Frari Assumption* to be the most beautiful painting in the world. When it was unveiled on May 19, 1518, it caused a sensation. The Venetians had been accustomed to static, portrait-style figures, and were unprepared for such drama. Perhaps better than any other treatment of this theme, this painting captures the upward movement of the Virgin as she moves into a glowing paradise. The vigorous motion is achieved, first of all, compositionally. The faces of the earthbound tier of figures are transfixed in wonder at the arc of *putti* that seems to be lifting the Virgin heavenwards. Reinforcing these upwards-thrusting movements is the triangle of brilliant red robes worn by the two apostles and the Virgin. Her posture is one of eager expectation as she rises towards the God whose arms are outstretched to receive her. A hovering angel holds her crown.

To view the painting, start at the bottom of the massive nave of this church. You can then appreciate one of the picture's innovations, which at first startled many viewers – the relatively large dimensions of the apostles beneath the Virgin. They were portrayed in this way so that they would appear in due proportion from the perspective of long distance. This device helped to establish the painting as the central feature in an enormous building which contained many competing attractions – the tombs of the Doges, for example.

Titian
Pesaro Madonna, c.1520

This was the second of Titian's early triumphs in the Frari. Like the Assumption painting, this one was designed to be in harmony with its context, a side altar, which required a different and innovative

VENICE AND SURROUNDS

solution. In order to attract the viewer approaching – as would normally be the case – from the left, Titian placed the Madonna and Child off-center to the right. From this vantage point, two primary orientations are established. For the Madonna, the orientation – diagonally downwards to the left to the kneeling donor, Jacopo Pesaro – is indicated by St Peter. For the infant, the orientation – also downwards – to other Pesaro family members is indicated by the gesture of St Francis. While this is another rendering of the hallowed subject of the *sacra conversazione*, its departure from the central placement of the holy figures so long established in treatments of this subject is a late but genuine Renaissance shift of focus. Although Titian had good pragmatic reasons for this shift, the painting was so successful that it led to a fashion for off-center Virgins, even when this design was not required for pragmatic reasons!

Donatello
St John the Baptist, 1438

Go to the Chapel of St John the Baptist to find a compelling representation of St John. Donatello made two sculptures on this theme – this wooden, polychrome statue, and the bronze that you'll find in the Siena Cathedral. John is depicted after his long years of penance and suffering in the wilderness, his face haggard and his body wasted. And yet there is still an authoritative air about the figure, as he raises his right hand to predict the coming of the Messiah: *Ecce Agnus Dei*! ("Behold the Lamb of God.")

A few steps away to the southwest are the Chiesa and Scuola Grande di San Rocco, with their splendid array of Tintoretto paintings.

Chiesa and Scuola Grande di San Rocco

Location: Campo San Rocco
Contact details: Tel. 041 5214864
Opening hours: 9:00 am–7:00 pm, Mon.–Sat., 9:00 am–2:00 pm, Sun.
Admission: Euro 5.50

Free audio guides are available at the Scuola, and it is worth using one. Begin in the church, where we will first view nine paintings that depict the life of the saint. Six are in the church; the remaining three are in the school. San Rocco was a 14th-century scion of the French aristocracy at Montpellier. Early in his adult life, he divested himself of his wealth and set out on a pilgrimage to Rome. On his travels, he encountered the plague, and devoted himself to the care of the sick. Near Piacenza, he became ill himself, but was sustained in a forest by a dog, which brought him daily rations of bread. When the pustules on his leg burst, they seem to have produced a form of immunization, so that San Rocco came to be credited with miraculous powers of healing. Because of this he became the patron saint of sufferers from the plague – both human and animal. Finally, the saint reached Rome and gained an audience with the pope. After more trials, he finally arrived back in Montpellier, only to become embroiled in a battle and thrown into prison, where he expired at a young age. The six paintings in the church portray significant scenes in this short but colorful life, culminating in his imprisonment. They are:

Tintoretto
San Rocco Healing the Plague-Stricken in Hospital, 1549
San Rocco Healing the Animals, c.1577
San Rocco Presented to the Pontiff, 1577
San Rocco in the Desert, c.1577
San Rocco Captured During the Battle of Montpellier, c.1577
San Rocco in Prison, 1567

Having reached the place where the saint is portrayed as close to death, cross the street to the school, and ascend the stairs. There you will encounter three final paintings – of the saint experiencing a vision shortly before death, and his glory after death – together with a portrayal of the saint by Tintoretto, the master portraitist. There are also many other Tintoretto paintings on Biblical themes and a couple of Titians as well.

Tintoretto
Apparition of San Rocco, c.1588
San Rocco in Glory, 1564
San Rocco, c.1577

Most of the remaining paintings we focus on are upstairs.

Tintoretto
Annunciation, 1583–1587

This painting invites comparison with Titian's more conventional treatment of the same theme. This is a curious picture: the startled Mary sits before a splendid bed under ornate ceilings – but next to a chair beginning to lose its seat of woven rushes. Gabriel has flown through the doorway of a dilapidated exterior, accompanied by an endless retinue of angels, and the Holy Ghost, in the form of a dove. If you think that two stylists are at work here, you are right: the Virgin's head, the robe of the heavenly messenger and the flying cherubs were executed by Domenico Tintoretto, the master's son.

Tintoretto
Baptism, c.1580

Tintoretto has produced another of his radical compositions in this version of the Baptism of Christ. The supposedly central figures of Christ and John the Baptist are relegated to the middle ground, leaving the foreground to a strangely assorted collection of figures, some of them apparently unfinished. In the background, illuminated by a burst of heavenly light, is a mass of ghostly wraiths. The postures of Christ and John the Baptist are also unconventional. Jesus, in particular, is kneeling in an act of submission rather than standing in serene acceptance as so often conveyed by the Renaissance mainstream. Yet the overall impact of this picture is powerful, perhaps especially for today's viewers with their modern tolerance of ambiguities.

Tintoretto
Ascension, 1577–81

Given its theme, this painting is appropriately *de trop*. Jesus, normally portrayed by Tintoretto as a boyish, slight figure is here much more substantial, making his ascension a weighty affair – though easily accomplished on the backs of sturdy angels. In the center of the picture, Moses and Elijah conversing are bathed in a sunny luminescence, but around the heavenly figures above them swirl darkly thunderous clouds. On the ground, the apostles – not surprisingly – are in startled disarray. The ascending figures have blocked out the sun, casting them in temporary shadow.

Titian
Christ Carrying the Cross, c.1510

This small early painting – now in poor condition – is often wrongly believed to have been painted by Giorgione. This scene is a curiously memorable one, no doubt because of its political resonances. Here we have the innocent Christ looking away from the fiercely oppressive glare of his custodian, representing the government that is about to put him to death. In the same room is another small but moving Titian of a Christ depicted as the Man of Sorrows.

Tintoretto
Crucifixion, 1565

Taking up the entire wall opposite the entrance of the Sala dell'Albergo is this huge picture, full of dramatic urgency. It is as though the executioners are eager to complete their gruesome business before an impending terrifying storm erupts. Even those not involved in the execution seem to have been caught up in whirling vortices of energy. Above the tumult on the ground hangs the solitary Christ. A heavenly aureole radiates from his cross, and, in a similarly radiating panorama, concentric circles of actors are incessantly moving, drawing us inexorably into the scene. Before long, the viewer is in the midst of the tumult – a participant, rather than a detached observer. The 'noise' of this picture is deafening: the restless horses fretting to our left and right; the hammering; the screams of the thieves as they are bound to their crosses and roughly thrust into place. Allow at least half an hour to experience this picture: you will need every second!

Titian
Annunciation, c.1540

This is a more orthodox treatment of this popular Renaissance theme than Tintoretto's version downstairs. The ethereal elements of the picture – the heavenly messenger alighting in front of Mary's *prei-dieu,* the beams of celestial light from the Holy Ghost – are balanced by the mundane objects of earthly existence – the half-open work basket, the quail trotting about, and the fruit. The Virgin appears to be cringing from the destiny that has been thrust upon her.

Tintoretto
Christ Praying in the Garden, 1578–81

Although this is characteristic of the work of the later Tintoretto – with its vivid chiaroscuro contrasts and ghostly procession of figures – this is also one of his most original compositions. The angel is descending from a psychedelic paradise. This provides a striking contrast with the Stygian gloom below, through which the arresting soldiers are advancing. The sleeping apostles, illuminated by the heavenly rays, serve to emphasize the loneliness of Christ.

Tintoretto
Resurrection of Christ, 1578–81

With its bright and dazzling light and figurative complexity, this painting is one of the most proto-Baroque of Tintoretto. In light such as this, the wraith-like ghostly figures so characteristic of the later Tintoretto have given way to a life-affirming band of angels.

Tintoretto
Last Supper, 1578–81

Tintoretto's several treatments of this theme are discussed under the entries for San Giorgio Maggiore (p.190) which contains his last, and in some ways most interesting, rendition of this theme.

The next pair of paintings takes us from the upstairs – where the paintings of Tintoretto are primarily concerned with the adult Christ and the Old Testament – to the ground floor, where he is mainly concerned with the Madonna and Child. However, first view the painting below, in the Upper Hall, and then compare it to the painting of the Magi on the ground floor.

Tintoretto
Adoration of the Shepherds, (upper hall) and *Adoration of the Magi* (ground floor), 1577–81

Two Tintorettos are at work in these two paintings. In the first, we observe the product of a down-to-earth craftsman. Mary and Joseph are at ease with their peasant companions. The supernatural is barely in evidence: the celestial beings above the rafters shed only a gentle radiance on the mother and the barely haloed child. In the second, ground-floor version of the Adoration, Tintoretto the metaphysical visionary has come to the fore. In the presence of their eminent visitors, the holy mother and her child are more assertive. The external environment has become turbulent: angels swirl overhead, and, in the background, a procession of Tintoretto's familiar luminescent wraiths approach the stable.

Tintoretto
Assumption of the Virgin, *1583–87*

Comparison of this treatment with the artist's much earlier one in the Accademia shows just how much the style of the older Tintoretto had evolved. In place of the more conventionally solid figures in the earlier work, we now have a more supple and dynamic Virgin ascending through a network of incessantly turning angels. On the ground, the apostles are also in full movement – toppled by the blast of wind that is transporting the Virgin heavenwards. The picture once more demonstrates the appropriateness of Tintoretto's title of the great colorist. The heavenly glow is punctuated by blues, grays, burgundy and rose-tints.

Now we embark on a walk that takes us to a number of churches and one museum, each which has one notable painting within it. Rather than list each as a full entry, the paragraphs below briefly describe this journey and the artworks you will see. You will end up at the vaporetto stop Zattere. As the sites are fairly close together, this portion of the Trail should not take more than a few hours.

About 400 yards a little north of east, on the Campo San Polo, you'll find the **Chiesa di San Polo:** There you will find another Tintoretto treatment of the theme of the Last Supper, discussed in greater detail under San Giorgio Maggiore. Continue on another 400 yards, this time, a little east of north, to Campo San Cassiano. Within the **Chiesa di San Cassiano** view Tintoretto's *Crucifixion* of 1568, a study in the banality of evil.

Walk yet another 400 yards – somewhat east of due south – and you are back at the Grand Canal, at the **Chiesa di San Silvestro**, located, predictably, in the Campo San Silvestro. Another Tintoretto – a *Baptism of Christ*, painted in 1580 shows John the Baptist and Christ in a work that is full of strong and full of subtle movement

Having enjoyed the very considerable riches of Santa Croce/ San Polo, you have some mopping-up to do in the vicinity of the Accademia, around Dorsoduro. About 200 yards west of Accademia is the **Chiesa di San Trovaso**, where you will find another Tintoretto. Like the other churches, this church is in a square named after it, the Campo San Trov'aso. There we find another treatment by Tintoretto of the *Last Supper,* this time from 1564. Again, we'll be discussing this theme in greater detail a few stops on. About 150 yards to the south, at the Fondamenta Zattere ai Gesuiti, is the confusingly named **Dominican Church of the Gesuati**, (not to be confused with the Jesuits' Church, Santa Maria Assunta, otherwise known as the *Gesuiti*, in Campo dei Gesuiti). This church charges a modest entrance fee, probably because of its wonderful Tiepolo murals. Inside is the smallest of the Tintoretto *Crucifixions*, (1565) depicting Christ on the cross, towering above a group of distraught women mourners.

Two hundred yards further, across the narrowing peninsula is the only Florentine painting in the Venice Trail. It is in the **Collezione Cini**, a small private gallery which you'll find on San Vio 864. Opening hours are somewhat irregular, so if you are particularly keen to see the *Madonna and Child with Angels, Saint and Donor* by Lippi in 1420, you might telephone ahead (Tel: 5210755). There is a modest admission charge. The small painting is a good example of the work of the young Lippi. It is experimental in its foreshortening and its treatment of forms. The heads of most of the figures – but not that of the Madonna – have the slightly bulbous shape so characteristic of early Lippi.

While you are in the vicinity, you may care to take some time out to visit the superb collection of modern art in the **Peggy Guggenheim Gallery**, which our Trail takes you past. It is about 100 yards to the east of the Cini – at San Gregorio 710.

A last stop before catching the vaporetto is the huge **Church of St Maria della Salute**, which is virtually on the very point of the peninsula of Dorsoduro – 300 yards beyond the Cini. There you can see Titian's *Descent of the Holy Ghost,* c.1546. In it the glowing dominance of the Holy Ghost is emphasized by the ecstatic postures of Sts Mark and Peter and by the architectural symmetry of the work. Shafts of heavenly radiance illuminate the upward-turned faces, and tongues of fire flicker from their heads. The containment of the scene within the small vaulted room strengthens the dramatic intensity of the picture.

From the Salute, take a walk along the southern side of the peninsula, along the banks of the Canale della Giudecca. About 800 yards along, quite close to Gesuati, is the Vaporetto stop, Zattere. Hop on board, and you are bound for the Isola and the Church of San Giorgio Maggiore (Church of St George the Elder).

San Giorgio Maggiore

Chiesa di San Giorgio Maggiore

Location: Isola di San Giorgio Maggiore

Inside the church go to the Cappella della Deposizione, the chapel named after the painting.

Tintoretto
The Deposition, (Deposizione), 1594

This was painted on the eve of Tintoretto's own death, and the dead Christ is presented as a man finally at peace after his terrible ordeal. The friends tending the body are not wracked with the emotions of mourners. Rather, they convey an air of resignation – even calm acceptance – unusual in earlier treatments of this theme, including Tintoretto's own. The strikingly elegant posture of the Virgin, physically well separated from her son, contrasts strongly with that of most Pietà Virgins. The long perspective of the picture reveals the thieves still hanging on their crosses in the dark of night.

Tintoretto
The Last Supper, 1594

The Last Supper was Tintoretto's favorite theme, to which he returned again and again over a half a century. It was a theme which permitted the painter to present a mundane activity – that of eating with friends – in a way that is redolent with a sense of dread for the suffering ahead. We have access to Tintoretto's treatments of this theme in youth, early middle age, late middle age and the time of his death in old age. The youthful treatment now in San Marcuola is unsurprisingly the most conventional. Christ sits in the middle of his apostles clustered around a table that stretches across the horizontal plane. Even at this early stage, however, Tintoretto uses a characteristic device by situating the backs of some of the figures so as to focus the eye on the bright center of the tablecloth and the Christ behind it.

By the time of early middle age, represented by the renderings in San Trovaso and San Polo, Tintoretto no longer uses the table as the central organizing structure. Instead, the dynamic interactions of the figures themselves place Christ at the center of an interpersonal vortex. The context has broadened too, with surreal vistas of mysterious outside worlds.

A decade or so later, in the painting in the Scuola di San Rocco, the social context and architectural contexts are more fully elaborated. In the background, there is considerable activity in the kitchen, while in the foreground the external world is represented by two beggars and their dog. The eye is strongly drawn to the illuminated back of Judas, but thence to the object of his intense observation, Christ. Even though he is positioned low down on a periphery, Christ thus ends up as the ultimate central focus. (Seven decades later, Velazquez – while purchasing some Tintoretto paintings for the Spanish court – took the trouble to copy this work for his king.)

Here, in the final treatment of this theme, the table reappears as an organizing structure, but performs a new function. Now it is obliquely angled and directs attention to a markedly celestial environment. In the Lucca painting (in the church of San Martino) the bright, cheerful colors and the golden luminescence of the void behind Christ suggest that the Last Supper is more a preliminary to his triumphant Ascension than impending suffering. A couple of years later, when Tintoretto himself was facing death, the colors have again become muted and somber, and the ghostly celestial beings seem to portend the impending tragedy.

When you return to the wharf, take a vaporetto to the Rialto stop, in the north of the San Marco sestiere. One hundred yards or so to the south is the Church of San Salvatore.

Chiesa di San Salvatore

Location: Campo San Salvatore

Titian
Annunciation, c.1560

In this relatively late work, heaven – and the Holy Ghost – have become much more prominent, and the surroundings of the Virgin less elaborate. However, the overall effect is one of opulence, with the rich golden light suffusing the central figures and their raiment. Is it the veil of ignorance that she is lifting to receive the message of a Gabriel with the physiognomy of a classical Greek messenger of the gods? Despite the near-Baroque turmoil in the heavens, the Virgin seems strikingly composed.

Titian
Transfiguration, 1560–5

Although this painting is in poor repair, it is included in our visit because it is a striking manifestation of Titian's style in his last phase. The brilliant hues of his earlier career are here giving way to a stark – almost monochromatic – coloring. This rather somber work does not convey the spirit of a great triumph that earlier suffused the Raphael treatment of the same theme.

Turn to the southwest and walk about 500 yards to find the Church of Santo Stefano.

Chiesa di Santo Stefano

Location: Campo Santo Stefano

Tintoretto
Last Supper, c.1578
Agony in the Garden, c.1578
Jesus Washing of the Feet of the Apostles, c.1578

Here is another of Tintoretto's *Last Suppers* (see San Giorgio Maggiore) What is of most interest here is that Tintoretto has treated the *Last Supper* as just one of a trio of paintings depicting that fateful night – the others being the *Washing of the Feet* and the *Agony in the Garden.* The century before, the three scenes might well have been included in the one picture (as in Masaccio's famous *Tribute Money* in Florence's Brancacci Chapel.)

Another 200 yards walk – this time to the east – brings you to the Piazza San Marco. On the western side of the Piazza is the Museo Correr. This is a vast gallery containing fabulous treasures. It can swallow you for days … we recommend a couple of hours at the very least. Although the Correr is not as strong as the Accademia in its Renaissance holdings, it rivals it in its collection of works representing the entire history of Venetian art – from medieval times to the 18th-and early 19th-century sculpture of Canova. Here we focus on four Bellinis.

Correr Museum (Museo Correr)

Location: Procuratie Nuove
Contact details: Tel. 041 5225625
Opening hours: 9:00 am–6:00 pm, daily
Admission: About Euro 9.50 gains admission to both the Correr and the Doge's Palace.

Giovanni Bellini
Madonna and Child (Madonna Frizzoni), 1460–4

Mary stares wistfully into the middle distance while the Christ Child is preoccupied with his own sad thoughts. The baby fingers of the infant's left hand grasp his mother's thumb, but his right hand touches his chest in a gesture of self-knowledge. Again, Bellini's parapet separates the Madonna and Child from the domain of the viewer, and, in contrast to some of his other Madonnas, Bellini here has made no attempt to include the viewer in the moment captured in the picture. This early Madonna is one of the most secular produced by Bellini. The simply ornamented red costume of Mary is in harmony with the demeanor of the Christ Child who, like his mother, is not flaunting his sacred status through haloes and the like. On the contrary, the infant's nakedness emphasizes his human vulnerability. There is little to recall Byzantium in the simple background of cloud and turquoise sky.

Giovanni Bellini
Crucifixion, c.1455

This is one of Bellini's earliest solo works. In this same room of the Correr, you will have the opportunity of comparing it with another treatment of the theme – by his father. (The teen-age Giovanni may have worked on Jacopo's painting as well.) While both paintings portray the musculature of the crucified Christ with great realism, Giovanni's work conveys the anguish of the participants much more graphically. Giovanni has juxtaposed the heavily populated supernatural world above the crucifix with a strikingly harmonious modern landscape. Jacopo's painting, in contrast, has much of the courtly atmosphere of medieval times.

Giovanni Bellini
Dead Christ Supported by Two Angels, 1460

The poignancy of Bellini's many depictions of Christ in Passion is without parallel. In this one, outside the walls of Jerusalem, the dead body of the Savior is to be laid to rest. The sad little angels with grief-stricken faces support the leaden arms. The hands droop listlessly: the vicious iron nails that had pinned them to the cross have been removed, and now lie on the lid of the open sarcophagus; but the fingers remain half-clenched, reminding us of unspeakable pain. The body is marvelously drawn. The sinews stand out still, and the musculature of the stomach remains tense: further indications of the agony of his suffering. His head, shaded by its own halo, sags forward, the mouth still open after uttering the final breath. In the middle distance, the citizens resume their banal daily lives. The picture is lit from the left with a pallid, gray-green light that gives the dead flesh a marble-like hue, like that of the sarcophagus into which the body is being lowered. Only the clearing sky in the top left of the painting presages the triumph that is to follow.

Giovanni Bellini
Transfiguration, c.1455

This painting, possibly Bellini's earliest surviving, was designed as the central panel of a triptych or polyptych. At the age of 25, Bellini was experimenting with an approach to which he would return frequently during his long career – the setting of devotional subjects in large, airy, outdoor spaces. His capacity to evoke atmosphere in this way was pathbreaking. The painting depicts a Gospel story. Jesus took Peter and James and James' brother, John (the Evangelist) to a high mountain, where, before their eyes, he was transfigured so that "his face shone like the sun and his garment became white as light." (Matthew 17,1-13). Moses and Elijah, the old prophets, then appeared with him, and a voice from the clouds said: 'This is my beloved son, with whom I am well pleased'. The disciples fell about, overcome with fear, until Jesus told them to get up and to stop being afraid. The six figures in the painting appear on a rocky outcrop, against a low-slung horizon and a big, turbulent skyscape. Christ's intricately folded garments shimmer in the eerie light. The prophets

Bellini's Transfiguration

gesticulate in avid conversation. But the three apostles cringe in terror. James, in fact, seems to be almost asleep – as indeed he will be during the Agony in the Garden.

Across the Piazza, on its eastern side, is the Palazzo Ducale, or Doge's Palace. While its art collection is patchy and cannot come close to those of either the Accademia or the Correr, there are many other reasons – largely historical – for visiting the Palace, from the meeting rooms long used by the rulers of Venice to the prison cells where their victims (such as Casanova) languished, and the Bridge of Sighs over which they passed on their way to incarceration. (Look for some of the prisoners' graffiti on the dungeon walls.)

Doge's Palace (Palazzo Ducale)

Location: Piazza San Marco
Contact details: Tel. 041 5224951
Opening hours: 9:00 am–7:00 pm, daily
Admission: About Euro 9 gains admission to both the Correr and the Doge's Palace.

Giovanni Bellini
Lament for the Dead Christ, c.1472

Has any painter succeeded so consistently in representing the drama and agony of Christ's crucifixion as has Giovanni Bellini? This Pietà fairly exudes grief. You can almost hear the wailing of the Madonna. John the Baptist's face – so distressed – turns away from the pain of the mother embracing her dead son. The figure of Christ is remarkable. His body – look at his cruelly twisted left arm and clenched hand – still bears the signs of his torture. His face conveys the impression that he suffers still. Bellini's often-present parapet is here the frame of an altar on which Christ is the Eucharistic sacrifice. Candelabra separate the central group of three figures from St Mark (on the left) and St Nicholas (on the right). In the dark space between the figures of the Madonna and Christ burns a candle – symbol of the presence of God. The drama of the scene is heightened by Bellini's palette: the umber-colored tones of the background and parapet are repeated with the warm browns and orange in the faces and they are also used to highlight the anatomical features of Christ's torso. The dark but brilliant reds of

Palazzo Ducale

the robes of Mary and the Baptist are reflected in Christ's halo – and, of course, in the blood issuing from his wounds.

Titian
Madonna with Child and Angels, 1523

Although this work, originally a fresco, was greatly damaged in the 19th century when it was transferred to canvas, the effect has been to bestow on it the haunting beauty of a primitive fragment. There is an ethereal flow to the faded garments of both Mary and of Jesus (and held by one of the angels).

Tintoretto
Dead Christ Supported by Angels, with Doges, 1581–84

At which point does slavish adherence to a tightly defined commission become a form of sycophancy? Wherever that point may be, Tintoretto must be close to it in this painting. The convincingly cadaverous Christ is incongruously placed in a luxurious ducal setting. If one does not take into account the positions of the rather weighty angels, pride of place – well ahead of the worthy saints – is seized by two Doges. This is not a treatment with much appeal to modern sensibilities.

Tintoretto
Paradise, c.1588

At about 184 square yards, this is one of the largest paintings in the world. So huge is it that the Renaissance orthodoxies of perspective and order are rendered largely irrelevant. Instead, Tintoretto uses celestial light as the basic organizing force – bringing into central focus the otherwise distant figures of Christ and Mary. The void behind them inspires vertigo – had Tintoretto known of the Big Bang, would he have rendered the dynamism of the cosmos much differently? And yet something important seems to be lacking. There is no sense of the dialectic tensions between light and dark and good and evil. We know that Tintoretto was much given to meditations on his mortality at this time. Could it have been that this massive work, for which he refused payment, served to reassure him that life after death would be ecstatic after all?

Further east, about 300 yards, you will arrive at the sestiere of Castello, and the Church of San Zaccaria, in the Campo San Zaccaria.

Chiesa di San Zaccaria

Giovanni Bellini
Pala di San Zaccaria, 1505

Bellini's last great altarpiece of the Madonna is the second of the paintings by Bellini that Ruskin declared were the world's two greatest pictures; it is the one that caused Dürer to claim that the 75-year-old Giambellino was still the best painter in Venice. We can half-close our eyes and imagine what it must have looked like in its original, no doubt splendid, frame – which now is missing. Even without it, Bellini's sumptuously decorated interior provides a magnificent church-like architectural setting for his Madonna and Child, sitting in *sacra conversazione* with the four saints: Peter and Catherine, Lucy and Jerome. Bellini has placed the group under another of his magnificent, painted-mosaic semi-domes, but, this time, he has opened the space to the trees and the sky, conveying a feeling of light and space, notwithstanding the close proximity of the figures. From the vaulted ceiling above the Madonna hangs a lamp: hanging from its chain is an ostrich egg, symbolizing the virgin birth of Christ. The women are martyrs: they carry their martyrs' palms in their hands, that is, they are offering their martyrdom to Christ. St Catherine's left hand is on a wheel – the instrument of her intended execution (it fortunately exploded before she was killed), and St Lucy carries her own blood in a crystal vase.

Tintoretto
Birth of St John the Baptist, c.1555

This is a youthful rendition of an infrequently painted subject.

We now begin the last walk on our Venice Trail. It has numerous stops in churches and museums, most of which have only one painting covered, so again, we do not devote a full entry to each. How long you take is up to you, but it is a very pleasant walk and can be broken by coffee or meal stops. The churches are all in a *campo* named after them, so they are easy to find on a standard map. First, walk 200 yards to the northwest to the **Fondazione Querini Stampalia** in the Campiello Querini. Like the Museo Horne, this gallery illustrates the difficulties faced by private collectors (however discriminating) who do not have the resources to compete with public institutions. However, the collection contains, amongst other treasures, a 1516 painting that may have been Giovanni Bellini's last: *Madonna and Blessing Child with St John the Baptist*. The museum charges around 6 Euros for admission.

Continue on: 600 yards to the northeast is the **Chiesa di San Francesco della Vigna** in Ramo San Francesco. There is a *Madonna with Blessing Child, Four Saints and a Donor (Dolfin Madonna)* that Bellini probably had a hand in, although he would have been very old at the time (1507).

About 300 yards to the west is the **Chiesa di Santi Giovanni e Paolo** – also called **San Zanipolo**. In it you will find a Bellini polyptych from 1464–68. In the top row, from right to left, are: *The Announcing*

Angel, The Dead Christ and *The Annunciate Virgin*. In the second row are *St Christopher*, *St Vincent Ferrer* and *St Sebastian*. The bottom row (the predella) shows scenes of miracles performed by St Vincent Ferrer. At first glance, this Annunciation seems not to be typical of Bellini. Because of the limitations imposed by the small panel format, there is no room for one of his characteristically psychedelic skyscapes, and the two Annunciation figures are in restrained poses. But closer inspection reveals some characteristically Bellinian ambiguities. The somberly clad Virgin could as well be a figure in a Pietà as in an Annunciation. And the angel's somewhat diffident expression suggests that he knows how much suffering lies ahead of the young Virgin before her ultimate triumph. The central panel depicts a poignantly rendered Christ, his human life's energy finally spent after his cruel torture and death.

A walk of 500 yards to the west brings you to the sestiere of Cannaregio, and the **Church of San Giovanni Crisostomo**, which contains a Bellini altarpiece, *Three Saints*, from 1513, his last grand religious composition. It is noteworthy, if for no other reason, than because of the interesting way in which the painter has resolved what could have been a difficulty in the composition: he has avoided painting 'three saints in a row' by placing St Jerome on a rocky outcrop, lifting him onto the second plane of the picture, backed by one of Bellini's wonderful skies and low-slung landscapes. St Christopher is on the left and St Ludovic, on the right.

Ahead is a long haul – over half a mile. Try to walk alongside the Grand Canal wherever possible to reach your destination, the **Chiesa di San Marcuola**, (Campo San Marcuola) where you will see another Tintoretto treatment of the Last Supper. Afterwards, a walk of 500 yards to the east brings you to the great Jesuit **Chiesa di Santa Maria Assunta – or Gesuiti**. Here you can see Tintoretto's striking *Assumption of the Virgin,* (c.1554) and compare it mentally to Titian's famous *Assumption* in the Frari. What has changed, and what remains much the same? Both paintings display the typical Venetian dynamism, as the Virgin rises heavenwards. In this version, however, divinity is not so directly present. But the heavens are heavily populated with Baroque cherubim. The crowding is also evident back on earth, where the individual apostles are more readily distinguished than they were in the earlier Titian. The proto-Baroque style of this work attracted much praise in the 17th century, when one critic lauded it as 'one of the truly exceptional works in the world'. By the time of the 19th century, even as great an admirer of Tintoretto as Ruskin had to express a preference for Titian's less flamboyant treatment of this theme.

VENICE AND SURROUNDS

Over half a mile to the northwest is our last site on this Trail, the **Chiesa della Madonna dell'Orto**, where Tintoretto is buried. A Bellini Madonna was stolen from this church in 1993. Inside, see Tintoretto's disturbing 1566 treatment of *The Last Judgment*. Effie, the wife of Tintoretto's great Victorian champion, John Ruskin, was so upset by this painting that she had to flee the church. In one sense, this was a perfect theme for Tintoretto, with his ambiguous treatments of light and darkness as representations of good and evil. Forebodings about his own ultimate destination were not yet strong enough to lead him to focus only on heaven, with the result that he presents a splendid picture of hell and its devils. Some critics have compared this work favorably with Michelangelo's famous treatment in the Vatican's Sistine Chapel, but it is also interesting to compare it with Giotto's treatment in the Scrovegni Chapel and in the Torcello Cathedral. Tintoretto's devils are much more human in shape than were their counterparts in preceding centuries, but they were no less evil-looking on that account!

You have now completed the Venice Trail. *Bravissimi!* If you have the extra half day to visit the islands in the lagoon, catch a vaporetto to Murano, and its Chiesa di San Pietro Martire. If, instead, you are returning to the Grand Canal, you may like to do so by walking nearly a mile due south to Cà d'Oro, where you can visit the Galleria della Cà d'Oro.

Cà d'Oro

Galleria della Cà d'Oro

Location: Calle Cà d'Oro
Opening hours: 9:00 am–1:00 pm daily.
Admission: About Euro 2

Mantegna
St Sebastian, c.1506

The legend of St Sebastian describes him as a member of the Pretorian Guard who used his position to bring succor to prisoners and to convert them to Christianity. Under a violent Emperor – Maximian – he was arrested and condemned to death by being shot with arrows. The story says that he survived the attempted execution and continued his illegal activities, only to be re-arrested under Diocletian, flogged to death and his body thrown in the sewer. St

Mantegna's **St Sebastian**

Sebastian was a favorite subject for Renaissance painters glad of the opportunity to paint a nude male, and Mantegna painted several. This one (allegedly dressed with a loincloth by Francesco, his apparently more prudish son) is portrayed as a tortured man in genuine agony. He seems suddenly to have broken away from his assailants, and is running through a door or window, perhaps crying for help.

Murano

On Murano, we are visiting the Church of St Peter the Martyr.

Chiesa di San Pietro Martire

Location: Fondamento dei Vetrai, Murano.

Giovanni Bellini
Immaculate Conception and Eight Saints, 1513

This painting, which was largely if not completely executed by the assistants of the octogenarian Bellini, is included here because of an interesting difference between the experts. The mainstream view is that this is a portrayal of the Assumption. However, a more convincing interpretation, supported by the static nature of the composition, is that Mary is here not ascending, but standing – probably as a representation of purity.

Giovanni Bellini
Pala Barbarigo, 1488

Bellini manages to infuse a formal commissioned work with the cheerfull sunlight pouring in from the rural countryside outside. At the foot of the Virgin, receiving the blessing of the child, is the sumptuously garbed Doge Agostino Barbarigo. On the one side of the Doge is his namesake, St Augustine, who is his sponsor; on the other is his patron, St Mark. Apparently it took nothing less than the Virgin and Child to reduce Barbarigo to obeisance; in real life he was widely disliked for his insistence on receiving the obeisances of others!

Another stretch on the vaporetto will bring you to Torcello, whose *cattedrale* contains, not only the last of the paintings in on this Trail, but more importantly, the famous medieval mosaic renderings of the Madonna and the Last Judgment.

Torcello

Cattedrale di Torcello

Torcello Cathedral

Tintoretto
Assumption of the Virgin, c.1552, *Mosaics* and a *Last Judgment*

This altarpiece has been described as clumsy, mannerist, restless, overcrowded and unattractive! If you wanted a demonstration of the force of our argument that Renaissance art was not superior to that of the Middle Ages, but different from it, Torcello provides it. For here you will find 12th- and 13th-century mosaics that – although much later than the famous works at nearby Ravenna, rival them for sheer beauty. At each end of the Basilica are striking images: over the altar a hypnotic portrayal of the Virgin and Child; at the rear, a horrific medieval *Last Judgment* that some claim is superior to both Michelangelo's version in the Sistine Chapel in Rome and Tintoretto's own in the Madonna dell'Orto in Venice. In one other respect do these masterpieces resemble those at Ravenna: the identity of the magnificent craftsmen who executed them has been long forgotten.

SECTION 2

THE INTERCITY TRAILS

View of San Gimignano

TRAIL 4:
Florence to Rome

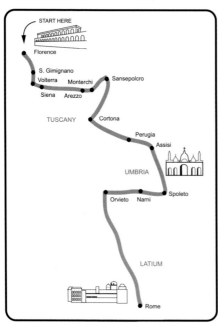

This is the shortest of the intercity trails – about 200 miles in length. From Florence, it proceeds in a generally southeasterly direction for about 130 miles – until it reaches the great religious center of Assisi. It then traces something of a question mark before ending in Rome.

From Empoli, a trip of 20 miles brings you to the superb hilltop town of San Gimignano, famed for its many towers, and featured in the film, *Tea with Mussolini*. Walk through the walls, up into the town, heading for the Center and the Collegiata.

San Gimignano

Collegiata, Chapel of Santa Fina

Location: Via Folgore 11
Contact details: Tel. 057 7940348
Opening hours: 11:00 am–7:00 pm, daily
Admission: About Euro 2

Ghirlandaio
Annunciation and Death of St Fina, c.1478

You will find Ghirlandaio's frescoes of Saint Fina in the Chapel named after her. The patron saint of San Gimignano, Fina was a 13th-century maid, who died at the age of 15. An extreme ascetic, she virtually starved herself to death. A week before her demise, she was visited by an apparition of St Gregory the Great, informing her of her impending release. One of the two main frescoes portrays this visit; the other depicts her lying in state after her death.

A further 10 miles to the west is another historic town, Volterra.

Volterra

Right in the center of town is the Palazzo Minucci-Solaini, which contains the Civic Gallery and Museum.

Pinacoteca e Museo Civici

Location: Palazzo Minucci-Solaini, Piazza dei Priori
Contact details: Tel. 058 887580
Opening hours: 9:00 am–7:00 pm, daily
Admission: Modest.

Ghirlandaio
Christ in Glory with Saints, c.1492

The majority opinion among scholars is that this painting was largely the product of the Ghirlandaio workshop. Its principal interest lies in its portrayal in the foreground of Sts Actinea and Graeciniana, for relics of these saints are preserved in the altar below.

Twenty miles southeast lies another of Florence's keenest historical rivals – the great Renaissance city of Siena, nowadays known for its (in)famous horse race in its Piazza del Campo – the Palio. Although Siena equalled Florence in painting and sculpture in the 13th and 14th centuries, it does not figure prominently in our Trail. The reason for this is that most of the important Sienese work – the paintings of Duccio, Martini and the Lorenzetti brothers and sculpture by the Pisano family – was too early to be considered Renaissance.

Siena

In the southwestern quadrant of the old city is the Duomo: a veritable treasure-house, with works by Michelangelo, Bernini, Nicola Pisano and Donatello – among others.

The Duomo (Santa Maria Assunta)

Location: Piazza del Duomo
Opening hours: 9:30 am–7:30 pm daily
Admission: Euro 5.50. You can purchase a composite ticket for the Duomo, Baptistery, and Museo for Euro 9.50.

You will find Donatello's *John the Baptist* in the chapel named after the saint halfway down the nave on the left-hand side. This is one of his trio of 'wilderness' sculptures. The others are his treatment of the same subject in wood in the Frari in Venice, and his haunted *Mary Magdalene* in the Cathedral Museum in Florence.

Donatello
St John the Baptist, c.1455

In stark contrast to the ornate, gilded wall that forms the backdrop for the sculpture, Donatello's bronze *John the Baptist* personifies extreme deprivation. His shaggy hair hangs in a mane over his shoulders, making it difficult to distinguish from the animal skin that reaches to his knees. His body – revealed through the slits in his garment – is wiry, but very thin. In his left hand, he holds his shepherd's staff. He is no mere shepherd but also the precursor of the Messiah, so he also carries the scroll bearing the *Agnus Dei* message. The forefinger of his right hand is raised to emphasize the message: "Behold the Lamb of God."

Set in the pavement on the left of the steps of the great altar, you will find Donatello's tombstone for Giovanni Pecci.

Donatello
Tombstone of Giovanni Pecci, c.1427

A three-dimensional pattern of brown, umber and cream terracotta tiles surrounds the inlaid bronze tombstone of the Bishop of

FLORENCE TO ROME

Grosseto. Interestingly, the figure of Grosseto does not seem to be lying in state, like those on other horizontal tombstones. Instead, his body is at a slight angle (notice his turned head and the differing positions of his feet), making him appear merely asleep on the stretcher on which he lies.

Across the nave is the Bernini-designed Cappella Chighi (the Cappella della Madonna del Voto – Madonna of the Vow): it has been *in restauro* for a while but you can still see the *ex votos* hanging on its walls. Inside, is Bernini's sculpture of St Catherine of Siena.

Cross the Duomo again. To the left of the entrance to the Piccolomini Library (next to the Chapel of St John the Baptist) is the Piccolomini Altar and:

Michelangelo
St Paul (San Paolo), 1481

This four-foot-high statue of St Paul is a work from Michelangelo's youthful career. He was commissioned, along with Baccio da Montelupo, to make 14 statues to adorn the altar in the chapel that would ultimately receive the remains of Cardinal Francesco Todeschini-Piccolomini (who had a brief period as Pope Pius III). In the event, only four of the statues were completed and of those, the *St Paul* is regarded as the only work that can confidently be ascribed to the young Michelangelo alone. The intensity of the expression on *St Paul's* face is said to anticipate *Moses* – the masterpiece of his later career – but one has to conclude that his apprenticeship was not yet over!

To reach the Baptistery, walk outside and around the back of the Duomo.

Michelangelo. Illustration Matt Morrow.

The Baptistery

Donatello
Herod's Banquet, c.1425

Donatello's remarkable representation of Herod's Banquet is a gilded bronze panel on the right of the baptismal font. The other panels were contributed by Ghiberti, Jacopa della Quercia and two Sienese goldsmiths. Donatello has chosen to record the moment when John the Baptist's head is presented to Herod (following the infamous dance of Salome). The presentation has been quite a party-stopper! The guests recoil in horror. Even Herod gestures as if to say, "Don't bring that thing any closer!" The sculptor's genius in conveying emotion is obvious – as is his skill in achieving great depth (sufficient for three parallel dining rooms) on a shallow surface.

Take the external steps leading from the road in front of the Baptistery to reach the **Cathedral Museum**. Open between 9:00 am – 7:30 pm, daily, the major reason for visiting it is to view the superb Maestá of the late medieval master, Duccio. The Museum also has a Donatello relief of the Madonna and Child which used to occupy a niche in the cathedral wall. The **Palazzo Pubblico** in the famous square contains important works by the 14th-century painters, the Lorenzetti Brothers and Simone Martini. The most interesting of these are Ambrogio Lorenzetti's *Allegories of Good and Bad Government*.

A trip of about 50 miles to the southeast brings you to the cultural center of Arezzo, birthplace of the poet Petrarch and the painter and critic, Giorgio Vasari. However, it is the work of a painter from the much smaller southern Tuscan town of Sansepolcro, Piero della Francesca, who attracts art travellers to this town. Our first stop in Arezzo will be the Cathedral (Duomo).

Arezzo

Duomo

Location: Piazza del Duomo, on the fringe of the Parco il Prato in the old town

Piero della Francesca
St Mary Magdalene, 1460–1466

A young, thoughtful Mary Magdalene stands – framed like a sculpture in a niche – under a delicately detailed marble arch. Only the blue sky behind her reveals this to be a doorway. Her gown and cloak fall in voluminous folds around her. In her hands she carries, like a lantern, the glass jar of precious ointment with which she anointed the dead body of Christ. Her hair, with which she has dried the Savior's feet, falls softly over her shoulders. The Flemish influence on Piero – a provincial painter with cosmopolitan interests – seems very evident in the ornamentation of the architecture and in the exquisite, perfectly rendered glass vial.

Donatello
Baptism of Christ, late 1420s

Here is another relief that demonstrates Donatello's genius in the technique of *rilievo schiacciato* (see Glossary). The sculptor has achieved real depth in the water in which Jesus stands and in the background landscape.

When you leave the Duomo, walk about 500 yards in a southwesterly direction, towards the city center to the Church of St Francis, where you will see Piero della Francesca's great fresco cycle, *The Legend of the True Cross*.

Chiesa di San Francesco

Location: Piazza San Francesco
Contact details: Tel. 057 520630
Opening hours: 8:00 am–noon, 1:30 pm–6:00 pm daily

There is something that prefigures grand opera in this great fresco cycle, in which an improbable legend is ennobled by sublime art. Unless you have a pair of binoculars, you will not be able to view the frescoes properly without getting close. Getting close means buying a ticket for a guided tour. Tickets are purchased from a special shop in the Piazza.

To get the most out of this cycle, you need to know who's who. The main identities in the story are:

Constantine, the first Christian Roman Emperor, who transferred the empire's capital (Byzantium, later Constantinople) to the East.
Maxentius, King of the Barbarians
King Solomon
The Queen of Sheba

Empress Helena, the mother of the Emperor Constantine
Heraclius, Christian king
Chosroes, the Persian king
Judas, (not Judas the traitor but Judas the Jew, who is tortured and
  forced to reveal the whereabouts of the True Cross)

This is not a traditional life cycle, able to be read chronologically. It depicts certain events as themes that can be followed in several different periods of history. (The *Legend* covers the period from Genesis to 628 CE, when the stolen cross was returned to Jerusalem.) The large paintings carry on the medieval tradition of representing several different scenes (which may have occurred at different times) simultaneously in the one picture. Even more confusingly, the fresco has to be read, not from left to right, but from right to left! Because the urge to travel sequentially through the story is very strong, we have listed the frescoes in as near to a chronological sequence as we can. But when viewing the fresco, it's always worth looking across to the opposite wall: the relationship between the companion pictures is always interesting. Use the numbers on the diagram to help you locate the frescoes described. Start with the lunette, high up on the right wall of the chapel:

Piero della Francesca
Legend of the True Cross (La Leggenda della Vera Croce), 1452–66

1. *The Death of Adam*: Adam, attended by his aging wife, Eve, and his children, lies dying: the death of the first human being. In the distant scene in the background, Seth, Adam's son, requests the Archangel Gabriel for sacred oil to prolong his father's life. Instead, he is given a shoot from the Tree of Knowledge that will grow into the tree from which the cross will be hewn. Seth returns to his father's deathbed, and plants the shoot in his father's mouth. Observe the dramatic gestures of the grief-stricken woman. Under this, in the middle register, you will find:

2. *The Adoration of the Wood and the Meeting between Solomon and the Queen of Sheba*: The Queen of Sheba, visiting the Holy Land, halts when she discovers that the holy wood has been cut into a beam used in the construction of a bridge that she and her stately retinue had been about to cross. She reverently kneels before the wood. Note the horses and groomsmen on the left of the elegant ladies, and Piero's marvellous use of color contrast. In the scene on the right, under beautiful Corinthian columns, the Queen and her female attendants meet the fabulously garbed King Solomon and his male courtiers.

Francesca's Legend of the True Cross

3. The Burying of the Wood: When the Queen of Sheba predicts that a man will be nailed to the wood of the tree, King Solomon orders that the precious wood be buried deep in the ground. One workman hefts the beam, striking a pose reminiscent of Christ carrying the cross.

4. The Annunciation: This is the companion picture to the Dream of Constantine. A somewhat haughty-looking Virgin reflects on the message of the Angel, reverently kneeling before her. Overhead, God the Father sends heavenly rays that bathe the Virgin's head in light.

5. The Dream of Constantine: Constantine, sleeping fitfully in his tent before his coming battle against the barbarians massed along the Danube River, dreams of victory. An angel appears with a banner showing the sign of the cross and the words, "In this sign thou shalt conquer!" Note the rows of tents against the eerie night sky, and the light (from a lantern?) falling on the soldier's helmet and the folds of the tent. This is reputed to be the first nocturne in Italian art.

6. Constantine Defeats Maxentius at the Battle of Milvian Bridge: Buoyed

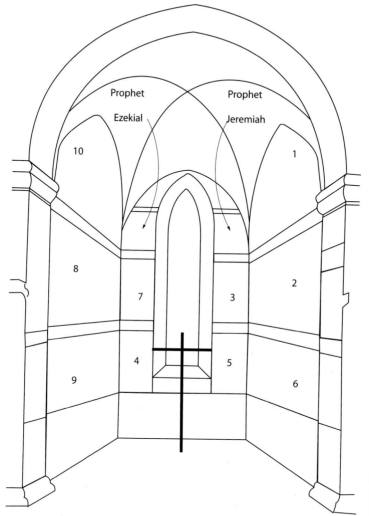

Piero della Francesca's Legend of the True Cross. *The frescoes from the choir of the main chapel, are numbered to match the descriptions in the text.*

by the visit from the angel, Constantine leads his army into battle, holding out his hand in which he holds the cross. Sadly, the picture is badly damaged, but it is still possible to contrast the orderly march of Constantine's army, lances uplifted and banners swirling, with the chaos in Maxentius' army, fleeing the scene before the battle has even begun. The soldier on the prancing white steed on the left of the viewer exudes confidence and eagerness.

7. *The Torture of the Jew, Judas*: The Jew alleged to know the whereabouts of the True Cross is made to reveal the secret by being lowered into a well and starved.

8. *The Discovery of the True Cross, and the Proof of its Authenticity*: Judas leads Helena to the spot where not one, but three crosses are uncovered, necessitating a test to determine which of them had carried the body of the Savior. (The man with the white belted gown and red headdress may be a self-portrait of the artist.) On the right of the picture, the test is applied. When the True Cross is held over the body of a dead boy, he miraculously comes to life. Helena spontaneously kneels. Now look across to the opposite wall and see the Queen of Sheba also kneeling.

9. *Heraclius Defeats Chosroes*: Chosroes, the Persian King, steals the Cross to adorn his throne (on the extreme right of the picture), opposite a black cock – parody of the Holy Ghost. Thus, once again, the forces of Christianity have to be mobilized to retrieve the Cross. On the extreme right of the picture, Chosroes kneels in submission, waiting to be beheaded. Meanwhile, the green-helmeted Heraclius plunges a dagger into the throat of Chosroes' son, and carnage abounds.

10. *The Exaltation of the Cross*: Heraclius carries the cross into Jerusalem, barefoot, emulating Christ's walk to Calvary. People kneel in reverence – one man hastening to remove his tall hat out of respect for the procession. A white-bearded man hurries to join the group of worshippers.

Monterchi

A little over six miles to the southeast is the village of Monterchi, which is strenuously promoting its major tourist attraction – the enigmatic Piero portrayal of the pregnant Madonna. The good citizens of Monterchi know what a treasure they have in Piero's painting: the signs you will see direct you straight to the Madonna del Parto, rather than to the town of Monterchi itself!

Civic Museum (Museo Civico)

Location: Via Reglia 1
Contact details: Tel. 057 570713
Opening hours: 9:00 am–1:00 pm; 2:00 pm–7.00 pm
Admission: About Euro 3

Piero della Francesca
The Pregnant Madonna (Madonna del Parto), 1455–65

What a picture this is! There stands the mother-to-be, heavily pregnant, her right hand indicating her precious burden (or perhaps showing you how her dress will no longer fasten over her swelling abdomen) Her left wrist rests on her hip in the characteristic pose of a woman about to give birth and needing to support her aching back. It's the expression on her face that draws you in. How is she feeling about her extraordinary pregnancy? Is she proud? Is she doubtful? She most certainly is serene – but gravely so. In the meantime, two angels – mirror images of each other, but with transposed colors in their wings and gowns – hold back the flaps of Mary's brocade tent, luxuriously lined with bear fur, a foil to her sensible blue dress. These days, the picture is displayed in such a way as to seem to be lit from behind: the curious glow seems to enhance the haunting mood of this great work. Many consider the picture to be a moving portrayal of rural motherhood. Perhaps it is: Piero's mother was born, and she died, in Monterchi.

After a drive of just 10 miles to the northeast you come to Sansepolcro, birthplace of Piero, and the community where he served for long as a councillor.

Sansepolcro

The Museo Civico is located in the main street, in the Palazzo.

Civic Museum (Museo Civico)

Location: Via Aggiunti 65
Contact details: Tel. 057 5732218
Opening hours: 9:30 am–1:00 pm, 3:30 pm–6:30 pm daily
Admission: About Euro 5

Piero della Francesca
Resurrection, 1464

An imposing Christ has planted his foot firmly on the rim of his sepulcher and prepares to lift himself out of his tomb and step forward into the world. He holds aloft a banner carrying the sign of the cross: Christ is risen! Behind him, the sun is also rising, tinting his cloak with its rose-colored rays. There are other signs of renewal: the trees on the viewer's left are bare, but on the right of the picture, they have sprung into luxuriant growth. The risen Christ is a metaphor of spring. Below the sepulcher, the guards are asleep, their bodies leaning back, as someone has said, "like the four quarters of an orange." The figure, second from the viewer's left, leaning his head against the tomb, may be a self-portrait of the painter. It was of course no accident that the city fathers of Sansepolcro – so named because the city claimed to hold the sacred relics of the Holy Sepulcher – commissioned this fresco.

The altarpiece below is shown in the diagram.

Piero della Francesca
Madonna della Misericordia, 1444–64

The *Madonna della Misericordia* occupies the central panel of a multi-panelled altar piece (a polyptych). In the panel above her, she is pictured as the grieving mother of the crucified Christ, accompanied in her grief by a distraught St John. (Observe the dramatic gestures of these two figures.) As *Madonna della Misericordia*, she is surrounded by a bevy of saints. The merciful mother is a monumental – and unforgettable – figure. Protectively, she holds out her vast cape, offering to enclose her followers. Interestingly, Piero, the painter/mathematician, has drawn the prayerful figures on a much smaller scale than that of the Virgin. This work of great mystic power took 17 years to complete. The scenes in the predella were painted by the Florentine, Giuliano Amidei.

Piero della Francesca
Saints Julian and Ludovic, 1454–58

These frescoes were discovered under layers of plaster as recently as the 1950s. The golden-haired young man of the huge eyes and troubled expression is St Julian, the Crusader, dressed, not in the armor of the religious knight, but as the elegant man-about-town.

St Ludovic, dressed as a bishop, may be a likeness of Ludovico Acciaioli, governor of Sansepolcro in 1460.

Cortona

Cortona is about 25 miles southwest of Sansepolcro. It is one of the oldest hilltowns in Tuscany and was the hometown of Luca Signorelli, a Renaissance painter much admired by his peers, and especially by Raphael. The Diocesan Museum is in the northwestern corner of the old town.

Diocesan Museum (Museo Diocesano)

Location: Piazza del Duomo 1

Contact details: Tel. 057 562800

Opening hours: 9:30 am–1:00 pm, 3:00 pm–6:30 pm, Tues.-Sun.

Admission: About Euro 4

Fra Angelico
Annunciation, 1432–34

The *Cortona Annunciation*, Fra Angelico's first undoubted masterpiece, is regarded as one of the great achievements of Florentine painting. The scene takes place in a gracefully arcaded loggia, bordered by Corinthian columns. The Archangel Gabriel leans earnestly towards the Virgin, speaking the words (from St Luke's Gospel) that are engraved on the painting: "The Holy Ghost shall come upon thee, and the power of the Highest shall overshadow thee." And Mary replies, "Behold the handmaid of the Lord; be it unto me according to thy word." When our eyes follow the perspective of the exterior of the building, we discover, in the top left corner of the picture, Adam and Eve being expelled from Eden. The scene in the loggia is bathed in a gorgeous golden light that illuminates the haloes of the Virgin and the saint and irradiates their rose and carmine garments. Best of all are the angels' wings: their graceful sweep slices across the strong vertical lines of the pillars, and their iridescent hues shimmer in the afternoon light.

You may wish to compare Fra Angelico's *Linaiuoli Adoration* in Florence with his rendition on the predella under the wonderful *Annunciation*, above.

Fra Angelico
Adoration of the Magi (Predella of the Annunciation), 1432–34

The composition of the *Linaiuoli Adoration* and this one have many similarities: in both paintings, the Holy Family, instead of occupying the center of the painting, is off to the right. Joseph engages in conversation with one of the Magi, and the identically costumed second Magi have removed their noble headgear to prostrate themselves at the feet of the Holy Infant. In contrast to the circular arrangement of the royal visitors in the *Linaiuoli*, the Cortona royal retinue approach from the left. The city walls behind the Cortona manger are more forbidding, having been built on a huge, barren rock. The jewel-like colors of Fra Angelico's palette are evident in both paintings, though somewhat more faded in the *Linaiuoli*.

Fra Angelico
Virgin and Child Enthroned with Saints, 1432–34

This is a beautiful polyptych (multi-panelled altarpiece) with Gothic pointed panels that frame images of the Madonna and Child and saints. The two St Johns are on the left panel: the Evangelist has quill in hand, and a stiff-looking John the Baptist carries a banderole with the words, "Behold the Lamb of God." On the right is a figure thought to be St Mark (with his own gospel and quill), and Mary Magdalene, possibly carrying the unguents with which she anointed the body of the dead Christ. The pinnacles of the outer arches carry an Annunciation, and, at the apex of the central panel is a Crucifixion.

Perugia

About 30 miles southeast of Cortona is the great Umbrian cultural center of Perugia. One of Perugia's most famous sons was the painter Perugino, pupil of Piero, friend and colleague of Botticelli and master of Raphael. Unsurprisingly, Perugino is well represented in the works of the National Gallery of Umbria. As part of the Palazzo dei Priori, the Museum is located in the main Piazza of Perugia.

Palazzo dei Priori

National Gallery of Umbria (Galleria Nazionale dell'Umbria)

Location: Palazzo dei Priori, Corso Vanucci 19
Contact details: Tel. 075 5741247
Opening hours: 9:00 am–7:00 pm Mon.–Sat., 9:00 am–10:00 pm Sun., closed first Mon. of each month.
Admission: About Euro 4

Fra Angelico
Virgin and Child Enthroned with Saints Dominic and Nicholas of Bari, 1437

These are the now-unframed panels of a polyptych originally painted for the chapel of St Nicholas in the Church of San Domenico in Perugia. A gentle-faced Virgin and her pale-bodied Child sit in a red-vaulted aedicule, attended by angels, their full-length, bird-feathered wings at rest. In a daring departure from custom, Fra Angelico has angled the lower body of the Virgin away from the viewer and allowed her right knee to occupy center-stage. In the left panel are the realistically rounded and flowing images of Sts Dominic and Nicholas of Bari.

Piero della Francesca
Polyptych of Saint Anthony (Polittico di Sant'Antonio), 1460–70

This very ornate polyptych is a symphony of religious feeling, fabulous decoration, splendid architecture, precise mathematical perspective, and artistic experimentation. Begin with the pediment, which contains a delicate Annunciation that threatens to be overshadowed by a fascinating, disappearing colonnade, a garden, and the Holy Spirit radiating from a clear blue sky. Yet this is no mere exercise in perspective: the respectful attitude of the angel and the submissive demeanor of the Virgin are sublime; as is Piero's attention to the play of light and shadow on the columns and floor. Moving to the central tier, you see the Madonna and Child (with intriguing, eliptical haloes) seated on an elaborate marble throne under a vault with rose-decorated coffers. The two central figures are flanked by four saints: on the left of the viewer, a stocky St Anthony of Padua and a weather-worn John the Baptist, and on the right, St Francis, showing the stigmata on his hands, and St Elizabeth of Hungary, carrying her the roses which miraculously

Legend:
1. Madonna and Child
2. St Anthony of Padua
3. St John the Baptist
4. St Francis of Assisi
5. St Elizabeth of
   Thuringia (with bread
   turned into roses)
6. Archangel
   Gabriel

7. Virgin Annunciate
8. St Clare of Assisi
9. St Agatha (carrying her
   breasts on a plate)
10. The miracle of St Anthony
11. The stigmatization of
    St Francis
12. The miracle of
    St Elizabeth

Polyptych of Saint Anthony: *Piero's work straddles the Gothic (the traditional form of the polyptych) and the Renaissance (the modern predella and the adventurous use of perspective in the upper panel).*

disguised the bread she illegally distributed to the poor. The two tondos just above the predella contain depictions of St Clare, who founded an order of nuns with a similar mission to that of the Franciscans; and St Agatha, carrying on a plate her breasts that were sliced off by the Romans. The pictures on the lowest level depict three miracles. On the left of the viewer, St Anthony cures a sick child. On the right, St Elizabeth rescues a child who has fallen down a well. But in the middle is St Francis receiving the stigmata. This is one of the few night paintings of the early Renaissance, and one which is punctuated by the sudden appearance of the crucified Christ, startlingly clothed in red, piercing the darkness like an angel of light.

Just over 10 miles southeast of Perugia is the great Christian center of Assisi, where St Francis is buried.

Assisi

This is the major stop on this Trail. The spirit of religiosity, which is everywhere, resembles that of Lourdes, but the Basilica of St Francis contains some of the most important works of 14th-century Italian art.

Basilica of St Francis
(Basilica di San Francesco)

Location: Although it is way on the northwestern end of town, the massive pile that is the Basilica is hard to miss.
Contact details: Tel. 075 813337

As you enter the church, do not be confused by one seeming anomaly: the obvious place to start is the Lower Basilica, through the main entrance. And yet the earliest works by Giotto are not there, but upstairs in the Upper Basilica. The reason is this: when the church was first constructed around 1230, the Lower Basilica was little more than a giant crypt, containing as it did the tomb of the saint. The Upper Basilica was initially the main church and it was here that the work of the most important artists, including the young Giotto, was first concentrated. It was only in the early 14th century that the Lower Basilica came into prominence, as a result of its having become the chief

FLORENCE TO ROME

Assisi

magnet for steadily increasing numbers of pilgrims. It was then that the Lower Basilica was modified so as to become the first point of entry for visitors and, once this had happened, the focus for artistic adornment by the likes of the older Giotto as well.

Giotto's earliest intensive work is here. On the walls of the nave of the Upper Church (Superiore) of the Basilica di San Francesco, he and other painters executed a series of frescoes depicting 28 stories of St Francis, as well as various scenes from the Old and New Testaments. The work was apparently begun around 1290, when Giotto was about 25 years old. There is continuing dispute about Giotto's authorship of this work, but the realism, the didactic style, the emotional force, and the fundamental humanity are very Giottoesque. The general consensus these days is that he was actively involved, but often with assistance. The diagram will help you follow the cycle.

In the Lower Church (Basilica Inferiore), you will find frescoes depicting, among other things, the Annunciation, two post-mortem miracles of St Francis, stories from the infancy and youth of Christ, a Crucifixion with Franciscans in attendance and more anguished flying angels. You will also find St Francis in glory; and the allegories of obedience, chastity and poverty.

The apse of the basilica, once denied to ordinary citizens, contains marvellous examples of the work of the Florentine painter, Cimabue (Cenni di Pepi, active between 1272 and 1302) who is often described as the teacher of Giotto. His famous wind-blown Crucifixion is there, as well as *Scenes from the Life of the Virgin*.

In the vault above your head as you enter the Upper Basilica is:

Giotto
Vault of the Doctors of the Church, mid 1290s

The four doctors – Sts Ambrose, Augustine, Gregory and Jerome – are here displayed in the most scholarly of modes, each dictating to his scribe. Most critics find St Gregory – the one furthest from the entrance – to be the one of greatest interest, for his portrait is one of an obviously aging man – an early indication of Giotto's characteristic striving for realism.

Giotto
The Legend of St Francis mid 1290s

These 28 fresco panels that cover the lower part of the nave present episodes in the story of St Francis. The episodes are more or less in the order presented in St Bonaventura's 13th-century Latin text, *Legenda Maior (Major Life of St Francis)*, which he prepared for devotional use. We have paraphrased Bonaventura in providing a brief description of each of the 28 episodes. They begin on the far right as you enter and proceed in a clockwise direction, ending on the far left (see diagram). The scenes are:

1. St Francis Honored by a Simple Man: In this first scene from the Franciscan cycle: a man from Assisi spreads his cloak on the ground in front of the Blessed Francis as a mark of respect, believing that one who is performing great works through divine inspiration should be honored by all. Behind his prostrate form stand two onlookers, barely disguising their skepticism. The symmetry of the picture is striking, the two medieval buildings and empty loggia providing a geometrically balanced yet pleasing context for the realistically rounded figures in the foreground.

2. St Francis' Gift of his Mantle to a Poor Knight: When Francis came across a man of noble birth who had fallen on hard times, he gave him his cloak. In this way, he helped relieve poverty and

Diagram of Giotto's **Cycle of the Legend of St Francis,** *Upper Basilica.* **The numbers below match the numbering in the text.**

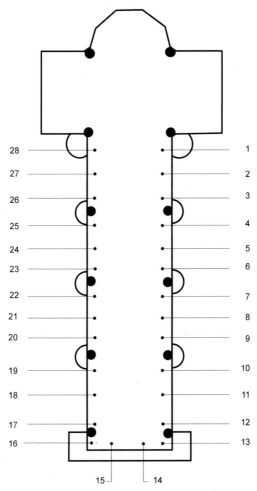

saved a nobleman from embarrassment. This is depicted in a rural setting, but not far from the towns nearby.

3. The Vision of the Palace Filled with Weapons: The following night as Francis slept, God showed him a vision of the reward he was to receive for his kindness to the nobleman – this magnificent palace!

4. The Prayer in Front of the Cross in San Damiano: This is a critical moment in the life of Francis. Having entered the near-derelict Church of San Damiano to pray, he heard the voice of Christ himself, ordering him to repair the church. This was the effective beginning of Francis' mission in life.

5. St Francis Renounces his Father's Inheritance: In his enthusiasm to renounce all that he was to inherit from his (very unimpressed) father, Francis shed all his clothes before his bishop. Out of compassion, the bishop covered him with the rough tunic of a peasant, thus creating the garb that henceforth was to be worn by Francis and his followers. This is one of the most famous frescoes in the series, because of the variety of emotions that it conveys.

6. The Dream of Innocent III: When Francis decided to seek papal recognition (a Rule) for the order he was bent on establishing, he went to Rome to wait upon Pope Innocent III. When the pope met the modestly attired Francis, he was reminded of one of his recent dreams, when he had seen a poor man holding up a tottering Lateran Basilica. He quickly came to the conclusion that the man in his dream had been Francis.

7. The Confirmation of the Rule: Although several of his cardinals had reservations about the Rule requested by Francis, the pope's dream had tilted the balance of considerations in favor of Francis, and he was granted his request.

8. The Vision of St Francis Borne on a Fiery Chariot: One night when Francis was praying, the Lord sent a fiery chariot of extraordinary brilliance to bring Francis to him. When Francis' followers saw this, they were confirmed in their resolve to accept the disciplines he imposed. This is probably as famous a set of images as Giotto created, and often features on the covers of books devoted to his art.

9. The Vision of the Throne Reserved for St Francis in Heaven: One night, a friar who had entered a deserted church to pray with Francis was granted a vision. He saw an array of heavenly thrones, among which one was outstanding in its place and adornment. The friar was then told that this throne, which had once belonged to an angel who had made the mistake of following Lucifer, was now being held for Francis.

10. The Expulsion of the Devils from the City of Arezzo: One occasion when Francis was visiting the fine city of Arezzo in southern Tuscany (soon to be famous as the birthplace of Petrarch), he found it in a terrible state of civic strife, stirred up by a horde of

Giotto's **The Expulsion of the Devils from the City of Arezzo**

devils. Francis instructed Brother Silvester to approach the town and order the devils to leave. Some of the Arezzo skyline here represented is still in place eight centuries later.

11. The Ordeal of Fire Before the Sultan of Egypt: Longing for martyrdom or glory, Francis travelled to the Middle East, seeking to convert the population to Christianity. He was seized and taken before the Sultan. Francis made him an offer: consign him to the flames, and if he emerged unscathed, agree to convert, together with his population. The Sultan did not accept this challenge.

12. St Francis in Ecstasy: When Francis was alone with Jesus, his followers would see him enveloped in a brilliant, supernatural light, the outward sign of the inner light that flooded his soul.

13. The Crib at Greccio: Three years before his death, Francis decided to celebrate Christmas with a crib re-enactment (which was something of an innovation in those days). One of those present, a knight of Greccio, later claimed to have seen Francis take the Infant from the crib and awaken it.

The next two frescoes are on either side of the entrance.

14. The Miracle of The Water Which Gushed from the Rock: Travelling to a hermitage, Francis felt weak and borrowed an ass from a poor peasant. It was a hot day, and the peasant who was walking along behind his ass begged Francis to get him a drink. After a brief prayer, Francis sent the peasant to a nearby rock, where he was able to slake his thirst.

15. The Preaching to the Birds: Near Bevagna, Francis saw a flock of birds and, in one of the best-known episodes in his life, preached to them to great apparent effect. Afterwards, he reproached himself for not having done so before.

16. The Death of the Knight of Celano: Once when Francis was visiting Celano, a village about halfway between Rome and Pescara, he was invited to dine with the local knight. Francis repaid this kindness by warning the knight to seek immediate absolution for his sins, for the Lord was about to call him. The knight did so, which was just as well, for in the middle of dinner he fell dead.

17. St Francis Preaching before Honorius III: On one occasion, Francis was to deliver a sermon to the pope and his cardinals. However, when the moment arrived, his mind went blank. He came clean with his distinguished audience, but the Lord then came to his rescue and gave him inspired words to deliver with the utmost eloquence.

18. St Francis Appears to the Chapter in Arles: As his order grew, Francis found it difficult to visit all his fellow friars. On this famous occasion, a congregation listening to St Anthony delivering a sermon in far-away Provence saw Francis standing in mid-air in the doorway, bestowing a blessing on them

19. St Francis Receiving the Stigmata: Two years before his death, Francis ascended a high mountain to pray and fast. There he had a vision of Christ crucified, and when the vision faded, he realised that he had been blessed with the same wounds – the stigmata – that had been inflicted on the crucified Jesus. This fresco may be the closest rival to that of the *Fiery Chariot* to serve as the single most recognizable stamp of Giotto.

20. The Death and Ascension of St Francis: Francis died surrounded by his brothers. One of them saw his soul ascending, borne on a white cloud, to heaven. In this fresco, both the body of Francis in the world below, and his soul in heaven above, are shown.

21. The Vision of the Ascension of St Francis: Here, the friar who has witnessed the ascension of Francis gives his account of it to his fellows.

22. The Verification of the Stigmata: After the death of Francis, a great crowd of local people assembled. Among them was a doubting Thomas – a reputable knight called Jerome – who was permitted to examine for himself the stigmata on Francis' body.

23. St Clare Taking Leave of the Remains of St Francis in San Damiano: As the body of Francis was being taken to the church of San Giorgio for his funeral, the cortège stopped at the church of San Damiano to enable Sister Clare and her fellow nuns to kiss the body. Modern feminists have shown a keen interest in Clare, the distaff side of Francis, who founded the Order of the Poor Clares.

24. The Canonization of St Francis: The pope was so convinced of the saintliness of Francis that he fast-tracked the process of his canonization, so that it occurred inside two years – no doubt, something of a record.

25. The Appearance to Pope Gregory IX: The new Pope Gregory was another doubting Thomas who remained skeptical about the claim that Francis had gained the stigmata. He was finally convinced when Francis appeared to him in a dream, showing him a glass full of the blood that was streaming from his side.

26. The Healing of a Devotee of the Saint: In Catalonia, a man called John was attacked and severely wounded by footpads (a Renaissance term for a person who robs on foot). He continually called for the aid of Francis, and when he was near death, the saint appeared and healed him.

27. The Confession of a Woman Raised from the Dead: A devotee of Francis had died with a terrible sin unconfessed. Thanks to the intervention of Francis, she was brought back to life to allow her the opportunity to confess her sin. Once she had done that, she died, happy in the knowledge that her soul would now go to heaven.

28. The Liberation of the Repentant Heretic: A man who had been incarcerated at Tivoli for heresy prayed to Francis and was rewarded when the saint came to him in his cell and struck off his chains.

Now descend to the Lower Basilica. The decorative program here differs from the Upper Basilica, for the works here are not concerned with the life of St Francis, but rather with his role and that of his Order in the progress of humanity towards salvation.

Giotto
Four Allegories in the Crossing Vault, 1316–19

Many critics hold this to be one of Giotto's most impressive works. In the quarter of the vault immediately above the high altar is St Francis, surrounded by angels in his heavenly glory. In the other three quarters are representations of the three cardinal virtues of the Franciscan Order – Poverty, Obedience, and Chastity. Of this trio, the first, which portrays Poverty as a gaunt woman to whom Christ is marrying Francis, is the most striking.

On your left as you turn back from the altar to face the entrance (ie in the north transept) is a series of scenes from Christ's childhood:

Giotto
Scenes from the Life of the Holy Family, c.1315

The scenes portrayed in this series are: the *Annunciation*; the *Visitation*; the *Nativity*; the *Adoration of the Magi*; the *Presentation in the Temple*; the *Massacre of the Innocents*; the *Flight into Egypt*; the *Young Jesus Disputing with the Doctors*; and the *Return of the Young Jesus to Nazareth*. There is also a sublime *Crucifixion*, and a representation of one of Francis' miracles: the *Death and the Raising of the Boy in Sessa*.

On the opposite side of the apse (ie the southern side, the same as the entrance) are two chapels with superb frescoes by the Sienese painters, Pietro Lorenzetti (south transept) and Simone Martini (the Chapel of St Martin). Turning back towards the entrance, the Chapel of Mary Magdalene is on your left, about half way between the altar and the entrance to the crypt containing the tomb of St Francis. Within it you'll find:

Giotto
Scenes from the Life of St Mary Magdalene, c.1310

There is no attempt at ordering chronologically the six episodes from the life of the saint. On the wall closest to the main altar are *Christ and the Magdalene in the House of the Pharisee*; the *Raising of Lazarus*; and (in a lunette) the *Magdalene Receiving Holy Communion*. On the wall facing are *Noli Mi Tangere*, the *Magdalene's Voyage to Marseilles*; and (again in a tondo), the *Magdalene in Ecstasy*. Among the other figures in the chapel, the most noteworthy are the four tondi on the ceiling, with busts of Christ, the Magdalene, Lazarus and Martha.

FLORENCE TO ROME

Giotto
Adorazione dei Magi, 1319

No stable for this Madonna! Instead, flanked by two angels, she sits in state to receive her kingly guests in an aedicule under a narrow, vaulted loggia. The Child seated on her knee bends to bestow a blessing on the white-haired dignitary who kneels before him and his mother.

Before you leave, look for the other five stories from the infancy of Christ – especially the heart-rending *Slaughter of the Innocents*, in which the mothers' screams of despair are almost audible. One woman, her dead and bleeding baby in her lap, has fainted at the sheer horror of the scene. You may care to compare this version with that in the Scrovegni Chapel, where the scene of the women trying to resist having their babies torn from their arms conveys the same mood of helplessness in the face of terror.

Spoleto

About 40 miles to the south is another major cultural center – Spoleto. Its most famous favorite son is an adopted one – the Florentine Filippo Lippi, a painter who came there to paint what turned out to be his last work, and who is buried in the cathedral which houses it.

Cathedral of the Assumption (Cattedrale di Santa Maria dell Assunta)

Location: Piazza del Duomo

After entering the cathedral, go to the apse, where you will find all the works covered below. The *Coronation*, almost psychedelic in its (doubtless restored) splendor, fills the semi-dome of the apse. On the walls of the hemicycle below are pictured the other highlights at each end of the life of Mary: the Annunciation, the Nativity, the Adoration of the Shepherds, the Dormition, and the elevation of Mary's body into heaven. Filippo's paintings of these scenes trace the life cycle of Mary, the chosen theme for the church.

Fra Filippo Lippi
Coronation of the Virgin, 1466–69

Painted at the end of Fra Filippo's career, the *Spoleto Coronation* is a wonder of design and a triumph over the constraints of the semi-circular space in which he worked. In a splendid cloak embroidered with gold motifs, Mary kneels devoutly before a white-bearded God to receive her crown. Behind them bursts forth a riot of golden light from a flaming, stylized sun and moon. A bejeweled rainbow of dazzling hues and its mirror image beneath their feet frame the two central figures with a circle of vibrant color. On either side, angels of great beauty sing and dance and, with other biblical figures, prophets, saints and sibylls, react to the scene with a variety of very human responses – curiosity, wonderment, reverence, happiness. This celestial party dwarfs the tips of earthly mountains, below.

Fra Filippo Lippi
Annunciation, 1466–69

To modern eyes, the Spoleto murals look psychedelic – a quality which had its origins in the mosaics of the Byzantine period. Spoleto was a papal town and Lippi had come to work in the sister church to that of Rome's Santa Maria Maggiore, which possessed splendid mosaics. While evoking the spirit of these mosaics, Lippi demonstrates his genius in depicting the varieties of human expressiveness. From his celestial realm, God the Father ensures the impregnation of the Virgin through the mediation of the (now faded) Holy Spirit. For her part, the Virgin seems assured of her role in all this. The *Spoleto Annunciation* has all of the Fra Filippo *ornazio* trademarks: elaborate (in this case, almost overbearing) architecture, decorative detail (especially in the *cosmati* floor) and a distant, disappearing garden.

Fra Filippo Lippi
Nativity and Adoration of the Shepherds, 1466–69

The *Spoleto Nativity* contains all the iconography of the nativity theme but in a delicately colored and symmetrical arrangement. The architecture of the stable frames the figures and the animals, but without dominating them. This is because their scale is appropriate for the buildings: the use of linear perspective and foreshortening also contributes to the naturalistic aura of the painting. The solemn grace of the figures is striking, their essential dignity projecting through an otherwise fairly standard treatment of this popular theme

Fra Filippo Lippi
Dormition and Assumption of the Virgin, 1466–69

Against a lush Renaissance landscape whose steeply climbing paths seem to link earth and heaven – a favorite theme of Lippi late in his career – the body of the Virgin lies on a bier, surrounded by apostles and praying mourners. At the foot of the bier, an angel carries a taper, part of the ritual for the dying. Some of the figures seem uncharacteristically static, such as the red-capped man standing to the right of the black-hatted man, believed to be Lippi himself.

After leaving Spoleto, you may wish to visit two towns. Fifteen miles to the southwest is **Narni**. There you may wish to visit the Town Hall (Palazzo Communale) which contains a splendid work by Ghirlandaio: his *Coronation of the Virgin*, 1484–86, in which an ornately cloaked Madonna receives her crown from her son while a golden sunburst erupts in the background.

About 40 miles to the northwest is the last stop before Rome – the superb hilltown of **Orvieto.** If you come to it by train – it is on the main Florence-Rome line – you will have the unusual experience of taking a funicular railcar up to the main town.

There, in the Duomo, is Luca Signorelli's masterpiece – a Last Judgment cycle in the same Cappella di San Brizio, which houses some earlier Angelico frescoes. In 1447, Pope Nicholas V, the great humanist scholar, was elected successor to Eugenius IV. Fra Angelico was invited to spend the summer months of that year in Orvieto, decorating the Cappella di San Brizio within this cathedral. Art critics consider the quality of the ceiling pictures to be uneven – possibly the result of the studio assistance the painter received in order to meet the very tight deadline of 14 weeks! The best of the works is *Majesty with Angels and Sixteen Prophets.*

This last stop before Rome – only 60 miles to the south – is an appropriate one, for Angelico is himself buried in Rome, no more than a couple of hundred yards from Raphael.

FLORENCE TO ROME

Orvieto

TRAIL 5:
Rome to Venice

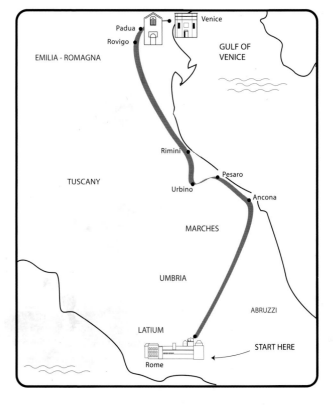

This Trail is a little over 250 miles in length. From Rome, it proceeds in a northeasterly direction for about 125 miles – until it reaches the major Adriatic port of Ancona. It then proceeds in a generally northwesterly direction for another 125 miles. Four painters are most prominent on this Trail: the Venetians,

Giovanni Bellini, and Titian, who had worked down the Adriatic coast, the local Piero della Francesco in the middle, and – most spectacularly of all – Giotto, in Padua. It makes a pleasant and not very demanding drive, but can also be easily accomplished by rail.

The first stop is about 125 miles northeast to the coast: the major port of Ancona, capital of Le Marche.

Ancona

If you stop off here, be sure to establish the whereabouts of *Christ on the Cross with Saints*. This hung for centuries in the Church of San Domenico but in recent years has been on display in the Civic Museum. The parish priest to whom we spoke was of the view that the painting would soon be returning to the church – a view not shared by the attendant at the Civic Museum! We have included it in our coverage of the Civic Museum.

Civic Gallery (Pinacoteca Civica)

Location: F. Podesti Palazzo Posdari, Via Pizzecolli 17
Contact details: Tel. 071 2225041
Opening hours: 9:00 am–7:00 pm Tues.–Fri. 8:30 am–6:30 pm Sat.,
3:00 pm–7:00 pm Sun., 9:00 am–1:00 pm Mon.
Admission: Euro 4

Titian
Madonna with Saints, 1520

This is a particularly charming Madonna. She sits on a cloud, restraining her very mobile infant, embraced by an angel – wings outstretched – and entertained by two tambourine-playing cherubim. The balance of the composition is enhanced by the open vista reaching back to St Mark's Square, where the campanile and the Doge's Palace are beginning to reflect the sun's golden glow. This is another of Titian's symphonies of light, color and movement, amply justifying his reputation as the supreme colorist. Although it might seem strange for Titian to have emphasized Venice in a painting for an Ancona client, it is possible that this was intended to bring out the shared Adriatic identity of the two cities.

Titian
Christ on the Cross with Saints, c.1560

The mood of profound anguish which pervades this dark work makes it one of the masterpieces of the old Titian. The funereal nun-like garb and disconsolate posture of Mary heightens this dark mood. At the foot of the cross, St Dominic has collapsed, wrapping his arms around it in a gesture of deepest despair. Titian has come to paint purely with color. The rich sky is streaked with dark ochres, burgundy and blue, with highlights of white cloud. So completely does this livid sky fill the background that it almost seems that the crucified Christ has already commenced his ascension into Heaven.

A further 40 miles up the Adriatic coast is the smaller, stylish resort town of Pesaro, birthplace of the composer Gioacchino Rossini. Rossini was a considerable collector and bequeathed many of his paintings – including *Eternal Blessing* – to the Civic Museum.

Pesaro

The Civic Museum is just off the main square.

Civic Museum (Museo Civici)

Location: Via Pizzacolli 17
Contact details: Tel. 290 7213 87541
Opening hours: 9:30 am–12:30 pm, 5:00 pm–8:00 pm Wed., Fri.–Sun., 9:30 am–12:30 pm, 5:00 pm–11:00 pm Tues., Thurs., closed Mon.
Admission: About Euro 3

Bellini
Pesaro Altarpiece (Pala di Pesaro; Pesaro Coronation of the Virgin), c.1475

This altarpiece, which once graced the Church of St Francesco in Pesaro, is probably Giovanni Bellini's first major work in oils. The light and color of the work suggest that the artist greatly enjoyed discovering the enhanced flexibility that the new medium could offer him. The central panel depicts a curiously subdued *Coronation of Mary* in the company of just four saints: Peter and Paul, the pillars of the church, on the left of the picture, and the confessor saints, Jerome and Francis, on the right. In this

Bellini's Pesaro Altarpiece

Coronation, there are no rejoicing choirs or angel-musicians: an air
of solemnity, even sadness, pervades the picture. Even the flying
cherubim are serious. In the central panel, Christ and his mother sit
on an elaborately carved, two-seater throne of white marble inlaid
with geometric shapes of brown, beige and terra cotta. The back of
the throne is actually a large, free-standing structure comprising
two pilasters and a lintel which frame the heads of the Virgin and
Christ, as well as the distant, fortified castle behind them. The

1. Pietà (now in the Vatican)
2. St Catherine
3. St Lawrence
4. St Anthony of Padua
5. St John the Baptist
6. St George and the Dragon
7. Conversion of St Paul
8. Crucifixion of St Peter
9. Nativity
10. St Jerome in the Desert
11. Stigmatization of St Francis
12. St Terentius, Patron of Pesaro
13. St Andrew
14. St Louis of Toulouse
15. St Bernadino of Siena
16. Blessed Michalina

Plan of the Bellini altarpiece in the Pesaro Civic Museum.

window in the marble frame is a reference to Mary as the "Window of Heaven," and the castle that we see through the window is the Heavenly Jerusalem – the Kingdom of God the Father.

Giovanni Bellini
Eternal Blessing, 1505–10

This panel may have been the upper section of a larger painting – perhaps of the Baptism of Christ – that has been lost. God emerges from the clouds, arms outstretched, conferring an eternal blessing on humanity.

Giovanni Bellini
Head of the Baptist, 1464–68

This gory little tondo depicts the decapitated head of John the Baptist.

Giovanni Bellini?
Crucifixion, 1464–68

This rather mannered rendition of the Crucifixion was, for a while, attributed to Bellini, but modern scholarship has cast severe doubts on this.

At this point, you must decide whether to take a detour inland to see more of the work of Piero della Francesca. If you have liked what you have seen in Florence and Arezzo, you should head inland for about 12 miles to the town of Urbino.

Urbino

The provincial center of Urbino was the birthplace of Raphael. The most famous ruler of Urbino, who died just before the birth of Raphael, was Federico da Montefeltro. Piero's portraits of him and of his wife hang in the Uffizi in Florence (see Trail 1).

The National Gallery is housed in the Ducal Palace (Palazzo Ducale) in the center of town.

National Gallery of the Marches
(Galleria Nazionale delle Marche)

Location: Piazza Duca Federico 3
Contact details: Tel. 072 22760
Opening hours: 9:00 am–7:00 pm daily
Admission: About Euro 3

The most famous room in the Palace is the Duke's Study, at the northwestern corner of the First Floor. This room is famous for its superb works of inlaid wood, some of which may have been designed by Botticelli. However, it is not the paintings in the study that have drawn us here. Down one corridor, in the Guest Apartment, is:

Palazzo Ducale

Giovanni Bellini
Sacra Conversazione (*Madonna with Blessing Child, Saints John the Baptist and Anna*), 1490

Scholars can't agree on whether this picture is actually the work of Bellini, though it closely resembles the more famous Frankfurt work, which was signed by the painter. (Scholars can't even agree on whether the figure on the right is St Anne, the mother of Mary, or her cousin, Elizabeth, the mother of John the Baptist!)

Even closer to the Duke's Study, in the Audience Chamber, are the two paintings most treasured by the Gallery:

Piero della Francesca
Flagellation, c.1470

This mysterious little picture has been called the finest small picture ever painted. It has everything – a dramatic subject; an adventurous use of perspective; beautiful architecture; decorative fabric; light emanating from several sources; a sun-filled blue sky. But such enigmatic figures! The main scene – after which the picture is named – is occurring in the background, and we can easily understand it – can't we? Christ is on the point of being scourged. But who is the figure in the Turkish hat, with his hands conspicuously flopping into his lap? Most think he is Pontius Pilate, dressed in the Byzantine costume of the Eastern Emperor, Mohammed II – possibly a reminder of the capture of Constantinople in 1453 by the Moslems. As if to drive home the point, the figure watching the torture scene with his back to the viewer is also in Moslem dress. But those three figures in the foreground – who are they? One of the enjoyable things to do with Italian Renaissance art is to collect the many different interpretations of this part of the *Flagellation*. Perhaps the three men are high priests who are refusing to enter the loggia as a protest at what is going on inside? Perhaps this is the apparently civilized discussion of prominent citizens turning their heads away from a central political fact – which is that all governments ultimately rest on violence? Perhaps the Greek dignitary on the left and the brocaded European figure on the right are meant to signify the meeting of the eastern and western religious traditions? Who is the middle figure? Is he Oddantonio, the younger brother of Piero's sponsor, Federico da Montefeltro, who'd been killed 30 years previously during a popular uprising? But note his similarity with the figure of Christ: is he then an angel? These are some of the possible ways you can interpret this fascinating picture.

Piero della Francesca
Madonna di Senigallia, 1470–85

This picture reveals that Piero was very much influenced by the Flemish painters and their depictions of realistic figures inside very detailed interiors. It is the most intimate of all his treatments of the theme of the Madonna. Piero has placed the Madonna in a domestic setting: she may almost have just picked up the baby from his afternoon nap in the bedroom behind – now with sunlight filtering through the shutters. Her attendants seem less like angels and more like neighbors who've popped in to see the baby. Only the child, wearing the coral necklace that symbolizes his coming passion, and with his characteristic gesticulation, reminds us that this is, after all, a religious picture.

Ghirlandaio
Virgin and Child and a Donor, c.1470

This wooden panel has been badly treated in its past life so that by now, the folds of the Madonna's robes are no longer visible. The figure of the donor has even been cut off the picture, leaving only his hands behind – a fact that would probably make him turn in his grave, given that he paid for the painting! What is still clearly visible, though, is the peaceful expression on the Virgin's face under her intricate veil, and the somewhat uncertain, sideways gaze of her infant son, who already wears a rosary – and crucifix – around his neck.

Further along the corridor, in the Duchess' Salon, are a further three significant works: a Raphael and two Titians. There is also an earlier Raphael: a picture of St Catherine of Alexandra standing on the wheel of her martyrdom – from which she was delivered by angels. The two Titians are closely related, and so are described in one entry:

Raphael
La Muta 1505–07

This portrait ("of a Gentlewoman") is often regarded as Raphael's own *La Gioconda*. Like Mona Lisa, she has a silent (*muta*) demeanor, but she lacks the enigmatic, half-smile of amusement captured by Leonardo.

Titian
Last Supper, 1542–44
Resurrection, 1542–44

These two small paintings were the two sides of a processional banner and present two of the high points of the final phase of Christ's time on earth. In the *Last Supper*, Titian emphasizes the sacramental rather than the dramatic dimension earlier made popular by Leonardo. This emphasis was in conformity with the spirit of the Counter-Reformation, so the Titian treatment became increasingly common in the succeeding century. As a composition, this may well have been the first painting to solve the design problem caused by the traditional lining up of the participants along a horizontally aligned table by placing the table diagonally across the picture. Later, Tintoretto was to adopt the same solution in his Lucca treatment of the theme. (Could the younger painter have picked this up during his ten-day apprenticeship with Titian?) In the *Resurrection*, Titian appears once again to have borrowed heavily from a Raphael masterpiece – in this case, the famous *Transfiguration*.

About 60 miles back east to the coast lies the largest beach resort in Europe – Rimini.

Rimini

Although its well-organized tourist industry is strongly focused on the city's favorite son, Federico Fellini, the city also boasts an intriguing ancient cultural center, the Tempio Malatestiano. Condemned by a pope as a temple of devil worshippers, this museum houses some fine religious paintings alongside Piero's sycophantic treatment of one of his patrons.

The Malatesta Temple (Tempio Malatestiano)

Location: Via IV Novembre
Admission: Modest

ROME TO VENICE

Giotto
Crocifisso, c.1310

Some regard this as Giotto's finest crucifix, a masterpiece produced several years after the one he made for Santa Maria Novella. Giotto's entire artistic life was a continuing quest to represent God in visual, human terms. Here, in the *Rimini Crucifix*, he has achieved his aim – perhaps more comprehensively than in any other work: the figure of Christ has even been compared to a statue of the golden age of Greece. The work reveals Giotto's fully developed mastery of chiaroscuro: a mellow light falls on the dying God-man, turning his hair to gold and causing his body to emerge, in high relief, from its flatter surrounds. His clenched hands indicate that his life has not yet finally ebbed away, but that the end is near.

Piero della Francesca
Malatesta and St Sigismund, 1451

This fresco had an explicit political purpose – to emphasize the legitimacy of Malatesta rule in Rimini. Even the relationship between Sigismund Malatesta and his patron saint was political: the figure representing the saint is in fact the Holy Roman Emperor who in feudal times had granted the Malatesta family their rule. In the space to the right are more political symbols. The fortress seen through the round window on the right represents the military might of the ruler. The two grayhounds, each facing a different direction, represent the loyalty of Malatesta's subjects, both by day (the white dog) and by night (the black dog).

About 200 yards to the north is Rimini's City Museum.

Museo della Cittá

Location: Via L. Tonini 1
Contact details: Tel. 054 155414
Opening hours: 8:30 am–12:30 pm, 5:00 pm–7:00 pm Tues.–Sat., 4:00 pm–7:00 pm Sun., closed Mon.
Admission: Euro 3.62

Giovanni Bellini
Dead Christ Supported by Four Angels, c.1474

In the rendition of the Dead Christ, all barriers between the viewer and the image have been removed. Christ's body leans across the diagonal of the rectangle, and rests on the front of the parapet – we are meant to feel that his legs, stretching towards us, would extend to somewhere near our own feet. In fact, it is not difficult to imagine that, if that little *putto* struggling to support Christ's slumping form doesn't receive some immediate help from his more insouciant colleagues, the body of Christ could topple over and fall right out of the picture into our own arms! One angel holds up the wounded left hand of the Savior closer to our line of vision, so that there is no avoiding its bloody stigma. The right hand has fallen listlessly to his side, but it is still clenched in the spasm of pain recalling the nailing to the cross. Despite the potential goriness of the picture, we are overcome by its beauty.

Ghirlandaio
Saints Sebastian, Vincent Ferrer and Roch, 1493–96

Under the sage blessing of God the Father (in the lunette) an eclectic collection of individuals celebrates the life of St Vincent Ferrer. They are, from left, the ubiquitous St Sebastian, displaying his customary *sang froid* about the arrows piercing his flesh; the saint himself, and St Roch, rolling down a stocking to display his cure from the plague. The main interest in this rather stilted painting is political. The donors at the front are members of the then ruling Malatesta family. After the fall of their dynasty in 1528, the donors were painted out of the picture and remained in this state of obscurity for four centuries. The repainting was removed in 1924.

You now have ahead of you a long, but beautiful, trip north along the Adriatic coast – 150 miles to Venice. On the way, you will pass through one of the great cultural centers of the world – the late Roman capital of Ravenna. Although it contains no Renaissance paintings of note, it is well worth spending one or two days studying its remarkable Byzantine mosaics. As you continue up the coast, before visiting the important art center of Padua, you may care to take a small detour inland – to the town of **Rovigo**, the southernmost town of the Veneto. While there, visit the Concord Academy, where you will find two Bellini paintings, although the authorship of one of them is disputed.

Padua (Padova)

Less than 20 miles north of Rovigo (and only a short train ride from Venice's main station, Santa Lucia) is Padua, site of one of the world's oldest universities and of a long-standing and renowned system of municipal government. Appropriately enough, it was the hometown of the great political philosopher of devolution, Marsiglio of Padua. We are heading, first of all, to the Arena Chapel, now usually called the Scrovegni Chapel after the its founder, Enrico Scrovegni, which contains the most substantial concentration of Giotto's work to be found anywhere, as well as many other delights. The authorship of these luminous works by Giotto is not disputed, as some of the other cycles we've seen are. The Chapel is about 800 yards south of the railway station.

The Scrovegni (or Arena) Chapel (Cappella degli Scrovegni)

Location: Piazza Eremitani
Contact details: Tel. 049 8204550
Opening hours: 9:00 am–7:00 pm daily
Admission: Euro 11 gains entry to the Eremitani Museum as well.

Around 1302, Enrico Scrovegni, a Paduan nobleman, commissioned Giotto to paint on the walls of his family's chapel a cycle of frescoes depicting the lives of the Virgin; of her parents, Joachim and Anna; and of Christ. Some say the building of the chapel was an act of expiation for the sins of usury committed by the Scrovegni family in accumulating their wealth. Whatever the motive, the Scrovegni Chapel is now a treasure house of early Renaissance art. The nave is decorated with dozens of intensely moving pictures by Giotto. On the altar in the apse of the chapel are three sculptures by Pisano – the superb *Madonna and Child with Two Angels*. The *Scrovegni Sarcophagus* is the work of Andriolo de Santi.

If you wish to read the frescoes as a narrative, you will have to be prepared to walk around the small chapel three times – or even four, if you wish also to make a separate study of the *Virtues* and *Vices* painted in monochrome on the dado. If you are facing the altar, the south wall (the one with the windows) is on your right. Turn to face it, and start with the top tier of paintings. Beginning at the top left-hand corner of the south wall, and moving to your right towards the west entrance (the

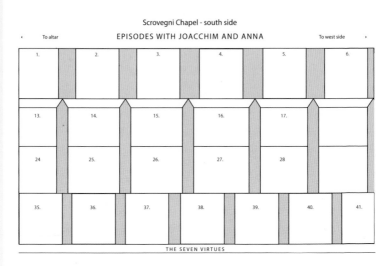

Scrovegni Chapel - south side
EPISODES WITH JOACCHIM AND ANNA

THE SEVEN VIRTUES

Scrovegni Chapel - north side
EPISODES FROM THE LIFE OF MARY

THE SEVEN VICES

The Scrovegni (or Arena) Chapel contains Giotto's luminous scenes from the Lives of Joachim and Anna, Mary and Christ: the most substantial concentration of the Maestro's work to be found anywhere. The numbers on the diagram follow the numbers in the text. Please note the altar is not shown in the diagram.

wall which contains *The Last Judgment*), you will find six paintings depicting events in the life of the parents of the woman who was to become the mother of Jesus:

Giotto
Episodes from the Lives of Joachim and Anna, 1302–1305

1. *The Rejection of Joachim's Sacrifice:* Joachim's offering in the temple is rejected because he is childless.
2. *Joachim among the Shepherds:* After the rejection of his sacrifice, Joachim withdraws, sorrowing, to the wilderness with his flocks and shepherds.
3. *The Annunciation to Anna:* While a maid sits spinning outside her door, an angel appears to the praying Anna and reassures her that she will indeed have a child.
4. *The Sacrifice of Joachim:* Out in the wilderness, under a mysterious hand of benediction, the angel appears also to Joachim to tell him that his sacrifice has been accepted.
5. *The Dream of Joachim:* While shepherds watch over him and his flocks, Joachim sleeps in the shelter of his hut. In his dream, an angel appears to tell him he is going to become a father.
6. *The Meeting of Joachim and Anna at the Golden Gate:* Anne and her women friends have set off to find Joachim. Meanwhile, he has returned home to be with his wife. They meet at the Golden Gate of Jerusalem, and embrace, rejoicing in their impending parenthood. Their companions display a variety of responses to the news of the pregnancy!

Keep walking to your right – past the entrance – and, still following the top tier, this time, on the north (windowless) wall, you will find the following cycle:

Giotto
Episodes from the Life of Mary, 1302–1305

7. *The Birth of the Virgin Mary:* Mary is born in the same room in which the angel had appeared to her mother, Anne. In a second episode of the same picture, the baby Mary, still in her swaddling clothes, is being cared for at the foot of her mother's bed.
8. *The Young Mary Presented at the Temple:* Mary, now an adolescent, is presented to the priests and elders at the Temple, where she will receive her education.

9. The Bringing of the Rods to the Temple: The High Priest stands in the choir of the temple, dubiously inspecting the rods brought by Mary's suitors. He is waiting for one of the rods to burst into blossom: as Mary's parents had dedicated her to God, the question of who would marry her was to be decided by a miracle. A tentative Joseph stands to one side, believing himself to be too old for Mary.

10. The Prayer of the Suitors for Mary's Hand: The suitors and the High Priest pray for the miracle to occur. If you have a really good pair of binoculars, you may be able to discern in the fading blue of the cupola the hand of God pointing to one of the rods.

11. The Marriage of the Virgin: The choir and cupola of the temple frame Giotto's picture for the third time: this time, the marriage of Joseph and Mary. The priest joins the hands of the betrothed while a subdued Mary rests her left hand on her stomach, a reference to her future pregnancy.

12. The Bridal Procession of the Virgin: A somewhat sombre wedding party walks to Mary's house, where, however, musicians greet them. The palm leaf flying from the balcony is a further reference to the imminent birth of Christ.

The narrative has now brought you back to the top picture in the Triumphal Arch, where begins another cycle:

Giotto
Episodes from the Life and Death of Christ, 1302–1305

God the Father Sends the Archangel Gabriel to the Virgin: At the apex of the scene on top of the arch, God the Father is painted on a wooden door, which was opened during religious festivals to release the dove representing the Holy Spirit. He is flanked by rows of ethereal, floating angels, swaying to the music piped by the little *putti* on the extreme right of the scene (and presumably, originally on the left as well).

Directly underneath, on either side of the Triumphal Arch, is Giotto's depiction of:

The Annunciation: The Archangel Gabriel and The Annunciate Virgin are presented as a pair of splendid pictures painted on either side of the top tier of the arch. Giotto has used symmetry to great effect. Each figure is framed by an identical medieval window, which in turn is framed by Gothic-arched balconies. What would otherwise be naturalistic touches become design features in the two mirror images – a white sheet that has blown in through a balcony window; an interior curtain casually knotted. The painted architecture of the picture merges with the actual architecture of the chapel: the real Triumphal Arch and the image of God the Father that sits above it unite the two separate pictures.

Directly underneath the Annunciata, also on the right-hand side of the arch, is:

The Visitation: This portrays the visit of the pregnant Mary to her cousin, Elizabeth, who is also pregnant (with John, later the Baptist). The picture is full of emotional intensity: observe the way in which the two women look at each other!

Walking always to your right, move round to face the south (windowed) wall once again, and lower your eyes to the middle row of pictures. Between the first two windows, you will find:

13. *The Nativity:* In a rocky, barren setting, the Madonna lies in the manger. A woman who has presumably helped at the birth, tenderly places Jesus in the arms of his mother. Mary stares intently at her new baby, who meets her gaze with an even expression, full of meaning. On the ground beneath them, like many a weary husband before and since, Joseph slumbers. An ox with knowing eyes and a gray donkey (with expertly foreshortened head) look on. In a second episode, the angels announce the birth to the shepherds.

14. *The Adoration of the Magi:* The three kings reverently present their gifts to the Holy Infant. One has removed his crown to kneel to kiss the baby's feet. On the left of the picture, a camel driver settles his charges.

15. *The Presentation of Christ in the Temple:* In this very natural depiction of the theme, the infant seems not to have enjoyed being separated from his mother, who reaches out to calm him.

16. *The Flight into Egypt:* This image is remarkable, among other things, for its depiction of lateral movement, and for the expression of strength on the Virgin's face – her back as firm and straight as the rock behind her, and her features set.

17. *The Slaughter of the Innocents:* The ground is littered with the bodies of innocent children as King Herod himself directs the slaughter from a balcony. The agony of the women is palpable.

Walk once again past the entrance, and, in the middle tier of pictures on the windowless northside wall, you will find:

18. *Christ among the Scribes*: Christ as a young boy engages the priests of the temple in lively discussion. They are rapt: only one of them looks up to observe the sudden appearance of Jesus' worried parents.

19. *The Baptism of Christ*: Christ stands up to his waist in the waters of the Jordan under the ministering hand of John the Baptist. In the sky above hovers the Holy Spirit (very faded) and God the Father. On the bank to the left, the apostles hold his clothes – a blood red tunic and a (once) celestial blue cloak, seemingly emphasizing the dual human and divine nature of their Lord.

20. *The Marriage of Cana:* Christ, seated on the left of the table, raises his hand to bless the water and perform his miracle. On the right of the blue-cloaked Virgin, the marvelling host samples the result.

21. *The Raising of Lazarus from the Dead:* A picture full of energy and movement: the ghostly figure of Lazarus, still embalmed, rises from the dead, apparently requiring at least two of the onlookers to cover their noses. The expressions on the other figures range from reverence to utter disbelief.

22. *The Entry of Christ into Jerusalem:* Seated on the back of a donkey, Christ triumphantly approaches the Golden Gate of Jerusalem with his serious-faced disciples. Two men climb the palm trees to strip the branches for their Hosannas; others hastily remove their cloaks to provide a carpeted entry to the city.

23. *Expulsion of the Moneylenders from the Temple:* A rope-flailing Christ confronts the moneylenders in the loggia of the temple while a sacrificial sheep takes advantage of the confusion to escape from its cage.

The next episode in the cycle is the middle-tier painting on the left-hand side of the arch over the altar.

Judas Receiving Payment for his Betrayal: The same group of scribes now convince Judas to betray his Master. Behind the yellow-cloaked Judas, who is clutching a sack of silver, lurks the Devil.

Also, look at the two paintings on the lower tier of each side of the pillars of the Triumphal Arch:

The Coretti: In these paintings Giotto has experimented with perspective to produce the illusion of a room beyond the arch, complete with vaulted ceiling and swinging chandeliers.

Now, to the right of the arch, the lower tier of paintings on the south, windowed, wall contain more episodes from the life and Death of Christ:

24. *The Last Supper:* When looking at paintings on the theme of the Last Supper, it is interesting to try to guess the actual moment being portrayed. Leonardo Da Vinci is often said to be the first painter to have emphasized the precise point when Christ revealed that one of his apostles was about to betray him. Giotto's 'moment' seems to occur a little later: the white-bearded St Peter is still in shock (a reminder, perhaps, of his later triple-betrayal). Another apostle – probably John, has collapsed onto Christ's breast, as recounted in the Gospel of St John: "Now there was leaning on Jesus' bosom one of his disciples, whom Jesus loved." (13:23). What followed, according to John, was that Peter suggested to that disciple that he should ask Jesus to identify the one who would betray him. Giotto's picture appears to capture the moment between Jesus' revelation that he was to be betrayed, and Peter's inquiry.

25. *Jesus Washing the Feet of the Apostles:* The focus of the picture is the exchange between Christ and Peter. Peter has raised his hand to his head, exclaiming at what his Master has just told him. In the meantime, his left hand gathers up the hem of his robe and, on the left of the picture, another apostle, oblivious of the dramatic exchange between his two leaders, calmly does up his sandal.

26. *The Judas Kiss:* The scene is one of turmoil. Soldiers wave weapons and fiery brands. Peter is in the process of cutting off the ear of the servant of the High Priest (who gesticulates in the right foreground). A simian-faced Judas, his limbs hidden by a yellow cloak, envelops Christ in an awkward embrace, puckering his lips to deliver the kiss that will identify his master to his enemies. Amidst this chaos, Christ is a figure of profound serenity and great moral dignity, his eyes penetrating the sham affection of the traitor. Giotto's capacity to pinpoint the pivotal element of each of the sacred narratives was unsurpassed.

27. *Christ Brought Before Caiaphas:* In a darkened room, Christ, looking frightened for the first time, is dragged before the High Priest, Caiaphas, who tears at his garments in anger. A soldier raises his hand to strike the helpless prisoner.

28. *The Flagellation:* Christ appears successively more defeated and submissive. Here, he has been dressed in a royal cloak and is being mocked and beaten by his vicious-faced captors.

Giotto's The Judas Kiss

The equivalent tier of paintings on the north wall contains:

29. *The Road to Calvary:* The crowd at once propels Christ towards Calvary and pushes his distraught mother to the back of the procession. An isolated Christ glances wistfully over his shoulder at his disappearing mother.

30. *The Crucifixion:* Christ hangs dying on his cross, while distraught angels fill the sky overhead. Mary faints into the arms of the apostles and Mary Magdalene embraces the foot of the cross, her veil having slipped to the ground to reveal her golden hair.

31. *The Lament Over the Dead Christ:* Without doubt, this is one of the most moving renditions of the Pietà theme ever painted. The expressions of agony on the faces of the mourners, the bodies leaning earnestly towards the dead Christ, convey unspeakable pain, yet the mood is one of great tenderness. There are many technical innovations here: figures set on different planes to convey filled space; the plastic mobility of the forms achieving hitherto unparalleled naturalism; the essential simplicity of the figures actually heightening the dramatic mood. But one returns, again and again, to the intense facial expressions, for they are the source of the picture's profound humanity.

32. *The Resurrection (Noli Me Tangere):* Mary Magdalene has recognized Christ, now risen from his tomb. She stretches her arms to embrace him, but, as he no longer belongs to this world, he says, "Touch me not." Meanwhile, the guards sleep on.

33. *The Ascension:* Giotto has painted an extraordinarily ethereal Ascension, which combines elements of the Byzantine tradition with radical innovation. Christ, surrounded by a golden aureole, seems to be floating rapidly heavenwards into blue space. The figure twists sideways from the hips, presenting the upper part of the body in profile so that the lift of the head and eagerly outstretched arms intensify both the upward movement of the painting and its general airiness.

34. *The Pentecost.* The apostles have gathered in a Gothic loggia. The rays of the Holy Spirit have descended and touched them, and peace and enlightenment transfigure their faces.

The dado that runs around the walls underneath the large colored frescoes has been painted to imitate panels of veined marble. Between the panels are small figures painted in monochrome to imitate sculptures – on the south wall, the *Virtues*, and on the north, the *Vices*. The first is found beneath and to the left of *The Last Supper.*

Giotto
The Virtues, 1302–1305

35. Prudence sits like an accountant at her desk, gazing into the mirror of knowledge.

36. Fortitude is an armed woman, ready to defend virtue.

37. Temperance stands gracefully and peacefully – with a sword in her hand.

38. Justice stands above a scene of peace and tranquillity, carrying the scales that weigh punishment and mercy.

39. Faith holds a crucifix and an unfurled scroll.

40. Charity holds a basket of fruit while God hands her a heart.

41. Hope is a winged female figure, receiving a crown from the hands of God.

On the north wall's dado are found the vices. The first is found beneath and to the left of *The Road to Calvary*.

Giotto
The Vices, 1302–1305

42. Despair is depicted as a woman who has hanged herself, and whose soul is now being claimed by a demon.

43. Envy is an old woman carrying a sack of money and standing in the fire of jealousy. Her head is horned and her disfigured ears enormous. A snake crawls out of her mouth and turns to bite her face.

44. Idolatry carries in his hand a false idol, which is also tied around his neck.

45. Injustice sits rigidly on his throne, gazing, unseeing, into the distance. The resulting picture of misery is carved on his plinth.

46. Wrath distorts her face and tears her garments in irrational, unproductive rage.

47. Inconstancy slips and slides about on a rotating disc and slanting floor. Her constant efforts to regain her balance causes her robe to fly about as she desperately waves her arms in the air.

48. Foolishness appears in a silly costume, wearing a fool's hat and a clumsy stance.

You can now turn your full attention to the paintings over the west entrance, Giotto's rendition of :

The Last Judgment: You do not see *The Last Judgment* when first you walk into the Scrovegni Chapel because it is painted on the wall that surrounds the door through which you enter. If you are disciplined enough to read the narrative of the lives of the Virgin and of Christ in chronological sequence, you will come to this vision of hell last of all. Like a scene from Dante's Inferno, the mood of this nightmare of Gothic horror could not be more different from that of the other paintings of the cycle, and it has a gruesomeness that is very uncharacteristic of Giotto. Evil personified as a large, bluish monster sits devouring unfortunate sinners, while others suffer a variety of alternative unspeakable fates. Over this terrifying scene and the corresponding picture of paradise presides the enthroned Christ, the Supreme Judge, framed by a shining mandorla, flanked by apostles and Judges of the Church. On either side are choirs of angels. Above them, on either side of the window, two roll back the firmament to reveal glimpses of the Holy City.

Look above the entrance, on the left of the crucifix that separates the elite from the damned, to see a portrait of Enrico Scrovegni, who kneels to dedicate a model of the chapel to the Madonna.

In the same complex as the Scrovegni Chapel are the:

Eremitani Museums (Musei degli Eremitani)

Location: Piazza Eremitani
Contact details: Tel. 049 8024550
Opening hours: 9:00 am–7:00 pm, Tues.–Sun. closed Mon.
Admission: Euro 11 gains entry to the Scrovengi Chapel as well

Giotto
Crucifixion, 1317

This elegant crucifix was painted in tempera on a wooden panel, and may well have come originally from the Scrovegni Chapel. In common with several other works attributed to Giotto, there is a continuing debate about its authorship. You may wish to compare its style with that of the figures in the Scrovegni frescoes.

Jacopo and Giovanni Bellini
Descent of Christ into Limbo, c.1450

With considerable uncertainty, this has been attributed to father and young son. We have included it in this Trail for no other reason than that the devils have a splendidly medieval panache to them, and it is rare indeed to see the miserable denizens of limbo receiving any attention at all, let alone a visit from the Redeemer himself!

About 1000 yards to the southwest is the Duomo, St Anthony's Basilica in the Piazza del Santo, with its Byzantine style domes and minarets. Among other interesting features (like the high altar which, if you are allowed near it, you will see is decorated by Donatello), you can see fragments of delicate frescoes, apparently painted, at the very least, by the *bottega* (workshop) of Giotto, as well as the Donatello works we focus on.

St Anthony's Basilica
(Basilica di San Antonio)

Donatello
Crucifix c.1444

When Donatello moved his workshop from Florence to Padua in 1443, it was in part to complete an important commission – the production of a large bronze crucifix for the Basilica of Sant'Antonio. Other such commissions were to follow the great success of the Crucifix, so his Padua sojourn (which lasted 10 years) also marks the time when the sculptor started working less in marble, and more frequently in bronze. He quickly demonstrated that his unequalled ability to portray human emotion was in no way impeded by working in this difficult medium.

Donatello
Altare del Santo, late 1440s

Donatello designed the original altar for the Basilica, but it has been altered many times.

Nevertheless, the figures of the saints on the top, and the reliefs in the base are probably a product of his workshop, even if they once were arranged in a different order.

Donatello
Madonna and Child with Saints, late 1440s

The figure of the Madonna has a medieval feel to it, possibly because of the brief given to Donatello by the donors. She sits square on her throne and holds her infant squarely to the viewer. The two are flanked by the two Franciscan saints: St Anthony and St Francis.

Donatello
Symbols of Evangelists, late 1440s

The symbols of the Evangelists used to be fixed to the sides of the altar. Matthew was symbolized by an angel; Mark, by the lion; Luke, by an ox and John, by an eagle. (The creatures selected relate to the point at which each of the four gospels started. For example, Mark's lion – a desert animal – refers to John the Baptist's description of himself as "a voice crying in the wilderness.")

Donatello
Putti Musicians, late 1440s

Donatello was the supreme creator of *putti* – in any medium! These 12 little bronze ones once bordered the altar (on the sides of each of the large relief panels). (Check out the cute little boots on the hymn-singing cherubs.)

Donatello
Dead Christ (Cristo Morto), late 1440s

Two sad little *putti* hold a cloth of honor behind the dead body of Christ. Their free hands cover their cheeks in an expression of grief. The finely modelled figure of Christ is very moving: His slumped head and exhausted, tortured expression suggest that his suffering continues, even in death.

Donatello
Burial of Christ, late 1440s

This plaque, from the rear wall of the altar, contains a chaotic scene at Christ's tomb – a sarcophagus inlaid with colored tiles.

Donatello
Miracle of the Ass, late 1440s

The story told here is that of an ass that had refused to eat. When

St Anthony held up the host, it knelt before him. The three vaulted cubicles are full of amazed onlookers.

Donatello
Miracle of the Repentant Son, late 1440s

Another miracle allegedly performed by St Anthony is depicted in this bronze panel. A young man has had his leg severed in an accident. Having repented his sins, he now has the leg restored by St Anthony.

On public display in Padua is one of Donatello's most famous works – his huge bronze equestrian statue of the Condottiere (Military Leader) Erasmo da Narni (nick-named Gattemalata, or Honey Cat). It is right outside the Duomo, dominating the Piazza del Santo.

Donatello's Condottiere Gattamelata

Donatello
Condottiere Gattamelata, late 1440s

The soldier sits proudly on his big horse, dressed in full armor and carrying his staff of military command – the first free-standing bronze equestrian statue since post-classical times. If you have seen the classical Roman statue of *Marcus Aurelius* at the Campidoglio in Rome, you will understand what inspired Donatello. Even Gattamelata's head – he's not the handsomest soldier you've ever seen – seems idealized in order to achieve that military bearing: not unlike the face on a Roman coin. His mouth has a determined set, and his hair, in the absence of a military helmet, is styled in the manner of a Roman hero.

While you are in Padua, you may care to visit a sad site right next to the Arena/Scrovegni Chapel: the Church of The Hermits (Eremitani) of St Augustine. The church was heavily damaged during World War II, and with it some priceless Mantegna frescoes – his earliest-surviving works – only vestiges of which remain. You will also see here photographs of the Church before and after the bombing, as well as a record of the continuing attempt at restoration.

Another 20 miles to the east lies the magic city of Venice.

Bologna

TRAIL 6:
Florence to Venice

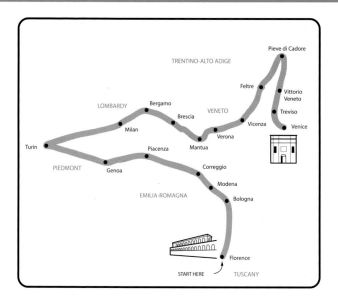

This is the longest of the Trails – over 600 miles in length. From Florence, it proceeds in a northwesterly direction until it reaches Italy's third largest city – Turin. It then swings eastwards ending in Venice on the Adriatic coast. On the way, it comes to the major stop on this Trail – Italy's second largest city, Milan.

Bologna

Sixty miles to the north of Florence is the major city of Bologna, an important cultural center which has given priority to collecting the works of its own favorite sons – from the 14th-century Vitale da Bologna to the 18th-century Giuseppe Maria Crespi – painters beyond the scope of this Trail. However, just over half a mile to the east of the railway station is the National Gallery. Although its speciality is the Baroque period, it does contain three works of Renaissance painters featured in this Trail.

National Gallery (Pinacoteca Nazionale)

Location: Via Belle Arte 56
Contact details: Tel. 390 632810
Opening hours: 9:00 am–2:00 pm Tues.– Sat; 9:00 am–1:00 pm Sun., closed Mon.
Admission: About Euro 5

Giotto
Bologna Polyptych, c.1330

This altarpiece was commissioned for Bologna's Church of Santa Maria degli Angeli. Perhaps that's why Giotto – from distant Florence – felt it necessary to identify himself as its author. Look for the inscription at the base of the central panel: *Opus Magistri Jocti de Florentia* (Work of Master Giotto from Florence). In her stunning blue robe, the enthroned Virgin gazes out at the viewer while the Child appears to be wriggling about in her arms, as if trying to gain her attention. This very human couple contrasts with the rather more wooden pairs of figures in the panels on either side, which may have been painted by Giotto's assistants. St Peter and the Archangel Gabriel are on the left – the latter in Annunciation pose although the moment of conception is obviously well past. On the right are the Archangel Michael and St Paul.

Titian
Christ on the Cross with the Good Thief, c.1566

Perhaps because this picture was never finished, there is a debate among art historians as to whether it is the work of Titian or someone else – perhaps even Tintoretto! The work is interesting, in part because its rough, unfinished state enables us to see the *alla prima* method in use; but also because the painter – whoever he was – has achieved great dramatic effect by affording us an unusual, close-up perspective on the exchange between the crucified Christ, and (a remarkably animated) good thief.

Raphael
Ecstasy of St Cecilia, 1514–16

This altarpiece was commissioned by a lover of music and mysticism, Bologna's Elena Duglioli dall' Olio. Its central figure is the patron saint of music, St Cecilia. Interrupted at her organ-playing by the strains of a celestial choir, she lets the instrument drop to listen more attentively. Only Cecilia can hear the heavenly music that is the source of her ecstasy. Behind her, St John the Evangelist and St Augustine exchange glances, while Mary Magdalene gazes out at the viewer. St Paul tugs thoughtfully at his dark beard, contemplating the broken instruments at Cecilia's feet – a reminder to the viewer, perhaps, that music made by mere humans is vastly inferior to that from the celestial spheres.

Modena

A further 25 miles to the northwest lies the industrial city of Modena. Modena is an intriguing blend of the old and the new. In medieval times, it was the seat of Queen Matilda of Tuscany. In the modern world, it is internationally famous for its racing cars and balsamic vinegar. It is also home to a renowned university, whose campus is close to the Estense Gallery.

Estense Gallery (Galleria Estense)

Location: Largo di Porta Sant-Agostino 337
Contact details: Tel. 059 4395711
Opening hours: 8:30 am–7:30 pm Tues.–Sun., closed Mon.
Admission: Euro 4

Tintoretto
Madonna in Glory, c.1550

In this large swirling work, the genders are clearly separated. In the celestial sphere, among the angels, Sts Catherine and Scholastica flank the Virgin in her glory. Down on earth, Sts Peter, Augustine, Paul, and John the Baptist admire from afar the resplendent Mary.

Bernini
Bust of Duke Francis I d'Este, 1651

Bernini once said that if someone were to dye himself completely white, then were to show himself to his friends, they would barely recognize him: "It is very difficult to achieve a resemblance in white marble." Considering that Bernini made this bust from portraits of the Duke – a process that took him 14 months – it is no wonder that he announced, when he'd finished the bust, that that was the last time he would work from portraits! Nevertheless, for all of Bernini's fatigue, he had accomplished a striking work that was also innovative in the way it balanced opposing forces.

The next few stops are only mentioned briefly, as there is only one work to note within each. Firstly, if you have the time to take a short detour of about 15 miles to the northwest of Modena, you will find an out-of-the-way treasure in the small town of **Correggio:** Go to Palazzo dei Principi, where you'll find the Civic Museum (Museo Civico). There you'll see Mantegna's *Christ the Redeemer*, a fragment of a larger work.

The ancient town of **Piacenza** lies about 60 miles northwest of Modena (somewhat closer if you've taken the side trip to Correggio), whose center is still laid out as it was in Roman times. In the center of town is the impressive Palazzo Farnese, containing the town's Civic Museum. The authorship of its Botticelli painting called *Virgin Adoring the Child with the Young St John the Baptist,* from around 1477, has been disputed. Most art historians believe that the figure of the Virgin and that of the Child are definitely Botticelli's; although it seems the young John the Baptist may have been painted by workshop colleagues. Some intriguing local politics surrounded this tondo in the 19th century. Shortly after the attainment of national independence, the new Italian government decreed that the painting should go to Turin. Defiantly, the mayor of Piacenza hung it in the municipal offices for three decades, after which its retention was assured.

About 50 miles southwest of Piacenza is the great port of **Genoa (Genova)**, where it is worth stopping to see a dramatic Caravaggio – *Ecce Homo (Man of Sorrows)* in the Palazzo Rosso, on via Garibaldi.

About 45 miles northwest of Genoa is the great industrial city of Turin (Torino).

Turin (Torino)

Although settled in antiquity, Turin did not come into its own until Baroque times. Because of this, its holdings of Renaissance paintings are meager. From the railway station, proceed about 600 yards to the northeast to the:

Pinacoteca dell'Accademia Albertina di Belle Arte

Location: Via Accademia Albertina 8

Contact details: Tel. 011 8177862

Opening hours: 9:00 am–1:00 pm, 3:00 pm–7:00 pm Tues.–Sun., closed Mon.

Admission: About Euro 4

Fra Filippo Lippi
Four Doctors of the Church, 1435–37

Unfortunately, it is impossible to view Filippo Lippi's *Four Doctors of the Church* with their central panel with which they formed a triptych, as the latter is in New York's Metropolitan Museum of Art. St Augustine and St Ambrose appear on the left wing of the former triptych, and Sts Gregory and Jerome, on the right. In this context, St Jerome is depicted in his scholarly – rather than his hermetic – mode, reflecting his role in producing the Latin (Vulgate) version of the scriptures. The lion from whose paw he extracted the thorn, and who then became his companion in the desert, is at his feet. Fra Filippo has tried to model the four Doctors in natural poses, though their very large eyes detract somewhat from his efforts. The ways in which the internal spaces have been architecturally enclosed in the two panels has been claimed as a design innovation for the 15th century.

Lippi. Illustration Matt Morrow.

From the Pinacoteca dell-Accademia, you proceed another 600 yards – this time to the northwest.

Galleria Sabauda

Location: Via Accademia delle Scienze 6
Contact details: Tel. 011 547440
Opening hours: 9:00 am–2:00 pm Tues., Wed. and Fri.–Sun;
1:00 pm–8:00 pm Thurs., closed Mon.
Admission: Around Euro 4

Fra Angelico
Madonna and Child, c.1433

In its very simplicity, this small painting vividly presents the central innovation of Fra Angelico – his ability to rework the traditional Byzantine elements of iconic poses in gilt settings in ways that conveyed an emerging sensibility. Here we have a warmly human mother and child, revealed by the opening of curtains to be seated in a tabernacle. The majesty of the couple is subtly suggested by the delicate gold embroidery of the curtains and the haloes.

Giovanni Bellini
Madonna with Blessing Child, 1475

This tender portrayal of one of Bellini's favorite themes can serve to illustrate the unfairness of geography. It is likely that this was the first of several similar treatments that Bellini produced in the latter half of the decade of the 1470s. The most famous in the sequence is the Contarini Madonna in the Accademia in Venice. This softer treatment stands comparison with that of its celebrated successor.

About a 75-mile drive north of due east from Turin is Milan, Italy's second largest city.

Milan (Milano)

Milan's original name – Mediolanum – meant "in the middle of the plain." Surprisingly, this great center, like the rest of the northwest, has not produced many painters of renown. Probably the best of the local crop was Caravaggio, who was born just outside Milan, but who hightailed it to Rome at an early opportunity. This Trail follows a more-or-less clockwise course, starting at ten o'clock in the north west, and finishing at eight o' clock in the south west. Six of our focus painters have works in this city. A quick note: to view Leonardo da Vinci's *Last Supper*, you need to make reservations ahead of time (tel: 199 199 100).

Commence at the grand Sforzesco Castle, in the north west of the central city, close by the Metro station, Porta Garibaldi. The Sforza family ruled Milan in the medieval period. The family derived its name from its founder, a peasant of legendary strength, who was nicknamed 'Sforza' (strength).

Castello Sforzesco

Location: Piazza Castello
Contact details: Tel. 026 2083946, 003 902877004
Opening hours: 9:00 am–5:30 pm daily

Within the grounds, you visit two separate sites. In the Pinacoteca, you will find the following paintings (among others):

Fra Filippo Lippi
Madonna of Humility with Angels and Carmelite Saints, mid 1420s

As Fra Filippo was, for ten years, a Carmelite monk, it is understandable that he painted several Carmelite pictures. The Carmelites were the religious order who wore white cloaks and who were supposed to have received their "life formula" from the patriarch of Jerusalem, St Albert Avogadro. In this early Lippi, a semi-circle of figures kneel and squat around the Madonna, with those at the rear appearing to jostle for a vantage point. Despite the rather rag-doll appearance of the Christ Child, (signs of an apprentice at work?) he has interesting hands, and the faces of the Madonna and the onlookers are wonderfully varied and animated. The haloed Carmelite saints are Blessed Angela of Bohemia on the left and, on the right, St Angelo (disconcertingly wearing the instrument of his martyrdom) and, carrying the lily, St Albert of Trapani (Sicily).

Giovanni Bellini
Madonna of the Apple (Madonna della Mela), c.1460

Although this was not the first of Bellini's 'portrait' paintings of his favorite subject, it is the earliest still on view in Italy. In one important respect – the aloof, rather asexual Mary – this painting set the pattern for what came to be seen as the cold approach of Bellini, which many critics compared unfavorably with the later voluptuous versions of Titian. But despite her distant expression, the Virgin holds her child on his cushion in a gently maternal way. The soft apricot tones of her robe provide the warmth that her expression lacks: they are reflected again in the background beyond the arched area of darkness against which the two figures and their golden filgree haloes stand out with great clarity. They are repeated in the velvety flesh of the child and his mother's peerless complexion.

To see Michelangelo's unfinished *Rondanini Pietà*, go to the Civiche Raccolte d'Arte Antica in the grounds.

Michelangelo
Rondanini Pietà, 1564

Michelangelo was still working on this piece in the last week of his nine decades of life. Here, the very workings of gravity seem to have been suspended (as they were to be in subsequent Ascensions by Christ and Mary). The spiritual love of Jesus and Mary appears to have produced a near perfect balance – the dead Jesus is supporting as much as he is supported. A circle has been closed with this work: in its rough, unfinished state, the sculpture possesses much of the iconic character of primitive Christian art.

Proceed due east for about 400 yards to the great Brera Gallery.

Brera Gallery (Pinacoteca di Brera)

Location: Inside the Palazzo di Brera at Via Brera 28
Contact details: Tel. 02 722631
Opening hours: 8:30 am–7:00 pm Tues.–Sun., closed Mon.
Admission: About Euro 6

The Brera, like such other great galleries as the Accademia in Venice and the National Gallery in Bologna, was begun in the Napoleonic era, in 1808. However, the Brera is proud to proclaim that, unlike some of its rivals, its collections were assembled by public-minded governments and citizens rather than the nobility. Our coverage begins in Room 6.

Sala 6

Giovanni Bellini
Madonna with a Blessing Child, 1510

The young Madonna sits in front of a green watered-silk cloth of honor edged with red. (The painter seems to have enjoyed the artistic challenge of painting its concave and convex folds.) On either side is a detailed, if dry, landscape, featuring a distant hilltop fortified town with a causeway over a ravine and two shadeless trees under which tiny, distant figures go about their daily lives. The figure of the Holy Infant is especially interesting: he appears as a mini-version of a Greek or Roman statue – nude, and is in the *contropposto* pose of the classical hero. He looks directly at us (a pose rarely adopted in Bellini's early Madonnas), and holds up his hand in blessing for those whose sins render his sacrifice necessary. A marmalade cat sits on top of the white stone block on the Madonna's right – on which Bellini's name has been carved.

Mantegna
St Luke Polyptych, 1455

This altarpiece was originally executed for the Chiesa di Santa Giustina in Padua, and the surrounding saints are those especially venerated in that city. The dominant figure of St Luke, hard at work writing his Gospel, dwarfs the dead Christ and mourners above.

Giovanni Bellini
Pietà, c.1465

Against the wan, opaline light of a sky just after rain, a gray-faced Madonna searches her dead son's face as if trying to gauge the full measure of his suffering. The picture speaks to us of profoundly felt emotion. Each of the figures' lips are parted – in fathomless sorrow, in painful death, in a sob of grief. When at last we avert our eyes from the intimacy of the mother's compelling encounter with her son, we notice the interplay of hands at the center of the picture. The Madonna, gently avoiding the wound in her son's side, moves his cruelly torn, but now relaxed right hand to a position of rest. The splayed fingers of John the Baptist support the Redeemer's torso. Christ's left hand, still clenched as it was on the cross, not only symbolizes the violence of his suffering but crosses the parapet that separates the viewer from the three figures in the picture. The daring innovation in this painting is in the unusual representation of Mary whose face demonstrates, so clearly, the disfiguring effects of grief. Her ravaged features epitomize anguish to an extent unsurpassed anywhere else in Renaissance art.

Mantegna
Virgin and Child with a Choir of Cherubim, c.1485

The Madonna's dark cloak is a foil for the pale flesh tones, the airy blue sky and puffs of clouds that separate the cherubim, but her flame-colored dress reflects the infra-red wings of some of the cherubs. She is the gentle mother, hands protectively clasping her infant son, who endearingly wraps his arm around her neck and joins in chorus with the cherubim.

Mantegna
Dead Christ, date unknown

This is probably Mantegna's best-known work. Although other contemporary artists were experimenting with techniques of foreshortening, none achieved a more dramatic effect than this. The somber colors and the grief of Mary emphasize the tragedy that has just occurred, and yet the posture of Christ's body holds out the hope of Resurrection. It has been said that those who look upon Mantegna's *Dead Christ* see their own death.

Mantegna's Dead Christ: *Another strikingly new Renaissance perspective – this time, on death itself.* Illustration Matt Morrow.

Giovanni Bellini
Madonna Greca, 1460–64

This is another of Bellini's famous portrait Madonnas. In the center of the picture is the Christ Child's hand grasping the apple, the symbol of sin and redemption. Behind hangs the cloth of honor, making the two figures seem nearer to us. Bellini's separating parapet is still there, though, in this picture, merely suggested by the position of the baby feet, which seem ready to venture into our world. But the Madonna's protective hands gently restrain him. This is an image of tragedy – the dark, brooding eyes of the Virgin, the vulnerability of her son. The sense of the Byzantine tradition, which is never really absent from Bellini's work, is here quite strong. Mary's cloak is a dark, velvety mass, the light picking up some of the delicate gold tracery of its border. In the background are the Greek letters from which the painting derives its name. Perhaps better than any other Renaissance work, this famous picture illustrates the complexities of the relationship between the Renaissance and the Byzantine tradition. Although the Byzantine style had originated centuries before the birth of the Renaissance, it retained great vitality in 15th-century Venice. Yet the painting was also daringly innovative, with the Christ Child apparently at the point of falling out of the frame.

Sala 8

Mantegna
St Bernardine of Siena and Angels, (San Bernardino di Siena con Angeli), late 1460s

Mantegna is responsible for the design of this picture and for the figures in its lower section. The unusual architecture may have been a *trompe l'oeil* extension of the real frame.

Sala 29

Caravaggio
Supper at Emmaus, 1605–06

On Easter Day, at a table in a gloomy inn, two travel-worn disciples on their way from Jerusalem to Emmaus sit down with a stranger to eat a simple meal. When he blesses the food they are about to eat, they recognize him as the risen Christ. The figure on the left has his back to the viewer, but his outstretched hand reveals his surprise. The disciple on the left has had such a shock that he grips the table as he rises to express his delight. The woman on the left looks suspiciously at him, while her companion, carrying a tray of cooked fowl, is not yet aware of the sensation he has caused. The depiction of Christ is fairly conventional by Caravaggio's standards, but his expression, in the half-light, exudes quiet strength.

Continuation of the easterly course will bring you to the Poldi-Pezzoli Museum, which is dominated by a gloomy trio of pictures.

Poldi-Pezzoli Museum (Museo Poldi-Pezzoli)

Location: Via Alessandro Manzoni 12
Contact details: Tel. 027 94889
Opening hours: 10:00 am–6:00 pm Tues.–Sun., closed Mon.
Admission: Euro 6

Fra Filippo Lippi
Pietà, early 1430s

This small, early panel – no longer in good condition – was probably the gable of a polyptych. Against a darkly mysterious wilderness background, the body of Christ is being supported by an anguished Mary and a red-gowned St John the Evangelist. The contortions of grief on the Virgin's face call to mind the most famous treatment of this theme, which is housed nearby – the Brera's *Dead Christ* by Lippi's near contemporary, Andrea Mantegna. The figure of Christ is quite unconventional – the awkward turn of his left wrist and hand a poignant reminder of the physical suffering he has endured.

Giovanni Bellini
Dead Christ, 1460

This is one of Bellini's most unforgettable images. In most Renaissance treatments of this theme, including Bellini's, the dead Christ is surrounded by mourners. This painting, however, focuses strongly on the isolated figure of Christ, but sets it in a populated landscape. In this way, Bellini conveys a sense of Christ offering salvation to ordinary humans going about their humdrum business. Deprived of the grieving companions present in the conventional Pietà, Christ here seems already to be suspended between death and life. His features seem almost in repose or in sleep. Intriguingly, this early painting is as close as Bellini ever came to portraying the Christian triumph of the Resurrection. While the portrayals of the dead Jesus and his grief-stricken mother are intensely moving, the most prominent figure (and the largest) is – most unusually – that of St John the Evangelist. The expression on his face raises the question that must have beset all the apostles at this time: Does the death of our leader mean that it has all been a waste of time?

Botticelli
Lamentation over the Dead Christ, 1490s

This is another of Botticelli's later, more religious paintings, but it is a marvellous work, a composition of extraordinarily dynamic complexity. Figures are moving in several directions, but the strong tendency is downwards, from the swooning Mary to her dead son. This is a very confronting picture: Botticelli positions the body of Christ in the central foreground of the painting, lighting it from the front, and leaving no space along which the viewer's eye can travel for a moment to prepare it for this dramatic depiction of the dead Christ and his distraught mother. The emotion conveyed by the pyramid of grief-stricken figures is therefore very direct and very powerful. John the Baptist leans forward to place his chin on Mary's brow and with his left hand, to tenderly stroke her face. Above them, an emotional Joseph of Arimathea, in whose tomb Jesus is to be buried, holds aloft the instruments of the Passion. Mary Magdalene cradles the injured feet of Christ, caressing them with her hair.

The mood is now somewhat lightened by Mantegna's picture of the Madonna and Child.

Mantegna
Madonna and Child (*Madonna col Bambino*), 1470

Mantegna painted two versions of this theme in 1470: the other is in the Accademia Carrara at Bergamo, not far away. Here, the

FLORENCE TO VENICE

Madonna lifts the head of her seriously sleeping infant as if to display her newborn to the viewer. Affectionately, she nestles her head against his, her sad gaze drifting into the middle distance. The little knuckles of his baby hands can just be made out poking from the folds of his swaddling clothes. The light on the infant and on her face contrasts with her dark blue cloak that almost merges into the even darker banner hanging behind.

Botticelli
Madonna of the Book (*Madonna del Libro*), c.1479

The book that Mary is teaching her infant to read is rather advanced: it is the *Horae Beatae Mariae, Mary's Book of Hours*! But this is a charming picture, evoking the intimate mother and child relationship represented so well by Botticelli. The pair sit at an open window through which can be seen a glimpse of a landscape. (Botticelli was much impressed by the detailed landscapes of the Dutch Renaissance painters, such as Jan van Eyck and Rogier van der Weyden.)

Piero della Francesca
St Nicholas of Tolentino, 1454–69

This striking representation is the only part remaining in Italy of Piero's great Sant'Agostino polyptych, originally commissioned for the church of that name in Sansepolcro (Other parts are to be found in Lisbon, London and New York.) The 13th-century saint, who was an Augustinian hermit credited with numerous miracles, had only recently been canonised, so the Augustinian order was eager to have their latest hero commemorated by Piero. The imposing figure of the saint carries a book and raises his right hand. He wears the inscrutable expression of many of Piero's figures.

Swinging in a southwesterly direction for another 800 yards will bring you to the center of the city and the Ambrosian Gallery.

Ambrosian Gallery

Location: Piazza Pio XI 2
Contact details: Tel. 028 645 1436
Opening hours: 10:00 am–5:30 pm Tues.–Sun., closed Mon.
Admission: Euro 7.50

Botticelli
Madonna of the Pavilion, 1490–92

This is one of several tondi that Botticelli painted in his late period. It is difficult to understand why he used the round form in this case: the composition makes virtually no concessions to it. The figures, too, seem carelessly proportioned: Mary's head seems too large for her body, for example. But it has been suggested that Botticelli, by this stage, was explicitly rejecting the Renaissance preoccupation with ideals of beauty and proportion, and returning, instead, to medieval values that related scale to the religious significance of the figure. The picture is beautiful, for all that. The motion of the angels' robes and wings and the liveliness of the toddling infant are charming. The colors, though showing less variety than in earlier works, are at once vivid and subtle. Memories of *La Primavera* are evoked by the landscape behind and the red fruit ripening in the trees behind the tent.

Titian
Adoration of the Kings, c.1560

Of Titian's four very similar treatments of this theme, this is the only one in Italy. (Of the others, two are in Spain and one in the USA, in Cleveland.) Fortunately for us, this is generally regarded as the best. Against the panoramic backdrop of a rose-colored sky, the Magi worship the tiny Jesus with great solicitude. The first king, in red jacket with white fur, stoops to gaze up intently into the face of the infant, hidden from the viewer. The oriental king, in white turban and crimson jacket, is a splendid figure as he waits on his white horse before paying his respects to the child. The figure of the Madonna is especially charming, though it seems that some of the other figures – that of Joseph, for example – may have suffered from over-zealous restoration attempts. The white horse occupying center stage appears to be paying its own homage to the holy family. The horseman on the far right is generally considered to be Titian himself.

Caravaggio
Still Life with a Basket of Fruit (Canestra di Frutta), early 1600s

Caravaggio was a prodigious exponent of the still life and his baskets of fruit appear in a range of his dramatic paintings – from *Bacchus* to *Supper in Emmaus*. But the Ambrosiana Basket of Fruit has no dramatic context, no mysterious lad carrying it about, no tipsy God to compete with it. The basket is perched (and indeed, protrudes over) a brown ledge. The pale creamy ground (again, unusual for Caravaggio) provides the perfect backdrop for his subject: note the geometric patterns formed by the leaves. The realism is astonishing.

Keeping on a southwesterly course for the best part of another mile will bring you to the Church Of Santa Maria Delle Grazie, whose refectory contains the most famous Renaissance painting of all – Leonardo da Vinci's *Last Supper*. Reservations are now mandatory. No less a figure than the great 19th-century historian, Burckhardt (whom some credit with the invention of the very term "Renaissance") had this to say of this painting: "A prodigious genius has here revealed the whole of his treasures to us."

Church of Santa Maria delle Grazie

Location: Piazza Santa Maria delle Grazie 2. The Cenacola Vinciano (Vinciano Refectory) that contains the da Vinci work is next to the church.
Contact details: Reservations are mandatory: 199 199 100
Opening hours: 8:00 am–7:00 pm Tues.–Sun., closed Mon.
Admission: Euro 7.50

For most of its long life, this wall painting has been in poor repair. Some attribute this to a daring technical innovation of Leonardo's: he had tried to blend the new medium of oil with the traditional medium of tempera. While this new technique had been reasonably successful with some panel paintings, it was to prove inappropriate for mural work. Hopefully, the sensitive restoration, which was completed to mark the 500-year anniversary of the work, will be more durable. Like much else of Leonardo's work, this picture achieved immediate celebrity. So much so that, following his conquest of Milan in 1499, the French king had to be dissuaded from removing the painting to Paris.

Leonardo
Last Supper, 1495–98

The unequalled dramatic force of this famous picture, painted on the wall of the monks' refectory, derives from the moment Leonardo chose in which to set his rendering of this venerable theme. Christ has just electrified his apostles by informing them that one of them is about to betray him. Most of the diners are fixated on the question of who the traitor could be. In four trios, the apostles wrestle in differing ways with the implications of their master's fateful words. The trio on the left comprises – from the left of the viewer – Batholomew, James the Less, and Andrew. The black-bearded Judas leans his elbow on the table while straining around to listen to the conversation between a shocked Peter and a devastated John. On the right of the central figure of Christ are Thomas, with one finger raised to reflect the Lord's prediction, while James the Great recoils in disbelief and Phillip questions, "Is it I, Lord?" At the far right are Matthew, Thaddeus and Simon. But other things, too, are happening in the picture: Christ himself has moved on, pointing to the wine that will soon come to represent his blood. Only the trio of figures on the right seem to be aware of the significance of the first Eucharist about to be performed by their Lord.

da Vinci's Last Supper *(pre-restoration)*

Bergamo

Another 30 miles a little north of east brings you to the charming hilltown of Bergamo, whose Carrara Gallery is one of the finest in northern Italy. As in many such towns in Italy, the old and the new are clearly separated. The Carrara is in the new town, beneath the sharply ascending rise to the old town. It is only a leisurely walk of 15 minutes or so from the Carrara to the funicular railway that takes you to the beautiful old town. At its center is the elegantly proportioned Piazza Vecchia, around which are the impressive cathedral, the 12th-century palace and the exquisite Colleoni Chapel (the same Colleoni who modelled the superb equestrian statue by Verrocchio in Venice's Campo Santi Giovanni e Paolo) Bergamo was also home to the 19th-century composer, Gaetano Donizetti.

Carrara Gallery (Accademia Carrara)

Location: Piazza Giacomo Carrara 82
Contact details: Tel. 035 399677
Opening hours: 9:30 am–1:00 pm, 2:30 pm–5:45 pm Tues.–Sun., closed Mon.
Admission: About Euro 3

Giovanni Bellini
Madonna of the Pear, (Madonna Morelli), c.1488

The Madonna and Child are arranged in a way that is characteristic of Giovanni Bellini: they sit before a cloth or panel which separates them from a background landscape (in this case, a fortified castle and its neighboring village) and behind a parapet, which separates them from the viewer. Despite the close configuration of these three elements of the picture, the horizon behind is set low enough for the painting of a huge sky, and in this way, the atmosphere is rendered full of air and light. Only a line of cloud, painted parallel to the horizon, interrupts the big, gray-blue sky. Christ looks beseechingly at his mother, touching his right hand to his chest, perhaps to indicate his sure knowledge of his destiny. His beautiful mother gazes at him, sadly but reassuringly. In the distance, people chat, ride horses: life goes on. On the parapet that separates us from the mother and child is the pear from which the picture derives its name.

Bellini's Madonna of the Pear

Giovanni Bellini
Lochis Madonna, 1480–90

A mighty painting in a small panel! Mary's blue mantle falls into deep, naturalistic folds, which, however, are highlighted with Byzantine strokes of gold, giving a fine ribbed appearance to the fabric and an iconic tone to the image of the Madonna. The Christ

Child appears to be trying to escape from his mother's grasp: he is restlessly moving across the parapet – an expression of his eagerness to accept his fate, perhaps? Or has he stumbled onto his left knee in an allusion to his future fall under the weight of the cross? Some further details are worth noting. The glimpse of the child's genitals reminds us of his humanity and therefore of his future Passion, including the circumcision – the first occasion on which his blood was spilt.

Giovanni Bellini
Pietà, 1460s

In this early panel, Bellini presents half-length portraits of the three major Crucifixion figures, their identity revealed (as though that were necessary) in the Greek characters inscribed on the dark backdrop. On the left, the sorrowing Virgin looks at her son through swollen eyes, painfully observing that he is no longer able to return her gaze. In the center is the unmistakable face of a dead man, his features already beginning to droop. Christ's head falls forward onto that of his mother, and the inconsolable John holds his cheek against his right hand. So closely observed are these anguished figures that we almost feel that we are invading their privacy.

Mantegna
Madonna and Child (Madonna col Bambino), 1470

This is the second of Mantegna's two 1470 Madonnas; the other is in the Poldi Pezzoli Gallery in Milan so you may have an opportunity to compare them. They are quite different. This Madonna is not as soft as her Milanese counterpart. Her eyes are quite focused and her lips are upturned in the suggestion of a smile. The expression on her Baby's face is – well – strange! Perhaps he is communicating with his Heavenly Father. But if it were not for his mother's half-smile, we would say he had colic!

Brescia

Another 30 miles to the southeast is the next site on the Trail: Brescia, which is the second largest city (after Milan) in Lombardy, and is aptly named the City of the Beautiful Fountains.

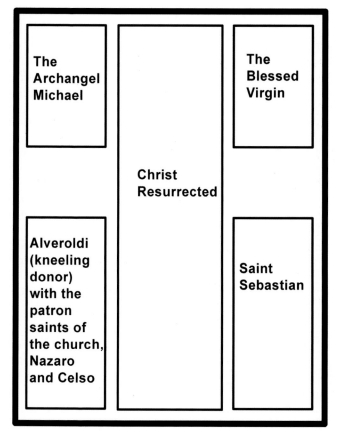

Diagram of Titian's Alveroldi Resurrection Altarpiece.

Chiesa di Santi Nazaro and Celso

Location: Corso Matteotti

Titian
Alveroldi Resurrection Altarpiece, 1522

This is a remarkable work when you consider the competing pressures that Titian had to reconcile while he was painting it. His patron, the papal legate, Altobello Alveroldi, wanted a traditional Venetian polyptych design, requiring the artist to paint different elements of the picture on different panels. In part because of

Titian's own preference for unified designs for altarpieces – however large – this design had fallen out of favor in Venice but, at Brescia, Titian triumphantly revived it – albeit with dynamic, unconventionally posed figures. In addition, he clearly wanted to experiment with the new sculptural forms that he had recently encountered in the works of Michelangelo. The central panel depicts a powerful Christ, rising, like the morning sun behind him, from his coal-dark tomb, his white loin cloth streaming out behind. The archangel in the top left panel is also in motion: wings still spread, sash and golden locks flying, brandishing his message of greeting to the inclined head of the Virgin in the top right-hand panel. The donor kneels bottom left with the patron saints of the church, Nazaro and Celso. The bottom right-hand panel, which was apparently painted some time before the other, contains the powerful contorted and sculptural figure of St Sebastian.

You may consider it worthwhile to detour to the southeast to visit historic Mantua (Mantova) – the setting for Verdi's *Rigoletto*. It was also the birthplace of the poet Virgil as well as Andrea Mantegna's home town, and the site of the only completely preserved room of (largely nonreligious) frescoes by Mantegna. You'll find them in the Palazzo Ducale which dominates the main piazza at the top of the town.

Mantua (Mantova)

The Palazzo Ducale (also referred to as the Castel San Giorgio) is a longish walk from the railway station – about 800 yards to the east.

Palazzo Ducale

Location: Piazza Sordello (the large main square)
Contact details: Tel. 037 6320283
Opening hours: 8:00 am–9:15 pm Tues.–Sun., closed Mon.
Admission: Euro 6.50

As you walk through the seemingly endless and ornate rooms of the Dukes of Mantua, remind yourself that you have a very special treat ahead of you: the Camera degli Sposi, or bedroom of the Marchese Ludovico, decorated sublimely by Mantegna.

Mantegna
Room of the Married Couple (Camera degli Sposi), 1465–74

The ceiling and two of this room's walls are covered in Mantegna's exquisite (and recently restored) frescoes. The wall frescoes depict aspects of daily life – and perhaps specific events (there are debates about this) – in the life of the Court. The *Meeting* picture is said to record the Marchese Ludovico greeting his son (now a cardinal), but there is disagreement about which of two such significant meetings (held a decade apart!) is occurring here. The backgound is an idealized version of Rome – perhaps an allusion to the family's great expectations for the Cardinal. There are further debates about the identity of the author of the letter held by the red-hatted Marchese Ludovico in the *Court Scene*. But why would you worry about that when there is so much else to divert you: courtiers; ladies of the court, one of them (standing by the knee of the aging Duchess Barbara of Brandenburg), a gray-haired small person; children; dogs; splendid furnishings; beautiful fabrics. Best of all, though, is the frescoed vault, with its *trompe l'oeil* opening to the sky and circular balustrade over which ladies look down at you and to which plump, naked little *putti* cling. There are some secrets on the west wall that you should ask the attendants to help you find: a self-portrait of Mantegna painted into the design of the painted pilaster and a procession of the Magi that has been discovered during a recent cleaning.

The **Cathedral** (**Duomo** or **Chiesa di San Andrea**) is our next stop, about 300 yards down the Piazza from the Ducal Palace, in the Piazza Sordello. This is the Mantegna's burial place. Once inside the Duomo, stop at the Cappella di Giovanni Battista – the first on the left as you enter the nave. However, you need to have sharp eyes to gain much from the visit, as the chapel is gloomy and behind a formidable grille. There are three works by Mantegna here. In the center is *The Holy Family and the Family of John the Baptist*, c.1505. On the right is the *Baptism of Christ*, c.1506; and on the left (you may have to squeeze your face against the bars of the grille to get any sort of a view) Mantegna's *Self Portrait Bust*, c.1505.

Leave Mantua and travel east for another 45 miles or so. During the trip you will pass the southern shore of Lake Garda, and soon you will reach historic Verona, famed for the performances of Grand Opera in its ancient arena.

Verona

We'll view works in two churches first. Five Euro gains entry to all the major churches in Verona, including the Duomo and St Zeno. Start at the 12th-century Duomo, which is about a mile and a half walk through the old town center northeast of the railway station. In the **Duomo**, buy your ticket, and then see Titian's 1535 *Assumption of the Virgin*. This work lacks the explosive dynamism of its celebrated predecessor in the Frari in Venice. The Virgin serenely ascends, while a gray-haired apostle searches the sepulcher to convince himself that Mary has really gone. Convention has it that Thomas is the apostle next

San Zeno

to him, gazing directly at the Virgin, with a girdle in his hand. The tonal quality of the picture is subdued. The Madonna is almost totally enveloped in her blue robe, and is surrounded by frothy white clouds. The only bright colors are to be found only in the red robes of the figures on the left and the young St John's orange-red and dark green garments. In the center of the picture, the white-headed St Peter, in his customary yellow cloak, turns to look above his left shoulder. The man with the long white beard behind him is almost certainly St Paul.

On leaving the Duomo, cross the River Adige and proceed in a southwesterly direction for about 800 yards until you again reach the river (which curves around). Just on the other side of the river is the **Basilica of San Zeno**, in the Piazza San Zeno. Your ticket from the Duomo covers this church as well.

Our main focus in the Basilica is the magnificent Mantegna *San Zeno Altarpiece*, from 1457–60. Mantegna's dazzling wooden triptych stands on the altar. The three scenes are quite distinct, but they are united by a common architecture (an ornately decorated loggia); a common sky, seen beyond the loggia, and one of Mantegna's inter-linking garlands that loops behind the pillars separating the three pictures of the altarpiece and is caught up by brilliant red hangers in the center of each frame. The Madonna and Child occupy the center panel along with caroling angels and instrument-playing *putti*. They are flanked by four saints in each of the side panels: from the left, Peter, Paul, John the Evangelist and Zeno; and in the right-hand panel, Benedict, Lorenzo (holding his ever-present grill), Gregory and John the Baptist. With his customary skill, Mantegna uses perspective to create great depth in the scene: the figures become smaller in size, the further they are from the viewer; the lines of the architecture disappear towards the distant clouds. The three paintings in the predella (*Gethsemane*; *The Crucifixion* and *The Resurrection*) are substitutes for those stolen by the Nazis during the war – now in the Louvre and the Musée des Beaux-Arts of Tours.

A stroll of about 300 yards (walk along the river in an easterly direction) brings you to the Castelvecchio Museum.

Museo di Castelvecchio

Location: Corso Castelvecchio 2
Contact details: Tel. 045 594734
Opening hours: 8:30 am–7:30 pm Tues.–Sun. 1:30 pm–7:30 pm Mon.
Admission: Euro 4.20

Bellini
Madonna and Child, 1475

This portrayal is similar to many others from Bellini's early to middle years, with the Virgin's left hand outstretched to protect the infant. In this version, Bellini omits the background landscape so typical of much of his work, replacing it with a clouded sky. This concentrates our attention solely on the melancholy communion between Mary and her doomed son. This picture was once owned by the great Venetian painter of the Baroque period, Tiepolo.

Mantegna
The Holy Family and a Saint (Sacra Familia), c.1500

This picture has been placed on an easel in the middle of the room, with no protective barrier at all, so you can have a completely unimpeded view. But don't expect to be cheered up! Four solemn faces greet you at eye level: a pensive, downcast Madonna, her sad-eyed infant, a wise-eyed but weary St Joseph, gazing off into the distance over the viewer's left shoulder, and a female saint, who stares wistfully out to the right. The Child's left arm encircles his mother's neck and she holds him to her, her horizontal left arm acting like the protective parapet – often painted by Giovanni Bellini, Mantegna's brother-in-law – between viewer and infant.

The next arch-shaped journey takes us briefly to five interesting towns, where we'll stop briefly to view one major artwork in each.

Thirty miles to the east lies **Vicenza**, whose built form has been heavily shaped by its most famous son – the 16th-century architect, Andrea Palladio. However, the Gothic church to which we direct you came from an earlier period – the 13th century. In the Contra' Santa Corona, you'll find the Church of Santa Corona, in which you can see Bellini's last altarpiece, executed when he was in his seventies. The work, *Baptism of Christ* was commissioned to honor John the Baptist, so Bellini placed the saint on a higher plane than Jesus. But there is no doubt that Christ remains the central figure in the composition. He stand serenely while the waters are poured over him. As is often the case with Bellini, the supernatural is enclosed in an expansive landscape evocative of a dreamworld.

About 40 miles east of north and into the mountains is the Renaissance town of **Feltre.** Its town center possesses a rare architectural unity, as it was virtually rebuilt in the early 16th century

The Basilica of Vicenza

FLORENCE TO VENICE

after being twice sacked by the invading Austrians. In Via Lorenzo Luzzo, you'll find the Civic Museum, which costs around five Euros to enter. See *Madonna with Blessing Child, Saints John the Baptist and Elizabeth,* executed by Bellini around 1516. Either this, or the painting of the same subject in Venice's Querini Stampalia Gallery, was Bellini's last painting because both were completed in the year of his death.

A further 40 miles into the mountains will bring you to Titian's birthplace – **Pieve di Cadore**. There, in the parish church (Chiesa Arcidiaconale), view Titian's gift to the town: *Madonna and Child with Saints Peter and Andrew, with Titian as Donor,* (c.1560). It has not survived the centuries all that well, but it retains an eerie quality, with Titian (as donor, dressed in black) in the company of the saint for whom he was named (the white and gold cloaked bishop). The artist's brother, Francesco Vecellio, apparently was the model for St Andrew (in the brown and red robe). The painting was badly cut during an attempted burglary in the early 18th century, and was later on the subject of a bitter ownership dispute among Titian's descendants.

About 30 miles to the south is the town formerly known as Serravalle, **Vittorio Veneto** which became the hometown of Titian's daughter after her marriage. Throughout his long life, Titian maintained links with the region of his birth, and this is the main village of the area. The town acquired its grand new name after it served as the site for a famous battle in World War I. There, in the Chiesa di Santa Maria Nuova, is a massive 1547 painting by Titian, *Madonna with Saints Peter and Andrew*, c.1547. Titian's borrowing from Raphael is most obvious here. The fishing scene in the background has been lifted straight from a Raphael tapestry, the *Miraculous Draught of Fishes* (in the Vatican Museum). Seated on a bank of cloud and surrounded by angels, the Virgin appears, at the apex of the picture, to the two saints, who form the human pillars of the arch-shaped composition. St Andrew carries a heavy Latin cross (rather than his customary X-shaped one), and St Peter, his yellow robe tinted pink in the sun, presents the keys of the church.

Our final destination of this Trail is **Treviso**, a further 25 miles to the south. It is a very attractive town which, like nearby Venice, is threaded with canals. The Duomo was founded in the 12th century, though rebuilt several times. The Duomo, where you'll find a Titian *Annunciation* (c.1520) is not hard to find in this small town. It features a sumptuously garbed Virgin, but the unimpressive archangel and the seemingly deformed donor – Broccardo Malchiostro – seem unworthy. In addition, the substantial depth of the middle ground is uncharacteristic of Titian. This has led some critics to speculate that a large hand in the composition may have been taken by one of Titian's assistants, the Treviso-born Paris Bordone. Because Malchiostro, the long-serving and pugnacious canon of Treviso Cathedral, was disliked locally, the worthy citizens of Treviso smeared the painting with pitch a few years after it had been completed.

If you enter Venice from this northerly Trail, you will find yourself very much at home, for you will encounter many more great paintings by artists who have been most prominent on this Trail – Giovanni Bellini and Titian – together with those of the Venetian Tintoretto, whose representation on this Trail has been thin.

Postscript

The Italians don't fuss about their art. Like their antique monuments and their religion, they integrate it into their daily lives. So it's not essential that the traveller in Italy should be an art expert. But the traveller who merely glosses over the Italian art experience misses out on a fundamental source of meaning for all Italians, whether they visit galleries or not. We hope that our book will encourage more travellers to drink from that same source, thereby enhancing their trip.

– Ann Morrow and John Power

Other Artists and Renaissance Writers

Alberti, Leon Battista (1404–1472): Florentine architect and humanist writer, who formulated the most influential treatment of perspective in painting.

Ammannati, Bartolommeo (1511–1592): Sculptor/ architect, close friend of Michelangelo and designer of the Pitti Palace in Florence.

Baldovinetti. Alesso (1425–1499): Painter who studied alongside Piero della Francesca in the studio of Domenico Veneziano.

Bellini, Gentile (1429–1507): Member of the leading artistic family in the Venice of his day, but overshadowed by his famous brother, Giovanni.

Bellini, Jacopo (c.1400–1470): Venetian painter who brought much of the spirit of the early Renaissance back to Venice from Florence. Overshadowed by Giovanni, his son.

Bandinelli, Baccio (1493–1560): Florentine sculptor much favored by the Medici.

Bologna, Vitale da (14th century): Favorite painter of the Bologna of his day.

Bordon, Paris (1500–1571): Venetian painter.

Bramante, Donato (1444–1514): Architect who designed the church of Santa Maria delle Grazie in Milan, and who made a start on the rebuilding of St Peter's Basilica in Rome.

Bronzino, Agnolo (1503–1572): Establishment Florentine painter much favored by the Medici.

Brunelleschi, Filippo (1377–1446): Architect most famous for the design and construction of the massive dome of the Duomo in Florence.

Buffalmacco, Buonamico. Artist of the early 14th century often credited with the famous frescoes in the Camposanto in Pisa where you will find the most terrifying – though faded – *Last Judgment* of all.

Cambio, Arnolfo di (13th century): Sculptor who exercised significant influence on Giotto.

Canova, Antonio (1757–1822): The most famous Venetian sculptor.

Castiglione, Baldassare (1478–1529): Author of *The Courtier,* the famous Renaissance text on statecraft.

Cavallini, Pietro (c.1240–c.1330): The most famous painter of 13th-century Rome, some of whose works are only now – in the 21st century – being recovered through refurbishment of church walls in such Roman churches as St Paul's Outside the Walls.

Cellini, Benvenuto (1500–1571): Florentine sculptor and goldsmith, best known today because of his famous autobiography.

Cimabue (c.1240–early 1300s): The most famous Florentine painter of his day, until he was surpassed by a man some believe to have been his pupil – Giotto. Represented in the Basilica di San Francesco in Assisi.

Cortona, Pietro da (1596–1669): Roman painter and architect who was one of the founders of the High Baroque style.

Crespi, Giuseppe Maria (1665–1747): Bolognese painter renowned for his use of chiaroscuro.

Dante, Alighieri (1265–1321): Florentine poet – and friend of Giotto – who is generally regarded as the father of the modern Italian language.

Duccio di Buoninsegna (c.1255–c.1318): The most influential religious painter in the Siena of his day – a worthy companion for Cimabue and Giotto in Room 2 of the Uffizi in Florence.

Duccio, Agostino di (1418–c.1481): Roman painter.

Dürer, Albrecht (1471–1528): Leading German painter and engraver.

Gaddi, Taddeo (1300–1366): Pupil of Giotto, best represented in the Church of Santa Croce in Florence.

Gentile da Fabriano (c.1385–1427): A very mobile and influential exponent of the International Gothic style of painting. As the well-travelled master of Jacopo Bellini, one of the painters responsible for the dawning of the Renaissance in Venice.

Gentileschi, Artemisia (1593–1652): Leading Baroque painter. When a biography of her less talented father was published, she was accorded – to the subsequent outrage of modern feminist scholars – a single sentence at its end.

Ghiberti, Lorenzo (c.1378– 1455): Florentine sculptor whose greatest accomplishment was the design and execution of the bronze doors of the Baptistery in Florence.

Giambologna (1529–1608): A widely travelled sculptor who spent the later part of his life in the Tuscan city of Lucca.

Giorgione (Giorgio da Castelfranco) (c.1478–1510): A contemporary of Titian, whose limited output of enigmatic paintings have made him a popular subject for modern interpretations.

Gozzoli, Benozzo (1421–1497): A pupil of Fra Angelico who went on to execute important works in San Gimignano and Pisa.

Lippi, Filippino (1457–1504): Product of the then scandalous liaison between Fra Filippo Lippi and his model-nun, Lucrezia Buti, Filippino went on to great accomplishments, especially in the Brancacci Chapel in Florence and in San Gimignano.

Lorenzetti, Ambrogio (1319–1347): A Sienese painter who executed the pictorial equivalent of Machiavelli's treatises in his superb *Allegories of Good and Bad Government* in the Palazzo Pubblico in his hometown.

Lorenzetti, Pietro (c.280–1348): Like his brother, Ambrogio, he was a daring innovator, but in his case these talents were most effectively exercised in the religious setting of Assisi.

Malatesta, Sigismondo: 15th-century ruler of Rimini.

Martini, Simone (1284–1344): A pupil of Duccio, the well-travelled Martini was the last of the great Sienese painters. He ended his life in the Papal court of Avignon, where he executed a famous – but long lost – portrait of Petrarch's Laura.

Masolino Da Panicale (c.1383–1440): A widely travelled painter, who is nowadays remembered principally for his work with his younger colleague – who may have been his pupil – Masaccio.

Michelozzo di Bartolomeo (1396–1472): As one of the architects favored by the Medici, he landed the plum job of planning the renovation and enlargement of San Marco in Florence.

Michelozzo, Bartolomeo di (1396–1472): Tuscan sculptor.

Montefeltro, Federico da: 15th-century ruler of Urbino.

Nelli, Plautilla (1523–1588): The leading woman painter of the Renaissance in Florence.

Palladio, Andrea (1508–80): Architect who devised his own distinctive style of Palladian design, which he developed most extensively in his adopted home of Vicenza.

Palma, Il Vecchio, Jacopo (1480–1528): Venetian painter.

Palma, Il Giovane (c.1548–1628): Venetian painter, great nephew of Palma Il Vecchio, who took a leading position in Venice after the death of Tintoretto in 1594.

Perugino (1446–1523): One of Perugia's favorite sons and well represented in its National Gallery. Also painted frescoes in the Sistine Chapel in Rome.

Petrarch (1304–1374): Born in Arezzo, one of Italy's greatest poets.

Pinturicchio (1454–1513): A close colleague of Perugino, who like him worked in both Perugia and Rome.

Pisano, Giovanni (1240–1320): Tuscan sculptor who studied alongside Arnolfo di Cambio in the studio of his father, Nicola Pisano.

Pontormo (1494–1557): A Florentine painter favored by the Medici, and other Florentine patrons.

Quercia, Jacopo della (c.1370–1438): The greatest of the Sienese sculptors of the Quattrocento.

Robbia, Andrea della (1435–1525): Nephew of Luca, and like him an artist who worked in glazed terracotta, he took over the thriving family workshop at the end of the 15th century.

Robbia, Luca della (c.1400–1482): Generally credited with establishing glazed terracotta as a medium for wall sculptures.

Sansovino, Jacopo (c.1486–1570): Florentine sculptor and architect who spent the latter half of his life as the state architect of Venice.

Savanarola: Famous Florentine Dominican preacher, who was executed in the Piazza della Signoria in 1498.

Sodoma (1477–1549): Piedmont-born, he was a painter who did most of his work in Siena.

Signorelli, Luca (c.1450–1523): A Tuscan painter, pupil of Piero della Francesca, and one of the first of the Italians to follow the Flemish in eschewing the use of bright colors.

Tiepolo, Giambattista (1696–1770): Spectacular – even in the age of the Baroque – painter of frescoes, especially on large ceilings.

Traini, Francesco (14th century): Muralist who played a leading role in the Camposanto in Pisa.

Uccello, Paolo (1397–1475): One of the earliest painters in Florence to experiment boldly with perspectives.

Van Der Goes, Hugo (d. 1482): A Flemish painter who caused a sensation in Florence in the 1470s with his Portinari Triptych, now in Rooms 10–14 of the Uffizi.

Van Der Weyden, Rogier (c.1400–1464): A native of what is now Belgium, van der Weyden became one of the most influential painters of the early Renaissance.

Van Eyck, Jan (1390–1440): Painter and diplomat, widely regarded as a founder of the Flemish school.

Vasari, Giorgio (1511–1574): Tuscan painter, architect and writer. Designer of the Uffizi, he is however best known for his *Lives of the most Eminent Painters, Sculptors and Architects.*

Velazquez, Diego (1599–1660): Spanish court painter who was greatly influenced by the Venetian Renaissance painters and indeed purchased several Tintoretto paintings for his king.

Veneziano, Domenico (1410– 1461): Venetian born, but rose to prominence in Florence, where he was master to Piero della Francesco and Alesso Baldovinetti.

Veronese, Paolo (1528–1588): Prominent Venetian painter who was in some ways the natural successor to Titian. Less important than his contemporary Tintoretto as a forerunner of the Baroque

Verrocchio, Andrea del (1435–1488): Sculptor and sometime painter who was Leonardo's master. Late in life, he moved to Venice to work on the famous equestrian statue of Colleoni.

Vivarini, Antonio (c.1418–c.1480): Venetian painter and designer who produced many elegant altarpieces.

Vivarini, Bartolomeo (c.1430–1490s): Younger brother and student of Antonio, who in partnership with him built up one of the most prosperous workshops in the Venice of his day.

Saints

Agatha: Third-century Sicilian martyr. Because of her gruesome end – her breasts were cut off – she is the patron saint of wet-nurses!

Ambrose: One of the four Doctors of the Church, Ambrose served as Bishop of Milan, from which position he was influential in securing the conversion of an even more famous Doctor of the Church – St Augustine.

Andrew: Initially a disciple of John the Baptist, Andrew became the first of the apostles when he was quick to apprehend the Divinity of Jesus at his Baptism.

Anne: The mother of the Virgin Mary.

Anthony Abbot: Born in Egypt in the 3rd century, Anthony was a hermit in the desert who attracted many followers and has thus come to be seen by many as the founder of monasticism.

Anthony of Padua: Lisbon-born, Anthony was originally an Augustinian monk. However, he later transferred to the newly formed Franciscans and became a famous preacher at Padua, of which he is patron saint.

Aquinas, Thomas: A Dominican priest who was the greatest philosopher of the Middle Ages.

Benedict: 6th-century Italian founder of a prominent religious order.

Bonaventura: 13th-century Franciscan monk who composed the authorized biography of St Francis – the *Legenda Maior*.

Bruno: 11th-century founder of the Carthusian Order.

Barnabas: A close associate of St Paul and, like him, admitted into the select band of the apostles even though he was not one of the 12 originally chosen by Jesus.

Catherine of Alexandria: 4th-century martyr who took her executioners with her when the wheel upon which she was being broken flew apart.

Catherine: 14th-century Sienese associate of the Dominican order, renowned for her mysticism.

Cecilia: Although there is considerable doubt about the existence of this early virgin-martyr, she is commonly recognized as the patron saint of music.

Christopher: A mythic 3rd-century man of giant proportions, who was called upon to carry a child – who turned out to be the Christ Child – across a difficult river.

Clare: A close associate of St Francis and founder of the distaff Franciscan order – the Poor Clares.

Cosmas: With his twin brother Damian, he worked as a physician to the poor in Syria, before being martyred there. The twins are patron saints of the profession of medicine.

Crescenzio: 4th-century Sicilian martyr.

Damian: With his twin brother Cosmas, worked as a physician to the poor in Syria, before being martyred there. The twins are patron saints of the profession of medicine.

Dominic: Spanish-born 13th-century contemporary of St Francis. Between them, they founded the two orders, the Dominicans and Franciscans, which were among the principal patrons of art in Renaissance Italy.

Elegius: Patron saint of goldsmiths.

Elizabeth: The cousin of the Virgin Mary and mother of John the Baptist.

Elizabeth of Hungary: 13th-century Queen of Thuringia, renowned for her charitable works, and speedily canonized after an early death.

Eugenio: 5th-century bishop of Carthage.

Francis: Assisi-based contemporary of St Dominic. Between them, they founded the two orders – the Dominicans and Franciscans – which were among the principal patrons of art in Renaissance Italy.

George: 4th-century martyr, most famous for his slaying of a dragon, and now the patron saint of England.

Gregory: The only one of the early Fathers of the Church who rose to become a 6th-century pope. He was a skilled diplomat and a man of wide culture.

Ignatius: Founder of the Jesuit order.

James: Brother of St John the Evangelist, and the first Apostle to be martyred, only a decade or so after the Crucifixion.

Jerome: A famous early Doctor of the Church and prelate, who late in life retired to the desert as a hermit.

Joachim: Father of the Virgin Mary.

John the Baptist: The forerunner or precursor of Christ. He was related to Christ, as Elizabeth, his mother, was a cousin of Mary, the mother of Jesus. He was six months older than his cousin, Jesus, but Renaissance painters and sculptors commonly ignored their relative ages. John had adopted the practice of baptizing repentant sinners in the River Jordan. When Jesus offered himself for Baptism, John initially demurred but then consented to honor the Son of God. John is often depicted wearing animal skins, signifying his period as a hermit in the wilderness. A more dramatic representation is as a decapitated head on a platter – the gruesome reward proffered by King Herod to Salome in return for her celebrated Dance of the Seven Veils.

John: Composer of one of the four Gospels, John (the Evangelist) was considered by many to have been the favorite apostle of Jesus Christ.

Lawrence: 3rd-century martyr, usually portrayed as having been roasted to death on a gridiron.

Lucy: 4th-century Sicilian martyr, often represented as having been blinded.

Louis of Toulouse: A member of the French nobility who was an early member of the Franciscan order and, as such, served as Bishop of Toulouse.

Ludovic: Better known as the 13th-century art patron and Crusader King of France, Louis IX.

Marina: 8th-century martyr, noted for her prior success in passing as the monk Marinus.

Mark: Although not an apostle, author of one of the four Gospels.

Mary Magdalene: Alleged to have been a former prostitute, Mary Magdalene became one of Jesus' most devoted followers and, unlike the male apostles, did not betray him at his time of execution. For this, she was rewarded with the first sight of the risen Christ, who exhorted her not to touch him – *Noli Mi Tangere*.

Nicholas of Tolentino: 13th-century Italian Augustinian monk, reputed to have been a prolific miracle-worker.

Paul: The most influential of the early Christian thinkers, noted especially for his dramatic conversion on the road to Damascus.

Paul The Hermit: 3rd-century Egyptian, who was one of the first Christian hermits, and who lived to a very old age.

Peter: The leader of the apostles and later the first pope, St Peter was a man with human frailties who greatly dreaded the impending execution of his master. When the time came for his own execution three decades later, he faced his ordeal with great courage, insisting on being crucified upside-down.

Peter Martyr: 13th-century inquisitor, and the first Dominican martyr. Often shown wearing the axe implanted in his head that had killed him.

Reparata: Third-century martyr, who became one of the patron saints of Florence.

Rocco: San Rocco was a 14th-century scion of the French aristocracy at Montpellier who came to be credited with miraculous powers of healing, and because of this became the patron saint of sufferers – both human and animal – from the plague.

Scholastica: Sister of St Benedict, and in the 6th century the first Benedictine nun.

Sebastian: An early Christian who was sentenced by the Roman authorities to be executed by being shot through with arrows, an ordeal which he (temporarily) survived.

Thomas: The most skeptical of the 12 apostles of Jesus Christ. After the resurrected Christ reappeared before his apostles, it was Thomas who insisted on receiving hard empirical evidence that he was indeed the person who had been crucified, thus earning the soubriquet of "Doubting Thomas."

Victor: 2nd- or 3rd-century martyr famous for the prolonged torture – perhaps as long as three years – to which he was subjected before execution.

Vincent Ferreri: 14th-century Spanish-born Dominican friar renowned for his oratory.

Zacharias: The father of St John the Baptist.

Biblical & Christian Characters, Stories, Places and Terms

Aaron: The brother of Moses, who became the first high Priest of the Jews.

Adoration: The newly born Jesus Christ was typically portrayed as receiving adoration from both humble local shepherds and from the Magi – 'wise men from the East', who came to call, bearing gifts of gold, frankincense and myrrh.

Agony in the Garden: After the Last Supper, Jesus Christ and some of the apostles retired to a garden near the Mount of Olives, where he contemplated his impending ordeal and where he was taken into custody. An important element of the story is that, while they were supposed to be supporting him, his apostles fell asleep.

Annunciate Virgin: Mary, after having received the news of her pregnancy from the Archangel.

Annunciation: Usually the occasion when the Archangel Gabriel appeared before the Virgin Mary to announce to her that she was to become the Mother of God. Occasionally, the Annunciation may be to Anna, informing her that she is pregnant with Mary.

Ascension: The culminating event of the Christian story: the Gospels explain that, after his Resurrection from the Dead, Jesus rose into heaven. The event was witnessed by the apostles, and, as such, was Christ's last appearance on earth.

Assumption: This refers to Mary being taken up into Heaven (on some accounts, before her burial, and on others, three days after). Renaissance artists liked to represent this event as one in a sequence – from her death (or Dormition) through to her Coronation (after the Assumption).

Baptism of Christ: John the Baptist, the cousin of Jesus, had adopted the practice of baptizing repentant sinners in the River Jordan. When Jesus offered himself for Baptism, John initially demurred but then consented. As he did so, the Holy Ghost appeared in the guise of a dove. It was this incident that persuaded several of the apostles that Jesus was divine.

Calvary: The hill, sometimes called Golgotha, where Jesus Christ was executed.

Christ among the scribes: This is the only episode from the boyhood of Jesus Christ recorded in the Gospels. At the age of 12, he astonished the learned men in the Temple with his knowledge of religion.

Cleophas: The uncle of Jesus, who was among the family group at the foot of the cross.

Crucifixion: The death of Christ on the Cross – a horrific and degrading form of execution usually reserved for slaves and non-Roman citizens. Interestingly, there are no images of the Crucifixion from the first 400 or so years of Christian art.

David: The famous Old Testament hero who as a youth slew Goliath and went on to become King of Israel.

Deposition: The taking down from the cross of the dead Jesus Christ, surrounded by his loved ones.

Elias /Elijah: A major Old Testament prophet, who railed against the apostasy of the kings of Israel of his day.

Entry of Christ into Jerusalem: At the beginning of the week in which he was to be crucified, Jesus Christ entered Jerusalem in triumph, with palm branches strewn before him – hence Palm Sunday, which commemorates the event.

Eucharist: The core of much Christian worship, commemorating the transubstantiation of wine and bread into the blood and flesh of Jesus Christ.

Expulsion of the moneylenders from the temple: This was one of the symbolically most potent of the acts of Jesus Christ, for he sought by it to restore the Temple as a place of worship.

Flagellation: The flogging of Christ during his Passion.

Flight into Egypt: When King Herod feared that the Messiah had been born, he ordered the slaughter of all new-born boys. Warned by God of this threat, Joseph took his small family – the Virgin Mary and the infant Christ – to Egypt, where they stayed until they learned of the death of Herod.

Gabriel: The Archangel who told Mary she was pregnant.

Gethsemane: The garden in Jerusalem where Christ endured his agony prior to being arrested.

Holofernes: A Biblical tyrant who was heroically despatched by Judith.

Holy Ghost: The third figure in the Trinity, often referred to as the Holy Spirit, typically portrayed as the transmitter of grace.

Holy Infant: The infant Jesus who appeared with his mother, the Madonna, in countless Renaissance paintings.

Immaculate Conception: The dogma that Mary conceived Jesus without the agency of man and thus was free of the taint of original sin.

Incarnation: The dogma that God became man in the person of Jesus Christ.

Isaac: The son of the Old Testament prophet, Abraham, who himself became a prophet. In his youth, he was on God's orders taken to a mountain to be sacrificed by his father, but God granted a last-minute reprieve.

Jesus Christ: As the founder of the Christian religion, the central figure in Italian Renaissance art.

Jesus washing the feet of the Apostles: After the Last Supper and shortly before his arrest, Jesus washed the feet of each of his apostles in order to teach them humility.

Job: The supreme Old Testament representation of patience. God tested his faith with a series of disasters, which Job bore with equanimity.

Joseph of Arimathaea: A prosperous member of the Jerusalem community, who disapproved of the persecution of Jesus and was allowed to have Jesus buried in the tomb he had intended for himself.

Judas Kiss: Having agreed to betray Christ, the apostle Judas arranged to identify his victim with a kiss.

Judas receiving payment for his betrayal: For his services to the authorities in leading their soldiers to Christ in the garden of Gethsemane, the Apostle Judas received a reward of thirty pieces of silver.

Judith: Old Testament heroine who slew the tyrant Holofernes.

Last Judgment: Renaissance painters loved to paint the Day of Judgment, when God separates the Faithful from the Damned and casts the latter unfortunates into the fiery furnaces of Hell. The most celebrated examples include Giotto's vision of hell in the Scrovegni Chapel in Padua, Michelangelo's in the Sistine Chapel, and that attributed variously to Francesco Traini and Buffulmaco in the Camposanto in Pisa.

Last Supper: A favorite theme of Renaissance painters, providing the opportunity to portray great drama and psychological tension. On the eve of his crucifixion, Christ gathered his apostles together for a final meal (often represented as the first Eucharist, or celebration of the sacrament of Holy Communion). This was the occasion on which Christ told his followers that one of them was about to betray him. The most famous version of the theme is that painted in Milan by Leonardo da Vinci.

Marriage at Cana: This was the first of the public miracles of Jesus Christ, when he turned water into wine at the marriage feast.

Mary (Saint): See entry below on the Virgin Mary.

Miraculous draught of fishes: This early miracle came to symbolize the leadership of Jesus. Several of those who were to become apostles were fishermen. One day, when Jesus was with them, they were bemoaning their lack of success. On his instructions, they cast their nets and were immediately rewarded with an enormous catch. It was then that Jesus enjoined Peter, "henceforth thou shall catch men."

Moses: The greatest lawgiver in the Old Testament.

Nativity: From the Year 336, the Nativity, or birth, of Christ in a manger has been celebrated on December 25 in some parts of the Christian world, and in others, especially in the East, on January 6, the date of the Epiphany and the date of his recognition by the three Magi. Consequently, these two subjects – the birth and the Adoration by the Magi – are often treated simultaneously by Renaissance artists.

Nicodemus: A friend of Joseph of Arimathaea who assisted in the deposition and burial of the body of Christ.

Noah: One of the most famous of Old Testament figures, because of his construction of a huge ark that enabled him to survive the Great Flood.

Passion: The sufferings of Jesus Christ before and during his torture and crucifixion.

Pentecost: The feast of this day marks the occasion after the ascension of Christ into heaven when the Holy Ghost descended to impart grace to the assembled apostles.

Pietà: A meditative representation of the dead Jesus Christ, usually in the arms of his mother, in much the same way as she sometimes holds him as an infant in depictions of the Nativity or Madonna and Child. The most celebrated example is the sculpture by the young Michelangelo in St Peter's Basilica in Rome.

Pilate: As the Roman governor of Judea, Pontius Pilate was the official who sentenced Christ to death.

Raising Lazarus from the dead: This was one of the most celebrated of the miracles of Jesus Christ, for Lazarus had been in his tomb at Bethany for four days before Christ arrived to raise him from the dead.

Redeemer: An appellation often used by Christians to refer to Jesus Christ.

Resurrection: One of the central tenets of Christianity – that on the third day from his crucifixion, Jesus Christ rose from the dead.

Salome: The woman who demanded as her reward for dancing before King Herod the head of John the Baptist.

Stigmata: The marks of the five wounds sustained by Jesus Christ in the course of his crucifixion, granted as a special mark of divine favor to a small number of saints, of whom St Francis was the first.

Virgin Mary: The Virgin Mother of Jesus Christ was the all-time favorite figure in Renaissance paintings, because of the endless opportunities she presented for painters to explore the ambiguities of, and tensions between, sensual beauty and holy abstinence.

Visitation: When the pregnant Virgin Mary came to visit, her also pregnant cousin Elizabeth greeted her with the famous words, "blessed is the fruit of your womb."

Glossary

academicism: A style of expression that was allegedly excessively abstract and unconnected to the real world.

aedicule: A recess like a small temple that often frames images of saints and/or the Virgin.

alla prima method: A method of painting oils straight onto the canvas with a single layer of paint, usually to enable the work to be completed in the one sitting.

apse: A semicircular section of the church, usually covered by a semi-dome.

bacchanale: A drunken party, often degenerating into an orgy.

baldacchino: Called "baldachin" or "baldaquin" in English, this is a canopy supported by four poles, or hung from the ceiling. It symbolizes status or power and often appears in paintings over the Madonna and Child. The most famous baldachin of all is that in St Peter's, made to Bernini's design from bronze stripped from the roof of the Pantheon.

banderole: A banner conveying a message, such as the one conventionally carried by the risen Christ in Renaissance painting.

Baroque: The style of cultural expression that succeeded the Renaissance and flourished especially in the 17th century. Closely associated with the Counter-Reformation in Rome, the Baroque style was heavier both in physical design and emotional content than the Renaissance that preceded it, although much of the Baroque was prefigured in the work of such late Renaissance painters as Tintoretto.

bas-relief: A sculptural decoration in low relief.

Byzantine: The art of the Eastern Roman Empire, centered on Byzantium (now Istanbul). Stylized and iconic, Byzantine art provided the matrix against which the Italian Renaissance rebelled but could not escape.

chiaroscuro: A style of painting which gives special consideration to the balancing of light and shadow.

choir: That part of the church set aside for singing, also those who sang in it.

contropposto: The stance of a figure that is posed with the upper half of the body turned in the opposite direction to that of the lower half.

cosmati: A style of working marble into a mosaic form, usually alternating white with other colors.

cupola: A rounded vault or dome interior constituting, or built under, the roof of the church.

dado: The part of a pedestal between the base and the cap.

diptych: A two-panelled altarpiece. (*dittico* in Italian.)

doge: The head of the Venetian State, elected by the city elite to serve for life.

finial: Ornament at the top of a post or pillar.

fresco: A method of painting on walls, perfected in Renaissance Italy (where the word means "fresh"). Although the method required careful preparation of surfaces, its application often achieved markedly spontaneous effects.

frieze: Horizontal band of decoration on a wall or pillar.

goldfinch: A symbol of Christ's Passion. The bird was thought to make its nest in thorn-bushes, and the patch of red on its head supposedly signifies Christ's crown of thorns.

Gothic: The style of architecture and, by extension, art, which originated in 12th-century France and came to dominate pre-Renaissance Western Europe.

humanism: A philosophical movement that made man and his gifts the primary focus of study, with special attention to the ancients and their wisdom.

impasto: thick paint sometimes applied with a palette knife.

loggia: A gallery or arcade open to the elements on at least one side.

lunette: A crescent-shaped picture, often positioned above a doorway or another painting.

mandorla: An oval or almond shape placed around a figure in glory.

mosaic: A design or representation executed in pieces of colored stone or glass, usually on the walls and ceiling of a church.

nimbus: An ancient term – still in use today in its original meaning as a type of cloud – which came in the Renaissance to be used to refer to less stultified representations of the haloes of saints.

ornazio: The delicate depiction of characteristic movement.

pala: Altarpiece

Pala d'Oro: This may well be the most beautiful altarpiece of all. Made in Constantinople (Byzantium, now Istanbul) in the 10th century and subsequently stolen by the Venetians, the Pala is a superb expression of Byzantine culture, as it draws upon a number of themes from Christian and indeed pre-Christian times. Located in the San Marco Basilica in Venice.

pendentive: Triangular section of load-bearing masonry in the corners of domed chambers.

pilaster: A projection from a wall presented as though it were a pillar.

polyptych: A multi-panelled altar-piece, usually consisting of a large, central picture on a grand theme (such as the Resurrection), with smaller panels depicting individual saints or sub-themes on either side. It often had, at its base, a predella, comprising smaller pictures carrying a narrative or images of further saints. (*polittico* in Italian).

predella: The strip of small paintings that can be found at the bottom of an altarpiece. The themes in these little paintings usually relate to the principal subject of the major painting.

prie-dieu: A prayer stool.

putto: (plural putti) A representation of a very young child, usually nude.

Quattrocento: Literally, the fourth hundred but referring to the 15th century. A famous example of the rather confusing Italian habit of referring to the centuries as though dating started in 1000 AD.

rilievo schiacciato: A way of achieving great depth from a shallow ground by finely grading a series of surfaces.

reliquary: Receptacles in which relics are kept.

sacra conversazione: "Holy conversation" is the term used to describe representations of the Madonna and Child shown surrounded by saints, donors and/or angels in a single space.

sarcophagus: A stone or terracotta coffin for the body of an important person.

seraphim: With cherubim, among the most important of angels, although typically portrayed in Renaissance paintings as chubby, winged infants.

shell: Symbolizes virginity because it was thought that some molluscs were fertilized simply by dewdrops. It was therefore often associated with the Virgin (like the one that decorates her prie-dieu in Leonardo's Annunciation), or the inverted shell-shaped aedicules that often sit, like canopies, over images of the Madonna and Child. Botticelli's Venus floats into shore on an up-turned shell.

Stella Maris: The star of the sea.

Sybil: A female prophet in antiquity.

tenebrist: A gloomy style of painting, emphasizing darkness and shadows.

tondo: A painting or carving of circular shape.

transept: In a basilica, the arms of the cross which separate the apse from the nave.

triptych: A three-panelled altarpiece. (*trittico* in Italian.)

triumphal arch: In church architecture, the portion of the wall around an arch that was used for prominent mural paintings.

vault: An arched roof.

Index